A gigantic roll of thunder rattled the windows. Before she could even think, Michele cried out and found herself in Ian's arms.

He drew her against him, close and hard, and his kiss was fierce and gentle at the same time. His lips seemed warmer than the glow from the fire, and Michele felt her own body flame. She felt herself go limp with desire, and knew that this night she would not deny Ian MacLeven.

'Michele, Michele,' he whispered, 'how I have longed to do that. You cannot know!'

I do know, she thought, but did not speak the words, only fitted her lips again to his. No words were necessary; she let her mouth and body speak for her.

Also by Patricia Matthews

MIDNIGHT WHISPERS (with Clayton Matthews)
FLAMES OF GLORY
EMBERS OF DAWN
TIDES OF LOVE
LOVE'S AVENGING HEART
LOVE'S WILDEST PROMISE
LOVE FOREVER MORE
LOVE'S DARING DREAM
LOVE'S PAGAN HEART
LOVE'S MAGIC MOMENT
LOVE'S GOLDEN DESTINY
LOVE'S RAGING TIDE
LOVE'S SWEET AGONY
LOVE'S BOLD JOURNEY

and published by Corgi Books

Patricia Matthews

Dancer of Dreams

DANCER OF DREAMS

A CORGI BOOK 0 552 12406 0

Originally published in Great Britain by
Century Publishing Co. Ltd.

PRINTING HISTORY
Century edition published 1984
Corgi edition published 1984

Corgi Books are published by Transworld Publishers Ltd.,
Century House, 61-63 Uxbridge Road, Ealing, London W5 5SA.

Made and printed in Great Britain by
Hunt Barnard Printing Ltd., Aylesbury, Bucks.

This book is dedicated to my number one fan Robin Slavitsky, and to all my other loyal readers who have sent me so many kind words and good wishes. God bless you every one.

With thanks to Elizabeth and Leo Whitaker,
my Scottish connection.

Dancer of Dreams

Chapter One

THE sound of the pianoforte, in the room above, came clearly through the open window, distracting Hannah Verner from the task at hand.

Placing her pen on the open page of the account ledger, she glanced up at the ceiling, as the sound of Andre's voice rose above the music.

His tone was peremptory: "No! No, Michele! Gracefully. Gracefully. *Mon Dieu!* You are supposed to be a sprite of the forest, not a lump of wood. Move your arms gently. So!"

Hannah, massaging the tense spot between her shoulder blades, smiled gently, thinking of her own long-ago lessons with Andre. Could it be twenty years? Yes, it was at least that. Andre Leclaire had come to Malvern in the year 1717 to teach manners and social graces to a raw, untutored girl, and the year was now 1737.

And yet Andre, despite the passage of the years, seemed little changed. He was as energetic and bossy as ever. Physically he was a little thinner, his face somewhat more lined; but the changes were few considering the number of years that had slipped past.

Upstairs, the music changed tempo, growing slower, softer, adding its particular inducement to the soft spring air that came through the window, moving the lace curtain, like a lover's caress; making her think of Michael and the wound of his loss that six months had not been able to heal. Michael, her handsome, vital husband, whom she had loved to distraction, and who was now gone, killed in a senseless accident.

Closing the account book with a weary gesture, Hannah got up from the desk. It was no use, she could not concentrate on the work, even though there was so much to be done, things that Michael had always taken care of in the past, which she must now handle herself.

Walking to the open window, she gazed out onto the lush grounds below, and then to the fields beyond, feeling the pleasure that she always felt upon looking at this land she loved so intensely, this land that was hers. Yes, although Michael was gone now, Malvern remained, and she must take care of it; but not today, not now. Now the lure of memory and the past were too strong. Spring should be forbidden, she thought, to those recently bereaved. It brought too many memories with it.

As the breeze caressed her face, bringing the scent of flowers, her mind's eye saw again the girl she had been when she first came to Malvern, the young Hannah McCambridge, sixteen years old, ragged and frightened, already having borne more suffering than many women ever had to bear, fleeing from the inn of that evil man, Amos Stritch, to whom she had been sold as a bond slave.

What would her life have been like if she had not been befriended by Malcolm Verner, if he had not married her, despite the difference in their ages and social status. Surely she would not be the mistress of Malvern today. Malvern, the plantation she had loved and coveted since childhood. Her thoughts moved back farther still, back to a time when she was only a child, when she and her mother had driven past Malvern in their broken-down cart, on their way to Williamsburg. Hannah could still remember the feeling of awe and pleasure she had felt at the sight of the great house, its two stories white and shining in the hot Virginia sun, shaded by great trees and surrounded by its dependencies, or outbuildings, and the huge, wrought-iron, ornamental gate, with the name, Malvern, hanging above it.

Who would ever have thought that that poor, ragged

child would one day achieve her dream, and become the mistress of all that splendor?

Hannah shook her head, trying to free herself of the past. Malcolm Verner was dead, stricken by a heart seizure only a short time after their wedding, and then there had been Michael, Malcolm's only son, whom she had loved with a passion that completely overshadowed the affectionate gratitude she had felt for his father. Michael, whom she had married, and whose child, Michele, she had borne.

But enough of that! Michael was gone, but she was alive, and so was Michele; and they must go on, no matter what the pain. All Hannah had now was Michele and Malvern, and she would devote herself to them both with all the energy that she could muster.

Tentatively, she moved back toward the paper-strewn desk; and then, on a sudden impulse, she turned instead and left the room, mounting the broad stairs to the second floor, heading toward the large room which had been turned into a practice room for Michele.

Dear Andre, he was such a good friend; and Hannah knew that she was fortunate to have him with her again, doing for Michele what he had done fo: her, coaching her in deportment, music, and the dance; although surely the task must be easier with Michele, who had been reared in the lap of luxury, and had never known true need.

In her own case, Andre had been working with a wild, willful, uneducated girl, who knew none of the social graces. Hannah smiled to herself, thinking that Michele too had that streak of spirit and independence in her, and occasionally gave her mentor a difficult time, just as her mother had.

The music was louder now, pouring through the open door of the practice room, and Hannah, approaching, could hear the sound of her daughter's slippered feet upon the floor.

Reaching the door, she peered into the long, sunlit room to see Andre seated at the new pianoforte, which had replaced the old virginal, nodding his head to the beat of the music he was playing as Michele, in a whirl of white skirts, moved gracefully across the smoothly polished floor.

Gazing at her only child, Hannah caught her breath. It seemed to her that each time she looked at Michele she was lovelier. She bloomed, like a rose, a bud which was opening, petal by petal, day by day. And it was Michael's face that looked at her, Michael's dark eyes that stared back at her from under a mass of hair as red-gold as Hannah's own.

"*One* two three! *One* two three!" Andre called out. "Keep the beat, Michele! Keep the beat!" He struck the last chord and lifted his hands from the keyboard in a theatrical gesture.

He is becoming more dramatic with his gestures and demeanor as he grows older, Hannah thought with a touch of amusement, if that is possible.

Michele, perspiring and rosy, was coming toward her, her red hair in disarray above her dark eyes, her slender, small-waisted figure reflected thricefold in the mirrors which Andre had installed on the walls so that she might watch her own progress. She wore a rather short white dress that ended just above her ankles, and black slippers on tiny feet.

Seventeen, Hannah thought, sighing. When I was eighteen I was already married, widowed, and carrying Michele. She looks *so* young! Surely, I looked older at that age, but then I was much taller and considerably more buxom.

From the corner of her eye Hannah critically considered her own image in the nearest mirror. Had she changed so much? Well, she *had* put on a bit of weight about the bosom and hips—a fact that Andre brought up at every opportunity—but her waist was still trim, her skin good, and her hair almost as colorful as ever. For a thirty-seven-year-old woman, she decided, she looked extremely well. Many of her contemporaries were old women by that age, with faded, graying hair and lined faces. She had been fortunate.

And then Michele was upon her, kissing her cheek, enveloping her in the mingled scent of warm girl and the rose-scented cologne she favored.

"Mama, did you see? It is a new dance. Did you like it?"

Hannah put her arm around her daughter's shoulders. "I only saw the end, but it looked very good. You are dancing well, Michele."

Andre clucked his tongue. "Dear Hannah, you should not tell her such things. She has just learned it, and her performance is full of flaws. You should save your praise for the times when she deserves it."

Michele made a pouting face. "Don't listen to him, Mama. If Andre had his way, I would never receive a kind word. A person needs *some* encouragement!"

Michele gave Andre a haughty look, kissed her mother's cheek again, and literally danced out of the room.

Hannah, laughing fondly, watched her go.

"Speaking of encouragement," Andre said in a scolding voice, "you, dear Hannah, encourage her willful behavior. *Mon Dieu!* She is spoiled, spoiled!"

Turning about, Hannah gestured. "In some ways, I may spoil her, yes. But then so do you." She came toward him. "Tell me, old friend, is it just a mother's fond prejudice, or is she very good?"

Andre cocked his head judiciously, but there was a twinkle in his eyes. "You are prejudiced, yes, milady, but you are also right. She is a natural dancer, as I have told you many times before. And with my tutoring, *naturellement*, she has become very good indeed, but you must never tell her that I told you so. The child is vain enough as it is. She is the dancer you might have been, Hannah, had you begun earlier and stayed with it longer."

Hannah shook her head. "No, Andre. I was never quite so graceful, so light on my feet. Even then, I was too big, too tall. Michele has the perfect body for it, as well as the skill and the grace."

"Which brings us to a subject I have been considering for some time." Andre's tone was suddenly serious.

"Hannah, I have told you that there will be little opportunity here for Michele's talents to reach full expression, not to mention being properly appreciated."

Hannah stared at him curiously. "Why, yes, you have, but Michele loves dancing, and obtains great pleasure from it. Isn't that enough?"

He shook his head. "No, dear Hannah, it is not. At least not any longer. Michele is *your* daughter. She is ambitious, she wants to do something with her life, and that something is dance. Dance professionally!"

"But there is little opportunity here, in Virginia. You just said so."

He raised a hand. "I said 'here.' Here a dancer is considered something lower than the best class, but in Europe, in France and in England, dance is considered an art form. There are companies in both France and England that would be overjoyed to have someone of Michele's caliber. And you, Hannah, you should see something more of the world than you have. I have often told you that."

Hannah's immediate reaction was to halt Andre with a firm refusal, but he hurried on, and would not give her the opportunity to speak.

"I have already discussed this with Michele, and she wants very much to go. I have many friends still, in France, many people who could help us. I have, over the years, kept up a correspondence with several of them, including Madame Dubois. Madame Dubois has money and a great deal of influence, and she is lonely since her husband died. Many times she has invited us to stay with her, and she could be very helpful to Michele, as she is extremely well connected. Besides, my dear, you need to get away from Malvern for a bit. It will ease the pain for you." His expression softened. "I know how hard it has been for you, how much you loved Michael. It would help you, believe me."

Hannah, touched by his sympathy, felt tears coming to her eyes. "But didn't you once tell me that you had to leave France because of some trouble, some difficulty?"

Andre smiled mockingly, his eyebrows elevated. "I don't believe I ever said that, in so many words, although it is nonetheless true. However, that was a very long time ago, and I'm sure that my youthful indiscretion has long since been forgotten. Tell me that you will consider this, Hannah. I know that your first instinct is to say no, that you cannot bear to think of leaving Malvern in the care of others, but think on it, and think about Michele. Shouldn't she have her chance to make the kind of life she wishes? The chance you never had at her age? Think of her talent, and how wasted it will be here. Think on it, I beg of you!"

He leaned forward and kissed her gently upon the cheek, and again she felt undone.

Pressing her hand to her face, Hannah quickly left the room. Andre could always see through her; he always seemed to know what she was thinking and feeling. And he also knows how to manipulate me, she thought, almost angrily. Well, she would do as he suggested, she would think about it. She could always, in the end, still say no.

As she moved slowly down the broad, curving staircase that led to the first floor, Hannah heard the clang of the huge brass knocker striking the front door. Now, who could that be?

She heard Jenny, the housemaid, opening the door; and as Hannah descended the last step, she saw Jenny turn away from the door, an envelope in her hand.

Jenny held the envelope out. "This just came, mistress. A messenger brought it from Williamsburg."

Mildly curious, Hannah took the envelope, experiencing a disquiet as she held it in her hand. The paper was of good quality, and the calligraphy on the front was quite elegant.

As Jenny left her, Hannah opened the envelope, and slid out the single sheet of paper inside. Why, it was a bill, a statement of some kind. She scanned it quickly, and her feeling of apprehension grew. It was definitely a bill, a statement rather, stating that a payment was overdue. A payment? She drew in her breath sharply as she looked at the amount owing. It was large, frighteningly large!

At the bottom of the statement was a brief note: "Please come to see me at your earliest convenience." It was signed: "Yrs. respectfully, Courtney Wayne," and the address was in Williamsburg.

Surely, it *must* be a mistake. And yet, her name was clearly written on the envelope—Mrs. Hannah Verner, Malvern. What could it mean?

Concerned now, she pocketed the letter, and hurried into the small room that had been Michael's study, and which now served as an office of sorts for the business of the plantation.

Hannah still had not gone through all the business documents, which Michael had kept neatly filed in a wooden cabinet. She had been too distracted by his death. In fact, it had taken some time before she could bring herself to look at them at all. Perhaps there was something among the documents that would explain this strange and frightening message from the mysterious Mr. Courtney Wayne.

It took her most of the afternoon before she finally located what she was looking for, and when she found it, her dismay was total. It was the copy of a loan agreement, for a large amount, with Malvern offered as security. It was signed by Michael, dated only a short time before his death.

Hannah felt the blood drain from her face. Why had he not told her? But she knew, even as she formulated the question. Michael had never wanted to bother her with the details of running Malvern, even though she had managed the estate after his father's death, and later, with the help of Henry, the ex-slave who had acted as overseer. But when she had married Michael, and he had taken over, Henry was dead; and Michael had said that he needed no manager, no overseer. He would see to the plantation himself, and she could supervise the house, and the upbringing of Michele.

The next question was, why had Michael borrowed the money? There had been a crop failure last year, but when she had expressed concern over it, Michael had assured her that all was well. But if this statement was accurate, if there was no mistake, she did, indeed, have something to worry about.

Her thoughts went back, back to the time Michael had been at home with his father, before she came to Malvern. Malcolm had told her about that difficult time. Michael had been wild, gambling recklessly, incurring huge debts. Finally, father and son had quarreled bitterly over this, and Michael had left home, not returning until Hannah was living on Malvern.

Had Michael, before his death, reverted to his old ways?

She forced herself to stop thinking in that direction; such thoughts seemed a sacrilege. Besides, this was not the time to place blame.

She must see this Courtney Wayne as soon as possible; and she would tell no one about it, not even Michele or Andre, until she knew what it all meant.

Once out of the practice room, Michele walked slowly down the hall toward the bedroom, wiping her damp face with the hem of her muslin skirt. The dress would have to be washed anyway; she always perspired heavily when she danced, and it was very warm today.

She knew that Andre was going to broach the subject of their going to France to her mother today, and Michele felt a bubble of excitement in her chest. Would Mama say yes? She simply had to! Michele had dreamed of France, of Paris, since her childhood. Andre's stories of the French court, of the ballet, the theater, the opera, the excitement of Parisian life, had been the stuff of her childhood dreams; in fact, they still were.

Andre had been her tutor, her companion, for almost as long as she could remember. She knew that he had performed the same services for her mother when Hannah had been a young woman; and that Andre had been with her mother when she, Michele, was born. She also knew that when her mother and father had returned to Malvern—Michele had been just a baby then—Andre had remained behind in Boston to run the inn that he and her mother had started. According to what she had been told, Andre had missed them, so he had finally come back to Malvern to stay—when Michele was six.

Although Andre was devoted to both Hannah and herself, and was reasonably happy at Malvern, Michele knew that he secretly yearned to return to Paris. He had hinted at this to her mother in the past; and although Mama had shown some interest, something always seemed to come up; also, her mother had not wanted to leave her father.

At the thought of her father, Michele's eyes filled with scalding tears, and a choking lump caught in her throat.

Angrily, she tried to blink the tears away. Why? Why had he died? Why did it have to happen to him, when there were so many bad people in the world? The injustice of it made her angry, and increased her pain. Much as she loved Malvern, Michele felt increasingly that she must get away from it, away from the memories that confronted her at every turn. How could Mama stand it? It would be best for all of them to get away, at least for a time, and this seemed, to her, the best opportunity. Mama could get someone, an overseer, to look after the plantation. Mama thought too much about Malvern anyway. A trip abroad was just what she needed. She simply *must* say yes!

Going into her room, Michele began to strip off the damp muslin practice dress. Once it was off, she pulled off the flat leather slippers and flung them into a corner, to be followed by her undergarments.

Lucy, the upstairs maid, had filled the water pitcher and set out clean towels. Michele poured the cool water into the china basin, dipped a linen face cloth into the water, and began to wash her perspiring body. The water felt cool and pleasant; and as she washed her high, young breasts, Michele felt the nipples spring to life, tingling at the touch of the cloth, and sending a slight current down through her body. It was a feeling that was pleasant and embarrassing at the same time; and she paused for a moment, staring at her reflected face in the mirror above the washstand.

Her cheeks were flushed, and she looked hoydenish, with her disheveled hair and pink cheeks. At times like this, when her body experienced this kind of feeling, Michele always tried to think of something else, something that would turn her thoughts in another direction. Often, she thought of her dancing, and that usually distracted her, but today, strangely, that ploy did not work. Instead, she could feel her body growing warmer, and her nipples remained erect, like two small sentinels searching for . . .

Quickly, she spun away from the mirror, and pulled on a clean chemise, her face flushing hotter still. Oh, she knew what her nipples were searching for, she need not pretend otherwise. And into her mind popped the image she had been trying to suppress.

It had been the night of the church social over a month ago, and there had been music and dancing, and a great deal of food. There had also been some drinking, outside by the men, despite the location of the social.

Michele had been dancing with Beau Thompkins, the tall, good-looking son of Lawyer Thompkins, and Beau had, without so much as a by-your-leave, danced her right out the door and into the yard, laughing all the while.

Before she could stop him, or even utter a word of protest, he had guided her into the night shadows of a large tree and pulled her close, so close that she could smell the drink upon his breath, and the not unpleasant man smell of him.

In the instant his mouth was on hers, and his hands were cupping her breasts, which had sprung to life, just as they had a moment ago, and she had felt for the first time that feeling she had grown to both enjoy and despise.

Of course, she had felt *some* stirrings before that night, but it had been mild compared to the hot feeling that had so thrilled her as she had stood clasped in Beau's arms.

In the end she had pulled away, and slapped his face,

for good measure; but by then it was too late—the damage had been done.

If asked, Michele could not have spelled out just what she meant by "damage"; but although she could not put her feelings into words, she knew deep inside what she felt.

It had to do with what she wanted in life, and what she did *not* want. She longed to be a dancer, a good one. She wanted to dance professionally, in front of an audience, and to have them *acknowledge* that she was good.

What she did not want was to marry some local plantation owner's son, and settle down to managing a household and raising children. She was odd in this, she supposed, for her friends often told her so. Since early childhood, the other girls had talked continually of first boys, then men. Their favorite subject was marriage, and their favorite daydreams were about when and with whom it would happen. They played house. They played dolls. They practiced in every way they could, training for what they all longed for—marriage and motherhood.

Michele had never felt this way. From the very beginning, when Andre had coached her in her first steps, dancing had been the most important thing in her life, except for her father and mother; and she knew, deep in her heart and soul, that these private feelings she experienced, these physical urges, would only lure her away from her dream and into the arms of someone like Beau Thompkins, where she would be lost forever, just another housewife planning meals and bearing children like a brood mare.

No! That life was not for her; and if it meant controlling her body's willful inclinations, well, so be it. She could do it. She was strong.

Calmer now, she reached for the brush to tidy her hair. They *would* go to Paris. Mama *would* say yes, and when they were in Paris, then, Michele knew, her real life would begin.

Chapter Two

HANNAH was on the road to Williamsburg early the next morning, not long after sunrise. It was a half-day's journey to the village.

She was alone in the coach, only a single coachman on the seat above keeping the four horses at an easy gallop, as the dust of their passing filled the road behind them.

For the first half-hour of the journey, Malvern's fields stretched out on both sides of the road. Clinging to the strap, Hannah gazed pensively out at the land. The field hands, men and women, were already at work. For years Malvern had grown only tobacco, but growing tobacco was brutal to the land, and a field had to lie fallow for a period after several crops had been raised. This process had seemed wasteful to Michael; and so of late years he had been planting about half the Malvern acreage in cotton, which was a fairly new crop in the South, although the market was growing steadily.

The trouble was, getting the final product to market was a slow, tedious process. After the cotton had been picked, the seed had to be separated from the cotton fluff, and only a pound of fluff was a good day's production for one man.

A cotton crop, from planting to harvesting, was several months of hard labor. The tender cotton plants had to be nurtured carefully through late spring and summer and into fall when the white balls burst open, like corn popping over a fire. A crop could easily be destroyed along the way—drought; plagues of insects; a hard rain; or a hailstorm. That was what had happened last autumn, not too long before Michael's death—a fierce hailstorm had destroyed the cotton crop about two weeks before picking time.

That was the reason only about half of Malvern acreage was in cotton; the rest of the land lying fallow or still planted in tobacco. Michael had been optimistic about cotton, he had believed that the future of the South was tied up in cotton. "Some day, Hannah, some ingenious fellow will devise some mechanical method of separating cotton seed from the cotton, and our land will produce untold wealth for all of us."

Dear, dear Michael, Hannah thought with a melancholy smile; he had always looked on the sunny side of life. That was undoubtedly the reason he had borrowed against Malvern, confident that the future could only be better, and he could pay off the loan with no trouble. And that probably would have happened, if he had lived.

But now she was in danger of losing Malvern. She shivered as if cold, although the morning was warm and humid. She could not, she *would* not lose the land she loved. There would be a way. She could handle it. She had faced hard times before.

She knew that all too many of her neighbors would not grieve a great deal if Malvern was lost to her. As far back as Malcolm's day, the Verners had been at odds with most Virginians on the slavery issue.

In point of fact, this attitude toward slavery was mostly Hannah's doing. Sold as a bond slave at an early age, she knew firsthand the terrible strictures of slavery, and she began to work on Malcolm Verner from the day she married him. In time, Malcolm had freed many of the slaves on the plantation, and Hannah and Michael had followed suit; today, all the laborers on Malvern were freedmen.

This did not make for good neighborly relations, since all the other plantation owners were slave holders, but this did not faze Hannah. She had never let the opinions of others sway her, if she was convinced she was right, and she was not about to change now.

She sat up, alert for what was to come, as the coach entered the outskirts of Williamsburg.

Before leaving Malvern that morning, she had asked John, the Negro coachman, what he knew of Courtney Wayne. Of all the Malvern employees, John was the most knowledgeable about Williamsburg and its inhabitants. It was his chore not only to drive the coach into the village during Hannah's infrequent visits there, he was also responsible for most household purchases, and he was familiar with the storekeepers, and was usually aware of the current gossip. John was a tall, dignified man of some sixty years, self-educated and well spoken, and had been the Verner coachman as long as Hannah could remember.

"Master Wayne is something of a mystery, mistress," John had told her thoughtfully. "He came to Williamsburg less than a year ago. He does not talk much of himself, but it is known that he is a wealthy man. He purchased a fine house, employed a large staff, and took up residence. But he does not mix socially, and naught is known of his past. He dresses well, when seen abroad, and is a fine-looking man, of mayhap forty years."

"But what does he do? What is the man's profession? He must do *something*."

John had shrugged. "He is a gentleman of means, that is all that is known. There are stories, of course. Stories that he was left a fortune by a wealthy father. Stories of his discovering buried treasure. Beyond that, nothing much is known."

Hannah snorted softly to herself. Gentleman of means, indeed! A true gentleman would not have taken advantage of Michael, and a gentleman certainly would not have penned that note she carried in her reticule.

She craned to peer out the window as the coach drew to a halt. They were on a shady, tree-lined street a distance from the commercial section of Williamsburg, and the coach was drawn up before an imposing, two-story brick structure, with a beautifully manicured lawn and well-trimmed hedges before it.

John opened the coach door and handed her down. She shook herself, settling the folds of her brown traveling dress, wrinkled from the journey, tucked a few stray wisps of hair under her bonnet, and strode determinedly up the steps.

At the sound of the knocker there was an immediate response. The wide door opened, and an impressive black man in butler's livery stood in the doorway.

Hannah said crisply, "Would you tell your master that Hannah Verner is calling, please?"

"Yes, Mistress Verner," the butler murmured, inclining his head. "Would you follow me, please?"

Hannah was a little taken aback. Was Courtney Wayne expecting her? Clutching her reticule to her bosom, she followed the butler down a long hall.

The butler paused before a set of tall doors, opened them, and said, "Mistress Verner is here, sir."

A deep voice said, "Please have her come in, Noah."

Noah stepped aside with a small bow, and Hannah swept past him. The room she entered was long, three walls lined with books, while the fourth wall was a series of French doors, all opening onto a flower garden, which was a profusion of bright colors, and from which the breeze carried the scent of many blossoms.

All this Hannah noted with her peripheral vision; the main thrust of her attention was on the figure of a man standing beside a desk. He was tall, commanding, with a shock of dark hair shot with silver, and piercing blue eyes. A rather large nose dominated his handsome face.

He was dressed rather elaborately, Hannah thought; with a great deal of lace at the sleeves and shirt front, velvet knee britches and waistcoat, dark stockings and buckled shoes, the buckles pure gold and gleaming. Hannah considered his attire foppish, but then his strong features and commanding presence gave the lie to that assessment—there was nothing foppish about this man.

"Mistress Verner? Hannah Verner?" He made a leg. "I

am Courtney Wayne. Would you care to join me in my midday meal?"

He gestured, and for the first time Hannah saw the table by an open French window, set with snowy linen and gleaming crystal ware. Did he honestly think that she, under the threat of losing Malvern, was going to eat and drink with him in a civilized manner?

She said tartly, "I did not come here to share a meal with you, sir!"

A glint of amusement struck his eyes. "But surely a cup of tea, madam?"

"No, thank you." She was fumbling in her reticule. She finally produced the dunning bill and the loan agreement.

He was going on, "In any event, please accept my condolences for your husband's untimely death."

"Condolences? Does this sound like condolences?" She thrust the documents at him.

"Ah, yes." He sighed. "I am sorry, Mrs. Verner, but I *am* a businessman. And out of respect for your sorrow, I did wait a respectable time. Five months, to be exact. I had hoped that a note would not be necessary, that you would bring the loan payments up to date without prompting."

"I didn't even know about the loan until I received your note, sir."

"Then I gather that your late husband did not inform you of the transaction?"

"He did not."

"Well then." He made a negligent gesture.

"For what purpose was this loan made, sir, if there was such a loan?"

"If there was such a loan? Are you questioning my word? I believe you have a copy of our agreement in your hand, madam, with your husband's signature. I also have a signed copy of the document."

"That does not answer my question. Why did my husband come to you for money?"

"I haven't the least idea, madam. If he did not see fit to confide in you, he certainly did not inform me. If you mean why he came to me, instead of someone else, I made it known that I have funds available, to certain select gentlemen. As I am sure you know, money lenders are considered . . . uh, shall we say unsavory? Perhaps deservedly so, perhaps not. I thought there was a possibility of such a business being conducted honorably, among gentlemen."

"Gentlemen, sir?" Her lip curled. "You are no gentleman!"

He flushed, and stood taller. "Perhaps your husband had his reason for keeping his need of funds a secret from you. Perhaps he owed a large gambling debt. Or perhaps he was supporting a mistress . . ."

Her hand flashed out and delivered a stinging slap to his cheek.

Instead of angering him further, the slap seemed to calm him. He nodded distantly. "I may have deserved the rebuke. If so, my apologies, madam. But that does not change the fact that your husband owed me an honorable debt. And since he used his plantation as security for the loan, the debt is now yours. As calloused as it may seem to you, I must insist on the payments being brought up to date."

"I must have time. I only learned about this on receipt of your note. I must have time to raise the money."

His blue eyes were cold as he contemplated her. "It appears that I am on the horns of a dilemma. If I refuse to grant you more time, I am heartless. And if I do grant you more time, I risk losing my money."

"You will not lose your money, Mr. Wayne. I will find a way to repay you, you have my word on that. I have battled for Malvern before and won, and I will win this time!"

Courtney Wayne smiled slightly. "I do admire your determination." He seemed to reach a sudden decision. "Very well, Mrs. Verner. You may have sixty days in which to make the payment, but no longer. I must be firm about this, do you understand?"

She nodded, relief making her weak. Trying to keep

her voice steady, she said, "You shall have your money, sir, that I promise you."

Returning the letter and loan agreement to her reticule, she turned to go.

Courtney Wayne spoke, "My invitation to share a repast with me still stands, Mrs. Verner. Now that our business is out of the way, is there any reason we can't talk of pleasanter matters?"

Hannah choked back a scathing retort, and said instead, "I thank you, sir, but I must be on my way."

He shrugged. "Very well, madam. I will have Noah show you out." He reached for the bell rope.

Courtney Wayne gazed after the departing Hannah Verner with an amused smile. He admired a woman with spirit and intelligence, and she quite obviously had both. Most women of his experience were subservient to men, often disgustingly so, and it was nice to encounter one who stood up for herself.

Only once before had he known a woman like Hannah Verner—Katherine, his wife of three years. Of course they had been nothing alike physically; Hannah was a large, robust woman, with red hair and a white complexion, whereas Katherine had been small and dark and delicate; but both were women of spirit and great intelligence.

Sighing, Court turned, his smile dying, to stare out into the garden, his mood turned melancholy by thoughts of Katherine. Dear, dear Katherine, dead now these ten years, her delicate body racked by a deadly fever contracted on a tropical isle in the Caribbean.

He had never loved another woman, before Katherine or after; even though he had made a solemn promise to her that last day, when Katherine, shivering under several blankets in humid tropic heat, had murmured, "Court?"

"Yes, my love? You should rest, not talk."

"There is something I must say before I die."

"Hush, my love, hush. Do not talk so. Your fever will go soon, and then . . ."

"You have never lied to me, Court. Do not do so now!"

she had said in that scolding voice she used when she was impatient with him about something. "I very well know that I am dying, and there is something I want you to promise me."

"Anything, Katherine, anything you ask of me."

"After I am gone, I want you to find another woman and marry. It is not good for a man to live alone." Her hand had closed around his with a burst of strength. "Promise me!"

"I promise, Katherine. You have my solemn promise. Now you must sleep."

Katherine had never awakened from that sleep, and he had yet to keep his promise. Yet how could he keep it? He had never found a woman that did not suffer grievously when compared to his wife.

Now, he stood straighter, frowning at himself. God's oath, why were such thoughts running through his mind at this particular time?

More importantly, why had he relented and granted Hannah Verner two months' grace on the loan payments? It was not good business practice. He had felt sorry for the woman, she was in an untenable position, yet that was really no excuse for his softening. By the time the two months had expired, she would be far behind on the payments, and he would have to act then anyway, there was little doubt of that. How could a woman alone, in this day and age, raise five hundred pounds? In point of fact, she would have to raise more than that; the full amount of the loan to Michael Verner had been fifteen hundred pounds, and Hannah would have to raise at least that much in order to make the current payment to him, and keep her plantation running the rest of the year, until she brought in a new crop.

Why had he returned to Virginia, anyway? He had sworn that he never would, yet the pull had been strong. It had to do, in part he supposed, with the fact that he had wandered the world for so long—rootless, homeless—and he was weary of it. He needed a place to call home; in a way, this *was* home; also, there were some old scores to settle.

It would, he thought, be nice to make his permanent home at Malvern, to be accepted as landed gentry, a country gentleman of property. And if that meant hardening his heart against Hannah Verner and asserting his right—pay her debt or he would take over Malvern—he could damned well do it!

A soft cough from behind him brought his head around. "Yes, Noah?"

"Shall I serve your food now?"

"Yes . . . No, I've changed my mind. I'm not hungry. Bring me a bottle of brandy instead."

As the dark face registered disapproval, Court's temper gave way. "Don't look at me like that, damn your soul! Do as I tell you. Who's the master of this house?"

Hannah was in a quandary on the ride home to Malvern. How on earth was she going to get the funds necessary to save Malvern? For the first time she halfway regretted alienating herself from her neighbors, several of whom were rich planters who might have helped her through the crisis; but she was not about to humble herself before them now. She would manage some way.

But what made her quandary even worse was the ambivalence of her feelings toward Courtney Wayne. He was certainly no gentleman, and he had the cold heart of a moneylender; yet Hannah had found him physically attractive. For the first time since the death of her husband she felt herself drawn to a man. That it should be a man of Courtney Wayne's caliber was infuriating!

It had been her experience that there were many charming rascals in the world, and a woman had to look beyond the physical facade of a man, probing for the person underneath. At least she would not have to do that with this man; he had already revealed himself for what he was.

As the coach wheeled up the driveway before Malvern, she forcibly rejected all thoughts of Courtney Wayne, and gave herself over to that warm rush of pleasure she always experienced when she saw the great manor house. Even if she had only been away for a few hours, she always felt a great delight when she saw those soaring white pillars, and knew that this place was hers.

But for how long, she wondered; dear God, how long?

Her thoughts were bleak as she swept through the front doors, and found Andre and Michele waiting for her in the entryway.

"Mama, Andre told me!" Michele squealed, and gave her a fierce embrace.

"Told you what, for heaven's sake?" Hannah said grumpily, and disengaged herself from her daughter's arms.

"That he had talked to you about all of us going to Paris, and you had agreed."

"He said that, did he?" Hannah said grimly, frowning at Andre, who returned her look with a shrug of innocence. "I agreed to no such thing, Michele. I only said that I would think about it."

"The child wants to go so badly, milady, that she gets carried away," Andre said. "So she misinterprets what I told her. She can hardly be blamed for that."

"You mean you won't agree, Mama?" Michele said in dismay, her face going pale.

"I did not say that, I said that I needed time to think about it."

"If you don't agree, I am going anyway." Michele assumed a stance of belligerence, her chin stuck out. "And you can't stop me, Mama!"

Hannah studied her daughter in silence for a moment, torn between admiration and annoyance. How so like herself Michele was! At that age Hannah also had been filled with fire and spirit. She finally said tiredly, "You might be able to run off, if you chose, except for one thing . . . Ship passage to France is expensive, my dear daughter. Where would you get the necessary money?"

"I will find it somewhere!"

Infinitely weary now, Hannah said dryly, "If money is

all that easy to find, Michele, perhaps you should advise me. I might find it helpful."

She started down the hall toward the study.

"Hannah?" Andre came hurrying after her, a look of concern on his face. "What is it, dear Hannah? Are you in financial trouble?"

For a long moment she was tempted to confide in him. He had been her friend and confidant for so many years. On the other hand, Andre had about as much money sense as a goose, and there was no point in burdening him with her troubles.

She smiled, and taking his hand between hers, she patted it maternally. "It's nothing to concern you, Andre. You and Michele, you may go to Paris, with my blessing."

A smile bloomed on his face. "Do you mean it, Hannah?"

"Of course I mean it. Have I ever promised you something I didn't mean?" she said crossly, already regretting her sudden, impulsive promise. "I beg one promise in return. It will take me a few days, perhaps longer, to arrange the funds for the trip, so I would very much appreciate it if you and Michele would not pester me about it in the meantime. Are we agreed?"

"Of course, Hannah, of course!" He was still beaming. "But you, you haven't said you're going with us."

"Someone has to remain behind and attend to business affairs. Besides, what need do you have of me? Now, off with you, Andre! I have things to do."

Briskly, she went into the study and closed the door in Andre's face. Inside, she collapsed into the chair at the desk, dismay almost making her ill. Why had she made such a rash promise? Still, what difference did it really make? She either raised the money she needed to pay Courtney Wayne or she did not. If she did manage to raise the money, it should be no problem to get additional funds, enough to finance the trip to Paris.

Sighing, she opened the account books and started in where she had left off yesterday. She spent the rest of the afternoon with them; twice Andre knocked on the door, and once the cook rapped, inquiring if she wanted something to eat. Crossly, Hannah sent them both away.

Finally, late in the afternoon, she leaned back, finished. She massaged the back of her stiff neck, staring numbly at the final figures. The plantation was in much worse financial shape than she had dreamed. There was almost no ready cash on hand, and there were a number of unpaid bills from shopkeepers. There were no ready assets on Malvern that she could sell to raise money. Ironically, she herself was partially responsible for that. Usually, when a plantation owner needed money to tide him over a bad situation, he sold off a few slaves. Hannah could not do that, since she had seen to it that they were all freedmen. And what made it even worse, the fifty-some people on Malvern were employees, and she had to pay them wages—wages that she did not have.

There was only one alternative; she had to borrow enough money from somewhere to see Malvern through until the next harvest, pay the delinquent payment to Courtney Wayne, and send Michele and Andre to Paris. Briefly, she again regretted her promise, then squared her shoulders. Her daughter deserved a chance at life; and if dancing in the ballet was what she wanted, Hannah intended to do everything in her power to see that she got it.

For the next three days Hannah went into Williamsburg every morning and spent hours going from one moneylender to another. Once she encountered Courtney Wayne on the street. He lifted his tricornered hat in a slight bow, and his smile was knowing, as if he was aware of every person she had petitioned.

At the end of the third day she was plunged into gloom as she rode the coach home. She had been rebuffed in every instance; the excuses varied, but it all came down to the same thing, she was certain. No one was willing to lend money to a woman.

She thought of going farther afield, to Jamestown,

Norfolk, or the newly founded city of Richmond, but she knew it would be a waste of time. If people in Williamsburg, who at least knew the Verner name, would turn her down, why should complete strangers react any differently?

She was tired, discouraged, and badly in need of a bath. It was with a feeling of dismay that she saw Andre waiting on the steps as the coach pulled up before the manor house. She was going to have to tell him, and Michele, that they would be unable to go to Paris. It would be a blow to Michele, she knew, but the longer she waited to tell her daughter, the worse it would be.

Andre hustled forward, opened the coach door before John could climb down, and helped her out.

In a low voice, he said, "I wanted to tell you, Hannah, before you went into the house, you have a visitor. He's been here most of the afternoon. I told him you were not at home, but he stubbornly said that he would wait. More, he said you would *want* to see him." Andre made a face. "I can't imagine why you would. He's an obnoxious fellow."

"What is this man's name?"

"Jules Dade."

She frowned, thinking, then slowly shook her head. "I'm not familiar with the name, but I suppose I should see him at least, since he's been waiting all this time."

"If you think it's wise." He shrugged. "I put him in the east parlor, out of harm's way. I'll hover close by, dear one, in the event you need assistance."

In the parlor the man who arose from the divan as Hannah came in was short, thin, and dressed in sober brown. He came around the divan toward her, removing his hat, showing mouse-brown hair—a peruke, Hannah realized. He moved with slow, deliberate steps, but in spite of his bulk, he seemed to be taut with nervous energy. His face was broad, and his expression phlegmatic. Hannah placed his age at close to fifty.

"Mrs. Hannah Verner?" he said in a colorless voice.

She got her first good look at his eyes. They were a pale gray in color and had a chill, depthless look. Unaccountably,

Hannah shivered. She said quickly, "Yes, I'm Hannah Verner."

"I am Jules Dade." He made a leg, sweeping the floor with the tricornered hat.

"I am unfamiliar with your name, Mr. Dade. Are you a stranger in Virginia?"

"Only a recent arrival to Williamsburg, madam. I am a Virginian, formerly in shipping out of Norfolk. I have retired from that."

Still mystified, Hannah said cautiously, "That is all very interesting, sir, but may I inquire as to what business you may have of me?"

"Ah, yes!" Dade clasped his hands behind his back. "I am here to be of service to you, Mistress Verner."

"Service? In what way, pray?" She eyed him suspiciously.

"It has come to my attention that you are seeking a business loan . . ."

She cut in, "How did you know about that?"

"Ah." He smiled, a thin gleam of teeth. "I have my sources. That is my business nowadays, loaning money. I have ample funds, and I seek to loan them out, at a reasonable but profitable rate of interest. It is also my understanding that you have so far been unsuccessful in your efforts."

"You seem to know a great deal about my business, sir."

He ignored her displeasure. "Mistress Verner, I am prepared to make you a generous loan, at three per cent interest." He smiled again, exhibiting an expression that failed to warm his chill eyes in the least. "Now what could be fairer than that?"

"Just like that?" She was still wary of the man, but despite her reservations, her heart was beginning to speed up at the prospect of a solution to her problems. "Nothing more?"

"Ah, well." Hands clasped behind his back, he rocked back and forth. "I will require a lien against your property, madam, but it is purely a technicality, in addition to the lien already existing, owed to Courtney Wayne."

"You know about Mr. Wayne?"

"I have some knowledge of him, yes."

"But another lien . . .," she said dubiously.

"Ah, but do not be fearful," he said blandly. "That is merely a protection that is good sense to require. I am confident that you will repay the loan. You have the reputation of being a reliable person. But consider, madam . . . what if something should happen to you, God forbid that it should, but I would need some assurance of recovering my money."

"I suppose there is no other way," Hannah said slowly.

A spark of light seemed to burn far back in Dade's eyes. "I am afraid that is the case. It is the proper way to do business." He shrugged his heavy shoulders. "It is true that some might be willing to risk their money, out of friendship perhaps, but it is not good business practice."

He spread his hands wide. "Consider this, madam. Our agreement will not include monthly payments. I am aware that, as a plantation owner, you are dependent on crop cycles, and will not be able to repay the loan until your next crop is in. Therefore, you will not be required to pay until such a time. What could be fairer?"

"I don't know," she said doubtfully. She turned her back and crossed to the window to stare out at the fields stretching beyond the range of her vision—Malvern fields. Would they fail her? She looked around at Dade thoughtfully. There were facets of his personality that she did not care for, but that could spring from her antipathy toward moneylenders in general. She did not like Courtney Wayne, either.

She came to a sudden decision, and a surge of confidence went through her. She could do it, she knew she could!

She faced fully around. "All right, Mr. Dade, I will accept your terms."

"Ah, excellent, madam, excellent!" He clasped his hands again behind his back, and rocked back on his heels. "You will not regret it, I am sure."

A short time later, the proper papers signed and a

money draft in Hannah's hands, she opened the parlor door and ushered Jules Dade out of the house.

Closing the front door with her back against it, she called out, "Michele? Andre?"

Andre appeared as if by magic from the side corridor. "Yes, milady?"

Michele appeared at the top of the stairs. "Yes, Mama?"

"Pack your trunks, the pair of you. You are on your way to France as soon as I can arrange passage for you!"

Chapter Three

ON the way back from Norfolk, after seeing Michele and Andre onto their ship, Hannah asked John to detour by Courtney Wayne's house in Williamsburg, so that she might pay the money due on Michael's loan. She found Courtney Wayne increasingly in her thoughts, and had decided it was because of the debt. Once she had paid him the money due, Hannah was certain that he would recede from her thoughts, and she would be able to get on with the business of making the money to pay back him and Jules Dade.

When the house servant opened the door to her knock, Hannah announced herself.

Noah looked down the hallway, and said uncertainly, "Master Wayne is, uh, engaged right now, Mistress Verner. Perhaps if you could call back later?"

Hannah breezed past him. "Impossible! I live a goodly distance from here. I'm sure Mr. Wayne will receive me. If you will tell him that I have rather pressing business . . ." At the servant's increasingly agitated look, Hannah's voice had risen.

And now a door opened down the hall. Courtney Wayne stood in the doorway, fastening his trousers. His hair was mussed, and his color was high. Hannah glimpsed a pale figure in the dimness behind him. Before he could close the door, Hannah realized the figure was female, nude from the waist up.

"What is it, Noah?" Court said as he strode toward

them. Then he gave a start as he saw Hannah. "Oh, Mrs. Verner! How do you do, madam?"

Hannah was secretly amused to see his composure shaken. In their prior meeting he had seemed self-possessed to the point of arrogance. But by the time he came down the hall to her he had regained his poise.

She said wickedly, "I must apologize, Mr. Wayne, for interrupting your *business*."

He regarded her calmly. "What can I do for you, Mrs. Verner?"

"I am here to make the delinquent loan payment, sir."

"Oh?" He elevated his eyebrow. "Perhaps we should talk in my study. Would you like some tea, Mrs. Verner? Or perhaps a glass of sherry?"

"No, thank you."

He placed his hand under her elbow, and Hannah experienced a tingle from his touch. She thought of freeing her arm from his grasp, but she waited until he had to let go of her arm in order to open the study door.

Inside the room she already had her reticule open and the money out before he had turned about from closing the door. As he came to her, she counted out the money she owed into his hand.

She said coolly, "It is all there, I believe. I would like a receipt, if you please."

He wore a look of astonishment as he accepted the money. "I'm afraid I do not understand, Mrs. Verner. How did you . . .?" Then he smiled. "You perhaps found some money that your late husband had secreted away?"

It was Hannah's turn to be astonished. It had never occurred to her that Michael might have hidden away some money. Was it possible? Without thinking she said, "No, I found no such money, sir. I borrowed the money."

"Borrowed? But it is my understanding that no one would grant you a loan."

"You seem well informed, Mr. Wayne," she said angrily. "But apparently not well informed enough."

"So it would seem," he said, his smile rueful. "But I would have been willing to wager that . . ."

"That no one would loan money to a mere woman?" she finished for him.

"Well, yes. I thought it highly unlikely, at any rate."

"Again, you were wrong."

"It would appear so."

"You apparently have a low opinion of a woman's ability to conduct business, sir."

"Our society poorly equips women for business, madam, you must admit."

"There are exceptions," she said proudly. "And I consider myself one of those exceptions."

"Still . . ." He looked again at the money in his hand. "I do find it difficult to believe that the hardheaded businessmen of Williamsburg would so bend their principles as to loan money, this much money, to a female." He looked up hopefully. "I know! A close and dear friend, am I correct?"

"No, you are *not* correct. A Mr. Dade apparently has more faith in a woman's business ability than you do, Mr. Wayne."

"Dade?" His look sharpened. "Not Jules Dade?"

"That is the one."

He said in obvious distress, "Mrs. Verner, you have made a grievous mistake. Jules Dade is a man of bad reputation. He is known as an unscrupulous individual. He has become wealthy as a moneylender, but not an honest one by any means."

Hannah felt a pull of apprehension, but then her anger drove it out. "He did not appear so to me, sir."

"Oh, well." He gestured negligently.

Her fury mounted. "You have little respect for women, do you, Mr. Wayne?"

"Madam, I defer to no man in my respect and affection for the female sex."

"So I noticed," she said icily. "I saw a wench behind you a bit ago, but that is hardly *respect*. You think women have no brains, no business sense. Well, I will have you know, sir, that I once ran Malvern by myself, and very well indeed. And I can do so again. If it is the last thing I do, I will prove you wrong!"

He looked at her pensively. "You may not believe this, Mrs. Verner, but I hope you do, I sincerely do."

Her temper abating, Hannah said, "One thing I am curious about, Mr. Wayne. You claim you do not know why my husband needed money, but why did he come to you, in particular?"

He shrugged. "I don't know that, either."

"Did you know Michael *before* he came to you?"

"No, madam, I had never met him before he came to me." His eyes were cool. "Did it ever occur to you that he may have come to me, in preference to doing business with a scoundrel like Jules Dade?"

Annoyed again, Hannah snapped, "I fail to see the difference between you, sir!"

He said indifferently, "Think what you will, madam."

"I will make the next payment on time, sir. Of that you may rest assured."

Court was in a melancholy mood after Hannah left.

Was he always to be plagued by Jules Dade? He had thought that the man was still living in Norfolk. Was it possible that Dade had moved to Williamsburg because he had learned that he, Court, now abided here? It seemed that Jules Dade was to be his nemesis for the rest of his life. Court was puzzled about one thing—why had Dade made the loan to Hannah Verner?

But of course the answer was obvious. Dade courted respectability, and what better way to become respectable than to own a plantation like Malvern? By making a substantial loan to the Verner woman he probably calculated that he would be able to eventually seize the plantation in payment.

And weren't you thinking much the same thing only a few days ago, he asked himself. He grimaced. It was true, he had, but after knowing Hannah Verner a little better, the idea was not nearly so attractive. Somehow Hannah, for all her quick temper and irritating stubbornness, appealed to him, and he found himself wishing her well. She was certainly going to need all his good wishes, and more, if she was going to be dealing with Jules Dade!

Court motioned angrily to himself and left the study, going down the hall toward the room he had quitted when Hannah came to call.

Why should he be thinking of Hannah when he had a comely, willing wench awaiting him?

As he opened the door, Beth Johnson spoke from the large divan, "Well, it's about time! I thought you were never coming back, Court."

"My apologies, Beth," he said, stepping out of his trousers. "I had some urgent business to attend to."

Beth Johnson, like Hannah Verner, was also a recent widow, her husband having died at approximately the same time as Michael Verner. But unlike Hannah, Beth did not grieve for her dead spouse. She was a lusty wench by nature, who thoroughly enjoyed being bedded. "That spouse of mine," she had told Court early on, "had about as much life to him as a dead fish. I married him when I was but a bit of a girl, and never knew what a real man was until he was gone."

In other circumstances, Beth would probably be considered a doxie, but fortunately her late husband had left her considerable property and a good income, so she could be discreet about her affairs with men.

Not only was she pleasing in bed, but she made no demands on a man beyond the sexual, which pleased Court immensely. Despite his promise to Katherine, Court very much doubted that he would ever marry again. However, he did have a strong sexual appetite, and a woman like Beth Johnson was welcome in his life.

Naked, he got onto the divan with her, and Beth enfolded him in her warm embrace. He said, "Now, where were we when we were so rudely interrupted?"

"From the feel of you, love, you might not have been interrupted at all." She laughed throatily. "As to where we were, I think we'd gotten about to this . . . point. Ah, yes, love! Yes, yes, that's fine!"

* * *

Hannah was still seething as the coach clattered toward Malvern. The infernal conceit and arrogance of the man! Just because she was a woman, Courtney Wayne thought she was silly, empty-headed, and utterly incapable of conducting the affairs of a plantation. Men seemed to believe that women were only useful in the kitchen and the bedroom. Even Michael had had some of that male prejudice, but in him it had not been quite so strong as in most men. Not only had she operated the plantation successfully, but during her time in Boston, she, with Andre's help, had operated a tavern, The Four Alls.

She could do it again, she *would* do it again! It was not going to be easy. She had thirty field hands to feed and clothe, plus a household staff of ten, and she had two substantial loans to pay off. She dismissed the thought of discharging a single one of the employees. All were black, and she well knew that it would be almost impossible for them to find employment in the area—freed slaves were looked on askance in Virginia. She felt an obligation to see them cared for.

As the coach drew nearer to Malvern, Hannah's mood gradually changed. The anger that had blazed up during the scene with Courtney Wayne began to subside, and doubts started to plague her. It was a tremendous load she was taking on, and she had to wonder if she could manage. She had no doubts about her ability to manage Malvern, but any number of things could go wrong. Another crop failure could occur, and it was not in her power—or anyone's—to prevent that from happening.

Also, in her mind was Courtney Wayne's warning about Jules Dade. If Dade was as unscrupulous as Wayne claimed, how could she cope with that, along with her many other problems?

Hannah was not given to rash, foolish decisions, but the feeling was growing in her that she may have acted rashly this time. Michael's sudden, shocking death, the disclosure of his debt, the need of funds for Michele's journey to France—all those pressures had pushed her too hard. She might regret it in the end.

Well, she had confronted hazard after hazard all of her life, and emerged triumphant. Would she fail this time?

To turn her mind away from present problems, Hannah thought of Michael's strange death, strange in that it was unexplained. It was the first time that she was able to bring herself to consider it objectively.

Michael had been returning from Williamsburg. Instead of taking the coach, he had ridden a horse into the village that day. It was established that he had finished his business—whatever it was—late in the afternoon, then stopped at his favorite tavern for a brandy. Hannah had talked with the owner of the tavern, and he had sworn that Michael had only imbibed two glasses. But now, thinking back on it, Hannah realized that the innkeeper had been deliberately evasive. Had Michael been intoxicated when he finally started for home?

Whatever his condition, no one had any knowledge of his movements after that. He had left the tavern after dark, presumably riding toward Malvern. His body had been discovered the next morning by a passing rider, in a ditch alongside the road about five miles from Williamsburg. His horse, Black Star, grazed peaceably a few yards away. Michael's neck had been broken; and after a cursory investigation, the constable from Williamsburg had concluded that Michael had been thrown by his horse, and killed by the fall. There had been a large lump on the back of his head, but the constable had also attributed that to the fall.

Michael, as superb a horseman as Hannah had ever known, thrown by his horse? And yet, it could have happened if Michael had been drunk; Black Star was a high-spirited stallion, and Michael had been one of the few people who could ride the animal. Yes, it could have happened that way, but there was no way of knowing for certain, and probably never would be. Since Michael had been riding alone, and the incident had been unwitnessed, how could anything else ever be learned? And what else *could* have happened? The constable had shaken his head when Hannah had mentioned foul play. And he was right, of course. Nobody had hated Michael, certainly not enough to kill him.

She sighed heavily, as the coach turned into the long driveway. Already the great house appeared empty and lonely. For twenty years she had been accustomed to Michael's booming laughter, to Michele's youthful exuberance, and to Andre's sly wit. Now they were all gone, and she would be alone, except for the servants. For just a moment she regretted her decision not to accompany her daughter to Paris.

Then she shook off the melancholy and the depressing thoughts, determined not to indulge in self-pity. She was going to be busy enough during the coming year to keep from feeling lonely.

As the coach drew to a stop and John got down to help her out, she said, "John, will you come to the study after you've seen to the horses? We need to have a talk."

"Of course, mistress," he said with an inclination of his head.

When John was admitted to the study a short time later, Hannah bade him to be seated, and then proceeded to tell him of the situation of her finances. She told him everything, except her fears that Michael might have lost a lot of money gambling. She did ask him, "Would you have any idea, John, why my husband would have made such a loan?"

"Master Verner did not confide business matters to me."

Hannah thought she saw a flicker of something in his dark eyes, but she did not challenge him on it. "This Jules Dade, John, what do you know of him?"

"Nothing that is good, I fear, but then of course, what I think of him is tainted by the fact that Master Dade is a slave trader. Or he was."

She said in dismay, "That is the way he made his fortune?"

"That is my understanding. Oh, he was not actively

engaged in the trade, to the point of going to Africa. But it was his ships that sailed across and brought my people over, and then Master Dade handled the sale here."

"Then the money I borrowed is blood money!"

"Mistress, that could be said about much of Virginia money," he said stolidly, "since Virginia's economy is a slave economy."

Hannah looked at him in surprise. She could not remember John commenting on slaveholding one way or another, and she had to wonder how much long-buried resentment he harbored. She said, "John, are you really that bitter, that unhappy with your lot?"

His look was sardonic. "In view of the other choice, slavery, I suppose you could say that I'm not all that unhappy. And whatever bitterness I feel, is not directed at you, mistress. You gave us our freedom and then decent employment. Bess told me, before she died, how hard you fought for her freedom, and she also told me something of your lot with Amos Stritch, when you were his bond slave."

Hannah's thoughts were shaded with sorrow for a moment. Bess was the black woman who had been Stritch's slave, cooking in his tavern. When Malcolm Verner had bought Hannah's freedom from Stritch, Hannah had insisted that he buy Bess' freedom as well. Bess remained Hannah's companion and friend up until her death three years ago.

Hannah sighed, shaking herself loose from melancholy. "If I don't make Malvern pay, so I can repay the debts I owe, there won't be employment for anyone, decent or otherwise. That's basically what I wanted to discuss with you, John. Before, when I ran the plantation by myself, Henry was invaluable, as my overseer. Do you think I should try to find an overseer now?"

John said slowly, "Did you have in mind doing the task alone? If so, I would advise against it, mistress."

"Why?"

"The workers, especially the men, do not take kindly to receiving their orders from a woman. Even if the instructions are actually yours, it would be better if they were delivered by a man."

"What you're saying is, they would rather take orders from a man, instead of a woman?"

He squirmed uncomfortably. "That is so."

Her temper stirred. "Why should that be?"

He gave a small shrug. "It is the way of things, mistress."

"But I've given the hands orders since Michael's death, and they obeyed. And the household staff doesn't seem to mind."

"The mistress of the house is expected to command the household staff."

"But not outside the house, is that it?" she said with a twist of bitterness. "But I suppose you are right, John. You know everyone on the plantation. Are any of the men capable of acting as overseer?"

He said promptly, "None, mistress. And it should not be one of us, but a man of your own race."

"Henry was black, and they obeyed him well enough."

"Henry was Henry, there were few like him. But I was thinking more of the other planters. You well know they do not approve of a black overseer."

"I care little for their opinions!"

"But you should, mistress, you should," he said softly. "It is the way of things. You will have difficulty enough, with the burden of debt on you, without the enmity of your neighbors."

Her shoulders slumped in defeat. "I know you're right, but still . . ." She straightened up. "Do you know a man, a *white* man, who would accept the job?"

He was silent for a moment, staring at her. "Perhaps I have heard of a man who might be available. I will see what I can learn, but you must not tell him, or anyone, that it is my doing."

Four days later, Hannah was interviewing Nathaniel Bealls in her study. In his early thirties, Nathaniel was stalwart, well over six feet, with smoldering black eyes, and a face almost classically handsome. He was dressed in high riding boots and rough clothing. He carried a riding crop in his right hand, which he struck against his thigh repeatedly. He had ridden up to the manor house on a great gray horse.

When he had been ushered into the study, and Hannah had risen to make him welcome, he had studied her with a bold, almost insolent appraisal, which had made her a little uncomfortable. Yet, at the same time, she was obscurely flattered that such a handsome, obviously virile man should find her attractive.

They had tea and cakes, the fragile tea cup incongruously tiny in his large hand. Hannah still felt a little flushed by his continued appraisal of her.

She said, "You do understand, Mr. Bealls, that Malvern's field hands are not slaves? They are freedmen."

"So I have heard, Mrs. Verner."

"And they must be treated as such, not as slaves."

He shrugged slightly. "So long as they perform the chores assigned to them, I foresee no problems."

"You have had previous experience as a plantation overseer?"

"I have worked as an overseer for some ten years, Mrs. Verner, throughout the South."

"Why aren't you employed at the present time?"

He gave a shrug. "The crop failure last year. The last plantation I worked on, the Tribow Plantation, had to sell off several slaves and Mr. Tribow let all the salaried men go."

Hannah had already known this, through John. Nathaniel Bealls, according to John, had a good reputation—a hard worker, and the land under his supervision flourished. However, last year's crop failure was universal. Nathaniel's only flaw, it seemed, was a tendency to be fiddle-footed; he seldom remained at one plantation for more than a year or so, before he became restless and moved on.

"I cannot pay more than a nominal salary, Mr. Bealls, until after the crops are harvested and sold. I'll be frank with you, sir, I am in sore financial straits. But when the crops are sold, I will reimburse you in full."

He shrugged again. "I require nothing more than food and lodging for now. Since your crop is already under way, I shall be working from dawn until dark."

"One thing troubles me . . ." She hesitated.

"And what might that be, Mrs. Verner?"

"That riding crop you carry . . ." She gestured. "I've seen men carry those around before, and usually they use it to discipline their slaves when they are displeased."

"This?" He lifted the crop and stared at it as though he had never seen it before. Then he laughed heartily. "Carrying this is simply a habit, Mrs. Verner. I've carried it around with me for so long that I often forget that I even have it. I would never whip anyone with it."

"Just so you don't. I will not allow my people on Malvern to be whipped. If someone has need of disciplining, you will come to me first. Is that understood, sir?"

His dark eyes studied her closely. "If I am to do my job as overseer, I must have authority to discharge any of your field hands that give trouble, or any who do not perform the work assigned to them."

Hannah nodded. "You have that authority, of course you do. I just will not allow any cruelty on Malvern." She got to her feet. "I will see you out, Mr. Bealls. John, my coachman, will show you to your quarters. I hope that our relationship will be to our mutual benefit."

She moved ahead of him to the door, and then led the way down the hall to the front door. There was a strange coach drawn up before the house, the coach horses shining with sweat. John was standing at the head of the coach, speaking up to the driver. Then he turned and opened the door to the coach.

Hannah stopped at the top of the steps, staring curiously as the door swung open, and an elegantly clad leg emerged, the foot groping for the step.

Finally the occupant of the coach fully emerged. It was Courtney Wayne. He straightened his hat, brushed off his clothing, and started toward the veranda steps.

Nathaniel Bealls was speaking, his back to the coach. She looked at him. "I beg your pardon, sir?"

"I was saying, I am sure that I shall enjoy working for you, Mrs. Verner."

He made a leg, took her hand, and raised it to his lips. Hannah darted a glance at the man coming up the steps, and she felt strangely pleased as she saw him stop, staring at Bealls kissing her hand.

Then Court came on. As he reached the top step, Bealls, made aware of the newcomer, turned to face him.

Hannah said, "Nathaniel Bealls, may I introduce you to Mr. Courtney Wayne? Mr. Wayne, Nathaniel is my new overseer."

As the two men shook hands, Hannah took note of a strange thing—the air between them almost literally quivered with hostility. She was confused for a long moment before the answer came to her—*she* was the cause of the hostility!

Chapter Four

As the smooth, wooden deck pitched under her feet, Michele slid across the cabin and struck the wall with bruising force, causing her to cry out. Andre, seated on a wooden bench near the door, slid quickly to the side, almost losing his grip upon the concertina, which let out a dreadful squall as his hands involuntarily contracted.

When the great ship began to right itself, Michele became aware of the sound of laughter, and looked around to see a man standing in the doorway to the salon, clearly convulsed with laughter at their plight.

A hot mixture of embarrassment and anger filled her. She hated to be seen in an unflattering light, and the pain of her bruised shoulder only added to her discomfort. She also disliked being seen in practice clothes, which had been chosen for comfort rather than fashion.

Cautiously, she stood erect, and glared at the interloper. He was young, although he appeared to be several years older than herself, and his sandy hair caught the light of the ship's lantern in the salon. The more he laughed, the angrier Michele became.

"You, sir," she cried, "are decidedly lacking in good manners! How dare you spy upon me? Have you no shame?"

The young man was bent over, clutching his stomach, trying to contain his laughter. "I am sorry, miss," he gasped out, "but it *was* amusing, particularly the concertina. It made such a peculiar sound."

"You had no right to be watching!" Despite her annoyance, Michele could not but help notice that he spoke with a strange but rather charming accent, one she was unfamiliar with.

Now he straightened, and she could see that his face was rather pleasant, with clear gray eyes and a strong nose above a well-shaped mouth. He said, "It was not intentional, I assure you. I happened to be passing along the passageway when your, uh, accident occurred. The cabin door was open, and I glanced in."

His expression hinted that he was about to break into laughter again, and Michele felt her anger mounting, and knew that it would soon be out of control.

"I will thank you then, sir, if you will please continue on your way. No gentleman would remain where his presence was not wanted!"

"Of course, Miss Verner. I shall immediately remove myself from your sight, and I do apologize most abjectly if I have offended you. I meant no such offense." Bowing low, he backed out of the salon, and disappeared into the dimness of the passageway.

Michele whirled on Andre, who had risen from the bench, and was staring at her in sympathy. "Andre," she cried, "this is impossible! I cannot work like this. I could break my leg. And that awful man! How dare he watch me like that? How dare he laugh at me?"

Andre stepped to her and placed an arm about her shoulders. "There now, *chérie,* I am certain that he meant no harm. He no doubt was, as he stated, simply passing by the open door as the ship rolled, and you must admit that it was a curious sight. *Mon Dieu,* the concertina did squall abominably!"

Michele, as the picture he painted formed in her mind, had to smile, but as her bruised shoulder twinged, the smile faded. "It is not humorous! I hurt myself, and for all he knew, badly. He is certainly no gentleman. And how did he know my name? We have never met."

Andre shrugged. "Perhaps you caught his eye when we

came aboard, and he asked the captain about you. You are a fetching wench, you know."

Michele rubbed the aching shoulder. "Well, he has a great deal of gall, in any case." Almost as an afterthought, she added, "He spoke in a rather strange accent, one I have never heard spoken."

"He is a Scotsman, Michele."

"Well, I certainly hope that we will not see him again."

Andre was smiling. "I fear that will be unlikely, my love. This is a large ship, but there are only a few passengers, and we are bound to meet at mealtimes, at least."

Michele favored him with a glare almost as cold as she had given the intruder. "Then I shall just ignore him, as best I can. Mayhap that will discourage him. At any rate, I can practice no more today. The ship is pitching too much, and this cabin is too small. I don't have space enough to even move!"

"Michele, my pet, you must learn to be more adaptable. You know that it is vital that you continue to practice, and this, the passenger's salon, is the only space available to us. The captain was most kind to allow us to use it. We will be at sea for five or six weeks, and if you did not practice during all that time, you would be in no condition to appear before Arnaut Deampierre. I have written him that you are a fine dancer. Would you embarrass me before him?"

Michele sighed. "No, no, Andre, of course not. I realize that I must practice. It's just that that man upset me, and my shoulder pains me."

Andre kissed her cheek. "You are simply tired. It has been a busy day, and you have yet to find what sailors call your 'sea legs.' After all, this is our first day at sea. We shall stop for today. But tomorrow, we practice. Agreed?"

Michele nodded consent. "Perhaps I shall feel better after a little sleep. If I *can* sleep with the ship pitching like this." She dredged up a smile. "Thank heavens, I have a strong stomach. It looks as if I shall need it on this voyage."

* * *

As Michele opened the door to her small cabin, she grimaced. The tiny cabin was dark and Spartan in appearance, the only light coming from a small porthole set in the other side. The narrow, hard bunk and her traveling trunk took up most of the room; although she understood that she had been very fortunate to get a private cabin at all, for the broad-beamed merchantman upon which they sailed had booked passage had room for only a few passengers. Andre had been forced to share a cabin with a portly businessman, who, he had said, smelled of liniment, and coughed continuously.

The other passengers consisted of a middle-aged couple from Norfolk, whom she and Andre had met as they came aboard, and, she had been informed, two men traveling together, one of whom she had evidently just met.

Michele rubbed her aching shoulder, and felt a rebirth of her earlier anger. She knew that she was oversensitive about being seen in a bad or embarrassing light—at least her mother and Andre often told her that she was—but in this case she felt that her annoyance was justified.

With a heartfelt sigh, she lay down upon the narrow bunk, and let her mind drift and relax, rather enjoying the rocking motion of the ship, which seemed restful to her when she was lying down. Drifting toward sleep, she wondered what it would be like in Paris; how it would be to dance on a real stage before an audience. She could easily visualize herself, reveling in the applause. There would be flowers, of course, presented to her after many curtain calls; and a party in her honor, at which she would be gracious and kind to all of her admirers. She went to sleep, smiling at her pleasant fantasy.

When Michele awoke, it seemed to her that she had slept for some time, for the light coming in through the porthole was dim and gray. Dinner, she had been informed, would be served at six, and she had to change her gown, and make her toilette.

Since it was to be her first real meal on board the ship,

she wanted to make a good impression, and debated what she would wear. Andre had cautioned her to keep only her most practical clothing in her cabin; for the journey would be lengthy, and laundry facilities were skimpy. He had also advised dark clothing that would not show soil easily, made of sturdy materials that would not easily crush or wrinkle; although he had conceded that she should take two gowns of a more elaborate style for evening wear, as they would take their meals with the captain.

She finally decided upon a green taffeta with the flounced ruchings and the laced bodice. She had chosen to bring this gown because the skirt was separate, and could be worn with different stomachers and fronts; and since it had no box pleats in the back, and was made to wear over relatively narrow hoops, it should be less cumbersome in the confines of the ship. Even so, when she was fully dressed, her skirts were pushing against the bunk on one side and the wall on the other, and she could scarcely move.

Leaning forward awkwardly, she looked at herself in the small mirror which hung over the washstand. As far as she could tell in the bad light, she looked fine. The green of her gown set off her red hair and fair skin, and brightened her eyes. Briefly, she wondered if the young Scotsman would be dining with them; but of course he would; all the passengers dined with Captain Hobart, she had been told. Why she should care about the Scotsman's presence, she could not imagine.

Just as she turned away from the glass, a knock sounded on the cabin door. She opened it, managing her skirts with some difficulty, to find Andre in the passageway. He too had evidently taken some care over his appearance, for he wore his light gray cueperuke, and his claret-colored suit and gray satin vest out of which his lace cravat foamed, like a waterfall tumbling over the brink of a cliff. His stockings were of gray silk, and he was wearing silver buckles on his new, pointed-toe shoes, which he had ordered from France.

"You look lovely, *chérie,*" he said, offering his arm.

"Shall we brave the good captain's table? I am certain that the food will be abominable, but we must accustom ourselves to it, and endure. I must confess that I brought along a supply of sweet biscuits, wine, and other such items to solace us if things grow *too* bad."

Michele's spirits rose immediately. Andre could be overbearingly bossy and high-handed, but he could also be amusing and comforting, and could usually, she was forced to admit, jolly her out of her occasional bad moods.

He stared at her in admiration. "You do look lovely, dear Michele. Green always becomes you; however, if I might be so bold as to make a suggestion, perhaps you should dispense with the use of your hoops while on board ship. I have seen the dining area, and it is small. Also, you will find it much easier to negotiate the passageways without them."

Michele looked down at her full skirts. The idea appealed to her immensely. "But the gown will be too long that way," she said dubiously.

"Then you will hold your skirts up with your hand while you walk. It will be easier than managing the hoops," he said. "Here, let me help you."

Together, they managed to remove the hoops and put them back into the clothing trunk.

"I wish that I never had to wear them at all," Michele confided, as she closed the trunk lid. "I always feel as if I'm in the middle of a hatbox when I have them on."

Andre laughed. "Styles change, *chérie*, and no doubt some day hoops will be out of fashion. But until then we must go along with it, if we wish to be fashionable."

Daintily, he removed a lacy handkerchief from his sleeve, and dabbed it to his nose as he raised his eyebrows and pursed his lips. Michele exploded with laughter. One of the characteristics of a man of current fashion was a mincing air; and Andre could mimic it so well. In most men who affected it, Michele found the fashion ridiculous; but somehow, with Andre, it seemed his natural metier, and was both amusing and graceful.

"Shall we go in to dinner?" he said with an exaggerated bow.

Still laughing, Michele took his arm, and they made their way down the narrow passageway to the dining salon.

Captain Hobart was a large, jolly-looking gentleman, with great puffs of red side whiskers cut in the mutton chop style. Since his face was florid, the whiskers were not too different in shade from his skin, and made his face look wider than it was long, giving his features a humorous appearance. He took an immediate fancy to Michele, commenting on her beauty, and ceremoniously seating her next to him. She was not pleased to see that seated upon her other side was the young man who had so rudely interrupted her dance practice that very afternoon.

"And on your left," Captain Hobart said in his booming voice, "is Mr. Ian MacLeven, from Scotland, returning to his native land, and on *his* left, Mr. Angus Lowrie, his traveling companion."

Both men rose from their seats and bowed. Michele felt her face grow warm as she met the gaze of Ian MacLeven, infuriated by the mocking glints she saw deep in his gray eyes. His traveling companion was somewhat older, with a stern but kindly countenance.

The captain continued with the introductions. "And on my right are Mr. and Mrs. Blakely, on their way to France, and Mr. Deering, whom I am sure Mr. Leclaire has already met, since they are sharing a cabin. The other gentleman is Mr. Higgins, my first mate." The first mate was a pleasant looking, youngish man, who seemed very shy.

The Blakelys, whom Michele and Andre had met upon boarding, were a dour, middle-aged couple, who looked as if a smile might crack apart the stern, sober set of their features. Mrs. Blakely was attired in a grayish bombazine that almost matched the shade of her skin and hair, and which was several years out of style. Her husband had a sallow, unhealthy complexion, accented by two very black eyes that seemed neither to receive nor emit light. Michele thought he looked dead, and could not suppress a slight shudder whenever she looked at him.

Oh, well, she thought, stealing a glance at the man on her left; at least I don't have to sit next to Mr. Blakely; he would ruin my appetite.

The meal itself, despite Andre's dire prediction, was quite satisfactory—a hearty soup for the first course, followed by roast chicken, fresh vegetables, and a large beef roast. For afters, there was a rich rum cake, of which Michele ate more than she should, ignoring Andre's warning glare.

The conversation at the table was casual and agreeable, and Ian MacLeven, despite her prejudice against him, proved to be a clever and entertaining conversationalist. All in all, it was a pleasant meal, and Michele found herself enjoying it.

When it was over, and she had retired to her cabin, she was thinking of Ian MacLeven, and not too unkindly.

They were six weeks making the crossing, but the time did not pass as slowly as Michele had feared.

Every day she practiced in the small salon—if the weather permitted—and after that she would stroll around the deck, enjoying the sun and the sea wind, if the weather was nice, or the salt spray and sea wind, if it was not. She discovered that she had a great affinity for the sea, and could understand how men could devote their lives to it. She also grew to enjoy the company of Ian MacLeven; he was the only passenger near her own age, and the only one except for Andre and Captain Hobart, with whom it was possible to have an interesting conversation.

Ian was, he told her, returning from a journey around the world; a voyage of experience, so to speak. He had been away from Scotland for two years, and now he must return to tend to the family business, a business about which he was very vague.

She in turn told him about Malvern, and about her dancing and the reason for the trip to France.

"Perhaps I will see you there," he said. They were standing at the stern, looking back at the perfect sunset spread out before them. "I often go to France. With whom will you be staying?"

"An old friend of Andre's, a Madame Dubois. Do you happen to know of her?"

He took on a look of surprise. "Aye. I have attended her salon. An interesting woman, with important friends. She should be able to help you make important theater connections."

Michele smiled. "That's what Andre says. Oh, I am so looking forward to it all! There is *so* much that I haven't seen, so much that I haven't done."

Ian's expression became serious. "Don't change too much," he said softly, raising his hand as if to touch her hair, then letting it fall again to his side. "I mean, perhaps it will sound foolish for me to offer you advice, but well, the life in Paris is very different from what you are accustomed to, Michele. Life moves very fast there, sometimes too fast."

She looked up at him searchingly, touched by his obvious concern. "You think I am naive, don't you? You think I am just a simple country maid."

His expression changed to one of chagrin. "Now I've made you angry. I'm sorry, I didn't mean to sound so pompous, or to lecture you."

Michele smiled impishly. "No, no, I'm not angry, not really. In fact, I do appreciate your concern, but I am not as naive as you may think. After all, I have been listening to Andre's stories since I was six years old, and I have been to Boston and other metropolitan cities." She neglected to tell him that she had been only a baby in Boston. "I realize that I have much to learn, and I will be cautious, never fear. But it *is* thoughtful of you to be so concerned about me."

They were standing quite near to one another now, and all of a sudden, she became acutely conscious of this fact. Ian turned his face away from her momentarily, toward the sea, and Michele could see the fine line of his profile.

He was a handsome man, and he was intelligent and witty. It was too bad that he was going home to Scotland now, and not to France. But what was she thinking of? She was the one who did not want to get emotionally involved. Even so, she experienced a strange pang when she thought that she might not be seeing him again; but then he had just said that he often went to France. Perhaps they *would* meet again. As friends, of course, just friends.

Suddenly, she noticed that Ian had moved closer, that he was almost touching her. She stared up into the face so close to hers; and then, before she quite realized what was happening, his hands had taken a firm grip on her shoulders, and she felt his lips upon hers, gentle yet insistent.

Feeling a maelstrom of emotions, Michele found herself responding, briefly, experiencing both pleasure and fear, and then fear was uppermost. She felt besieged, and quickly, with all of her strength, she tore free of his embrace, her face flaming.

"How dare you, sir!" she said in a choked voice. "What makes you think I would permit such liberties?"

He raised his hands in a placating gesture. "Forgive me," he said miserably. "I couldn't help myself."

"A poor excuse. Isn't that what men always say? I thought we were friends. I thought I could talk with you!"

He turned his face toward the sea. "I am your friend, Michele, despite what you may think. It's just . . . My God, lass, don't you know how beautiful you are, how desirable? Being here with you, seeing you every day, is sheer torture! Have you no idea how it affects a man?"

Michele, now insulated by her growing outrage, held up a staying hand. "That is quite enough, sir. I wish to hear no more. There are only a few days left of our voyage, and I will thank you not to approach me again during that time." She started off.

"But Michele . . ."

His voice followed her, thinned by the rising wind.

Quickly, she went below decks to her cabin, still supported by the righteous anger. She had been right! It was impossible to be just friends with a man. It was a good thing that he would be going on to Scotland. If he came to Paris, she would simply have to avoid him.

Still, in her narrow bunk that night Michele dreamed of him, dreams that she could not, or would not, remember in the morning.

As the ornate coach which Madame Dubois had sent to the ship for them clattered through the crowded streets of Paris, Michele kept her face to the open window, straining to see everything at once.

She felt a hot rush of embarrassment when she remembered herself saying proudly to Ian that Paris would not overwhelm her, for she had seen Boston and other large cities. He must have thought her the worst kind of provincial idiot! How amused he must have been, for there was simply no comparison between the places she had seen and this ancient, magnificent city with its elegant *places royales*, its splendid residences, churches, and palaces; and of course the river itself, the Seine, with its great bridges, and barges and boats.

She could not suppress a cry, as she saw in the distance the towers of the Cathedral of Notre Dame, which she recognized from illustrations she had seen in her books at home. She turned to Andre, her face flushed with pleasure and the wind that came in through the open window, her eyes sparkling. "Oh, Andre! It is so wonderful! Even more beautiful than I ever imagined."

He smiled indulgently, and patted her hand. "*Naturellement*. You have seen but little yet, Michele. When we are settled in, I will take you on a real tour of Paris. At night, Paris well deserves its name as the City of Light. You shall see everything, that I promise you, dear Michele. Ah, look! We are here."

The coach had turned into one of the large *places*, and the driver was bringing the vehicle to a halt in front of an imposing edifice of red brick and white stone.

"*Place des Vosges*," said Andre, his voice aquiver with a powerful emotion. "This, my dear Michele, is the home of

Madame Dubois, and ours for the time being. What do you think of it?"

Madame Dubois' house stood elbow to elbow, in a manner of speaking, with the others on the square, with no space in between. All the buildings were the same—four stories of artistically patterned red brick and white stone. All severely elegant, they presented a united front to the square. It was so different from home, from Malvern amid its many acres, from Williamsburg; yet it had its own rather intimidating beauty.

"It's lovely," she said breathlessly.

In front of the building where the coach had stopped stood a housemaid and a footman, and as the footman helped Michele down from the coach, she felt excitement leaping in her. This was it! This was the beginning of a new life!

The housemaid opened the door, and they were shown into a large, rather ornate entryway, crowded with a variety of magnificent *objets d'art*—statues on marble pedestals; large paintings in heavy, gilt frames; ornamental vases—all very beautiful, but seeming to Michele's Virginia eye much overcrowded.

She barely had time to scan the room before a woman swirled in with a flurry of motion so energetic that Michele unconsciously drew back.

She was a small woman, shorter than Michele herself, but much plumper in the face, shoulders, and chest. She was splendidly attired in a green kincob gown, worn with a stomacher of white silk. The gown was of the fashion commonly known as a Watteau saque, and it had two large pleats in the back, which hung over the rather large hoop skirt. Madame Dubois—for it must be she—wore her hair in what was known in the colonies as "French curls." Her hair was powdered, and the soft white set off her dark eyes and suspiciously rosy lips and cheeks.

As she swept toward the spot where Andre and Michele were standing, she lifted her skirts delicately so as to avoid the base of a statue; and Michele could see that her shoes were made to match her dress, having the same rich brocade upon the high heels, and straps of the material drawn through the silver buckles. A strap of wide silver galoon ran up the front of each shoe, and at the back from heel to counter. It was altogether a magnificent ensemble.

"Renée!" Andre exclaimed. "*Mon Dieu*, you are as young and beautiful as ever!"

The woman gave a soft cry. "Andre! You are back with us at last. Oh, how I have missed you all these years! The time among all those savages in the colonies has changed you little."

Quickly, she reached toward him, kissing him soundly on both cheeks. "Andre, you will be a godsend to me. Things have been so dull since poor Jean died." Her voice was surprisingly deep for such a small woman, and her French was rapidly spoken; still, Michele could understand most of it. "And this must be your pupil, the lovely Michele you have written so much about. Welcome, my dear. You must feel entirely at home here."

Michele found herself enfolded in two soft arms, and was overwhelmed by the scent of strong perfume and powder. "Oh, it will be exciting having you both here! It has been so quiet, so dull. Things will become more lively now, I am certain. I will give a party to introduce you to my friends. We shall have a grand time."

She gave Michele's arm a squeeze. Michele, almost overcome by Madame's ebullience, could only nod dumbly and smile until her face hurt.

Andre shook a scolding finger. "Now, now, Renée. That is all very well, but the girl is here for a purpose. She must work, work! It is what we came here for."

Madame Dubois waved her hand, and pulled a face. Seeing her up close like this, Michele realized that she was not a young woman. The powder and face paint disguised, but could not erase the lines around the eyes and the mouth, and the skin beneath her pointed chin had the unmistakable droop of encroaching age; still and all, she was a handsome woman.

"I realize that perfectly well, my friend," Madame Dubois was saying. "After all, it was I who arranged for Arnaut to interview her, was it not? He is only awaiting word that you have arrived, which I shall convey to him this very day. If he likes her, if she is talented, there is a place for her in his company. He has assured me of this, and Arnaut is a man of his word."

She turned to Michele. "You are a fortunate girl, Michele. Not every dancer is allowed the opportunity to audition for Arnaut Deampierre. If you are as good as Andre tells me, there should be no difficulty."

Michele felt the sudden chill of uncertainty. Was she as good as Andre thought? Would she be able to compete with the European-trained dancers? She had had no other teacher than Andre. She gave a slight start as she felt his hand on her shoulder.

"She is good, Renée," he said confidently. "She will pass the audition."

Michele smiled brightly at both of them, but at that moment she felt no certainty that Andre was right.

Madame Dubois tapped Michele's other shoulder with her fan. "But I am remiss. You are certain to be tired and sorely in need of refreshments after your long journey. Michele, I have prepared for you the Blue Room. I think you will like it. Andre, my friend, you are down the hall, in the Gold Room. I hope that you both will be comfortable. I had trays of fruit and cheese placed in your rooms, and a nice, light wine. Dinner will be served at eight. Michele, once you are settled in, we must have a long chat. We must become acquainted."

Michele smiled, a touch shyly. "I should like that."

She meant what she said, for she found Madame Dubois warm and friendly, and she was looking forward to asking her a great many questions about Paris, and the ballet here.

The room to which the maid showed Michele was large and richly furnished. As the name of the room suggested, the materials used to decorate the room were blue, which gave it a restful quality. There was a high four-poster bed, with a blue satin canopy with silver roses. The same material framed the high windows, and the chairs and settee were upholstered in a matching shade of soft velvet.

A beautiful little desk stood near the window, and Michele thought how nice it would be to write her mother from here. The carpet was an Aubusson, in pale blue, silver and rose, laid over a beautifully inlaid floor, and one entire wall was covered by a magnificent Gobelin tapestry.

Michele had never seen a bedroom so richly appointed, and it was to be hers for as long as she stayed with Madame Dubois. She was indeed a fortunate young woman.

Chapter Five

ON Malvern things appeared to be going smoothly for Hannah. Into summer now, the cotton stalks were reaching their full growth, and there had been no serious problems. The weather had cooperated beautifully; there had been no hard rains, no hailstorms, and the insects were at a minimum.

Her initial uncertainty concerning Nathaniel Bealls had subsided. He was working out very well. He certainly knew his job, and he worked long hours, seven days a week. Insofar as Hannah could learn, he was getting along with the workers. Of course she well knew that they were close-mouthed, accustomed from birth never to complain about one white person to another. But Hannah had asked John to let her know at once if there was any underground unhappiness about Nathaniel.

John had reported, "Everything seems all right, mistress. Mr. Bealls is a hard taskmaster, yet he doesn't drive those under him any harder than he does himself. He does have a temper, which he loses easily if he catches anyone disobeying a command, or not working hard enough. But so far the only goad he has used is a sharp tongue. No one has informed me that he has abused them physically, only verbally."

"If there are any incidents, John, let me know at once."

So, Hannah was reasonably content. She sorely missed Michele and Andre; she had yet to hear from her daughter, but she had not really expected to this quickly. It was a long voyage to France, and even if Michele had written immediately upon her arrival, there had not been enough time for a letter to arrive at Malvern.

One factor in Hannah's contentment, although she would have denied it vehemently, was Court Wayne. Despite their original antagonism, Court had become a frequent caller at Malvern. Rarely a week passed that he did not ride out to call on her.

On that first call, the day she had hired Nathaniel Bealls, Court had said with a charming grin, "I do have an investment in Malvern, madam, and I ask the privilege of visiting it. Your charming presence only makes it more enjoyable."

She had been caught off-balance by his expressed intention of calling on her, and had agreed, against her better judgment. But as the visits continued and she came to know him a little better, Hannah found Court a charming, witty man, although rather reticent about his past. For all that he had told Hannah, he might never have had an existence beyond the day he came to Williamsburg. Questions about his past he turned aside with the same remark: "My past is very dull, Hannah, of no interest, I assure you."

Hannah had to admit, to her secret self, that Court's presence set her heart to hammering and her pulse racing. She began to look forward eagerly to his weekly visits. When he was with her, she seldom thought of Michael. The ache of Michael's loss grew less with every passing day. But that was as it should be, she concluded. She could not mourn the past forever; she was still in the prime of life, and had many years before her.

On an afternoon in mid-July she was awaiting Court's arrival with anticipation, for they were going riding. Court was a superb horseman and loved to ride. There were several riding horses on the plantation, but Court had selected Black Star, Michael's horse, the one he had been riding the night of his death. No one had ridden him since that night. A couple of the stablehands had tried, and had been thrown. No one but Michael had ever ridden the animal, and it seemed that he had turned outlaw since Michael's demise. But strangely enough, the stallion took to Court at once, and now seemed to look forward to Court's visits.

Hannah also loved to ride, but had not indulged herself much of recent times. She did not like to ride alone, and had not had a riding companion since Michael. Now that was changed, and she rode with Court at every opportunity.

She was already dressed in her riding skirt when Court's coach rolled up the driveway shortly past the noon hour.

He emerged from the coach, elegant as always, his clothes fitting his lean but muscular figure snugly. He never wore a hat or a wig when he went riding with her, and she had never seen his hair powdered.

"Hannah, my dear Hannah." He bowed over her hand. "You look ravishing today, as always."

"Thank you, Court," she murmured. "Shall we go? The horses are saddled and waiting."

Court gave her his arm, and they walked together to the stables. The groom had the horses waiting for them. Black Star snorted and rolled his eyes when he saw Court. Court stroked him alongside the neck, murmuring something to him, and the spirited animal quieted down. Then Court turned and gave Hannah a hand up onto the brown mare she usually rode. The groom opened the pasture gate, and they rode at a trot across the pasture.

Hannah could not help but think back twenty years, to another time she had ridden across this pasture. That time she had been riding Black Star's sire, the original Black Star, a much more spirited animal than she rode today, and she had been thrown and rendered unconscious. When she revived, she found herself cradled in Malcolm Verner's arms, and learned that Malcolm truly cared for her. She became his wife not long after that.

"You're lagging behind, Hannah!" Court shouted back to her.

Laughing, Hannah urged her horse to a faster gait, and soon they were galloping headlong across the pasture, headed toward the line of trees at the far edge, which marked a stream meandering across the plantation. Hannah's hair streamed out behind her, and she was thoroughly exhilarated by the time she reached the trees. The stallion had beaten her by at least three lengths, and Court reined him in, waiting for her in the shade of the oaks. Hannah pulled back on the reins, and Court leaned out to seize the reins of the mare and pull her to a full stop.

"You're not competitive enough, Hannah," he said in a teasing voice. "How can you ever expect to beat me in a race, if you don't even try?"

"Oh, I'm competitive enough, when it counts," she said with flashing eyes. "Just try me some time. But tell me, Court, how *would* you react if I beat you in a horse race? Most men would be furious."

"I would not mind in the least, Hannah, if you won fairly. You would have my sincere congratulations."

He slid off his horse and came to give her a hand down. He tied the two horses off where they could graze, and then they strolled arm in arm under the dappled shade of the great oaks, to the glade where the brook burbled over mossy rocks.

He said musingly, "Katherine, my wife who died many years ago, was very competitive. She tried to best me at everything. Unfortunately, she was a far more delicate woman than you, Hannah, and in poor health, which resulted in her early death. As a result, she rarely ever bested me. Oh, I could have let her win, of course, but Katherine had a faculty for knowing when I did my best, for knowing when I tried to lie to her."

Court stood slightly apart from her now, gazing down into the water of the brook. Hannah did not resent his reference to his departed wife as being more delicate; she well knew that she was a healthy, robust woman, and was grateful for it. He was silent for a long time, and Hannah held her breath, fearful that if she spoke he would stop talking of his past. It was the first time that he had spoken of himself; she had not even known that he had once been married.

But finally she sensed that he was not going to speak

again of himself, and she said, "Did you have any children, Court?"

He gave a start and looked over at her with a frown. It was a moment before he spoke, and then his voice was curt. "No, Hannah, we never had children. Katherine was too delicate to bear children."

He fell silent again, returning his gaze to the brook. Then, with an abruptness that startled her, he turned to her and took her hands in both of his. His blue eyes became warm and glowing, and his voice dropped down to a husky register. "Hannah, I've been coming out once a week now for over two months. I've enjoyed our rides together, more than I would ever have thought."

"And I as well, Court." Hannah found herself strangely breathless. She tried a laugh that did not quite come off. "Much more than I thought I would, too, especially with a moneylender who holds a lien on Malvern."

His smile turned faintly rueful. "In the beginning I told myself that I was merely riding out here in a business way, to see how you were faring, if you would be able to repay the loan. But last night, I finally admitted the truth to myself."

"The truth, Court?"

"Yes. I haven't been coming out here to check on the plantation at all. I've been coming out here to see you, my dearest Hannah, and only you."

His hands were on her shoulders, strong, capable hands that held her in a grip almost painful, and he began to pull her slowly toward him. Hannah stared into his eyes, and was lost to everything else. She tore her gaze away from his eyes and looked at his mouth, and that was no help. His lips were well formed, with a fullness that hinted at sensuality, and now they parted slightly to show even white teeth. His breath was warm and scented faintly of mint.

Then his mouth was upon hers. His lips were warm, and the touch of them on hers started a turmoil in her blood. A part of her mind wanted to resist, but the feel and texture of a man's lips on her mouth after such a long span of time was so thrilling that any resistance soon melted away, and she let herself go soft and pliable in his strong arms.

He was holding her so closely now that she could feel the strength of him through his clothing. Without speaking, without taking his mouth from hers, he raised one hand to the back of her head. He ran his fingers through her unbound hair, and took his mouth away from hers to murmur, "Your hair, dear Hannah, is so lovely, and so soft, like fine silk."

He cupped her head and brought her mouth to his again. Now his other hand moved slowly down her back, caressing the muscles there. With her riding habit, she was without a corset, and the material of her blouse was thin enough so that she could feel the heat of his hand, the stroking fingers, the hard heel of his palm moving in ever-widening circles.

She tensed, a sigh escaping her, as his moving hand reached the jut of her buttocks, and pressed there, gently, oh so gently at first, then moving on down to the fullness, kneading in ever-increasing demand. He pressed harder, and she arched in against him. A gasp was wrung from her as she felt his male hardness, throbbing like a heartbeat against her mound.

A weakness took hold of her, and she knew that she had no will left to resist him if he decided to take her, right here under the trees. Always a passionate woman, Hannah had not had a man since Michael's death, and this man's touch had set up a wanting in her that was so fierce it was an ache deep within her.

Court's mouth left hers, and his lips made a trail of fire along her neck and to a most vulnerable spot just below her ear. As the tip of his tongue probed at the spot, she moaned softly, and opened her eyes.

And there, astride his great gray horse at the edge of the trees, was Nathaniel Bealls, staring at them. He was unsmiling, his eyes burning. Then, as their eyes met, he smiled, ever so slightly, a knowing smile. He tipped his hat, tapped the horse lightly on the flank with the riding crop, and rode off. Court had not seen him.

Flustered, Hannah tore herself free of Court's embrace, feeling embarrassed and somehow ashamed. She stepped two paces back. "No, Court, no!"

Face flushed, he blinked at her dazedly. "What do you mean, no? You liked it, you were responding, I know you were."

"Perhaps so, but that doesn't make it right."

His eyes turned cold. "Why not? We're both mature people, with no spouses, no attachments of any kind. At least that's true with me, and unless you haven't told me everything, the same holds true with you. So where is the harm, if we are attracted to one another?"

She shook her head stubbornly. "It's still not right."

"Don't play the coy maiden with me, Hannah!" he snapped. "You liked it, so do not play the coquette with me. It ill becomes you!"

Her own anger ignited. "I'm not playing the coy maiden, sir! You have no right to assume that I am as willing to be tumbled as the wench I saw in your house that day!"

"I made no such assumption, madam," he said icily. "And if I have offended you, I make my apologies, and give you my assurance that you will not be troubled with me again."

He turned and marched to his grazing horse, back stiff as a poker. Hannah could not believe that he was actually leaving her, until he had vaulted into the saddle, and turned Black Star about.

Belatedly, she took a step after him, hand held out. "Court, don't go like this!"

But he had already sent the horse into a startled gallop, and probably had not heard her. If he had, he chose to ignore it.

Angry at herself for reacting so unreasonably, and also angry at Nathaniel for spying on them, Hannah did not mount her own horse at once. Instead, she sat on the bank of the stream, staring down into the water.

Of course she was being unfair to Nathaniel. He *was*

the overseer, after all, and had a perfect right to ride anywhere on the plantation in the performance of his duties. But had that been the reason he was there? There were no fields close by, and no hands working here. Casting her thoughts back, Hannah remembered that she had seen the overseer watching from a distance several of the other times Court had come to call. Perhaps her first thought was right—perhaps he was spying on her. But to what purpose?

She finally decided that Nathaniel had stumbled upon the scene purely by accident. She did not know whether to be angry or sorry about the interruption. Certainly it had succeeded in stopping the embrace from proceeding further, but had she really *wanted* it to stop?

Hannah had no ready answer to the question. Over the past two months her attitude toward Courtney Wayne had changed drastically. She found his company pleasant, and she was drawn to him physically. She had not been certain of this fact until now, after what had happened here today. Not once, in all his visits to Malvern, had Court mentioned the loan, except in passing, and he no longer seemed concerned about getting his money back.

Getting up, she mounted the mare and rode at a sedate walk back to the manor house. She had grown somewhat accustomed to Michele's absence now, yet she still had lonely times. Court's visits had helped assuage this loneliness. The question now was—had she driven him away for good, or would he return next week?

At that moment, riding in his coach toward Williamsburg, Court was telling himself that he would not visit Hannah Verner again. Damn the woman, anyway! She had led him on, setting his blood on fire, then backing off at the last possible instant. He detested women who did that. Court prided himself that he knew women better than most men, and he knew that he was good at the seduction game. What made the incident with Hannah so particularly galling was the fact that he could always tell when a woman was on the verge of giving in to him, and he would have sworn that Hannah had been well past that point.

No, he would see Hannah Verner one more time, the day she repaid her debt to him, and then he was well quit of her.

All of a sudden Court began to laugh at himself. His pride was a little battered, that was all. Perhaps he had been a touch overconfident of his charm, and had moved too quickly. He knew he would come calling on Hannah again.

Aside from the fact of her sexual charms, he had grown fond of Hannah, perhaps more fond than was wise. Certainly he thought more of her than of any woman since Katherine. Yes, he knew he would return. Perhaps she would not spurn him the next time.

Meanwhile, he was in need of a woman. The feel of Hannah's ample curves in his arms, the taste of her mouth, and the clean smell of her hair and skin had aroused him to the fullest. And it had been two weeks or more since he had had a woman.

As the coach entered the outskirts of Williamsburg, he leaned out the window and called up to the driver. When the man's dark face peered down at him, Court directed him to go by Beth Johnson's house.

When Michele's first letter arrived, Hannah took it to her bedroom so that she might read it without interruption.

Eagerly, she tore it open and began to read: "Dear Mama; I am writing this in the most elegant bedroom you have ever seen, at a beautiful little desk in front of a window that looks out onto a large square.

"Madame Dubois' home is quite magnificent, and furnished with beautiful things, so many in fact that it seems to be a bit overcrowded, but I am told that it is considered the utmost in elegance here in Paris.

"Madame Dubois has been very kind, and has done everything in her power to make us feel at ease. Andre is in seventh heaven. I had not realized how much he had missed his homeland during all those years with us.

"Tomorrow, Andre will take me to audition for Monsieur Deampierre. I am so excited about it that I know I shall not sleep this night. I shall do my very best, you may be sure of that, and I will write you as soon as I know.

"Paris is very beautiful, and grand, and there is so much to see and do. I wish that you were here with us, Mother, so that you could share our experiences. I am having a wonderful time, but I do miss you so. I hope that things are well at home, and that you are busy and happy. Perhaps, when you have things in order at Malvern, you will be able to join us. I can think of nothing that I would like more.

"Take good care of yourself, Mother dear, and write to me soon, in care of Madame Dubois. I promise to write regularly.

"Andre sends his love. Dear Andre, I do not know what I would do without him!

"Wishing you all the best, Your loving daughter, Michele."

Hannah sighed, reading the letter again. How wonderful it would be to travel as far away as France! The farthest Hannah had ever been from Virginia was the one time twenty years ago, when she had gone to Boston, and there had been nothing very enjoyable in that. It had been her responsibility to feed and clothe a number of people; she had never worked so hard in her life. How nice it would be to travel to some distant land, casting aside all responsibilities, and simply enjoy herself!

Well, perhaps she might do just that, if the coming year turned out well for her, and for Malvern.

Chapter Six

THE dance studio of Arnaut Deampierre was located in a shop district, and was situated in the upper story of a building that housed a millinery shop and a dress shop below.

As Michele climbed the steep stairs, with Andre behind her, she could feel her heart thudding with excitement and apprehension. Would Arnaut Deampierre like her? Would she be good enough? What if she had come all this distance only to be told that she was not acceptable? The thought made her heart pump even faster, and dried her throat.

"We are here, *chérie*," Andre said softly. "Now pause for a moment, relax and breathe deeply. Do not be afraid. You *are* good enough, believe me. Believe in yourself, Michele. And do not let Arnaut disturb you unduly. He is a man of stern manner, as seems to be usual with most ballet masters, but I knew him when he was but a member of the corps de ballet, and he is not really unkind. Hold your head up now. Back straight, and remember all that I have taught you."

Michele did as Andre instructed. Head high, shoulders back, she marched through the door that Andre held open for her, although inside she was quaking.

She entered the largest practice room she had ever seen. There were huge panes of glass in the slanted ceiling, and even though the day was overcast, the room was flooded with light. One wall was mirrored to about the height of six feet, and there were barres on three of the walls. Along the fourth wall was a row of wooden benches, and in one corner was a pianoforte, with an elderly gentleman seated at the keyboard.

There were at least a dozen people in the large room, all in practice clothes, but the only one that stood out instantly was a man who had to be the ballet master, Arnaut Deampierre. He came toward them, moving gracefully on well-muscled legs, and Michele could see that he was magnificently built, with wide shoulders and a narrow waist.

At first she could not see his face, for the light was behind him; but as he drew close to her she could see that he was not a young man, probably near her mother's age. He had a strong, high-cheekboned face and slanting Slavic eyes of surprising darkness. His face was arresting rather than handsome. He was unwigged, and a streak of white, which slashed through his black hair from forehead to nape, added to his theatrical appearance.

His voice, when he spoke, was deep, but rather harsh. "Andre, my old friend. So you have finally come home after all these years?"

Andre bowed slightly, with an ironic smile. "Yes, Arnaut. The prodigal son has returned."

Deampierre kissed Andre on both cheeks, then stood back and clapped the smaller man on the shoulder. "It is indeed good to see you again, my friend. And it is also nice to know that even though you did not continue with a promising career, you have still used your knowledge to teach others. This, I am sure, must be Mademoiselle Verner, the young woman that you wrote me about?"

"Yes," Andre said proudly, putting an arm around Michele's shoulders. "Is she not lovely, Arnaut?"

Deampierre's expression was noncommittal; and Michele, ablaze with embarrassment and anger, wished that she dared give Andre an elbow in the ribs for his comment.

"That is quite true, my friend. However, it is not her beauty that is at question here, but her ability to dance." Deampierre turned to Michele. "Mademoiselle, would it embarrass you to dance before the members of my company? Or would you prefer that I dismiss them? It is your decision to make."

Michele wished that she had the courage to tell him that she would not be bothered by the presence of the other dancers, but truth was to the contrary. Trying to keep her voice as steady as possible, she made a slight curtsy, and said, "If you please, monsieur, since I am quite nervous, I would prefer to dance for you alone." Her words came out clear and strong, with no note of servility, and Michele was pleased to see a flicker in his eyes that could have denoted respect.

He inclined his head slightly. "As you wish, mademoiselle." He turned his head and raised his voice. "Students, you are dismissed for the space of time it will take to perform a solo number. Do not go far. When we are finished here, we must rehearse *Les Indes Gallantes*."

With many curious, sidelong glances, the students began to file from the room, and Michele experienced an immediate feeling of relief. They had been watching her during the exchange between Deampierre, Andre, and herself, and she had not received the feeling that they were at all friendly toward her. She had been doing her own watching—more cautiously, of course—and had noticed with dismay how young most of them were. Many of them were younger than she was, some by several years. She knew that dancers had to be young, particularly the girls, and at seventeen she considered herself so. Yet some of these dancers could not be over twelve or thirteen. Even so, their faces expressed calculation rather than simple curiosity; and Michele realized that they were sizing her up as competition. It was a rather intimidating welcome, and one not calculated to put her at her ease.

When the other dancers had left the room, Deampierre gestured at the pianoforte and the seated accompanist. "Do you wish my accompanist, Monsieur Duval, to play for you, or would you rather that Andre accompany you?"

Michele again spoke in a firm voice, "Andre, if you

please, monsieur. I am used to him. I will be performing a selection from *The Loves of Mars and Venus*."

Deampierre agreed with a shrug, and Andre went to the pianoforte, and placed the music upon the stand.

Michele closed her eyes for a moment, took a few deep breaths, and tried to make herself believe that she was dancing at home, in her own practice room.

Andre struck the first chord, and she opened her eyes and began to dance.

When she was finished, Michele felt that she had done well; still, she hesitated to look at the ballet master, afraid she would see displeasure or outright rejection in his eyes.

As the last chord faded away, there was a long silence before Deampierre spoke. "She is graceful, Andre, and she has good line and execution. However, she still has much to learn."

Michele felt her heart begin to hammer, and she finally looked at Deampierre so that she might see his expression as he pronounced what to her were damning words. However, his expression was merely thoughtful, as he studied her with his chin propped on his fist.

"You have been away from the ballet a long time, my dear Andre, and there have been many innovations, many changes in style since you were last in Paris. However, since she has the talent, and the basic skills, I should think she would have no great difficulty catching up on these things."

He gestured to Michele. "Be here tomorrow, mademoiselle, eight o'clock sharp. I do not tolerate tardiness. Wear something practical and simple, for I promise that I shall make you perspire. You should also bring a lunch, and something to drink, for we will work well into the afternoon. Oh, and yes, bring a wrap so that you will not get chilled during the periods when you are not active. Now, if you will pardon me, I must return to work. Andre, I am free tomorrow evening, if you should like to meet with me and discuss old times."

Andre rose from the pianoforte, his face radiant. "I

should indeed like that, Arnaut. Shall we meet here, or at our old cafe?"

"Here, at five o'clock."

"Five o'clock it is then," said Andre, gathering up his music. "And thank you, Arnaut, for your time and patience. Thank you very much!"

Deampierre nodded, rather brusquely, Michele thought; and in another moment she and Andre were outside in the corridor, where they were greeted by the curious eyes of the returning dancers.

As they went down the narrow stairs, Andre suddenly laughed aloud. "You were accepted, *chérie*! Accepted by the foremost ballet master in all of Paris. Your future is assured."

Michele was feeling rather let down, and a little angry. "He didn't seem particularly pleased with me," she said slowly.

Andre embraced her. "My dear Michele, do not be misled by Arnaut's abrupt manner. It is just his way. Why, coming from Arnaut, what he said was a real compliment."

"But he said I had much to learn!"

"And so you do, my love, so you do. So have we all, for that matter. What he said is true. I could only teach you what I knew, and I have been away from Paris and the ballet for a long time. But he said himself that you should learn easily what you do not know."

"He's very arrogant," Michele said, still unconvinced. "He practically commanded you to meet him tomorrow. He didn't even ask if the time was agreeable to you!"

Andre laughed lightly. "It is just his way, my pet. Just his way. Do not fret yourself. Just see that you obey his directions and do not talk back to him the way you do to me. *Mon Dieu*, please do not do that!"

Michele made a small sound of discontent, but said no more. She had been accepted, she should be ecstatic, she supposed; but all she felt was a sense of confusion. What *had* she been expecting? She was not certain, but somehow the experience had left her feeling vaguely discontented and unsatisfied. Perhaps it was because of the reactions of the other dancers, their seeming hostility. She had halfway hoped that they would welcome her, accept her. Well, no matter. She had been accepted by Arnaut Deampierre. She would work hard, and she would excel; on that point she was determined.

"Ladies and gentlemen, your attention! I wish to introduce someone to you." Deampierre's voice echoed in the large practice room, and the other youngsters gathered around obediently. Michele was made uncomfortable by the combined pressure of their stares.

Deampierre continued. "I wish to introduce our newest member, Michele Verner, from the state of Virginia, in the English colonies. I trust that you will all make her welcome, and will give her any advice and assistance that you can. You may introduce yourselves later, during our midday period. Now, take your places at the barre, if you please!"

The dancers quickly dispersed to evidently familiar places along the wooden barre, leaving Michele to find what was the least desirable spot, the most distant from the ballet master. Michele realized that despite his admonition to make her welcome, and to help her, they were not going to go out of their way to be polite. Well, if that was the way it was going to be, she would simply ignore them. She did not need anybody, except Arnaut Deampierre.

Holding her chin up high, Michele took the cramped place left to her, and fixed her gaze upon the ballet master.

"And now! We will start with the *pliés*. Duval, are you ready? Now, bend, stretch! Bend, stretch!"

Michele, watching Deampierre closely, began to do the exercise. Three hours later, drenched with perspiration, and feeling the breath rasping painfully in her lungs, she was relieved when Deampierre gave the order to halt for the midday break.

Trying to breathe evenly, Michele mopped her face with the linen kerchief she had brought along for that purpose, and gazed around the room. To her delight, the other dancers seemed to be as winded and tired as herself. So she *had* kept up, at least after a fashion.

Wrapping her shawl tightly around her shoulders, she saw that the other dancers were hurrying to the cloak room where they kept their lunch hampers. Well, so much for "introducing themselves"!

Michele felt both annoyance and depression. She was used to being popular and sought after, a person of consequence; back in Virginia she certainly was. This attitude of the other dancers was both hurtful and cruel. Were they all so worried about their own position, their status in the company, that they could not risk a kind word to a newcomer?

Feeling dispirited and weary, Michele waited until the cloak room was clear, and then went to get her own basket, which Madame's cook had prepared for her.

She picked up her basket—it was quite large, and smelled delicious—and turned to leave the narrow room, then stopped short. Standing in front of her was one of the dancers, a young man, not particularly tall, but beautifully proportioned, with a wild tangle of black hair, and strange, light-green eyes.

He bowed low. "Mademoiselle Verner, may I present myself? I am Louis Lascaut, at your service."

Michele, flustered, made a curtsy. "Thank you for introducing yourself. You are the first to do so."

Evidently, he caught the bitterness in her voice. He smiled, and his rather somber face lit up, making him look quite boyish. "Oh, the others will come round. They consider it unfashionable to appear to be too interested, or too polite." He leaned toward her conspiratorially. "Actually, they are dying of curiosity. They want to know all about you. But I have defeated them!"

She looked at him, answering his smile. "Oh, and how is that, sir?"

"By eating with you, and asking all sorts of impertinent questions. That is, if you do not object?"

Michele shook her head quickly. "On the contrary, I

shall be delighted." She hefted the heavy wicker basket. "I think Cook packed enough food for a whole troop."

Laughing, he reached over and took her basket. "Come, let's find a quiet place, away from the others. It will make them even more curious, for they will think that we are sharing secrets."

Michele, feeling much buoyed in spirit, followed Louis into the next room, which contained several small, curtained alcoves, set around window seats. Louis chose one in a far corner, and they sat down with their baskets, and opened them on the padded cushions of the window seats.

Michele felt her stomach contract. The smells of the food made her realize that she was famished.

"Wonderful!" Louis exclaimed, as she pulled out half a roast chicken, a slender bottle of pale wine, pears, plums, a sweet tart, crusty French bread, a large square of cheese, pickled onions, and several pieces of marzipan.

"You must share it with me," she said, holding the chicken out toward him, "especially the chicken and the cheese. I'll admit that I'm starved, but there is far too much for me."

Louis smiled. "Gladly. My own meal is rather spare today, and I have never been one to look askance upon unexpected bounty."

Eagerly, they tore into the food, and in a surprisingly short time there was nothing left except a small quantity of wine in the bottle, which Michele insisted that Louis drink.

"Now," she said earnestly, leaning toward him. "I have a favor to ask of you."

He patted his stomach. "Anything, my dear, anything. I am forever in your debt for that marvelous meal, although I may not be able to dance a step this afternoon."

"Tell me about the others, their names and all, and what they do. I mean, in the company."

He belched softly, and lounged back against the window seat. "Well, that is simple enough to do. I'll start with myself. I am Louis Lascaut, *premier danseur*."

Michele sat up straighter. "Really? You are really *premier danseur*?"

Louis laughed softly. "Well, almost, shall we say? Actually, our *premier danseur* is that arrogant fellow leaning against the wall, over there. His name is Roland Maraise."

Michele followed the direction of his pointing finger, to where a tall, muscular, yellow-haired young man was standing. His expression, his very stance, did express arrogance, and he moved, she had noticed, with the lithe assurance of one who knows that his place in the world is not only secure but enviable.

"He is a prime bastard, if you will pardon my crudeness, and you would do well to steer clear of him, for he is extremely jealous of *anyone* who shows talent."

Michele continued to study the young man in question. He was very handsome, in a cold, rather self-centered way. And then, belatedly, the import of what Louis had said penetrated. "Then you think I have talent?"

He smiled mischievously. "Did I say that? Well, it must have slipped out. How remiss of me." He looked over at the dancers. "Now, the young girl next to him, that is Denise DeCoucy. She is one of our most accomplished dancers, next in line to our prima ballerina, Cybella, who is not present today; but Denise is a cold witch, with no more heart than a clockwork doll. I believe she inherits her nature from her mother, who is even more of a witch than her daughter. Still, Denise gets on well with Maraise. That should tell you something about them both."

The young woman to whom Louis referred was small, quite slender, and very blonde; a delicate-looking girl of perhaps sixteen, whose general appearance was belied by cold gray eyes and a narrow, thin mouth. Michele agreed with Louis' appraisal—Denise DeCoucy looked cold and ungiving.

"We have two other excellent male dancers in the company, of which I am one, if I may be so immodest, and the other is Maurice Decole, commonly known as Café au Lait, for obvious reasons."

Michele followed the direction of his gaze, and saw a very tall young man whose skin, indeed, had the color of coffee thinned with milk. His hair was tightly curled, and he had a certain fullness to the lips that spoke of Negro blood. She looked at Louis questioningly.

He shrugged. "His father is a nobleman, close to the king. His mother is a beautiful, half-black dancer. His father supports him well, but will not acknowledge him as his son."

Michele was about to ask him who the pretty, brown-haired girl was, when Arnaut Deampierre's voice trumpeted throughout the room: "Time is up! Back to the barre!"

As the dancers began to file back into the practice room, the brown-haired girl came up to Michele, smiling. "I wanted to introduce myself," she whispered, touching Michele's arm. "I am Marie Renaud."

Her smile was open and friendly, and Michele could not resist smiling in return. "I'm happy to meet you," she said.

"I would like to talk to you at length sometime, perhaps at break time one day, about your colonies. I am much interested."

"I would like that," Michele said, and then they were in the practice room, and there was no further time for conversation.

Over the next two weeks, Michele's life fell into a taxing routine of practice and rehearsal. The company was working on *Les Indes Gallantes*, which Deampierre was preparing for production in the near future, and he was pushing the company hard.

Michele would be dancing with the corps de ballet; and since she had come late to the production, she was hard-pressed to catch up with the others.

She watched the prima ballerina, Cybella Manet, with despair and envy. Cybella, whom Michele estimated to be a year or so older than herself, had perfect control and grace. Rather tall for a ballerina, she had long, slender, perfectly formed legs, a graceful torso, and seemingly boneless arms, which could assume any pose and gesture. Her dark brown, perfectly straight hair was parted in the middle, and pulled back from her classically featured face. She even *looks* like a ballerina, Michele thought wistfully; wondering if she would ever attain the perfection that Cybella seemed to possess.

Since Roland Maraise was dancing in two of the current ballets, Deampierre had given Louis the leading role in *Les Indes Gallantes*, opposite Cybella. Michele, watching the two together, realized that Louis was an exceptional dancer—strong, graceful, and athletic. He and Cybella danced beautifully together, and Michele admired that fact, while wishing that she might be dancing the role instead of Cybella. And she noticed that she was not the only one having such daydreams. The little blonde, Denise DeCoucy, watched Cybella with unfriendly gray eyes, envy written large upon her cold, little cat face for all to see.

Despite the grueling schedule, and despite Deampierre's stern manner and hard discipline, Michele enjoyed both the practice sessions and the rehearsals. She was slowly becoming one of the company, getting to know the other dancers, who were beginning, in the main, to accept her as one of them. Most of them were friendly toward her now, particularly Marie Renaud, who had a seemingly endless curiosity about the colonies and the life there.

All in all, Michele felt that things were going very well. She was progressing, slowly and painfully, catching up to the other dancers, learning the ballets currently being performed by the company. She hoped that soon Deampierre would tell her that she was ready to take her place in the corps de ballet for these productions.

So far she had been too busy to devote much time to sightseeing or her social life. Madame Dubois had informed her just last evening that she must begin to be seen socially, starting Sunday next, when Madame would be holding one of her famous salons, at which Michele and Andre would be guests of honor. She had invited many of Andre's old friends, and Andre was looking forward to the occasion with considerable pleasure, as was Michele. Now that she was settled in, so to speak, with the ballet company, she wanted to see and get to know Paris and its people; and from what she had overheard, there was no better way to embark on this endeavor than to attend one of Madame's salons.

The day of the salon, the weather was quite overcast, but the guests who assembled in Madame's home more than made up for the day's lack of color.

Michele, feeling overdressed but elegant, added her own color to the gathering. When she had shown Madame the dress she intended to wear, her water-green luster, she had expected Madame to comment favorably, but Madame made a moue, and shook her head.

"The color is lovely, my dear, and the fabric also, but you must allow my dressmaker to make some alterations."

Since the dress had been made just prior to her departure from Virginia by the most fashionable dressmaker in Williamsburg, who had assured her that it was in the very latest style, Michele was taken aback. "What do you mean?"

"For one thing, it will not fit over the new, larger hoops. The skirt must be made fuller."

"But the dressmaker assured me that it was the latest French fashion."

Madame smiled somewhat condescendingly. "Yes, my dear, and I am sure that it is, in the *American* style. But you must realize that it takes many months for our fashions to reach the colonies, and even more time for those fashions to be copied. The style now is for the large hoops, and there are other changes as well, minor ones to be sure, that will take only a few minutes for my dressmaker to do, but which will make all the difference in the world. Trust my judgment, Michele. I shall also have my personal maid, Jeanine, do your wig and paint you. She is very good. I wish you to look your very best. You are a beautiful girl, and I wish to show you off to the best advantage."

Although Michele appreciated Madame's desire to help her, she rebelled at the wig, which she considered uncomfortable and unbecoming, and she had demanded that her own hair be arranged instead.

Both Madame and Jeanine had insisted upon powder, however; and so now Michele, gowned, her hair floured, and with her face lightly painted and artistically patched, sat with the other guests in Madame's large salon, frankly staring at the illustrious assemblage gathered there.

They were, she thought, as bright and noisy as a flock of exotic birds. The men in their wigs, satin coats, and fitted breeches, their coat skirts flaring above silk-stockinged calves, were as ornamental as the women. Ruffles cascaded from their sleeves and at their throats.

Andre, Michele noticed, had taken particular care with his grooming, and was elegantly attired in a coat of purple velvet laced with silver, with breeches to match. His waistcoat was of a rich, flowered silk on a white ground. He looked, she thought, more effete than he had at home in Virginia; and she noticed that his tendency toward feminine gestures and expressions appeared more exaggerated, but then so did the gestures of many of the other gentlemen present. Watching Andre and the other men, she realized that they were, as a whole, almost as pretty and delicate looking as the women; and she decided that she much preferred the way the men looked and dressed back in Virginia; however, Andre was obviously in his element. His face fairly shone with pleasure at being again among his own people.

Michele turned her attention toward the women, most of whom had arrived at the door wearing velvet masks to protect their complexions against the damp weather. They were, to the last one, splendidly gowned and wigged; however, none of them eclipsed Madame Dubois, whose gown put all the others to shame. The garment was of a richly embroidered white satin, and Michele could only wonder how many hours had gone into the making of it.

The bottom of the petticoat had been worked into the

semblance of brown hills, covered with plants; and depicted upon every panel was the stump of a tree that ran almost to the top of the petticoat. The tree stumps were broken and ragged and worked with brown chenille, and round them twined nasturtiums, honeysuckle, periwinkle, and all kinds of twining flowers which spread and covered the petticoat; and vines, dappled by the sun, all only a little smaller than nature. The sleeves and the rest of the gown were worked in a pattern of twining vines, and the robings and facings were like green banks covered with all kinds of growing things. Many of the leaves were finished with gold thread, and the trunks of the trees were highlighted in gold, so that they looked as if the sun was striking the wood.

Madame wore very large, round hoops that would scarcely go through a doorway, and her wig was bejeweled and ornamented in a fashion to complement her elaborate gown. She was heavily painted and patched, and Michele felt uncomfortably as if the woman she knew had mysteriously disappeared beneath this pile of finery.

However, the rather deep, husky voice was the same, and Madame was now entertaining the company with a rather naughty story, to which they all listened eagerly. Michele, also listening, was shocked, for the story appeared to be about the king, Louis XV, and had to do with his reputed sexual prowess.

She found herself blushing furiously, and began to fan her burning face. She was distracted from her embarrassment by the sound of an amused male voice at her elbow, "I see that Madame's tale has made you uncomfortable."

She looked around to see a slender, elegant man in pale blue satin. He had a thin, dissolute face with world-weary gray eyes that expressed sardonic humor.

Michele, deciding that he seemed pleasant enough, did not try to make a witty reply. "I am afraid that I am not accustomed to such tales," she said simply; and then, with a smile, so that he would not think she meant offense, she added, "Do the French often speak this way of their king?"

The gentleman laughed; hearty, rolling laughter for so delicate looking a man. "Oh, but yes, dear lady. Positively. In fact, it is one of the chief pleasures of the populace. The king's doings, his love affairs, his peccadilloes, down to the last seduction, are common knowledge and open game for comment. It has always been so, did you not know that? It is one of the duties of a king, to provide diversion for the masses, and that our good King Louis provides very well."

Michele laughed delightedly. The man was droll, and seemed charming enough, but she did not even know his name. "With whom do I have the pleasure of speaking, sir?"

He bowed low, and she could see the crown of his rather elaborate wig, which appeared freshly powdered, but was none too clean.

"Albion Villiers," he said, gesturing with his lacy handkerchief. "At your service, mademoiselle. And you, you pretty creature, are Michele Verner, Madame's guest, and student of my old friend, Andre Leclaire."

"Oh, you are a friend of Andre's! How nice. Perhaps I can prevail upon you to tell me something about Andre. I know so little about him, despite the fact that he has been with my family since before I was born. What was he like when he was young, here in Paris?"

Albion seated himself in a small, gilt chair, and took out a jeweled, golden snuffbox. He did not answer her question until he had applied a small pile of the pungent tobacco to the back of his left hand, and sniffed it into his right nostril. A hearty sneeze followed this procedure. He then wiped his nose on the lace kerchief.

"Oh, there is so much to tell, dear lady. I hardly know where to begin."

"Have you known him long?"

"Since we were but lads, mademoiselle."

Michele, divining that this man was a gossip, and loved to talk, hoped that she could get him to reveal the reason Andre had left Paris. She had always been curious about this, but Andre would never speak of it except in the most general terms. She glanced across the crowded room, hoping that Andre would not come over to them now, but he seemed engrossed in Madame's tale about the king.

"When did you last see him?" she asked slyly.

Albion looked thoughtful. "Just the day before he left Paris to go to your colonies. And to think that would be the last time I would see him for so many years! It was all a very sad affair, but Andre brought it upon himself. I remember telling him, 'Andre, leave that young man alone. There are many others willing and eager for your love. Why endanger yourself for one such as that?' But no, he would not listen, but then what man in love ever listens? It was the young man's father, a straitlaced statesman of high position, who forced Andre to leave France. Such a pity. Andre was at the height of his career as a *premier danseur*, and he . . ."

Michele thought that she must have misunderstood. Had Albion said "young man"? Surely not . . . But he *had* said "*premier danseur*," and she fastened onto that. "You say Andre was a *premier danseur*?"

Albion arched his scant eyebrows. His world-weary eyes now sparkled with the excitement of imparting juicy gossip. "Did he not tell you that? How remiss of the dear boy! Did you not wonder how he obtained the skills to teach you so well?"

"Not really. I just accepted him as he was. We all did."

Albion's expression grew sly, and Michele had the uneasy feeling that he was about to tell her something that he hoped would shock her. She had begun to have grave misgivings about starting this conversation, but she was in too deep now to back out. Still, she was determined that she would not let Albion know that she was distressed.

The little man pulled his chair closer to hers. "But you *do* know that Andre is an *arracheur de palissade*? You *must* know that?"

Michele turned the phrase over in her mind, nonplussed. She understood the words, but not the context in which they were used. "I'm afraid I'm not familiar with the term," she said warily.

"Well," Albion leaned nearer still, "the term was coined when our King Louis was a mere lad. He and several of his playmates were caught in the Versailles wood . . . uh, experimenting with one another, shall we say? To put it as delicately as possible. Oh, it was the scandal of all Paris!" Albion tittered behind his hand. "The other boys were discreetly removed from court, and the ringleader, the Marquis de Rambures, was jailed in the Bastille. When King Louis asked where his playmates were, he was told that they were being punished for knocking down picket fences, and the term, 'picket fence puller,' *arracheur de palissade,* therefore became a euphemism for a man who makes love to other men. Surely you knew this about Andre?"

Albion's malicious gaze clung to Michele's face, and it was all she could do to maintain her composure. Andre, a man who made love to other men? *Were* there such men? She was deeply shocked and angry at this nasty little gossipmonger. How could she have thought him entertaining? Andre's friend? With such a friend one would not need enemies. She felt upset and disgusted, yet it was her own fault. She *had* urged him on.

As the silence stretched, she noticed Albion studying her with an expression of smug satisfaction. Despite Michele's attempts to disguise her feelings, Albion knew that he had struck his mark. She wished with all her heart that she might hit him, but she knew that would never do.

She finally said, speaking firmly. "Of course we knew! As I said before, we accept Andre as he is, and care for him, as one of the family."

"Oh, I'm sure," he said dryly, dabbing at his forehead with the ubiquitous handkerchief. "And now I must leave you, mademoiselle. I see someone I must speak with. If you will excuse me?"

Getting to his feet, he made a low bow, and scurried off

to join the group surrounding Madame Dubois, and Michele leaned back in her chair with a sigh. Perhaps undue curiosity *was* a sin. She wished, again, that she had never asked Albion Villiers about Andre; but she could not think on the matter now, for Madame Dubois was bearing down on her with two women in tow, one of whom looked familiar to Michele.

Chapter Seven

IT was not until the three women were almost upon her that Michele recognized the youngest of them as Denise DeCoucy, looking somewhat unfamiliar out of the practice clothing in which Michele was accustomed to seeing her.

Like all the other women present, Denise was wigged, powdered, painted, and elaborately attired. Her gown was made of pink brocade, which suited her; but the heavy paint upon her face gave her the appearance of being much older than her sixteen years.

"Michele, my dear," said Madame Dubois, when they were almost upon her. "Here is a young friend of yours from the dance company."

Michele smiled dutifully, as if Madame's words were true. Actually, from the beginning she had felt an instinctive antipathy toward the younger girl, who had shown Michele only minimal courtesy, and certainly had made no efforts toward establishing a friendship. In fact, the only feeling Michele had received from Denise was that of hostility.

However, this was a social occasion, and so Michele smiled and curtsied to the older woman, whom—since there was a strong resemblance—she assumed to be Madame DeCoucy, Denise's mother; a supposition which proved correct as Madame Dubois introduced the other woman.

Madame DeCoucy appeared to be as cold and unfriendly as her daughter, as Louis had told Michele. She nodded as Madame Dubois made the introductions, but did not smile. Her face was so heavily made up that her skin appeared to be as white and hard as porcelain; and Michele was reminded of the fashion dolls which were sent from France to the colonies so that they might copy the latest French fashions.

"I will leave you to chat," Madame Dubois said, patting Michele's shoulder; and Michele watched her leave with feelings of dismay. What would she say to these two?

Madame DeCoucy began the conversation. "Madame Dubois tells me that you are from the English colonies," she stated, in a tone that sounded almost accusing.

She barely moved her lips as she spoke, and Michele was certain that this was because any real movement would have cracked the heavy mask of her makeup. This mannerism was most disconcerting, creating the eerie illusion that her voice issued from somewhere other than her body.

"Yes, that is correct," Michele answered as pleasantly as she could. "I come from the sovereign state of Virginia."

Madame DeCoucy nodded again, still unsmiling, and Denise still said nothing, only watched Michele with those cold, calculating gray eyes.

"You were very fortunate to be accepted into Arnaut Deampierre's company," Madame DeCoucy said.

"I agree," Michele said. "I consider myself very fortunate indeed."

Madame DeCoucy elevated her penciled eyebrows. "Denise has been with the company since she was twelve, and she has been dancing leads since she was thirteen."

The woman's gaze dared Michele to compete with this feat, but Michele was determined that she would not be drawn into what she saw as a childish game. "That is most admirable," she said quietly.

"She would be *première danseuse*, if it were not for favoritism."

"Favoritism?" Michele asked in some surprise. What on earth was the woman talking about?

Madame DeCoucy nodded vigorously, causing her wig

to tremble precariously. "Cybella, of course. Cybella and Monsieur Deampierre are lovers. Everyone knows this. But he will weary of her eventually, and then Denise will take her rightful place."

Why, Michele asked herself, do I feel as if I am being issued a not-so-subtle warning?

Denise still had not spoken, and Michele, to change the subject, directed a question at the other girl. "Have you always wanted to dance, Denise?"

Denise's pale eyes showed no change of expression. "Yes," she replied, in her high, childlike voice. "Always, as long as I can remember. I intend to be the most famous *danseuse* in the world. I will be as well known as Salle and Camargo!"

"Humph!" her mother said contemptuously, her eyes bright above the barely moving lips. "Camargo is an ill-formed acrobat, and Salle lacks the most rudimentary technique. Everyone knows that. Denise is far superior to them both, and the world will soon know it."

Her sharp gaze challenged Michele to contradict her, and Michele did not know what to say. She had to admire Denise's dedication and purpose. Naturally, she had observed Denise in class, and had seen that the younger girl possessed a masterful technique and precision, plus great determination. If she had a failing as a dancer, it was that her coldness of character was projected by her dancing, making her seem somewhat mechanical; still, she was young, perhaps time would mellow her; perhaps experience would give her some heart. However, there was a massive arrogance in both mother and daughter, and Michele decided that such outrageous boasting should not go entirely unchallenged.

"I suppose that is every young dancer's hope, to be a *première danseuse*," she said coolly.

Madame DeCoucy gave her a haughty stare. "That may very well be," she snapped, "but Denise is not just any young dancer, such as yourself. My daughter is special!"

Michele, feeling her own temper begin to stir, clamped her lips shut. If she said anything more, it would likely only make this woman angrier, and she did not want to cause a scene and spoil Madame Dubois' salon. And then, like a gift from heaven, she saw Andre approaching. She had never been so glad to see him.

Andre gave Madame DeCoucy his most charming smile. "Madame, if you will pardon me, I must intrude upon your *tête-à-tête*. There is someone to whom I *must* introduce Michele."

Michele stood up quickly, grabbing Andre's arm in a firm grip. "It was a pleasure," she said in a sweet, insincere voice, which she hoped left no doubt as to her real meaning. And as they moved away, she said *sotto voce* to Andre, "Thank you, Andre. You have no idea what you saved me from!"

Andre's eyes twinkled. "Oh, yes, I do, *chérie*. I could see *that* look upon your face clear across the room."

She raised her eyebrows. "*That* look?"

"Yes, my pet, the very same look you give me when you are about to rebel against something that I have told you. I thought that I had better come to the DeCoucys' rescue."

"The DeCoucys' rescue! Hah! Those two women do not have a whole heart between them! When I first met Denise, I believed her to be the coldest female I had ever met, and I maintained this idea until just a few minutes ago, when I met her mother."

Andre laughed. "They are a calculating pair, I must admit. I knew Madelaine in the old days in Paris, before she married DeCoucy, and she was the same then. If anything, I'd say she is even more of a cold-hearted witch today." His expression became serious. "But do not underestimate them, *chérie*, and do not antagonize them, difficult as that might be. Madelaine DeCoucy has considerable influence, and she can be a very dangerous enemy."

Michele made a moue. "But they are so unfriendly and so rude. How can I hold my temper when they insult me?"

"With patience, my pet, with patience. Now, let us

change to a more pleasant subject. How are you enjoying the salon?"

Michele shrugged carelessly. "The only people I have really talked with have been the DeCoucys and a horrid little man named Albion Villiers, who claimed he was a friend of yours."

"Ah, so you have met the Asp!" Andre laughed at her questioning look. "That is what we called him in the old days, because of his poisonous tongue."

"An apt name," Michele said with a sniff. "And he still merits it, if our conversation was typical. He called himself your friend, but he said the most awful things about you."

Andre's smile died. "Yes, I can well imagine what he told you, Michele, and I have known you far too long not to know that it has upset you. We will talk of it later, when we are alone, but now I wish to introduce you to some pleasant and entertaining people who will take your mind from this unpleasantness."

Thereafter, in bewildering succession, Michele was introduced to the rest of the guests, many of whom more than fulfilled Andre's promise. The men paid her outrageous compliments which she enjoyed even though she did not wholly believe them, and both men and women were full of interesting anecdotes and stories, which she found generally amusing.

However, before the afternoon was over, Michele was beginning to find the excessive powder and paint, the elaborate mannerisms, a bit cloying; even though a part of her enjoyed all the attention, and the obvious interest she engendered.

It was while she was talking to a too handsome young man, who had just told her that he was soon to be presented at court, that she became aware of the uncomfortable feeling that someone was watching her, staring at her.

Smiling politely to show her continued interest in the young man's monologue, she slowly turned to meet the dark gaze of Arnaut Deampierre, who was standing behind her, leaning against the damask-covered wall.

He stood out among the ornately dressed throng, for he was wearing a plain suit of dark gray velvet, and a modest gray wig tied back with a ribbon of matching hue. His smile, as he caught her eye, was sardonic, and he nodded as if to acknowledge her recognition.

Michele returned his smile, thinking how handsome and distinguished he was, even with his striking dark hair hidden under the wig.

As she returned her attention to the young man, she could see out of the corner of her eye that Deampierre had left his place against the wall, and was approaching her.

She felt a heady bubble of excitement begin to rise within her. Deampierre had intimidated her at first, but as she had come to know him a little better, she had been duly impressed by the ballet master's teaching ability and his vast knowledge of the dance; and she found him very attractive. However, in the class, or during rehearsals, he seldom exchanged more than a few words with her, and then only to correct some flaw in her performance. But never a compliment! She was beginning to doubt that he was capable of a compliment.

Michele knew that most of the girls in the company hung upon his every word, and lived for a personal comment from him; and although she had never admitted it, she felt somewhat the same. And now, it seemed, they were about to meet as social equals; and then he was standing next to her, his dark eyes ignoring the young man whose flow of words suddenly stopped.

"Mademoiselle Verner," said Deampierre, with a slight bow of his head. "How nice to see you here."

Michele nodded, trying to appear as calm and sophisticated as he. "It is good to see you, also, monsieur."

"Are you enjoying the salon?"

"It is very . . . interesting, monsieur. Very different than what I am accustomed to."

His eyes, she noticed, seemed to see right through her. He smiled, and said, "I should imagine so."

The young man, ignored, moved reluctantly away. To Michele's astonishment, Deampierre took her arm. "It has grown quite warm in here, and the scent of all this perfume is making me ill. Shall we take a brief turn about the garden?"

He was already propelling her toward the door, and for a moment Michele felt resentment at his bland assumption that she would accompany him; but it *was* warm inside, and she was thrilled at the chance to really talk with him.

It was quite cool outside, but to Michele the change felt refreshing. The garden, which was located at the rear of the house, was quite formal, an affair of hedges and ordered banks of autumn flowers. As they walked side by side down the path, Michele was very conscious of Deampierre's proximity; and as she attempted to control her wide skirts so that they should not catch upon the hedges, she felt very awkward and out of her depth.

The clouds had begun to disperse in the western sky, and the late afternoon light was golden and pleasant, bathing the hedges and flowers in a lambent glow; and as Michele looked at them, she felt a stab of homesickness for the rambling lawns and plantings of Malvern so different from this ordered garden.

Beside her Deampierre took a deep breath, and stretched his arms, high and wide. "Ah! This is more like it. A man cannot draw a decent breath in there, the air is so thick with powder and scent that it clogs the nose and tightens the throat. I have heard it said that all the poor of Paris could be fed with the flour that adorns the heads of nobles, and I am inclined to believe it."

He spoke with disdain, and it was clear to Michele that he felt scorn for the courtiers and ladies inside. This conclusion made her more curious about him. "It would seem that you care little for the social life, monsieur," she said tartly, not yet sure how outspoken she might be with him.

He smiled, and then laughed, a sharp bark that clearly did not express amusement. "I suppose you might say that, particularly social life as practiced in salons such as this."

"Then why did you come?" she asked in confusion.

"Because I am made a coward by expediency," he answered with a scowl. "I need the patronage of Madame Dubois and the others like her to maintain my company and my school. I am not proud of it, but my company is important enough to me, so that I will do whatever is necessary to maintain it."

Suddenly, his scowl changed to a lighthearted smile. "You see, mademoiselle, it is my misfortune to love the dance more than I hate the company of the 'men of good company' and their ladies. I am a slave to my art!"

Michele drew in her breath. He was a fascinating man, but very confusing at times. His baffling moods seemed as changeable as the wind.

"But come," he said, taking her arm, "I should not be talking so to you, who are experiencing our social round for the first time. You must pardon me, I am becoming old and cantankerous."

"You are not old, monsieur," Michele blurted out, and then fell silent in embarrassment. "I mean, you are still a strong, vital man. I mean . . ."

Laughing, this time heartily, he guided her toward a stone bench nearby. "Thank you, my dear Michele, but sometimes, alas, I feel very ancient indeed. You are, what? Seventeen? Why, I could be your father! But come, let us talk of more pleasant things. Tell me, what do you think of our fair city? Tell me honestly now."

Michele felt herself color under his scrutiny. Her tongue felt thick and awkward in her mouth, and her usual facility with words seemed to desert her.

He looked at her curiously. "Come now, I did not take you for a timid person."

This last remark, uttered teasingly, made her feel even more ill at ease. She took a deep breath, determined that he should not see her as rattled as she really was. "Paris is very interesting," she said thoughtfully, "and yet, at the same time, very strange to me. The way you live, the way Parisians live, is much more . . . lavish. In a way the people that I have met seem less serious, more interested in the pursuit of their pleasure, than the people I know at home."

He nodded gravely. "That is because you have met only the upper classes. They are not the real Paris, the real France."

"That may be true," she said, "but most of the people I know at home are of the upper class, also, and yet they are still working people. Back in America, everybody works. I mean, those in the upper class, if you wish to call them that, manage plantations, or run businesses. We don't have a royal or noble class, you know, people who don't work at anything."

"Ah!" he said. "There it is, you see. You have put your finger on it. And I'll warrant that your country is the healthier for it, for that is our malaise, I do believe. Our lives have grown soft and overripe, like a rotting peach, since Louis took the throne. His father now, knew what it meant to be a king, but Louis thinks only of his women and his pleasures."

"Still I have heard others say that he is a *good* king."

Deampierre shrugged. "Some see him so, because it is in their own best interest to do so, but you will notice that there is no popular name for him as there was for his father, who was called 'The Sun King.' "

"Have you ever met him?" Michele asked.

Deampierre nodded shortly. "I have been presented at court, and I have danced for the king, both at Fontainebleau and Versailles. I have observed him and his court at play, a gaggle of chameleons, wind-sniffers, and tablecloth hangers! Parasites, that provide no useful purpose except to serve the king as sycophants. They do not entertain a serious thought or perform a useful deed."

"What does he look like, your king?"

Deampierre's tone was disparaging. "Oh, he is handsome enough, I suppose. Dark of eye, a fine, Bourbon nose, but a weak mouth, and his face has grown a bit soft. Yet it is not really his face that is flawed, but his character, for he is morbid, cruel, and totally lacking in courage."

Michele, her curiosity fully aroused, pressed on. "In what way is he cruel?"

Deampierre's gaze was fixed upon some distant spot. "King Louis takes pleasure in the suffering of others," he said flatly. "He often torments his courtiers with small cruelties, and he has a morbid interest in death and dying. If he would only pay as much attention to the running of the country as he pays to his mistresses! But enough of this. You must be getting chilled. We will return to the festivities inside, and attempt to maintain an agreeable attitude."

He looked at her strangely. "I do not know why I spoke to you of such things. It was not my intention to cast a pall over your first exposure to the social life of Paris."

Michele, feeling grateful that he was talking to her at all, smiled brightly. "I have enjoyed our conversation," she said truthfully.

"Then perhaps you will grant me the favor of being my companion at dinner?"

She was startled by the proposal, and so delighted that she had difficulty hiding her reaction. "I should be delighted, sir!"

Together, they returned to the salon, and for the next hour she was totally unaware of whom she spoke to, or what was said, for her mind was filled with only one thing—the voice of Arnaut Deampierre.

The next day was Monday, and going in to class, Michele's heart beat fast at the thought of again seeing the ballet master.

At dinner at Madame's salon, they had enlarged their acquaintance. Deampierre had been charming and witty at the table, showing none of the cynicism and anger he had exhibited in the garden, and Michele had thoroughly enjoyed both the meal and his company.

The food had been as lavish and ornate as the guests and the surroundings. Among the items served were pig's tongue stuffed with staghorn jelly; pheasant stuffed with carp and iris root sauce; and the sweet came to the table in the form of a small tree with a caramel trunk and marzipan branches and leaves, ornamented with candied flowers; the recipe for which Madame Dubois assured everyone had come direct from the king's own Department of the Mouth.

At the end of the meal, of which Michele had partaken little due to her excitement, Deampierre had taken his leave; and although Michele was loath to see him go, her heart was light. Of all the women among all the guests he had chosen her to spend time with! She had never dared dream it would happen!

So now, as she prepared to enter the practice room, she was filled with a tingling anticipation. Inside, the very first thing she looked for was Deampierre. He was standing near the mirrored wall deep in conversation with Denise DeCoucy and Roland Maraise.

Michele stored her lunch basket in the cloak room, and then returned to the practice room, where she sat on the bench to put on her dancing slippers, waiting all the while for Deampierre to notice her.

At last he finished his conversation and turned to look around the room, but his glance slid over Michele just as it did over the others, with no special sign of recognition.

"All right!" he said, clapping his hands together. "Up to the barre!"

Michele rose from the bench, swept by disappointment. She had expected *some* sign from the ballet master—a smile, a nod, anything! After the attention he had lavished on her at Madame's salon, Michele had thought . . . What exactly *had* she thought? That he liked her? Enjoyed her company? He had certainly seemed to. But if that was true, why was he so aloof today?

She took her place at the barre. Perhaps he simply did not want to single her out during class. Yes, perhaps that was it, yet she had often noticed him talking to one dancer or another.

Remembering what Madelaine DeCoucy had told her about Deampierre and Cybella, Michele experienced a hot wave of anger. Perhaps what Madame DeCoucy had said was true. Perhaps Deampierre had only talked to her yesterday because she was the lesser of several evils.

Deampierre's sharp voice brought her back to the present. "Michele, be alert! Pay attention! You are slumping!"

Face flaming, she straightened her back and raised her chin. Why was she acting this way? What was the matter with her? Clearly, she had misread Deampierre's attentions, and he had no interest in her whatsoever, except as a member of his company. Well, she would give him no cause to reprimand her again. After all, it was the dancing that was important, that was what really mattered. She determined to keep her mind on that, and nothing else.

Still, for the rest of the day she kept hoping for some sign from him, which never came; and at the end of the class, when she saw him talking to Cybella, their faces close together in an implied intimacy, Michele felt as if a cruel hand was squeezing her heart. She left the practice room with dragging footsteps.

Chapter Eight

ON Malvern cotton bolls were beginning to open, and before many weeks passed, it would be picking time. The pace of work on the plantation had quickened. Hannah was pleased with Nathaniel Bealls; he had more than lived up to her expectations.

And Court, after a three-week absence, had resumed his weekly visits. He returned without apology for his actions by the stream that day, and without apology for his absence. Secretly pleased about his returning, Hannah was happy enough to accept his terms, if such they were. He made no further overtures, and strangely enough, this disappointed her. She refused to examine her reasons for this discontent. There was one slightly disturbing note—it seemed that Nathaniel always managed to be around the manor house when Court's coach arrived. However, she did not catch him spying on them again during their weekly rides, and had concluded that the previous time had been inadvertent.

She had not heard a word from Jules Dade, which puzzled her more than a little. The little brown man—as she had begun to think of him—did not seem concerned about his loan. In fact, his nonappearance, and the optimistic signs of a bumper cotton crop, succeeded in lulling any fears she might have had about Dade, to the point that she even forgot about him, and the loan, for days at a time.

Consequently, she was quite surprised and a little

disturbed, when Dade drove up before the manor house one afternoon in an open carriage, driving it himself. As it happened, Hannah was on her way from the stables to the main house when she saw the dust roiled up by the carriage as it wheeled up the lane.

She paused, shading her eyes against the sun. Her first thought was that it might be Court, but this was not the day he was scheduled to call. When she saw that it was an open carriage instead of a coach, she knew she was wrong. Then, she saw Nathaniel's big gray, galloping after the approaching carriage, and for a moment she felt a pulse of annoyance. Did Nathaniel have nothing better to do than to keep watch on any visitors she might have? Of course, unless he was on the far side of the plantation, the dust from any approaching vehicle was clearly visible to him in the fields.

The carriage came through the archway, and she could finally make out that her visitor was Jules Dade. With some apprehension she waited on the veranda steps as the carriage wheeled up to a full stop.

Dade lifted his tricorn and called out, "Afternoon to you, Mistress Verner." He began to get down from the seat.

"Good afternoon, sir." Keeping herself outwardly composed, Hannah waited until he had climbed halfway up the steps, before saying, "To what do I owe the pleasure, Mr. Dade?"

Nathaniel had wheeled his big horse in alongside the carriage, and sat easily in the saddle, his gaze fixed upon her, idly swishing the riding crop against his booted leg.

Puffing slightly, Dade reached the top step and stood alongside her. He was smiling slightly, a smile that did not quite reach his eyes. As usual, he was a study in brown—brown wig, brown clothing, including his boots.

In a slightly condescending manner he said suavely, "I had business to transact nearby, and I thought I would pay you a brief visit."

"Loan business, I imagine?" she said caustically, and immediately regretted the remark, as a baleful light glowed briefly in his eyes. It was foolish of her to antagonize him; she sensed that he would make an implacable enemy, and that she did not need. She said hastily, "Would you care for a cup of tea, Mr. Dade, and perhaps some cakes?"

"It would pleasure me to accept your hospitality, madam," he said equably enough.

She stepped to the door and gave the bell rope a yank. She was reluctant to invite him into her house. Turning back, she said, "It is a warm day. Perhaps we should have our tea on the veranda?"

He dipped his head in a slight bow, but not before she had glimpsed again the displeasure in his eyes. "Whatever you desire, madam."

He was a shrewd man, much shrewder than she had given him credit for—he had divined her reason for not inviting him inside. But why should she concern herself with his wounded feelings? She must do business with him, but that did not mean that he was welcome as a guest in her house.

The door opened, and one of the house servants emerged. "Yes, mistress?"

"Mary, would you serve us tea and cakes out here on the veranda?"

The girl bobbed her head. Hannah escorted Dade to the wrought-iron table and chairs down at the end of the veranda. Dade sat down, removing his tricorn, and Hannah sat across from him. Even sitting Dade gave off a sense of energy and power so forceful that it was almost frightening.

Controlling her nervousness, Hannah said, "As you must have observed on your way up to the house, the prospects for my cotton crop are very good, Mr. Dade. I believe I shall have no difficulty repaying your loan, in the event you were concerned."

"Ah, yes, so I observed," he said with a slight smile. "And I am pleased for you. Regardless of the reputation we moneylenders have garnered, it does not pleasure me when a client of mine is forced to default on a loan. That is not my nature, madam. In my estimation a man in my business serves a useful function, and it does gladden my heart when a loan is repaid on time. I am a businessman, of course, but I am always pleased when a loan is repaid. Ah, yes."

Privately, Hannah was not so sure of his expressed benevolence, but she was content to have him think she believed him. She noticed that he was staring past her. Hannah turned her head, and saw that Nathaniel still sat his horse by Dade's carriage. Annoyed, she opened her mouth to call for him; but Nathaniel, as though divining her intention, tipped his hat, kneed his horse around, and rode away.

"Who was that young fellow?" Dade asked. "He seemed inordinately curious about my presence here."

"That is Nathaniel Bealls, my new overseer. I must credit him, to a large extent, for bringing in a bumper crop. He probably was being protective of my welfare, since you are a stranger to him, sir."

"How fortunate you are, madam, a lady such as yourself, all alone, without a husband, to have such a strapping fellow watching over you," Dade said in a dry voice.

Hannah was saved a response by the appearance of the maid with the tray of tea and cakes. After Mary had poured the tea in delicate cups, and served them each a plate of tiny, delicious cakes, there was a silence for a little time. Hannah noticed that, for such a small man, Dade ate with good appetite. But she could not say much for his manners; she watched with barely concealed distaste as he drank his tea with a slurping noise, and dribbled cake crumbs down his front as he ate, popping whole cakes into his mouth at a time.

Finally, the cakes on his plate were all gone. He burped without covering his mouth, brushed carelessly at the crumbs, leaned back. "Very good, madam, ah yes, very good indeed."

Hannah was impatient for him to be gone. Her dislike of him pushed her into being incautious. "I have been told, Mr. Dade, that you made your fortune in shipping?"

He looked at her through narrowed eyes. "That is correct, madam. I was in shipping out of Norfolk. I still have some interest in the shipping line I founded, but I am no longer active. I turned the line over to a younger fellow. Shipping is a risky trade at best, subject to many hazards."

She recklessly pushed ahead, somehow driven by a need to goad him. "Your shipping line was involved in slaving, I have been told."

"You have been told?" He leaned forward tensely, his face showing anger. "Who might have told you such calumny, madam?"

"Calumny? Are you denying the charge then?"

"I do not have to defend myself to you, Mistress Verner. Slave trading is a common practice along the southern coast." His thin lips shaped a slight sneer. He indicated the plantation with a sweep of his hand. "After all, your plantation depends on your slaves."

"Not true, sir!" she said spiritedly. "All the people on Malvern are freedmen, and women. Are you not aware of that?"

"No, madam, I was not so aware. In my judgment, I would say that is rather foolhardy."

"I have never held with slavery."

"That, of course, is your privilege. Ah yes." He leaned forward, his eyes malevolent. "You did not answer my question. Who informed you that I was a slaver? I would imagine that it was that rogue, Courtney Wayne. Is my surmise correct?"

She frowned at him. "What do you know of Courtney Wayne?"

"I know him as a villain and a blackguard." Dade grinned unpleasantly. "I also know that your late husband negotiated a substantial loan with him. Again I ask, did your information come from this man?"

Her head went back. "My source of information is none of your affair, Mr. Dade!"

He shrugged his narrow shoulders. "But then you have answered my question, haven't you, madam? Ah, yes. I would suggest to you that you would fare better if you had as little to do with this man as possible."

She got to her feet. "My personal life is none of your concern, sir!"

He laughed harshly. "Your *personal* life, Mistress Verner?"

Hannah felt herself flush. "Now you are being offensive. I would suggest that you take your leave!"

"If that is your wish." He also got to his feet, and bowed to her. "I bid you good day, madam."

Hannah stood rigid, keeping her temper with an effort. She did not relax until he had entered his carriage and started up the driveway. Her anger subsided then, and she was filled with a feeling of dread. She knew that she had probably made a grave mistake in offending Jules Dade.

But then what could he do to her, so long as she repaid the monies she owed him? She gestured contemptuously, and went into the house, calling for the maid to clear away the dishes.

Jules Dade was seething as he drove away from Malvern. In his business dealings, nefarious or otherwise, Dade had learned over the years to control a ferocious temper; he calculated that it gave him an edge over any opponent to conceal his anger. But he gave it free rein now, heaping vile oaths on the heads of Hannah Verner and Courtney Wayne, most especially Wayne. He had run afoul of Wayne several times in the past, and almost every time Wayne had gotten the best of him.

He vowed to himself that he would deal with Wayne in good time. He would see Wayne discredited and disgraced in the eyes of Hannah Verner and the community of Williamsburg, so that he would have to flee in shame.

But first things first. He had to gain possession of Malvern. Now that he had actively retired from the slave trade, he courted respectability, and the best means of gaining that was the ownership of a plantation such as

Malvern. He had long coveted it; and when the Verner woman had agreed to the loan, Dade was convinced that the way was open to him. With the death of her husband, how could she, a mere woman, hope to run a vast plantation profitably? He had been confident that she would default on the loan, and he could take possession of Malvern.

Now it appeared that it would not be that easy. He had not taken into consideration the possibility that she might employ an overseer, and a competent one at that. Dade had been sure that none of her black field hands could handle the job. No, he had figured that Mistress Verner was one of those stubborn, strong-minded women who considered themselves competent to do a man's job.

Now that was all changed. He could no longer sit back and let matters take their natural course; he had to become actively involved in seeing to it that the plantation failed.

About a mile from the house, still on Malvern property, Dade saw the overseer sitting his horse in a field close to the road, directing several field hands at work weeding out the cotton plants.

Dade drew the carriage to a halt by the side of the road, and called, "Sir! Could I have a few words with you?"

Nathaniel Bealls turned his head with a scowl. He did not respond.

"It will only take a few minutes of your time, sir," Dade said in a wheedling tone. "And it will be to your advantage, I promise you."

The overseer turned the big horse and urged him to the side of the road, alongside the carriage. "I am far too busy to pass the time of the day in idle conversation," he said stolidly.

Dade smiled ingratiatingly. "It will not be idle conversation, I assure you. Mr. Bealls, I believe you are Mistress Verner's overseer?"

"That is correct."

"My name is Jules Dade. I have a business arrangement with your employer. A loan, in point of fact."

Bealls struck his booted leg with the riding crop he carried. "I fail to see what that has to do with me, Master Dade."

"Ah, yes. Well, to be blunt, sir, it would be to my advantage to see Mistress Verner's current crop fail to pay dividends."

Bealls stared at him with narrowed eyes. Taking a twisted cheroot from his pocket, he lit it. "That still has naught to do with me."

Dade said slyly, "It does if you were somehow instrumental in that crop failure. Surely you are knowledgeable about such things. There must be a number of things you can do. You would be rewarded handsomely, I assure you."

"I am in the pay of Mistress Verner."

"But you are to be paid only after the crop is harvested and sold, am I not correct?" Dade said shrewdly.

Bealls shrugged. "There is nothing unusual in that, sir. Such arrangements are customary."

"But if you did my bidding, you would be paid much sooner, and much more handsomely."

"My loyalty is to Mistress Verner," Bealls said stoutly.

"Loyalty? Do not play the dolt, my good fellow. Loyalty is a virtue of little value in this world. Loyalty is always for sale, should the price be dear enough."

"Perhaps to some that might apply, but I am not for sale." Bealls made to turn his mount about.

"Admirable, sir, very admirable. Wait, Mr. Bealls!" Dade said sharply. "All I ask is that you consider my proposition, consider it very carefully, *then* decide where your best interests lie."

Bealls studied him for a moment in silence, then he smiled tightly. "I wonder, sir, how she would feel were I to tell her of your proposition?"

"Ah, yes." Dade smiled back. "It would not be in your best interest to do so, Mr. Bealls. It would not have an adverse effect upon me, since Mistress Verner does not seem to have a particularly high opinion of me at present.

In any event, I would simply deny that any such proposition had been made. She might not believe me, but there would also be a tiny seed of doubt planted in her mind about you, Mr. Bealls. It is the belief of many, rightly or wrongly, that no man is ever approached with a dishonest proposal unless he invites such a proposal. Ah, yes. I advise you to think about that, sir. Also, please consider my proposition carefully. It may appeal to you, after due consideration."

Dade clucked to the horse and started the carriage in motion. He could feel Bealls' gaze on his back as the carriage clattered away. He did not deign to look around, but rode on, smiling to himself.

Nathaniel Bealls sat his horse staring after Jules Dade long after the carriage had vanished from sight, idly striking the crop against his thigh.

He was not angered, or even insulted, by Dade's proposal. In different circumstances he might have found it attractive. Nathaniel had never been troubled by moral scruples as he made his way through life. He always had his eye out for the main chance, and there were not all that many for a man of his station.

However, there was something on Malvern that was of more immediate interest to him than money or advancement in the world, and that something was Hannah Verner. Although she was a few years older than he, Hannah was a fine figure of a woman, and Nathaniel lusted after her. He had coveted her since the very first time he had laid eyes on her; it was the main reason he had consented to become her overseer. When he had learned that the blacks on Malvern were all freedmen, his first inclination had been to get up and walk away. Nathaniel had grown up on various plantations, and one thing he had learned early—not only was it foolish to give a black man his freedom, it was dangerous; he could turn on you at any time. As a slave, he would not dare do such a thing; but granted his freedom, he suddenly placed a value on himself, and such a man could be dangerous to any white person over him.

But Nathaniel's desire for Hannah had been stronger than his reasons for spurning her offer, and he had remained, biding his time until the right moment came to make his move. Up until three weeks ago, he had been a little worried about the rivalry that the dandy, Courtney Wayne, posed for him. He had finally convinced himself that Hannah was merely dallying with Wayne, passing the time, waiting for a real man. Then he had come upon them at the creek, with Hannah in Wayne's arms, and his optimism had been dampened. But when Wayne did not appear at the plantation for some time after that, Nathaniel's hopes soared again—evidently Hannah had rebuffed Wayne's advances.

Watching Dade's carriage recede into the distance, Nathaniel decided that now, today, was the time to make his long-planned move.

Now that he had reached the decision, he became impatient. For the first time since he went to work on Malvern, he left the hands unsupervised for the rest of the afternoon, and rode at a gallop to the manor house. He stabled his horse, let himself into his quarters behind the house, and summoned one of the servants to prepare a tub of hot water. He stripped off his field clothes, and scrubbed himself thoroughly in hot, soapy water, then got into fresh clothing. As a final touch, he polished his other pair of boots to a high gloss, and tied his hair back into a plait with colored ribbon.

He debated a moment about carrying his riding crop. At the last moment he decided to take it along—it had become as much a part of him as his arm. He strode briskly toward the main house, swishing the crop against his thigh. It was late afternoon now, the shadows lengthening.

In the house the downstairs maid informed him that her mistress was occupied in the study. Nathaniel said brusquely, "No need to announce me, girl. I'll manage."

He strode down the hall, pausing at the door to take a deep breath, then knocked on the door.

* * *

At the knock Hannah leaned back at her desk. Knowing that she had annoyed Jules Dade that afternoon, she had begun to worry about the money she owed him, and had retired to the study to pore over the books. She had gone over them twice and of course had learned little that was new. She still owed the same amount, but she now realized an unsettling fact—the money she had borrowed from Dade was being eroded rapidly by the day-to-day expenses of operating the plantation. She purchased as much food and other supplies as possible on credit until her crop was in, yet there were some items she could not buy in this fashion. There was only one cheering note; another month, six weeks at the most, and she should be reaping the benefits of an abundant cotton crop.

If nothing dire happened between now and then, she should be able to scrape through . . .

It was then that the knock sounded on the door, and she welcomed the distraction, whatever it was. She called out, "Come in!"

The door opened to admit Nathaniel Bealls. The possibility of some disaster occurring was so much in her mind, that she asked in some alarm, "What is it, Nathaniel? Has something happened?"

On his way across the room, his step slowed, and he looked faintly startled. "No, there's nothing amiss, madam."

She sighed, pushing her fingers into her hair. "It's just that I've been so upset since that man came here, that I . . ." She broke off with a short laugh. "There's something about that man that hints at imminent disaster."

"Jules Dade, you mean?"

"Yes . . ." She broke off again, staring at him closely. "How did you know his name?"

He shuffled his feet, and removed his hat. "He stopped by the field where I was overseeing and introduced himself."

"That's all? Just introduced himself?"

"Oh, we passed the time of the day, and he inquired about the cotton crop."

Somehow she had the feeling that he was not being entirely truthful, but she decided not to press it. "What is it you wished, Nathaniel?"

He took a few steps closer, until he was looming over her. Instead of looking at her, he stared off, out the window. "I have been in your employ some months now. Is it your opinion . . .?" He swallowed. "Are you satisfied with my work?"

"Oh, yes, Nathaniel, very satisfied. I don't know what I would have done without you."

Now he hesitated, finally looking at her. He had a strange, intent look about him, and she noticed a sheen of perspiration on his forehead. All at once she became aware of the scent of horse and male about him. The scent was almost overpowering, and she felt faintly dizzy.

She said quickly, "Is it money, Nathaniel? Do you need some money for something? My financial condition is not good, but I can probably find my way clear to paying you something in advance."

"No, no, it isn't money," he said roughly. "Hannah, do you know how hard it is for a man to be around you for so long and not want you?"

Hannah could only stare at him, stunned. It had never entered her head that he might have yearnings toward her. True, there had been a few times she had awakened in the lonely hours of the night when she had felt the long-denied urgings of her own body, and her thoughts had turned to Nathaniel. He was a handsome man, exuding an aura of virility like the scent of musk. He was a few years younger than she, but it was not all that unusual for an older woman to take a younger man into her bed.

However, that had been a passing fancy, never seriously entertained when she was awake and busy. And of late any romantic day dreams she experienced mostly involved Court.

Nathaniel was speaking again, "You're a handsome, healthy woman, Hannah, long deprived of a husband in your bed. You want me, you know you do!"

"Sir, you are being too forward!" She drew herself up indignantly. "You do not know what is in my mind."

"I have had much experience with women," he said somewhat smugly, "and I can read the signs. Yes, you have thought of it, I am sure."

He tossed the riding crop onto the desk, and then his hands moved quickly, reaching down to seize her shoulders in a powerful grip. He drew her to her feet before she had a chance to resist, and put his lips to hers roughly. His mouth was hot, and as he drew her close against him Hannah could feel the swelling of his maleness.

A glow of heat suffused her body, and a weakness born of desire swept through her. His physical presence was strong. How easy it would be to give way to his demand, and let him take her, let his raw animal attraction ease the flaming need she was experiencing. Yet a small, sane part of her mind knew full well that it would be a terrible mistake. It would be an act committed without love, for she knew in that moment that this man was incapable of such feelings. And by giving in to him, she would give him sway over her. She realized that one time would not end it; whenever he felt the need, he would come to her, expecting her to accede to his demands.

She began to struggle. His arms tightened around her brutally; and Hannah knew that if she did not stop him now, this very instant, it would be too late. He would overpower her, take her by force if necessary. Outrage blazed in her, driving out any desire she might feel.

She tore her mouth away from his, turning her face aside. "Stop this, Nathaniel! Stop it right this minute!" she cried.

His only answer was a grating laugh. He took her face in his strong, cruel fingers, and began to force her head around so he could find her mouth again.

In a last, desperate effort, Hannah brought her knee up into his groin with all her strength. As her knee connected, he yowled in agony, and let her go, stepping back, doubled over with pain. Trembling, Hannah also moved back, putting the desk between them.

"I'm sorry if I hurt you, Nathaniel," she said coldly. "But you deserved it. You acted like an animal."

He slowly straightened up, his face pale and sweating, his features still set in a grimace of pain. His eyes burned at her. "An animal, is it?" he said in a venomous whisper. "You were quick enough to cock your leg for that Wayne fellow."

She recoiled. "That's not true!"

"Don't forget I saw you, that day by the creek."

"You saw nothing. I stumbled, and Court caught me to keep me from falling."

"Oh, you fell, I'm sure," he said with a sneer. "After I left, you fell to the ground with him, then the pair of you went at it like two *animals* in rut!"

Furious, she whipped around the desk, and slapped him hard across the face, her hand leaving a scarlet imprint on his cheek.

He snatched the riding crop up from the desk, and raised it high, advancing on her.

Hands up before her face, Hannah retreated. "Nathaniel, if you strike me with that, you're through here. You'll leave here without the money owed you. If you stop now, just turn and walk out of this room, I'll put out of my mind what happened here today. I'll put it down to a spell of temporary madness on your part, and we'll go on as before."

He stood for a long moment, the riding crop still raised, his face mirroring conflicting emotions. Finally, he drew a deep breath, and slowly lowered the riding crop.

Hannah said, "I value you as an overseer, Nathaniel, and I want you to continue. To be honest, I need you. But *only* as an overseer. I do not love you, and I want you to understand that clearly. I'm willing to forget this little episode, to forget that it ever happened. Is that understood?"

His expression had smoothed out now, and she could read nothing in his eyes. He said flatly, "It is understood, Mistress Verner."

He turned smartly and marched out of the room, his back straight.

Hannah drew a relieved breath after he had quitted the room. She had to wonder if she was making a mistake. It might have been better to have discharged him for his forwardness; she certainly had never given him any cause to expect her to respond to his advances. Yet she had come to depend on him, and it would be difficult, if not impossible, to manage the plantation by herself, at least until the crop was in. It galled her to have to admit this, and but for the money owed to Jules Dade, she would have taken the risk. She determined to discharge Nathaniel Bealls the moment the money was repaid.

Court was due to call on her the next afternoon, and as was customary now, Hannah looked forward to his visit eagerly.

The day had started off well, but it clouded over shortly after noon, and by the time Court was due to arrive, it was raining heavily. She wondered if he would still come.

At the usual time of his appearance Hannah was standing at the front window, peering out at the long driveway through the curtains. At least it was not raining hard enough to harm the cotton, but certainly hard enough to make it uncomfortable riding.

Then she saw his coach coming up the driveway. Her heart began to beat faster, her pulse rate accelerating. She stepped away from the window—it would never do to let him know that she was *waiting* for him! She started down the hall toward her study, catching a glimpse of the downstairs maid. The girl giggled behind her hand, and scampered back out of sight. Hannah sailed on serenely. She supposed that Court's visits provided juicy gossip for the servants, as well as the field hands. Well, there was nothing she could do about that.

She was bent over her desk, staring unseeingly down at the account books when Mary knocked on the door. "Yes, Mary, what is it?"

The door opened a crack. "Master Wayne has come calling, mistress."

"Show him into the parlor, Mary. I shall be right in. Oh . . . Perhaps you should ask Mr. Wayne if he would care for some sherry."

She dawdled for a few minutes, examining herself in the glass behind her desk. She had put on her riding clothes earlier, but had changed when the rain began. She was wearing one of her prettiest dresses, but without the hoop, and had powdered her face carefully, attaching a beauty mark to her cheek. Finally, satisfied with her appearance, she walked regally down the hall and into the parlor.

Court got to his feet when she came in. "Good day to you, Hannah. The weather is inclement, so perhaps we should forgo our ride today."

She nodded. "Yes, I have already changed from my riding habit."

"It was a fair day when I left Williamsburg. If I had known what it would turn into, I might have postponed my visit."

"I'm glad you didn't, Court." She was crossing the room toward him. "I would have missed you."

"And I you, dear Hannah." He looked her up and down. "It's rarely I see you nowadays without your riding habit, and I must say you look charming today."

She stepped before him, very close. "You're sweet to say so."

"Not at all, madam. It is the truth."

The memory of yesterday's encounter with Nathaniel rose vividly into Hannah's mind, and strangely the arousal she had felt briefly was now transferred to Court. She sensed that it would not be wise to tell Court about the incident; he might insist on calling the overseer on it.

She stared deep into his eyes, and they were so close that she could feel the warm exhalation of his breath on her cheek. She swayed slightly, murmuring, "Court, oh my dear!"

And somehow, without any recollection later of exactly how it happened, she was pressed tightly against him, his mouth on hers in a tentative, undemanding kiss.

It was not enough for Hannah; a wild, sweet madness invaded her blood, making her greedy for sensation. She moved as close to him as possible, her arms going around him, her fingers working along his back.

"Hannah," he said hoarsely. "A man can only take so much."

"It's all right, Court," she said softly. "This is not like that day by the creek, I promise you."

She took him by the hand and led him down the hall to her study. She did not dare go upstairs to her bedroom. The servants were busy on the second floor with the day's cleaning. To take Court into her bedroom would cause gossip to sweep across Malvern like a firestorm. There was an old divan in her study, that she used to nap on occasionally. It would do nicely.

Inside the study she carefully bolted the door, and turned into his arms. "That day wasn't so easy for me, either. A day doesn't pass that I haven't thought of it, and regretted what I did."

"Regretted, Hannah?" he said with raised eyebrows.

"Yes, regretted!" she said fiercely. "If that makes me a wanton, so be it!"

His hands were on her shoulders. "Methinks you will make a fetching wanton."

His mouth descended, and the sweet fire began in Hannah once more. She squirmed to get closer, wanting to be inside his skin. She had left her corset off when dressing, and his hands found her breasts through the thin material and cupped them.

She wondered hazily if she had had this in mind when changing from her riding habit. Perhaps not in her mind, but her body had known.

With a gasp she stood back and with fumbling fingers began unbuttoning her dress. She crossed to the study window and drew the curtains. It was still raining, the water sluicing down the window panes. As she faced around, she saw Court on the divan taking off his boots.

Her gaze clung to him as he removed his clothing. By

the time she had removed everything but her undergarments, Court was already naked. His body was slender, very trim for a man of his age. Muscles rippled under his smooth skin, and even unclothed he seemed elegant, his movements economical and graceful.

He was fully aroused, and Hannah shivered as she studied him. Her own movements were heavy and slow now, and she had the fancy that she was moving under water. Stepping out of her last garment, she moved toward him. She shuddered again as his gaze roamed over her.

"Dear Hannah, you are as beautiful as I imagined you would be," he said in a thick voice. "I have dreamed of this moment, almost from that day you came to my house."

He took her into his arms, his hands sliding down her back. Her skin seemed unduly sensitive to his touch, and she gloried at the silken feel of his flesh against hers.

He kissed her, and then his lips moved down the column of her throat. Her head arched back, a moan escaping her, as his mouth found her upthrust nipples. His tongue brushed across them; she locked her hands behind his head, and forced his mouth against hers. The tip of his tongue flicked across the undersides of her breasts, and in the valley between.

Then he fell back onto the divan and pulled her down with him. She was prepared for him to take her, but he was not to be rushed. He caressed her body with his lips and fingers, making love to her with consummate skill. Michael had been a good lover, as had been Joshua Hawkes, the lover she had taken in Boston; both had been strong men, capable of being tender at times, but often rough and demanding. Court was a strong man as well, but he was incredibly gentle, and seemed as much concerned with giving pleasure as taking it.

Before long Hannah was deaf and blind to everything but the waves of searing pleasure that consumed her. She became urgent, pleading with him with her hands and lips.

"Please, Court. No more. Please, now!" she said in a guttural voice.

"Yes, Hannah. Dear, dear Hannah," he muttered with heated breath, and rose to take her.

The rapture she felt as she took him into her was almost unbearable. They adjusted to each other's rhythms without undue difficulty, as if they had been lovers for time unmeasured.

Now he became potent and demanding, as virile and strong as a man half his age. Their pace quickened, and quickened yet again. Little cries of pleasure came from Hannah. Her fingers stroked his arching back, and then she clutched at him powerfully, as her pleasure crested and broke in an overwhelming tide of sensation. As the final spasm of ecstasy seized her, she reached up and brought his mouth down to hers, smothering her tiny cries of pleasure.

Court went rigid, a stuttering cry coming from him, and then slowly went lax. As Hannah cradled his head on her shoulder, she realized that neither had made a declaration of love. She knew by this time that Court was not a man who made commitments easily. As for her own feelings, she was uncertain; but she did know that this man in her arms was very dear to her, and she could love him easily.

But for now this moment was enough; whatever happened in the future she would cope with when the time came.

"You know something, Court?"

"What is that, my dear?"

"I'm glad it rained today." Her laughter was rich and full. "This was much more enjoyable than riding."

Outside the study window, Nathaniel Bealls stood, the rain running off his bared head. There was a tiny slit in the drawn curtains where they met, just wide enough for him to see what was happening inside. A sullen rage boiled up in him as he watched the pair locked together on the divan.

So Mistress Verner was too good for him, was she? She had lied to him—the foppish Wayne *was* her lover!

She would rue this day, he would see to that. He remembered the scene yesterday in this same room, and his mind shuddered with humiliation. Oh, she would humble herself before him when he was finished with her!

His gaze fastened on the man and woman in the throes of passion, Nathaniel lashed his thigh repeatedly with the riding crop, the blows measured and savage; in his mind appeared the pleasing image of Hannah writhing under those blows.

Chapter Nine

DURING the next few weeks, Michele noticed a peculiar thing. Although she often felt dissatisfied and vaguely depressed, her dancing was improving. This was not just her own opinion, but the opinion of others as well. Even Deampierre had remarked upon it, although with customary abruptness. Of course she *had* been working very hard, anxious to prove to Deampierre that she was good, wanting him to take notice, determined to prove that he had no reason to complain of her.

Her nonworking days had been busy also; for Andre and Madame Dubois were determined that she should see all of Paris, and on Saturdays and Sundays, Madame put her carriage and coachman at Michele's service so that she might see the city in comfort.

Andre had taken her to see the Louvre which—although it was no longer the king's residence—was still very impressive. He had taken her to the Grands Galeries; the Tuilleries Gardens; the magnificent Nôtre Dame Cathedral; the Pont Neuf; the Ile de la Cité; the elaborate Place Royale—all of the beautiful and romantic places.

They traversed the broad boulevards as Michele savored the names which rolled off her tongue with such grace. They visited the Outre-Petit-Pont where the university was located, and the Outre-Grand-Pont, which was the center of business. They examined grand hotels and monuments, and even drove out to Versailles so that Michele might see where the king and his court lived. In fact, Andre kept her so busy that she almost, but not quite, forgot about his promise to speak with her about Albion Villiers' remark that Andre was . . . What was it? An *arracheur de palissade*, that was it, a man who made love to other men. It was an embarrassing subject, but one which Michele felt that she must pursue if her mind was to be put to rest; but Andre had so far shown no inclination to discuss the matter, and she did not press it at this time. Her mind was still too full of the puzzle of Arnaut Deampierre to concentrate on anything else.

Still, her conversation with Albion Villiers had made Michele aware of certain things. In the past she had noticed that certain men and boys, like Andre and the boy in the company called Café au Lait, were different, that such men had a number of effeminate mannerisms and gestures; but she had ascribed it only to a personal eccentricity of manner. Now she observed more closely, and had seen that the interplay between certain men; for instance, the relationship between Café au Lait and his special friend, Raymond, a boy from the chorus, was very like that between a man and a woman. She found this knowledge both fascinating and baffling, and she had to wonder about the mechanics of it. How *would* a man make love to another man, and more importantly, why would he want to?

She was equally confused about her own feelings concerning Arnaut Deampierre. First of all, she was not certain just what they were! Michele found herself wishing that she had someone with whom she could discuss the matter, while at the same time feeling so embarrassed by her feelings that she did not wish to share them with anyone. The whole matter upset her greatly; she was a young woman accustomed to knowing her own mind, and not to be able to make a decision was pure agony.

And then, one afternoon, what she had been longing for happened—Deampierre spoke to her as they were beginning their mealtime break.

She was talking with Louis, and did not notice the ballet master until he was upon them. She turned and saw his face, which was serious, and her heart sank, as she thought he was about to reprimand her for some error or lack.

Instead, he spoke the words she had been longing to hear. "Michele, I have been watching you closely, and I believe that you are now ready to take your place in the corps de ballet. Be prepared to appear with them this Friday."

With those few words, he departed, leaving Michele speechless.

Louis burst into laughter. "Michele, you should see how you look! Just like a fish! But congratulations! We must celebrate. I will go downstairs and get a few bottles of wine, and we will invite the others to join us. Would you like that?"

Michele nodded, although she was really not all that thrilled about having a celebration. For some strange reason the elation she had imagined she would feel upon this occasion was lacking. She could not understand it. This was what she had wanted, what she had been working toward, why was she not happier?

Still, she rather enjoyed it when the dance troupe gathered round and toasted her new status in the company. Even Denise DeCoucy and Roland joined them, although their manner was distant and a little cool, as if they were doing it against their better judgment. The others, however, more than made up for Denise's and Roland's reserve, and for the first time, Michele really began to feel that she was a part of the company.

The rest of the afternoon went quickly, and Michele had finally begun to feel a little of the pleasure she had anticipated at her acceptance. After rehearsals were over, the thought came to her that she should thank Deampierre for what he had done for her. It would only be the polite thing to do, would it not? Madame's carriage would be waiting to take her home, but the driver understood that sometimes she was delayed when rehearsals ran late. He would wait.

As she decided to act upon the idea, her heart began to

beat faster in excitement. Surely he would not think her forward for simply thanking him!

As the others left, one by one, or two by two, Michele lingered, slowly removing her slippers, fussing with her hamper, dawdling over everything, until they were all gone except for Deampierre, who was busy at his desk in the far corner of the room.

Feeling uncomfortably nervous and excited, Michele slowly approached Deampierre's desk. He was concentrating upon some document before him and was seemingly unaware of her presence. Was he ignoring her purposely, or was he truly unaware that she stood there?

Beginning to feel that she perhaps had made a mistake, she was turning away when he glanced up. His dark eyes were bemused and his expression faintly annoyed, and her heart sank.

"Yes, Michele? You wished to speak to me?"

Face flaming, she nodded quickly, feeling tongue-tied now that he was finally looking at her. "I . . . I wanted to thank you. For all that you have done for me . . ."

Her voice trailed off, and she began to fidget with her hands. What was wrong with him? He had been so friendly at the salon. Why was he so cold toward her now?

His expression relaxed a trifle, and he smiled slightly. "That is not necessary, you know. You have studied well, and you have worked very hard. You have most certainly earned your place in the company."

"Thank you," she said somewhat lamely; and then, in a burst of feeling, "Why have you been avoiding me? After the salon, I thought . . . Well, I thought we were friends!"

She flushed again in embarrassment, as she realized how nakedly pleading she had sounded. He would think . . . What *would* he think? She should never have lingered behind. If she wanted to thank him, she should have sent him a formal note. He must think her a complete fool!

She watched his face, fascinated, as his expression changed from surprise to tenderness.

"My dear Michele," he said gently. "My sweet child. I

never thought . . . I didn't mean to . . ." He smiled ruefully at himself.

Michele stood frozen in her tracks as he came slowly toward her.

He framed her face tenderly with his strong, warm hands, and looked deep into her eyes. "I am your friend, Michele, and it is because I *am* your friend that I have avoided you as much as possible." His voice took on a musing tone. "It would be so easy, so very easy to . . ." He broke off, staring over her head. "Michele, I will speak to you honestly. As ballet master of this company, I must not become involved with my dancers. I am interested in having the best ballet company in all of France, in all the world, and to accomplish that, I must make some personal sacrifices. I have worked in many other companies in the past, and I have seen what happens when a director becomes romantically involved with one of his dancers. It can often mean destruction for the dancer, for when the affair is over, particularly if there are any bad feelings, it is the director who will remain, of course. I confess that I took the risk in letting myself get to know you, but we were meeting outside of the company, in Madame's salon, and I thought there was no great harm in it. I'm sorry."

He paused again, and his voice took on a pleading quality. "What I am doing is for your own good, Michele. Believe me."

Michele, very conscious of his hands upon her face, knew only that he was expressing tenderness toward her. Unthinkingly, she leaned toward him until their faces and bodies touched. His hands tightened upon her face, and he groaned softly; and then his lips were upon hers, and it was the sweetest feeling Michele had ever experienced; and then he was pulling away, but only so that he could press his mouth into her hair and whisper into her ear, "Ah, *chérie*, my sweet Michele, how I have longed to do this!"

And now his mouth was again upon hers, moving softly, seeking, pressing; and as his tongue touched hers, she felt a sharp wave of pleasure and arousal so strong that she instinctively arched her lower body in against his, and was startled to feel a hardness at his groin that was beyond her experience.

For an instant she knew a flash of fear, but the pleasure and the flaming need were the more powerful emotions, and she did not move away.

Deampierre's breathing had grown rough and agitated, and Michele could feel the drumming beat of his heart as his hands began to explore her body, moving first to her shoulders, then to her waist and buttocks with ever increasing demand.

She could hear her own breath coming faster now, and could feel her own pulse pounding madly. She was not quite certain what was going to happen, but whatever it was, she knew that she wanted it.

His body was now moving against hers, causing delicious friction that inflamed her senses; and then, in the next instant, she was in his arms, and he was carrying her into the cloak room where there was a small cot, kept there for emergency illness.

Deampierre placed her on the cot, gently, and smoothed her hair, and his lips were again upon hers, and the weight of his body; and then somehow, her dress was off, followed by her undergarments; and she was lying, naked and amazingly unashamed under his caressing hands, which began to stroke and touch her in places she had been taught were forbidden. Strangely, all she could think of was how thrilling it was, how *good* it felt; and although she trembled with the newness of it, she unconsciously responded, rising to meet his hand, moving her body to his touch.

This seemed to arouse Deampierre even more, and she could feel his excitement mount until the moment came when he stood back to strip away his own clothes. Michele lay in a daze, befuddled by the new and startling sensations in her body.

Then all thought ceased as he lay atop her, warm and heavy, the strange but exciting hardness at the juncture of his thighs against her mound. She felt his body rise, even while his lips were still upon hers, and his hands were sure in their touch, gently pushing her thighs apart; and then the hot, hard strength of him was an insistent pressure upon her, broaching her, and she gasped at the pressure and the unexpected, brief stab of pain; and then he was inside her, and all her senses were concentrated upon that part of her body as he began to move more and more rapidly. Her pain was forgotten as her own excitement spiraled to an almost unbearable crescendo, and she cried aloud as a gripping spasm clenched her lower body in a paroxysm of intense pleasure.

At her cry, Deampierre's thrustings became more frantic, and even though this caused Michele some discomfort now that her own body was relaxed, she gloried in it, knowing that he was obtaining pleasure from her, and was pleased by the fact that she could cause this riot of emotions in a man usually so icily controlled.

And then Deampierre's body went rigid as he gasped and cried out. He thrust into her once more, and she could feel him throbbing inside her. For a long moment he lay lax atop her, and then rolled away, breathing unevenly.

Michele felt strangely bereft as he moved away from her. He had been heavy, but she had been more than glad to bear his weight. Turning her head to look at him, she saw that he had one arm flung across his eyes, and that his face was turned away from her.

Despite the drowsy relaxation that she was enjoying, Michele felt a pulse of apprehension, for his position seemed to separate them by more than just the distance between their bodies. She wanted to ask him so many things, but did not quite dare to break the silence, which seemed to be growing into something quite frightening.

At last she could bear it no longer. She had to know if the experience had been for him as shattering as it had been for her. Tentatively, she reached out and touched his shoulder. "Arnaut?" Her voice was trembling. "Arnaut, speak to me. You are frightening me!"

Slowly, he lowered his arm, and turned toward her. His expression was unreadable. "I am sorry, *chérie*," he said. "I did not mean to do that."

Michele's throat felt dry. She swallowed. Why was he being so *serious*? "Do not push me away, Arnaut," she whispered. "We were so close, and now . . . Now . . ." Her voice broke. "You make me feel alone again!"

"Ah, *chérie*." He pulled her close against his chest. "It was certainly not my intent to make you feel that way. Forgive me. I was being selfish, thinking only of myself, forgetting that for you it was the first time."

He kissed her tenderly upon the forehead, and Michele tried to tell herself that it was all right, that things were going to be fine; but somehow, deep in her heart, she knew that something was amiss, that Deampierre was now going to tell her something that she would not wish to hear.

He pulled back from her, and looked deep into her eyes. "Michele, what just happened was wonderful for me, I want you to know that. Being close to you, loving you, was a very beautiful experience, and I will always remember it so."

Michele felt her heart begin to hammer. Why was he talking this way? It was as if he was never going to see her again!

He sighed. "I hope you will understand this, *chérie*, although I much doubt that you will." He sighed again, and touched her cheek with the tip of his finger. "You are so very, *very* young."

Michele clutched at him and burrowed her face against his chest. She began to weep.

Gently, he stroked her hair. "Michele, what I am trying to say is this . . . This must not happen again. As much as I wanted it, as much as I enjoyed it, it cannot happen again."

Michele's voice was a wail, muffled against his chest. "Why, Arnaut, why?"

"Because it never should have happened in the first place, my dear. It is not only that you are the ward of a very dear friend, or that you are so young. You are a member of my company, and as I told you before, I have always made it my policy never to become emotionally involved with one of my dancers. Today was happenstance, I did not mean for it to happen. My only excuse is that I am human, and fallible, and you are very beautiful, my dear, and desirable."

Michele's sobs were uncontrollable now. A happenstance? An experience which had been the most beautiful in her life. How could he say that, feel that?

"Why?" she sobbed. "Why does it matter if I am one of your company?"

"I have already answered that, Michele. I cannot afford to have bad feelings in the company. If, for instance, I should eventually give you a starring role, everyone would say it was because we were lovers, and there would be jealousy and bad feelings. You would not want that, would you?"

Michele shook her head against the warmth of his chest. "I wouldn't care."

He shook her gently, pushing her back so that he could see her face clearly. "You don't mean that, child. You only think you do because you are upset."

Michele hiccupped. She felt betrayed and despairing. "Anyway, they already say things like that," she said accusingly. "Madame DeCoucy says that you and Cybella are lovers!"

Deampierre sighed in exasperation. "Madame DeCoucy is not known for her truthful statements," he said angrily. "I can tell you honestly that this is a canard, child. Madame DeCoucy is blinded to everything else by her consuming interest in her daughter's career. She thinks that there must be some nefarious reason why Cybella and not Denise is our *première danseuse*, when the truth of it is simply that while Denise is good, Cybella is better. How could you believe such nonsense?

"Now, you must collect yourself. You must wash your face, tidy yourself, and go home, or Andre and Madame

Dubois will begin to think that something has happened to you. Come now. Stop your weeping, Michele!"

She tried, yet the tears still kept coming. "You mean that what happened just now will make no difference in our . . . our relationship? We will go on as if it had never happened?"

He nodded, his expression stern but kind. "That is exactly what I do mean. We must not even speak of it again. You must not think of me as anything but your ballet master. It may be difficult at first, but it will be better for both of us, you will see. I know you, Michele. The dance is for you what it is for me, the most important thing, above all else. You must always remember that. Now do as I have told you. I will fetch you some water and a cloth."

Later, Michele could remember very little about the moments that followed, or the ride home in the carriage with the patiently waiting driver.

Once home, she greeted Andre and Madame automatically, and she must have seemed to be all right, for neither of them commented upon her tardiness, or her appearance.

Pleading no appetite and extreme fatigue from rehearsing late, she proceeded directly to her room, and after removing her clothing and putting on her night rail, she fell into bed, burying her head in the pile of pillows, seeking sleep and sweet oblivion.

For the next few weeks, Michele was unhappier than she had ever been, save for that sorrowful period following her father's sudden death.

In many ways, she felt the same now as she had on that occasion. There was the same feeling of loss, of abandonment by someone she loved; the same feeling of cold heaviness around her heart.

Still, life went on. She attended her practice and rehearsals faithfully, and on evenings and holidays went out socially with Andre and Madame Dubois, just as if nothing was troubling her. It is so strange, she thought: I have changed so much, I am suffering so much inside, and yet no one notices. It does not show! She had now known a man's love, physically, and yet her face in the mirror remained unchanged.

Strangely, her dancing did not suffer, but was, in fact, showing even more marked improvement. She was too proud to let Deampierre know how much he had hurt her, and too stubborn to want to give him a chance to correct her dancing, so she worked harder than ever; still, she was angry at herself. She was the one who had promised herself that she would not be caught up in the trap of love; that she would never let some man become so important to her that the attachment might threaten her career! And yet here she was, mooning over the ballet master like some lovesick idiot. What was wrong with her? Why could she not control her feelings, and her life?

So, the days passed, one by one, and then it was time for the performance in which she would participate as a member of the corps de ballet.

As that fateful day approached, she found her spirits rising, in spite of herself. Andre and Madame Dubois were getting together a large group of friends to attend the performance, and it was impossible not to experience some of the excitement that they generated.

On the night of the performance, as she stood in the dressing room backstage with the other girls, Michele realized that for the first time since that evening with Deampierre, she had not thought of him for hours.

The realization caused her to smile to herself, and Marie Renaud, who was dressing next to her, looked around and smiled also. "Oh, Michele, it's so good to see you smile! You have been so gloomy these past weeks. But isn't this all so exciting? I love it so, the smell of the theater, the sounds of the orchestra tuning up, and then the dancing, knowing that the audience is out there, beyond the footlights!"

Michele let her smile widen. "Yes, it is exciting, although I admit to feeling very nervous. This will be the first time I have actually danced in front of a real audience. I just hope that I don't do anything awkward or foolish!"

Marie, slipping into her costume, laughed with a toss of her head. "We all worry about that, Michele, but I think you have less to worry about than the rest of us. You are already much better than most of the corps. You really should be doing solo work, and you will be before too much longer, I am certain."

Michele felt her face grow warm. Picking up her own costume, she slid it over her head and shoulders, and then turned so that Marie might fasten her. "Marie, you shouldn't say that. What if some of the others should overhear you? You know tonight is my first appearance on a real stage!"

"I don't care," Marie said stoutly. "You have been dancing a long time, and now that you have caught up on the things you did not know, you are very, very good. Why do you think Denise dislikes you so intensely?"

Michele sighed and sucked in her breath as Marie fastened the waist of her skirt. "I think Denise dislikes *everyone*, at least every other female dancer!"

"No." Marie's tone was positive. "She does not waste her dislike on those she considers not good enough to offer competition for her. You might say that her dislike is in direct proportion to the talent and skill of the person involved, and she seems to dislike you very much indeed, Michele."

"Then it might be said that her dislike is a great compliment."

Marie, finished with the fastenings, turned Michele around to face her. "That is true, in a way, but Denise can be a dangerous enemy, don't you ever forget that. She has no heart, no care for anyone save herself. Be very careful of her!"

Michele, realizing that Marie was serious, nodded soberly. "I have been told that before, but I really don't know what it means. After all, what could she do? Has she done something to someone in the past?"

Slowly, Marie nodded. "Although it might be difficult

to prove in a court of law, there have been strange happenings. There was one girl, Renée, a very good dancer, one of the corps de ballet. Denise was in the corps, too, in those days, and she and Renée were about equal as dancers. There was a part coming up, a small part for a featured dancer, and Monsieur Deampierre was making up his mind concerning which girl, Renée or Denise, would get the role.

"At the next performance, Renée tripped over something as the corps entered the stage, breaking her ankle, and Denise, of course, got the role. Perhaps it was simply coincidence that Denise happened to be standing in front of Renée in line as the dancers prepared to go on stage, perhaps not. Nothing was ever proven, but there was a good deal of speculation."

"But as you said, it could have been coincidence," Michele said with puckered brows.

Marie looked at her levelly. "Once, yes, it might have been a coincidence, but this kind of thing has happened again and again, and *always* to girls who were in Denise's way. That is why I felt you should be warned."

Michele, feeling somewhat alarmed by Marie's story, nodded slowly. "Thank you, Marie. I will watch out for myself, you can be sure. I shall keep a close eye on Denise."

A knock upon the dressing room door signaled that they had but a few minutes before curtain time, and Michele turned to the mirror to finish her toilette, her heart pounding wildly in her breast.

This was it! This was the day that she had been working for. A sudden surge of gratitude and gladness filled her; and then it was time to go on stage and face an audience for the first time in her life; but it was also time to face the future she had dreamed and prayed for for so long.

Chapter Ten

As Michele, dressed in her elegant, hooped costume, stood in the wings with the rest of the corps de ballet, awaiting her cue, she looked around her carefully, wanting to remember always the way it was this first time. It was dark in the wings, but the darkness made the stage seem all the lighter. In the steady glow of the hundreds of candles based around the stage, their lights reflected from brass shields, the sets looked magical and alive, the solo dancers larger than life.

And then it was their cue, and the corps de ballet moved out onto the stage, one by one, moving on and with the music; and Michele felt such a swell of happiness that she could hardly bear it.

Briefly, she thought of Marie's warning about Denise; but since she was not dancing near the other girl, she put it out of her mind and concentrated upon her dancing.

All too soon it was over, and they took their bows to thunderous applause. Because of the lights, she could not see individual members of the audience, but she recognized Andre's voice, his shout sounding above the others: "Bravo! Bravo!"

In the crowded dressing room, sweaty and almost swooning with excitement, Michele jostled and fought to find space to change her clothing and make her toilette. All of the girls were chattering and laughing, including Michele herself. Then she looked up and met the glance of Denise

DeCoucy, who was staring at her in speculation out of her cold, gray eyes.

Michele forced herself to look away, and heard Marie Renaud saying, "It came off well, don't you think? Didn't Louis dance beautifully? I thought he looked well with Cybella, didn't you?"

Michele nodded. "Louis was marvelous! Of course, so was Cybella, but then she always is."

At that moment there was a knock upon the door, which was simultaneously opened and used as a shield by a partially clothed dancer who had been standing nearby.

Because of the crush, Michele could not see who was at the door, but she could hear the oohs and aahs of those who could, and then she heard her name being called.

It took another moment for the girl who had opened the door to reach her, carrying a huge bunch of roses; their odor hung heavy in the small room.

"These are for you, Michele," the girl said, her eyes wide. "A messenger just brought them."

All of the girls were exclaiming and crowding around now, and Michele felt herself flush with embarrassment. Although it was not unusual for the leading and specialty dancers to receive dozens of flowers after a performance, it was an event for a member of the chorus.

They have to be from Andre, Michele thought; and he shouldn't have. The other girls would think that she believed that she was something special, better than they.

"Who are they from?" Marie asked, reaching for the card tucked in among the blossoms. "Let's see!"

Michele watched with misgivings as Marie read the card. Why were they making so much of it?

Marie's face broke into a smile. "It says: 'To a very lovely lady, and a superb dancer. Will you join me for supper?' "

"Well, who is it from, you ninny?" cried another of the girls. "What is it, a big secret?"

Marie's eyes grew quite large. "They are from the Englishman, Lord Bayington."

Michele, expecting to hear Andre's name, felt the shock

of complete surprise. "Lord Bayington?" she said, in confusion. "Who is he?"

She was answered by a gale of laughter. Marie shook her head, smiling fondly. "Oh, Michele, really! He's only one of the handsomest and wealthiest men in all of England, and he's been visiting his aunt here in Paris for the past few months. You *are* an innocent! Don't you ever pay any attention to the current gossip?"

She handed the roses to Michele, who took them gingerly.

"You had best beware, Michele," said Felice, a small, dark-haired girl with lively eyes and a pixie smile. "He is said to be a terrible *roué*. However, it is also said that he is very generous. Are you going to accept his invitation?"

Michele, more embarrassed than ever at being the focus of so much attention, shook her head. "Andre and Madame Dubois are planning a little supper for me, and besides, I do not know the gentleman."

"It is not necessary to know a gentleman before going to supper with him." It was Celeste, one of the older girls. "I only wish he had asked *me*. I could use a wealthy and generous suitor. Oh, could I!"

The other girls laughed, and Michele buried her face in the blossoms to hide her flaming face. As she did so, she felt a touch upon her shoulder.

It was Marie. "You will have to at least make some response, Michele. The messenger is still waiting at the door."

Michele raised a dismayed face. "But I don't know what to say!"

Marie smiled. "I'll help you. You don't wish to make him angry, I'm sure, even if you feel you must refuse his invitation. Tell the messenger that you are desolated, but that you have a prior engagement that you cannot break. Perhaps another time, if he would be so kind as to ask you again."

Michele looked at her in horror. "But that isn't true! I mean, I am not desolated in the least, and I certainly don't wish to encourage him!"

Marie sighed. "Oh, Michele, you are so . . . so American! It is only a game, you know, and it would do wonders for your reputation to have it bruited about that such a man as Lord Bayington was courting you."

Michele shook her head obstinately. "No, I will not lie. Tell the messenger to relay to Lord Bayington that I thank him most sincerely for the flowers and his kind words, but that I have a prior engagement, and that is all."

Marie shrugged in defeat. "Very well, if that is what you want, but that is certainly not the way the game is played!"

Michele watched her go to the door. Why was it that relationships between men and women always seemed to have to be a game? Could not a man and woman be straightforward with each other? Was it so difficult, so unusual for this to be so?

For the first time that evening, she thought of Arnaut Deampierre and herself, and found, surprisingly, that the thought of him no longer made her feel like weeping.

The roses were so beautiful that Michele could not bring herself to leave them behind; and so she had them with her when she came out of the dressing room to meet Andre and Madame.

Andre, his face alight with pleasure, hugged her to him, flowers and all. "You were wonderful, *chérie*!" he said explosively. "You looked so beautiful, didn't she, Renée?"

Madame bobbed her head, smiling widely. "Michele, you were marvelous! You should have heard the comments from the audience!"

Michele, pleased but embarrassed by their effusiveness, kissed them both upon their cheeks. "Sssh, now, both of you. Don't say such things. I was only a member of the corps. Who would notice me?"

Madame laughed and tapped Michele on the shoulder with her fan. "Well, someone obviously did, or perhaps you found those hothouse roses growing in your dressing room, eh?"

Michele blushed. "A gentleman sent them . . . He wanted me to have supper with him."

"How delightful!" Madame said with raised eyebrows. "Who was this gentleman?"

"An Englishman, a Lord Bayington, his card said."

Both Andre and Madame began to laugh.

"You see," Andre said, wiping his eyes with his lacy handkerchief. "We told you that you were noticed. You have caught the eye of one of the richest men in England. And he was not the only one. I too heard the comments, the least flattering of which was that you stood out from the corps de ballet like a rose among cabbages, which makes your bouquet seem most appropriate, most appropriate."

Michele shook her head in distress. "How could they say that? There are many excellent dancers in the corps. How could they particularly notice me?"

Andre's expression was serious. "I am not teasing you, or flattering you, *chérie*, whatever you may think. What we say is the truth. You have a special quality, a special talent. No matter how you try to conform, to blend in with the other girls, you stand out. You are noticed. It is perhaps not a good trait for a member of the corps de ballet, but it is an excellent one for a featured dancer, or a *première danseuse*."

Michele looked down at the floor. "But I am not a *première danseuse*, not even a featured dancer. I am not *supposed* to stand out. Monsieur Deampierre will be furious with me," she said dispiritedly. "He tells us often that in the corps de ballet we must act as one, move as one, that we are always a unit!"

Andre took her arm. "Do not worry about it, *chérie*. You may have to struggle to be unnoticed in the corps, but you will not be dancing with them long. Soon you will be a soloist, you will see!"

Although Michele had been upset by Andre's statement on the night of her first performance, within a few short weeks his prediction came true.

At first, of course, Deampierre had lectured her, telling her precisely what she had told Andre he would say; and she, knowing he was right, had tried to hold herself back, to conform to the movements of the other dancers; and to a degree at least, she had succeeded; yet she was still noticed, still talked about, still the recipient of letters and notes and flowers in such amounts that it made her feel guilty to be so singled out for attention.

When she spoke to Madame Dubois about this, Madame laughed. "Oh, my dear! Do not feel badly because you are noticed. It happens all the time. The audience has its favorites, it is part of the pleasure of attending the ballet. How do you think Camargo and Salle got started on their brilliant careers? They, too, were at one time members of the corps de ballet. It was their specialness that made the public pick them out, and it was their popularity that made them at last *premières danseuses*! So, do not worry. Be happy that they notice you, for it means that soon you will be dancing featured roles, and then leads, and your career will be made."

Madame's words comforted Michele to some extent, but she still had to face the jealousy of the other dancers. Some, of course, like Marie and Louis, were happy for her, and others just accepted her growing recognition with resignation, knowing that it was the way of the world. Others, mainly Denise DeCoucy and Roland Maraise, were openly hostile, and Michele was often reminded of Marie's warning concerning Denise. She tried to avoid the other girl as much as possible, but so far there had been no attempt to engineer an "accident," at least as far as Michele could tell.

Deampierre now had her understudying some of the featured roles, along with Denise, and Michele was happier that she had been in a long time.

She was now resigned to the fact that Deampierre was not going to allow a recurrence of their brief, romantic encounter; but he allowed her to see that he was genuinely fond of her—although he always maintained a stern manner with her; and this was almost enough. For now her whole being was concentrating on her dancing. She at last felt that she was really becoming good at it; that she no longer need feel that she was behind the others in ability, skill, or technique. She felt that she was coming into her own.

And then Deampierre announced that he had created a new ballet, based on an old folk tale, *Beauty and the Beast*.

This news created a tension and excitement among the dancers, who were all wondering who would be cast. Although most of them assumed that Cybella and Roland would play the leads, there were the supporting roles, and everyone, no matter how minor their position in the company, secretly hoped to be given one of those.

Deampierre finally put an end to the suspense: "I have given much thought to the casting of this ballet. Cybella will play Beauty, and Louis will play the Beast, for he is a good actor as well as a dancer, and will bring the necessary sensitivity to the role. It is necessary that the Beast be sympathetic.

"Now, to the other roles. Roland, you will play the father, for you are large and tall, and will add authority to the role. And you, Michele, will play Beauty's sister. It is not a large role, but it will give you a chance to see how you do as a solo dancer. Now, to the barre, all of you! Tomorrow, we will start to work on the new ballet!"

Michele could not believe what she was hearing. She had been given a featured role! She could hardly contain her excitement, and looked quickly over to Louis to share her delight with him. In doing so, her glance crossed that of Denise, who was glaring at her with naked hatred, so fierce that Michele almost cringed at the blaze of raw feeling exhibited by the other girl. But then she steeled herself and gazed coolly back. Why should she let herself be intimidated by this girl? If Denise, as Marie suggested, had staged accidents for her rivals, well, Michele was forewarned, and could take precautions. Denise would not find her an easy victim, of that she was determined.

There were other glances of envy, of course, but most

of the dancers complimented Michele, and wished her well. It was, she thought, one of the happiest days of her life.

And now her days became busier than ever, for there were special practice sessions for the new ballet; and Michele literally had no time for social life at all; but she did not mind, for she loved the new ballet, and the solo, which Deampierre had created for the sister, was lovely, graceful and sprightly, and Michele gloried in working on it. In fact, there was nothing about the ballet that did not please her, and she awoke each morning filled with a sense of delight and purpose.

She wrote to Hannah, in Williamsburg, telling her mother of her great good fortune and pleasure, and wished that her mother was here in Paris, so that she might attend the opening performance. Hannah wrote regularly, but it took so lengthy a time for a letter to cross the ocean that the news conveyed was always months out of date. Only the messages of love and caring were impervious to the long journey, and Michele knew that Hannah missed her as much as she missed her mother.

Michele had almost forgotten Marie's warning concerning Denise, when an unpleasant incident occurred. Michele was in the habit of sharing her bountiful lunches with one or another of her friends, usually Louis, Marie, or Café au Lait, or some of the girls from the corps de ballet.

On this particular day, she was sharing her lunch with Louis and Marie, when Marie, halfway through the meal, suddenly complained of feeling ill.

Michele looked at her in concern. Indeed, Marie's face was quite pale, and there were beads of moisture on her brow. She clutched at her stomach, and bent double, moaning. Michele and Louis tried to comfort her. At last Michele was forced to take her into the dressing room, where Marie vomited, violently, into a wash basin.

After Marie had been eased down upon one of the pallets in the dressing room, Michele returned to the other room and Louis. "What do you think is wrong with her, Louis?" she asked helplessly. "She was perfectly fine before we began to eat."

Louis, his expression grave, leaned toward her. "I think that is the answer, 'She was fine *before* we began to eat.' Look!" He held out the remainder of the rice pudding which Marie had been eating. "Smell this, Michele."

Gingerly, Michele leaned forward over the pudding, and inhaled. She could smell a strange, rather acrid odor, which seemed very out of place. She looked questioningly at Louis.

"I think something has been added to the pudding," he said. "Something to make *you* ill."

Michele felt a cold quiver of anger, laced with fear and distaste. "Make *me* ill? But who . . . ? Oh!" she said softly but explosively, and then her gaze turned, unwillingly, toward the corner where Denise and Roland sat together. They were not looking in her direction, but had their heads together in a low-voiced conversation.

"Do you mean Denise?" Michele said to Louis.

He nodded grimly. "It is possible."

"It was intended for me?"

"I should think so. Don't you? You are just fortunate that you do not care for rice pudding, and did not even taste it."

"And poor Marie is not so fortunate. If this is true, how could she do such a terrible thing? Marie warned me that Denise had caused accidents to other girls whom she considered a threat, but to *poison* someone . . . !"

Louis shrugged. "Probably not poison. It's probably just something to make you good and ill, so that you could not dance for a few days, and then Denise, of course, could step in. She is quite capable of it, believe me."

Michele stared in dismay at the rest of her food. "I wonder if the pudding is the only thing that was tampered with?"

"There is no way of knowing for sure, except by using the nose. I have a very good one, and I have smelled everything. There was only one other thing that smelled suspicious, and that was the chocolates. I believe the rest to be safe. Here, you've hardly eaten anything, Michele. Have some of the chicken, it is delicious."

But Michele waved the food away. She had lost her appetite completely. How could anyone, even Denise, be so despicable as to attempt something like this? It was upsetting and frightening. Denise should be exposed, but how? If she went to Deampierre, Michele knew that she would be labeled a tale bearer; and besides, there was no proof, only supposition. She would just have to watch very carefully; and that was a depressing thought—that she should have to protect herself from one of her fellow dancers.

It was only a few days later that Michele found the sliver of glass in her dancing slipper; a sharp shard that would have cut her badly, if she had not noticed it as she was putting on her slippers.

She showed it to Louis, who shook his head angrily. "You know, I have half a mind to do the same to *her,*" he said. "Somebody is going to have to stop that witch before she hurts someone badly."

Michele touched his arm. "No, Louis. If you do that, you will be as bad as she is. There *must* be some other way."

But as she thought of Marie, still ill in bed from the effect of whatever had been in the food, Michele almost changed her mind. Perhaps that was all such people could understand, violence to answer their own violence, hurt to match the hurts they inflicted on others, but her better judgment made her bide her time. There was still no proof, she thought, no real proof. If only someone would catch Denise in the deed, that would end it. Meanwhile, they could only wait.

And so Michele went on with practice and rehearsals, pretending that nothing had happened, but watching Denise more closely than ever.

And then it was time to try on the costumes, which were being made for them. Louis' costume was magnificent. Made from a tawny cloth that was the color of a lion's pelt, and topped with a manelike headdress, it made Louis look both frightening and appealing, the effect that Deampierre had wanted the costume to achieve.

The girls' costumes—both Beauty's and her sister's—were very simple, almost Grecian in design, and occasioned many a startled comment from the dancers, for they were very different from the usual hooped and panniered women's costumes.

"Why, they will show the form!" Marie said in a low voice to Michele. "This soft material will cling."

"Yes!" said Deampierre, who had overheard the remark. "It will cling, and it will also flow and move with the body. I have long wanted to get away from the usual type of costume, and this ballet affords me the opportunity to do so. And after all, it will not be a first. Salle did it."

"And caused a scandal," said Denise, rather loudly. "Well, I am only glad that I do not have to dance in such shameful garments!"

Michele and Marie exchanged knowing glances. "She would only *die* to be doing it," Marie whispered.

I only hope that *I* don't die doing it, Michele thought wryly.

This thought set her to thinking about Denise again. There had to be some way to stop Denise from setting her little traps. She simply had to think of something. After much thought on the subject, Michele finally decided that Louis had been right. She would have to fight Denise on her own level, no matter how repugnant that might be.

That night, she approached Andre and confided her problem.

"I think you are right, *chérie*," he said after some thought. "The only way to thwart her is to show her that two can play at her dirty little game. Come, I will get you something that will not harm her, but will make her *wish* that she was dead, at least for a spell of time."

The next day, armed with Andre's concoction in a small vial, Michele waited until the others were all in the practice room, then approached Denise's lunch basket unobserved. Following Andre's instructions, she uncorked the bottle of red wine, and poured the contents of the vial into the bottle. She shook the bottle vigorously so that the two liquids would mix well.

She was late getting up to the barre, but took Deampierre's scolding with good grace. It would be worth it, she thought, when she saw Denise's face at mealtime.

During the noon break, when everyone was settled with their food, she whispered to Louis and Marie, "Watch Denise, but do not let her notice. I have done something to even the score!"

Louis smiled widely, and Marie smothered a giggle behind her hand. "At last! What did you do, Michele?"

Michele said, "Just watch. You'll see."

The break time went all too quickly, as usual, and Denise did not seem to notice that three pairs of eyes were fixed upon her. She ate well, and drank freely from the wine bottle, and each time she did, Michele felt a small gratification. Now, if the potion only worked as Andre had promised it would . . .

"Look!" Louis said suddenly. "Look at Denise!"

Michele looked and saw for the first time some expression on the other girl's face. Denise's face was pale, and her brow wrinkled in obvious distress. She was clutching her abdomen in agony, and then, with a groan, she jumped to her feet and ran ungracefully toward the dressing room.

Louis turned a glowing face to Michele. "That was wonderful! How did you manage it?"

Michele was smiling. "Just a little concoction that Andre gave me. A physic, a strong one. Denise will be kept occupied all afternoon, and perhaps most of the night. She should be well chastened by tomorrow. Then I will tell her that two can play at her game, and that if she will promise to see that no further 'accidents' occur to me, I shall do the same for her."

"Marvelous!" Louis applauded softly. "I told you that the only way to fight fire was with fire. Did I not?"

Michele nodded. "Yes, you did, you bloodthirsty villain, but I want you to know that I still do not wholly approve of this. It was simply that in this case it seemed the only solution."

"It is poetic justice," Marie said benignly, daintily nibbling on an apple. "I adore things that balance out. It is so *just*!"

It was that same evening—when Michele reported to Andre the success of his physic—that she and Andre finally had the conversation that he had promised her on the afternoon of Madame's salon.

It was while they were laughing at the picture of Denise running continually to the chamber pot, that Michele put her hand on his arm. "Andre, this is the first chance we have had to actually talk during the past weeks. Do you remember, at Madame's salon, you promised that we would speak of your 'lurid past.' " She smiled as she spoke the words, to ease the sting.

Andre's smile faded. "*Naturellement, chérie,* I remember all too well, and I wish that I had never made such a promise."

Michele shook her head in annoyance. "Now why do you say that, Andre? Surely we are good enough friends, you and I, so that we might talk of this. Besides, it was *you* who said you would speak of it to me. I did not ask you."

He took her hand. "You are right, Michele, but I spoke in haste and perhaps foolishly. It is . . . It is a very difficult subject for me to discuss. Very painful."

Michele pressed his hand between hers. "Andre, you know I love you. You have been like an uncle, or an elder brother, to me, and now that Papa is gone, you have taken his place, also. I don't want to cause you pain, you must know that, but I do not think that I can bear knowing just a little bit and not all. It has baffled and worried me."

He sighed. "Very well, *chérie*. We will talk about this once, and that will be the end of it. I only hope that you will not hate or despise me after my tale is done."

"I cannot conceive of anything that would change my

feeling for you, dear friend." She leaned across to kiss his cheek.

He sighed again. "I pray that that is so, but there are many things in this world beyond your experience, Michele, and you may find them difficult to understand."

She gave his hand a slight slap. "Andre, are you saying that I am naive? Because if you are, I shall be properly insulted!"

"No, my pet, you are not really naive, but you have lived a life that might be referred to as 'protected.' Williamsburg is rather a staid village, by European standards, and you have spent most of your life on the plantation, at Malvern, where life is gracious but sheltered. There are certain things that simply have never come to your attention."

"Like 'picket fence pullers'?"

He got a pained look. "Yes, like 'picket fence pullers.' The first thing I must do, I suppose, is to tell you what that means."

"Oh, your *friend*, Albion Villiers, did that well enough. He told me the story about the young king, and his friends, but I still do not clearly understand!"

Andre looked directly into her eyes. "It is a simple thing, *chérie*, although, as I said, outside of your experience. There are certain men, and certain women too, who for some reason are unable to romantically love a person of the opposite sex. Such men and women can only love someone of their own sex."

Michele attempted to take this in. "You mean they really love . . . You mean, they physically . . . ?"

Andre smiled sadly. "Yes, my dear Michele. Physically also. They love one another just as a male and female would."

Michele pondered this for a moment, and her face grew warm with some embarrassment. "But how?" she said at last, in a small voice.

Andre bent a stern glare on her. "Now *that*, I am not prepared to discuss with you. It is bad enough that I must speak of this to you at all."

"And you are one of these people? These men who love other men?"

"Yes, Michele, I am. I am not necessarily pleased to be so, but it is the way I am, the way I was born. As long as I can remember, I have known that I was 'different.' "

"Ever since you were a little boy?"

"Yes. Ever since I was a little boy. Often I used to think that some mistake had been made, that I was really a girl inside a boy's body. This condition has caused me much unhappiness, but I am powerless to change it, no matter how much grief it has brought me."

Michele was experiencing a mixture of feelings that confused her, but sympathy for her old friend was uppermost. "Monsieur Villiers told me of the incident that was the cause of your leaving Paris," she said slowly. "I am sorry, Andre."

Andre shrugged expressively. "Well, things very often work out for the best in this life. If I had not left Paris, I would not have met your mother, or yourself, and you two have meant more to me than any transient love affair I might have had. It is difficult sometimes for a man of my kind to find a lasting relationship with a lover, but you and your mother have given me the best kind of a relationship, a family."

"But in Virginia, weren't you . . . lonely for someone of your own kind?" Michele said, attempting to put the question as delicately as possible.

His smile was melancholy. "Oh, I found solace here and there, although I was very careful never to be obvious about it. Even in the colonies there are such men as myself, although they are more circumspect about it than in this country. Here it is, if not accepted, very often tolerated. It was my misfortune to choose a lover with an intolerant father. In some cultures, such as the Greek culture, it was quite accepted, in fact, encouraged. Many Greek men used women only to bear children, and saved their best and truest love for other men.

"And so, my dear Michele, that is the story, as sordid as

it may sound to you. I can only hope that you do not hate me too much, now that you know."

Michele, who had found the story bizarre but fascinating, shook her head quickly. "I will confess that I do not understand everything you told me. I cannot imagine, for instance, making love to another woman, but it does nothing to change my feelings toward you, dear Andre. You are still my good friend and beloved teacher, and what you do in privacy is none of my affair. As you said, we will talk of it no more, but I do thank you for confiding in me and setting my mind at rest."

The confrontation the next day with Denise proved much less difficult than Michele had anticipated. As Andre had predicted, Denise was back in class the next day; but she looked pale, and did not have her usual energy.

When they broke for the noon meal, Michele approached the other girl. "They tell me you became ill yesterday while eating. I find that rather strange, don't you?"

Denise stared at her with surprise and hostility.

Michele went on, "The same thing happened to Marie last week, you know, only she was forced to stay home several days. I do hope that it doesn't happen again. But then I suppose what happens to one person can easily happen to another. If you take my meaning."

Denise's gray eyes had gone flat and hard, and her lips were a thin line. She did not respond, but Michele was certain that the girl understood the veiled message.

"I think," Michele continued, "that if any more such sudden 'illnesses' occur, or any 'accident,' they will very likely occur to more than one person, so I strongly hope that no further misfortune comes to any member of our company. Do you not agree? Denise, do you not agree?"

Finally Denise answered, in a sullen voice, eyes cast down. "Yes, Michele, I agree."

Michele went to meet Louis and Marie, feeling somewhat better. At least now Denise knew that her schemes were recognized for what they were; and that if she continued her present course, she could expect retaliation in kind. Hopefully, the problem was solved.

It was the night of the premiere of Deampierre's *Beauty and the Beast*. Michele, in the dressing room, felt the now familiar flutter of opening night nerves. Everyone she knew in Paris was in the audience, or here backstage, and they would all be watching as she made her debut as a solo performer.

Would she do well? Would she commit some error?

At the moment it seemed to her that she could not even remember the first steps that would take her out onto the stage. Her mind seemed to be a quivering mass of fears and doubts, and she feared that she might swoon dead away at any moment.

She glanced down at her costume. It was beautiful and graceful, but it would not be what the audience was accustomed to. Of course, in her first appearance on stage tonight, she and Cybella would appear together, and Cybella's costume was just the same, except that it was in a different color; so it would not be as if she was facing the audience alone. Still, Michele felt very daring in the flimsy, soft material, and very exposed without her corsets and hoops. It was true that Salle had appeared in similar garb some years earlier, but the audience had been shocked then, and they would no doubt be shocked now. Still, it was too late to turn back. She was committed.

She could hear the overture now. With trembling hands she finished her toilette, patting her hair into place. And then it was time for her to take her place in the wings, time for her entrance, with Cybella, who smiled at her and touched her hand; and then they were on stage and Michele forgot everything except the music and the movement.

The applause was deafening, and shouts of "Bravo, bravo!" arose. Deampierre's *Beauty and the Beast* was clearly a resounding success.

There had been some gasps from the audience in the

beginning, when Cybella and Michele had appeared in their filmy draperies, but these had come from only a few people. The rest obviously enjoyed the sight, and appreciated the freedom such dresses gave to the dancers.

If Michele had been embarrassed at the notice paid to her in the corps de ballet, she now felt overwhelmed. She had never seen so many flowers. And the notes! Some of the notes begged for assignations, others requested her company at dinner, at the opera; but all declared undying passion for Michele.

She felt both like laughing and crying, and did not know which to do first.

The only flaw in the evening, the only thing she wished for was her mother. If only Hannah was here to see and share in her triumph! Michele wondered what her mother was doing right now, back home on Malvern.

Chapter Eleven

IT was cotton-picking time at Malvern, and to all appearances, it was going to be a bumper crop. All the people on the plantation, with the exception of the house servants, were busy in the fields from daylight until dark plucking the fluffy, white bolls; even the children worked at cotton-picking time. The workers dragged a long sack behind them, held by a strap across the shoulders; and when a sack was full, or became too heavy to be dragged by the children or the women, it was emptied into a high-sided wagon parked at the end of the long rows.

Hannah was also up at dawn and out in the fields until work was finished for the day. Nathaniel Bealls could be seen on his big gray, always around. Hannah had had no further difficulty with Nathaniel.

They spoke nowadays only when necessary, and Nathaniel was excessively polite; but once or twice she had glanced at him unexpectedly, and found a smoldering anger in his eyes. She knew that he resented her for humiliating him that day in her study; and she had watched him closely for some time, fearful that he would do something to damage the cotton crop. But he continued to go about his duties, diligently, and she slowly relaxed her vigilance. But she was still determined to discharge him when the cotton harvest was finished.

There had been no further visits from Jules Dade, nor had she received any word of him. She was looking forward eagerly toward the day when her cotton was sold, and she could pay her debt to him. To hasten that day along, as soon as two thirds of the cotton had been picked and hauled into the cotton sheds, Hannah set about half of the work force to the tedious and slow process of separating the seed from the cotton fluff. She was taking a grave risk in doing this, as Nathaniel Bealls was careful to remind her.

"Mistress Verner, I would advise against this," he said with a stern countenance. "We have been very fortunate with the weather, but that could change at any time. With the cotton bolls fully fluffed out now, a hailstorm, even a hard rain, could strip every shred of cotton from the stalks. I would advise finishing with the picking before we start the seed separation."

"You are the overseer, Nathaniel," she said somewhat haughtily. "But I *do* still own Malvern, and the final orders are mine to give."

"Very well, madam." He lashed his booted leg with the quirt. "If that is your wish, so shall it be. But I wish it clearly understood that it is against my advice."

Standing erect, Hannah nodded coldly. "It is understood, Mr. Bealls."

She was far from feeling as confident as she appeared, for he was correct—the remainder of the crop could be destroyed in a half-hour of bad weather. Perhaps she was being headstrong and unwise; but she simply *had* to get out from under her debt to Dade, and that could not be done until the cotton was sold. In one respect she was fortunate—the price of cotton was the highest it had ever been.

During the two weeks that the picking took, Hannah saw Court only once. She had asked him not to come out, since she would be so busy she felt that she could not spare the time for him.

He remained away the first week, but on his usual day of the second week, she saw his coach rolling down the lane. Although her heart began to beat faster in anticipation, at the same time she was somewhat annoyed. She had been out in the fields since sunrise, and the day had been hot and dusty.

She hurried to her horse tied to a nearby tree, mounted up and rode toward the house at a gallop. She arrived just as the coach came to a stop. She jumped down as Court emerged from his coach. She greeted him formally in front of the coachman and led the way toward the house.

In a low voice she said, "Court, I told you that I wouldn't have time for you until the picking was done."

"My dear Hannah, it's been ten days. I've missed you, damme if I haven't, much as it galls me to say so."

"I've missed you, too, darling, but I shouldn't spare the time."

"Surely you can spare the time for us to be together for a little while." His eyes gleamed hotly, and his smile was insinuating. "The state I'm in, it won't take long, that I can promise you."

Despite her annoyance, Hannah felt the heat of passion begin in her. "We're like two young lovers, do you know that? It's unseemly at our age!"

"Around you, Hannah, I feel young again."

In truth being in Court's arms, being desired by a man again, made her also feel young again, but this *was* an inopportune time. They were inside the house now, and he started to lead the way toward the study.

Hannah held back. "Court, I've been in the fields all day. I need to bathe and change clothes."

He turned to look her up and down with that crooked grin. "You look fine to me. In my younger days I often worked with women in the fields. Many a wench I've tumbled in a haystack. Impromptu, in a manner of speaking. It adds spice to the whole proceedings."

She sniffed. "A gentleman never speaks of the ladies he has lain with."

"As I've mentioned before, my dear, I've never laid claim to being a gentleman. And the wenches I made mention of would hardly qualify as ladies."

"Then I should think you would be ashamed to mention them at all!"

"I've done things in my life which have caused me to feel shame afterward, but never for tumbling a woman, of any stripe." He took her hand. "Now come along, Hannah. I want you just as you are, smelling of the fields, of the sun, and hard work."

As usual, his mere touch had inflamed her passions, and she went along without further demur. In the study he bolted the door and turned to take her into his arms. His kiss was demanding, and sent thrills racing along her nerve-ends.

Somehow, the very furtiveness of the situation, stealing away during the middle of an important working day, made it more erotic; and it appeared to have the same effect on Court. Kissing, caressing, fumbling ineptly with their garments, all the while moving toward the waiting divan, their mutual need reached such a pitch that neither took time to get fully unclothed.

On the divan Court managed to push his breeches down; and shoving up Hannah's skirts, he tore away enough of her undergarments to reach the core of her, and he entered her at once.

On fire, Hannah's hips rose to meet his first thrust. She wrapped her legs around him, clutched at his back with rigid fingers, and they moved into a frenzied rhythm of love. It was quick and intense for both of them, Hannah crying out her ecstasy, Court groaning aloud, and shuddering mightily.

As they lay together, clothes impossibly rumpled, a warm lassitude stole over Hannah, and she no longer had any interest in what was taking place in the fields. Nathaniel was capable enough to see to everything.

Ten days of hard labor, in addition to the just completed seizure of pleasure, made Hannah realize that she was exhausted. She cradled her head on Court's shoulder, and he stroked her hair, murmuring nonsense words of love into her ear. She slipped into a light sleep.

She came partially awake when his hands began to stroke her thighs again, and he was fully aroused before she awoke completely. She murmured, "Again, so soon?"

"It's not all that soon, my love. It's dusk." He nodded his head toward the window. "You slept for a long time. You must have been exhausted, poor darling."

"Oh, good heavens!" she said in agitation. "I should have been up and out in the fields."

She started to sit up, but he put his arms around her, pulling her back down. "Why? It'd be dark before you got there. It would be much more pleasant here." He touched her intimately. "Now, wouldn't it?"

"Ah, Court, my darling Court!"

She subsided, giving herself up wholeheartedly to his adroit ministrations. In a very short while they were both ready for love once more, and locked together in a coupling that was gentler, if no less urgent.

Court prolonged it this time, thrusting slowly, then stopping, holding her still on the divan, until she was almost out of her mind with need for that final explosion of rapture.

And then it happened, happened for both of them. At the very height of his ecstasy, Court said softly, "Hannah, my dear, dear Hannah, I do love you."

It was his first vocal expression of love; but Hannah's body was in such a fever of pleasure that only a small part of her mind made note of his admission.

It was some minutes later, when they both lay with heaving breasts and pounding hearts, that she remembered. She started to say, "Court, did you just say that you . . . ," when there was a sharp rap on the study door.

Hannah sat up, trying to push her skirts down, then she remembered that the door was bolted. "Who is it?"

"It's Nathaniel Bealls, Mistress Verner. I wanted to tell you that we have finished picking for the day."

"Then what do you want with me, sir? I am . . . am indisposed. Too much sun, I think."

There was a pause before he replied, "I just wondered if you had any instructions for me."

"No," she said curtly. "No instructions, Mr. Bealls. I shall see you in the morning."

She listened with bated breath, imagining him swishing

that riding crop repeatedly against his thigh. Then she finally heard his heavy, deliberate footsteps going down the hall, and she breathed a sigh of relief.

She turned to Court. "He didn't believe me, you know. He knows you're in here with me. How could he not know, with your coach and coachman still awaiting you?"

Court shrugged negligently. "What matter if he does know? It is none of his affair. He is your overseer, Hannah, and you are the mistress of Malvern."

"You don't know how he is . . ." She caught her breath, instantly regretting her rash words.

He caught her wrist in a firm grip. "I don't know how he is? What does that mean? Has he done or said anything to you? If he has, I shall see that he regrets it!"

"It's just that he . . ." She hesitated, wondering if she should tell him, but she had gone too far to stop now. "It's just that he saw us that first time we kissed, down by the creek . . ."

Court reared up. "Why, the sneaking poltroon! Wait until I . . ."

"No, no." She placed a finger over his lips. "I'm sure it was inadvertent, that he just happened to stumble upon us, but he did somehow get the idea that he could approach me. But don't worry, I put him in his place at once."

"He still needs a sound thrashing, Hannah, and I intend to see to it."

She sighed. "No, Court, I don't want that. Not now. That's why I haven't mentioned it, fearful that you would react just this way. If you do or say anything, he may leave Malvern, you see. And I can't have that now, not until the cotton is all in. Then I shall discharge him. I had already made up my mind to that course of action. But whatever Nathaniel's faults, he *is* a good overseer, and I need him. Now, promise me you won't do anything rash."

His face had flushed, but his temper gradually receded. "All right, Hannah, if you insist. But it may be foolish of you in the end. A man like that, he cannot be trusted."

"I can handle him," she said, with far more confidence than she felt.

* * *

If Hannah had been privy to Nathaniel's thoughts at that moment, she would have been much upset.

Nathaniel was raging. Damn the wench! Did she think she was fooling him one bit? He knew very well that the dandified Wayne was tumbling her in the study.

This was the last humiliation he would suffer at her hands. He had been debating Dade's proposition since the proposal had been made, but he had not reached a final decision. Now he had.

He skipped supper, went to his quarters directly from the manor house, and changed into fresh clothing. It was almost dark when he slipped out to the stables, saddled his horse, and rode hard for Williamsburg. The ride into the village and back to the plantation would take some time, and cause him to lose some sleep; but he could still do his job tomorrow without trouble. If perchance, Mistress Verner noted his absence, he would simply tell her that he had felt the need of a wench's services, and had ridden into Williamsburg for that purpose. She should be able to understand *that*.

He did not know Dade's place of residence, but inquiries in a tavern made it known to him. He was surprised to see the house where Dade abided. It was a small, mean house on the edge of town, with a weed-grown yard, and was made of scabrous brick. It was close to midnight when he arrived, and the house showed no light.

He did not hesitate, but dismounted and strode up to the front door, giving it a thunderous knock. When there was no immediate response, he knocked again, and kept knocking until he saw the flickering of candlelight through the grimy front window, and heard an irritated shout: "I'm coming, I'm coming, damn you!"

Nathaniel waited impatiently, tapping his leg with the quirt. After a time the door opened a crack, and Dade's face peered out from behind a candle flame. In a grumbling voice, he said, "Who is it at this time of the night, disturbing a Christian man's slumber?"

"It's Nathaniel Bealls, Master Dade."

"Mr. Bealls!" Dade stepped back, opening the door wide. He was wearing a long nightshirt, not quite clean, and a tasseled cap, the tassels falling over his eyes.

As Nathaniel stepped inside, Dade said, "What can be of such urgency that you could not await some decent hour, sir?"

"This is cotton-picking time on Malvern, if you will recall, and I am busy from dawn until dark. As it is I will be losing half a night's sleep, while you will only lose an hour or so, as we talk. However, if you cannot be bothered, I can easily turn right around and ride back to Malvern."

"No, no, you're here. It would not be Christian of me to turn away a man after such a long ride."

Nathaniel had seen the glint in Dade's eye, and was not fooled. The moneylender was aquiver to learn his business here.

Dade led the way through a cluttered parlor and to a cramped room in the back of the small house, a room with a dusty desk and ledgers piled high around the walls. Dade went behind the desk, placed the candle and holder before him, and sat down. There was no other chair in the room, so Nathaniel had to stand. He stood with his feet set apart, hands folded across his chest.

"Now, sir," Dade said, "let us attend to your urgent business."

"You know what my business with you is, Dade." Nathaniel spoke now with conscious insolence, out of dislike for this mean little man. Dade needed *him*, not the other way around. "It is about the proposition you made me."

"Ah, yes. You have considered it, have you?"

"I have considered it, and have decided to accept."

"I made mention of it some weeks ago. Perhaps I have changed my mind, after so much time has passed."

"I think not, Dade. You wanted to see to it that Hannah Verner did not profit from her cotton crop, and that crop is not yet ready for marketing."

"But the time grows short, Mr. Bealls." Dade pushed a tassel away from one eye and peered slyly at Nathaniel. "Methinks action should have been taken ere this."

"Not for what I have in mind," Nathaniel said stolidly. "What if you not only thwarted her, but turned a tidy profit as well?"

Greed blazed in Dade's eyes, but he spoke warily. "That would be nice, sir. Ah, yes. But exactly how do you plan to accomplish that?"

"First, we must discuss terms. We must reach an agreement as to my share of the venture."

"I promised that you would earn more than the Verner woman will pay you in wages."

"That is not enough. As I said, what I have in mind will not only place her fate in your hands, but turn a pretty penny. And of that, I want a half."

"A half!" Dade reared back. "Do not be greedy, sir!"

Nathaniel said calmly, "You are a fine one to speak of greed, Master Dade."

Dade looked at him craftily. "Before we can strike an agreement, I must be told your plan. Ah, yes. You cannot expect me to buy a pig in a poke."

"If I tell you first, then you would likely have no more need of me."

"You don't trust me, Mr. Bealls?" Dade assumed a hurt expression. "We are partners in this endeavor, are we not? A true partnership cannot flourish without trust."

"We are partners in crime, if partners at all, and I would not trust you out of my sight, Dade. No, first we must sign an agreement."

Dade sighed, looked put upon, and fussed with papers on his desk. "This plan of which you speak, it will bring about the Verner woman's ruin?"

"It will, my word upon it."

Dade sighed again, then reached into his desk for a blank sheet of paper, drew quill and inkwell toward him, and began to scribble on the sheet of paper. After Nathaniel had read the agreement—with much difficulty, since he had had little schooling—he demanded some changes. After a half-hour of haggling back and forth, they reached an agreement, and both men put their signatures to the contract, in which it was agreed that Nathaniel would receive half of any proceeds from his scheme.

Straightening up, he said, "It has been a long ride, and I have still a long night before me. Can we not toast our agreement with a glass of port, or perhaps something stronger?"

Dade said virtuously, "I have no drink in the house, Mr. Bealls. Strong drink is a device of Satan to muddle men's wits."

Nathaniel felt some amusement; Dade was too stingy to keep liquor in his house for guests; it had nothing to do with Satan. His dislike for the man increased, but that would not deter him from doing business with Dade.

Dade said eagerly, "Now, Mr. Bealls, your plan!"

Nathaniel quickly outlined what he had in mind. Long before he was finished, Dade was nodding his head in agreement. At the end he rubbed his hands together in great glee. "Ah, yes! It should work splendidly! Not only shall we turn a tidy profit, but it will bring the haughty Mistress Verner to her knees, and Malvern will be mine, all mine!"

When the cotton was picked, Hannah set everyone to work separating the seed from the fluff. Leaving Nathaniel in charge, she made a journey into Williamsburg, and met with several cotton buyers. They were all much interested, and promised a good price for her product. Cotton growing was still a minor industry in the South, and the demand from the mills in England, and the few mills in the northern states, was growing. Hannah blessed Michael's foresight in turning part of Malvern's acreage into cotton.

And then she had an idea. Why not follow the lead of the tobacco growers and have an auction, with several buyers present to bid against each other for her crop? It worked well with tobacco, so why not with cotton? She decided that when she returned home, she would immediately pen letters to all the buyers, inviting them to the auction two weeks hence. The cotton would be ready for sale by then.

It was late afternoon by the time she had seen all the buyers. She did not want to return to Malvern right away; such was her euphoria that she wanted to share it with someone.

As John helped her into the coach, she said, "John, I'm not going home right now. Drive by Mr. Wayne's residence."

John's face remained inscrutable. He merely inclined his head, and said, "Very well, mistress."

Court would not be expecting her, but then he had made her a surprise visit, had he not? A disturbing thought intruded into her mind. What if he had another woman with him? She tossed her head, refusing to entertain such a possibility.

Court answered the door himself. "Why, Hannah! This is a pleasant surprise." He frowned. "I do hope there is nothing amiss?"

"No, no, everything is grand, just grand." He had stepped back to let her in, and Hannah craned her neck to look behind him, and down the hall to where she had seen the nude woman on the bed on her last visit.

"There is no woman here, Hannah," he said amusedly.

Hannah flushed. "I was only wondering why you answered the door yourself. Where are the servants?"

He shrugged slightly. "They have gone to market." His eyes glinted at her. "But there *could* have been someone else here, my dear. People who pay surprise visits sometimes receive unpleasant surprises."

She refused to be baited. "I have such good tidings I had to share it with someone." She clutched at his arm in her excitement.

His amusement increased. "What tidings might that be, Hannah?"

He ushered her into the parlor as he voiced the question, and she waited until they were seated side by side on the divan before turning to him. Quickly, she told him of her plan for the cotton buyers to bid against each other for her crop.

"I must say, my dear, that you do show a head for

business at times." He shook his head in admiration. "Even if you do have a lapse now and then, like going to Jules Dade for a loan."

"I admit that was a mistake, but this will help rectify it. With a good price for my crop, I will be able to repay him. And the crop is harvested, so nothing can happen to it now. It's only a matter of waiting until the seed separation is finished. Oh, Court, I feel such great relief!"

She threw her arms around his neck, and kissed him soundly. He returned the kiss with vigor, and as always their passions ignited. Soon, he was leading her down the hall to the back room. On the threshold she held back, looking dubiously at the divan against the wall. "The last time I had a glimpse into this room, there was a naked woman. You had just left her embrace."

He propelled her into the room and firmly closed the door. "That is all in the past, my dearest. It was before I knew you, if you recall."

She said tartly, "Well, just so long as it *is* in the past."

Without speaking he led her to the divan and began to divest her of her clothing. She stood without resistance. When he got down to the last remaining garments, his fingers touched lingeringly on exposed flesh, followed by his lips. Hannah shivered in exquisite delight. When her breasts were fully exposed, he kissed the rigid nipples, and took one between his teeth, worrying it gently.

"Court, Court!" she said softly. Entwining her fingers into his hair, she pressed his face closer to her breast.

Then finally, they were both nude and locked together on the divan.

"Do you love me, Court?" she whispered fiercely. "Tell me!"

"Yes, yes, dear Hannah, I love you! I love you with all my heart."

"And I love you, my darling. Oh, yes!"

In a moment they were united in passion. Court moved slowly, but with ever-growing urgency, and Hannah uttered small cries at the glorious friction.

* * *

The night before the auction Hannah went to bed totally exhausted. She had been moving at a fast pace since before the sun rose. But everything was ready. The separation of the seed from the fluff had been completed on schedule, and bins of fluffy cotton were lined up in the long shed, ready for the buyers' inspection, like piles of virgin, newly fallen snow.

Although she did not expect any trouble during the night, Hannah thought it best not to take any chances, and had left three of the hands on guard all night, with instructions to let nothing near the cotton shed, man or beast.

Hannah sank into a bone-weary, dreamless sleep at once; she slept so deeply that her wits were slow and befuddled when a loud knocking on her bedroom door awakened her. She raised her head groggily. What was amiss? Pale daylight spilled in through the window. The auction was not due to begin until that afternoon, so why was she being awakened?

She called out, "Who is it? What's wrong?"

"Mistress, it's John! You should come at once."

"What is it, John? What's wrong?"

"The cotton, it's gone!"

"Gone?" She sat up in bed. "But that can't be!"

"It's true, I swear! Please come!"

Fully alert now, she scrambled out of bed, and quickly threw on her clothes. Opening the door, she saw John's usually impassive face looking miserable and deeply troubled.

She cried, "What happened to my cotton?"

"I am not sure. Please come out to the shed, mistress."

She flew down the broad stairs, almost tripping in her haste, with John right behind her. It was just short of sunrise when she reached the outside. She sped toward the shed, skidding to a stop just inside. The bins were empty. She ran from one to the other, but they were all empty. The cotton was gone!

She stood in stunned silence, gazing about in disbelief. It was as if some evil magician had visited the shed during the night, spiriting her cotton away. It was then that she noticed the bodies of the three men she had left on guard, sprawled on the ground at different locations. Her glance went to John.

"No, they are not dead," he said somberly. "They sleep the sleep of the dead, but they are not dead. I would surmise that they were given a strong sleeping potion."

Suddenly, she knew. She gestured to John. "Come."

She hurried across the yard to Nathaniel's quarters. The door stood wide, confirming her guess. She looked inside the small room, and saw only the empty bed. His clothing, which usually hung on pegs along one wall, was gone.

She turned slowly to John, and said in a stricken voice, "It's Nathaniel. Court warned me, I should have listened. In some manner a mystery to me, he managed to steal all the cotton during the night. He must have been planning this for weeks, just waiting for this night. Oh, John, I am ruined! Without my cotton, I have no means to pay my debt to Jules Dade!"

Chapter Twelve

AUTUMN had descended upon Paris, bringing with it chill winds, and cloudy days.

As the coach made its way across the countryside, Michele could see that the trees were touched with red and gold, and that the fields were turning brown.

Against the chill of the day, she wore a rose-colored, velvet gown, with a matching cape and hood. In her gloved hand she held a black, velvet mask which she had removed so that she might better see the countryside, which reminded her very much of Virginia.

From the seat opposite her, Andre smiled at her. "What are you thinking, *chérie*?"

"Of Malvern. Of home. The countryside here is not all that much different."

He leaned forward to peer out the window. "The leaves are changing, I see. You don't notice it so much in the city. Well, it is almost winter, after all."

He sighed. "So much has happened since we arrived in Paris, Michele. It hardly seems possible, in such a short time. *Mon Dieu!* When we arrived you were an unknown, now your name is on the lips of everyone in Paris. And today, today we are on our way to Fontainebleau, so that you may dance before the king! Oh, if only your mother could be here! That would make everything absolutely perfect!"

Michele returned his smile. "It would, wouldn't it? Oh,

Andre, I am so nervous! We are to be presented to the king!"

Andre's smile widened. "I know, my pet, I know. I am in awe as well. But isn't it marvelous? And to think that twenty years ago, I left Paris under a cloud! It is amazing!"

Michele said bemusedly, "And to think, we will be staying at Fontainebleau for three whole days. I do wish the whole troupe was staying."

Andre shrugged negligently. "There are a great number of them, and even in a palace such as Fontainebleau there is a limit to the number of guests that may be accommodated. There are always many guests there. You should be grateful that the principals of the company were invited to stay. It is a great honor, *chérie*, and a wonderful opportunity for you to see what life is like among the royalty. What tales you will be able to relate when you return home! This fact alone, that you have been a guest of King Louis at his chateau, is enough to bring you fame."

She made a moue. "I would far rather be renown for my dancing!"

Andre laughed. "You will be, I am confident. Not everyone cares about dancing, Michele, but *everyone* wants to learn about how a king lives, behaves, and *mis*behaves. Now, shall we go over it again, *chérie*? What will you say when you are presented to the king?"

Michele went through her rehearsed responses, but her mind was not on the words she spoke. She was thinking of the afternoon, only a week ago, when Arnaut Deampierre had announced to the troupe that the king had requested that they perform the new ballet for him in his country residence at Fontainebleau, where he had gone for the hunting.

Deampierre did not have to tell the dancers that it was a great honor, and the rehearsal room was filled with the buzz and hum of their excited voices.

Furthermore, Deampierre had told them, the king had requested that the principal dancers be his guests for the weekend following the performance.

Louis had been unable to contain himself, and had gone leaping about the room like a creature gone mad. Roland had contented himself with a grunt of approval, and Cybella, usually so staid, had leapt into the air and executed several quick *entrechats*. Michele could only stand there, stunned. She was still reeling from all the attention heaped upon her since the opening night of the ballet. Now she, along with the other principals, was going to dance for the king of France! It was simply too much to take in all at once.

And now, here she was, in Madame Dubois' coach, approaching the famous chateau with Andre at her side, as her "guardian." She was afire with excitement; and she was pleased that Andre had been allowed to accompany her, for it meant even more to him, she knew, than it did to her.

"There it is!" Andre said in a voice of awe. "Straight ahead! No, Michele! Don't stick your head out and stare like that. You won't want to appear a country bumpkin!"

Michele paid him no heed. With her head partially out of the coach window, she was staring ahead at the chateau, which looked to her not like one building but a small town—a row of buildings connected together, each with its own chimney pots, bays, and garrets. In the center of this long line of buildings was a magnificent, horseshoe-shaped staircase that sloped gradually upward to frame the entrance in graceful curves; and leading up to the staircase was a long, wide, cobbled drive, along which they were now traveling. On either side of the courtyard were formal plots of grass, ornamented with neatly trimmed and shaped shrubberies.

"It's very elegant," Michele said breathlessly, pulling her head back inside, and settling back into her seat, regaining as much dignity as she could under the circumstances.

"Wait until you see the inside," Andre said. "I have heard that it is a veritable treasure house! Filled with great paintings, sculpture, priceless rugs and hangings.

This is the opportunity of a lifetime, *chérie*, for both of us."

Michele reached over and touched his hand. "I am so glad that you have this chance to share it with me, Andre. I would have been terrified going by myself, even though the others will be here, also. I feel much more secure having you with me."

Andre beamed paternally, and seemed to swell with pride. "I shall look after you, never fear. Even so," he said more sedately, "you had best be on your guard, my dear. King Louis is noted for having an eye for a pretty wench, and you had best keep this fact in mind at all times. He is, after all, the king, and accustomed to having whatever he desires. He does not take kindly to being denied."

Michele shivered suddenly, feeling cold. Life is so strange, she thought; even in the midst of pleasure and triumph, there could be something dangerous lurking for the unwary, something that you must watch out for and defend yourself against. Perhaps it was simply the way of the world; but if that was so, it made life very complicated indeed, and thinking about it depressed her.

Now the coach was stopping, and she could hear the horses stamping and snorting as they came to a halt upon the hard cobblestones directly in front of the staircase.

Michele allowed herself to be helped down from the vehicle by the footman, all the while attempting to appear as if she were accustomed to visiting the houses of royalty every day; but her heart was beating unnaturally fast, and she could feel that her cheeks were flushed.

Andre, with a lordly air that made her giggle, took her arm; and together they ascended the great stone steps up to the entrance doors through which they would enter into a world that few young ladies from the colonies had ever been privileged to see.

When the maid had finally left her alone, after unpacking and hanging up her clothing, Michele stood in the center of her room, simply staring in awe. She had thought

Madame's house in Paris elegant and ornate, but it was nothing to compare with this. The room was decorated in soft greens and gold. All four walls and the ceiling were ornamented with stucco molded in the form of cupids, flowers, and leaves, surrounding magnificent frescoes of sylvan scenes.

The bed, which rested against one wall, was not large, but had a high headboard and footboard, and a magnificent canopy, which originated from a frame upon the ceiling, falling in graceful folds and swags, adorned with silk tassels.

The rest of the furnishings were equally elegant. Michele smoothed her hand over the rose satin that covered one of the gilded chairs, and marveled at the silken feel of the expensive fabric. She had never witnessed such a display of wealth. It almost overwhelmed the senses. As she gazed about her, Michele felt a prickle of unease. Madame Dubois had chosen her wardrobe for the occasion, but would her clothes be grand enough for this setting? Would she look out of place among the noble and royal guests? It was with a mixture of anticipation and fear that she stretched out upon the bed to rest before the evening's performance. Surely, this was going to be one of the most exciting nights of her life!

Lying upon the bed, Michele tried to relax, but found that she was much too excited and nervous to lie still. She was still trying to make herself comfortable, when there was a knock upon her door. Grateful for any distraction, she jumped up from the bed, and in her stocking feet and dressing gown, went to answer the knock.

She opened the door to find Louis, Café au Lait, and Marie standing upon the threshold. It was obvious they were all in a high state of excitement—their faces were flushed and their eyes were bright.

Louis stepped forward and gave Michele a great hug, so fierce that she feared he would crush her ribs. "Michele!" he exclaimed, "Isn't all this wonderful? Who would have ever believed it, that we would be here, at Fontainebleau?"

Michele, laughing, pulled out of his grip. As Louis had

held her close, so that she felt the warmth and strength of him, she had suddenly become acutely aware of him as a man, a male, and this awareness had embarrassed her; but now they were all crowding into the room, exuberant and excited, and she had no time to analyze her feelings.

"Oh, Michele! We have been looking at the different rooms, and they are all so grand!" Marie said, her eyes shining. "Have you looked around the chateau yet?"

Michele shook her head. "We only got here a short time ago, and Andre suggested that I should rest before the performance."

Café au Lait, his honey-colored face alight, grinned at her, showing perfect, white teeth. "But you can rest when you are dead, Michele. This is an important event, being at Fontainebleau, and I, for one, mean to make the most of it. Besides, all of us except the principals will have to leave after the supper tonight. I mean to see all that I can before that time arrives."

Marie settled herself upon one of the gilt chairs. "Oh, Michele, you should see the ballroom, where we are to perform. It is magnificent! There are great pillars along the walls, huge ones, and the most beautiful frescoes of the mythological gods. The floor is inlaid in the most exquisite designs, just like the designs of the ceiling above. It is so smooth we shall glide over it like the gods themselves."

"It is truly amazing," said Louis, taking Michele's hand unself-consciously. "Above the musicians' platform is a marvelous painting depicting a concert, and at the other end, over the fireplace, is a painting of a nobleman killing a wolf."

Michele, a bit embarrassed by Louis taking her hand, gently pulled her hand from his grip. "It sounds very grand. I am still trying to recover from the effect of *this* room." She motioned around her, and the others followed her gesture with their eyes.

"It is lovely!" Marie said, her eyes wide. "And to think that you have it all to yourself. The corps de ballet has been given one room for all of us, as a dressing room, and it is not so grand as this. Even Cybella's room is no grander!"

"There will be a supper following the performance," Louis said. "I have been told that it is customary."

"And the king himself will be there," Marie said, clapping her hands together. "Just think! We will all get to dine with the king! Oh, I am so excited that I do not know if I will be able to dance at all!"

Michele, nervous enough on her own, now caught their excitement as well. "And the queen, will she be there also?"

Louis laughed. "The queen? No, I should think not, although probably the king's mistress will be in attendance."

Michele looked at him in confusion. "The king's mistress? Do you mean he permits himself to be seen with his mistress in public?"

The others began to laugh.

"Oh, Michele," Marie said, smiling widely. "Sometimes you seem as if you come from another world.

"Of course, the king is seen in public with his mistress, and often. It is quite the accepted thing to do. You see, it is the custom for the king to marry a foreigner, for reasons of state, and her purpose is to bear an heir for the throne. It is a practical matter, you see. It is said that our King Louis married his queen, Marie Leczinska, a Pole, when he was but fifteen, and she seven years older. She has fulfilled her duty well, bearing him ten offspring. She is a dull woman, I am told, and plain. So you see why he would naturally seek his love and pleasure elsewhere."

Michele shook her head in disapproval. "It is very different in my country. There, we marry for love!"

Louis glanced at her with a mischievous twinkle. "Ah, Michele, you are a romantic. Are you so certain that your countrymen *never* marry for such practical reasons?"

Michele felt some confusion, for her common sense told her that this indeed must sometimes happen. "I suppose such marriages do occur, now and then," she said slowly. "But if they do, no one admits it, or talks about it."

The others burst into laughter, and she was forced to

join them, for it was obvious that such an attitude was hypocritical in the extreme, certainly in the eyes of the French people.

When their laughter subsided, Michele asked, "And the king's mistress? What is her name? Is she very beautiful?"

Café au Lait began to snicker, and Louis and Marie smiled.

"Her name is Madame de Mailly," Louis said. "As to whether or not she is pretty, well, you may judge for yourself tonight when you see her."

Michele glanced at each in turn, uneasily; it was clear that they were enjoying some jest at her expense, but even when she cajoled them, they would tell her no more.

A knock sounded on the door, interrupting their conversation. Michele opened the door to a stern Andre, who ordered them all to go to their rooms where a light repast was awaiting them. "You will then get into your costumes, and meet Monsieur Deampierre in the grand ballroom, where he is presently discussing the music with the musicians."

Andre put down the tray he was carrying, which held fruit, cheese, and wine. "This is for you, Michele. Now, the rest of you, out!" He gestured widely. "Out!"

The three young people left, calling their goodbyes to Michele, and then she and Andre were alone.

He smiled and indicated the plate of fruit and cheese. "You had best have something to eat, *chérie*. It will be a long while before supper, and you will need a little something to give you energy for the performance."

She returned his smile. "I will try, but I'm so nervous, Andre . . ."

"*Naturellement!*" He put his hand upon her shoulder. "But you mustn't get overexcited, my pet. Try to think of this as just another performance. If you keep thinking about the fact that you are performing before the King of France, and his court, you will make a wreck of yourself.

It will all go splendidly, you will see. You have danced the ballet several times now, and you know your part perfectly. Trust your old friend."

Michele tried her best to follow Andre's advice, and by the time she was costumed and had joined the others in the ballroom, she was feeling somewhat calmer and more sure of herself.

Marie had been right about the ballroom. It was truly a marvelous thing to see. A simple set had been arranged in the area they would use for performing, in front of and below the musicians' platform; and in front of the performing area, rows of chairs had been arranged for the audience, with a grand, heavily ornamented chair in the center of the front row, which Michele assumed was for the king.

The dancers would remain out of sight, hidden by the huge, pillarlike consoles which supported the ceiling. The consoles had benches along the sides, upon which the dancers could rest when not on stage, and which made an excellent substitute for the wings of a theater.

Deampierre had them walk through the opening scenes, so that they might get the feel of the space, as the king's musicians ran over the music, which they were not familiar with.

It was, Michele thought, a strange mixture of the familiar and unfamiliar. She waved to Louis, who was warming up on the other side of the room, for his entrance would be made from that side, and then looked around for Cybella and Roland.

She saw them nearby, doing stretching exercises. Cybella looked quite calm, in full control as usual. Nothing, it seemed, Michele thought enviously could ever disturb her aplomb. Denise was standing near Roland, her triangular little face looking tight and set.

Roland appeared nervous and a bit pale, but at least he was not scowling, as was his custom, and that was a definite improvement. Perhaps he will be too worried about his performance to be nasty and unfriendly as is his wont, Michele thought. Besides her solo, Michele had a *pas de deux* with the character of the father, performed after Beauty has gone to the castle of the Beast; and although she had to admit that Roland danced well, Michele was always conscious of his disdain, even as they danced together. It was not easy for her to pretend the solicitude that she must show toward the character of her aged father in the face of Roland's attitude; but she had been doing her best to put her own feelings toward Roland aside while they danced. She was all too conscious of being at his mercy, to a certain extent, during the lifts. If he dropped her . . .

Well, she was just glad she had had that conversation with Denise, for Denise would certainly have told Roland about it. But at any rate, now was not the time for such thoughts. She should be warming up, for the time for their performance was rapidly approaching.

She began to bend and stretch, limbering up her limbs and body, feeling a part of the group, the movement, at the same time feeling separate and alone; and then the musicians struck up—a stately piece with which she was not familiar—and she turned, with the rest of the troupe, to peer around the huge consoles to see the royal party entering through a door at the other end of the room.

First came a group of guards in ruffs and plumed hats, looking very forbidding and military, and then a number of gentlemen all in blue jerkins and red, silver-trimmed breeches. Marie, who had crept up behind Michele in order to see over her shoulder, whispered in her ear, "Those are the king's guards, and his personal guard of nobles. Aren't they grand?"

Michele nodded, wondering what they were protecting the king from, here in his own residence.

After the personal guard came a gaggle of elegant men and women, all dressed in the height of fashion. Never had Michele seen so much color, so much powder, such magnificent jewels, even at the *soirées* held by Madame Dubois.

"They look like peacocks!" she whispered to Marie, who

giggled. "And look at their faces. They are painted like clowns. Even the men, for heaven's sake!"

"Shh-h," said Marie. "Here comes the king!"

As the nobles framed the doorway on both sides, two trumpeters in gold and blue livery appeared to take up their positions. The orchestra finished the last notes of their piece, and the trumpeters sounded a fanfare. As they did so, a man came striding through the doorway, and Michele strained forward to catch a glimpse of his face.

He was, it seemed to Michele, a rather smallish man; but that might have been because of the wide skirts of his brocade coat, which were so full that they looked like the skirts of a short dress. His face, under the powder and paint, seemed to be even-featured and rather pretty, set off by large, dark eyes, a rather plump face with a small, sulky-looking mouth like a rosebud.

He looks just like any other man, Michele thought; and to think he rules a whole country, and people bow and scrape to him!

The orchestra had started up again, this time playing the introduction to the ballet, and Deampierre was motioning to the dancers to take their places.

Michele could feel the flutter of nervousness in her stomach, rising in her throat, and resolutely choked it down, thinking of Andre's reassuring words; and then, abruptly, the introduction was over, and the entrance music began for her number with Cybella, and Michele forced her legs to move, as Cybella smiled at her and took her arm for their entrance.

As they moved out from the shelter of the console, Michele wished that she might flee back to its concealment. Extremely conscious of the royal audience, she worried about the smoothness of the floor. Would she slip? Would she fall, shaming herself and the rest of the troupe?

She felt Cybella squeeze her arm, and became acutely aware of the music, which moved smoothly into the graceful passages of the sisters' dance, and suddenly she was all right. The floor was wonderful, and she felt herself glide more gracefully and easily than she ever had before. Blocking everything from her mind but the movement and the music, she entered into that marvelous state that existed for her only when she was performing well.

It seemed only moments before her dance with Cybella was ended, and Roland was coming on stage, the father returning from his journey, being greeted by his daughters.

And then it was time for Michele to make her exit. Deampierre was waiting behind the console; he handed her a handkerchief, so that she might wipe her brow. He smiled at her, and touched her shoulder, and Michele knew that she had danced well—it was one of his rare compliments. She felt fine now. There was no more fear or nervousness.

She watched as Cybella and Roland completed the scene, where the father tells Beauty that he has promised her to the Beast, and Beauty dances out her fear and sorrow. Michele thought that Cybella was perfect for the part, even as a part of Michele wished enviously that she might have a chance at the other girl's role.

It was not until Cybella's solo was over that Michele finally spared a glance toward the royal audience, trying to guess which of the overpainted, overdressed women was Madame de Mailly, the king's mistress; but she could not see very well from where she stood, although she did notice a tall young man, who stood out from the rest of the audience because of his dress; instead of the flared coat and knee breeches worn by the other men, he was attired in a bright tartan kilt and cape, and wore a cap upon his unpowdered hair.

Although his clothing was different from the satins and brocades worn by the other males, Michele did note that his shirt was ruffled at the waist and neck, and that he was wearing heavy gold buckles on his shoes, and at his waist. He was evidently someone of importance; oddly, he looked somehow familiar to her; but she was forced to give off studying him at that point for it was now time for the *pas de deux* with Beauty and the Beast, and Michele wished to watch and learn it, for it was not an impossibility that

Cybella would some day be unable to perform, and in the back of Michele's mind was the thought that she might, just might, be chosen to stand in for Cybella.

As she watched, Michele was moved as always by this particular dance; it was a masterpiece of choreography, showing both Beauty's growing fondness of the Beast, and the Beast's bittersweet adoration of Beauty.

And then the corps de ballet came on, depicting the magical servants and attendants of the Beast; and Michele's gaze went first to Marie, then Denise, whose expression spoke of her anger at being forced to dance with the corps instead of dancing a featured role.

And then it was time for Michele's solo, and she was onstage, alone, in front of the royal audience. She did not look at them, concentrating strictly upon the dance, and what it was supposed to say, thinking only of the music and the steps and the feeling that she was supposed to portray.

She left the stage to tremendous applause, no less in fact than that accorded Cybella and Louis. Louis, who was waiting for her, gave her a big hug; Marie and several other girls from the corps de ballet hurried over to offer congratulations.

It was a thrilling moment, and one, Michele felt, that she would always remember and cherish.

When the ballet was completed, the dancers came forward for their curtain calls, to loud acclaim.

Michele had imagined that such a sophisticated crowd, which surely must have seen everything, would be somewhat cool in its reception, but the truth was entirely the opposite. The royal audience, including the king, gave them a standing ovation. They could not seem to applaud loudly enough, and their expressions, which had been cool and disdainful in the beginning, were enlivened by smiles and laughter. They were, in fact, the most appreciative audience Michele had ever seen.

When it was Michele's turn to take her solo bow, she found herself directly in front of the king, and she could not help noticing, as she made her deep curtsy, that his gaze roamed over her thinly clad form in a decidedly lustful manner.

As she raised her head, at the end of her curtsy, he nodded at her and smiled knowingly, causing her to blush deeply, and almost causing her to lose her balance, for she was remembering what she had heard about him.

As Michele turned her head slightly, her gaze met that of the young man in kilts, who was smiling at her warmly; and with a shock she recognized him at last, despite the different clothing. It was Ian MacLeven, the young man she had met on the ship!

Whatever could he be doing here, at Fontainebleau?

Chapter Thirteen

"BUT monsieur, we must change out of our costumes first!" Cybella's expression was one of puzzlement, and she glanced at Michele as if for corroboration.

Deampierre shrugged expressively. "That is what I told His Majesty, but he insists that you come to supper dressed as you are. He said that it would be amusing."

Louis, wiping his forehead with a piece of cloth, gave a bark of laughter. "It will be amusing, perhaps, but not for me. For me it will be very awkward, and I shall no doubt shed pieces of my mane into all the dishes served!" He shook his head, and wisps of hair and yarn flew from his mock mane, for the costume, although marvelous to see, had a tendency to shed.

"It's the girls' costumes," Roland said with a sneer. "Cybella's and Michele's. Our dear King Louis just wants them at the table half-dressed, so that he may ogle them at will." He scowled at Michele and Cybella, as if the costumes were their idea, and it was their fault that the rest of them would have to go to the table without changing. Denise nodded quick agreement, although Michele felt quite sure that the other girl would go to the king's table quite naked, if that would secure for her the recognition she felt she deserved.

Cybella sighed heavily. "Well, I suppose there is no help for it."

Deampierre laughed. "No, my dear Cybella, there is not. It is the king's command. It is only a whim, no doubt, but the whims of kings are as powerful as the laws of ordinary men. So, put on your wraps, so that you do not chill, and we will be on our way to the king's table!"

The king's table was awe-inspiring, Michele thought, as she peered past Louis' shoulder at what seemed like an acre of white, linen cloth, covered with gold plate, crystal ware, and flamboyantly decorated china.

She, Cybella, Louis, Roland, Andre, and Deampierre were directed to places near the head of the huge table, above the salt, as it were, but separated from one another by several other guests. The rest of the dance troupe was seated at a smaller table.

Michele took her place, feeling very exposed and uncomfortable in her skimpy costume. She had grown accustomed to it on the stage, never giving a second thought to it, but this was a different matter entirely. She pulled her shawl closely around her shoulders, attempting to cover as much of herself as possible.

Surreptitiously, she studied the ladies and gentlemen now taking their places at the table. Seen up close, the effect of the paint and powder was overwhelming, to the point of being repulsive; and she could see that some of the more elaborate arrangements were already beginning to crack and run. It was an ugly custom, she thought to herself; and also uncomfortable.

A plump, dandified gentleman was now taking the chair next to hers, smiling at her jovially. "I must say, my dear," he said in a melodious voice, "you all danced spectacularly! I haven't enjoyed myself so much in ages and ages!"

"Thank you, monsieur," she said, dipping her head demurely. "You were a most appreciative audience."

The man laughed as he fussily settled the skirts of his coat around his chair. "That is because we are starved for *divertissement*," he said, still smiling; in fact, it appeared as if that was his permanent expression. "Life can get very boring here at times. We search continually for something new in the way of amusement. It is hard, my dear, hard indeed!"

Michele was nonplussed. Boring? Life was boring here, at Fontainebleau? How could that possibly be?

"It is rather like being on a great ship," a voice said from her other side. "You see only the same people, day after day, and any routine, even a pleasant one, can become boring."

Even though it had been some time, she recognized the voice; and she turned to see the amused gray eyes of Ian MacLeven focused upon her.

She felt herself flush. "Mr. MacLeven," she said rather more curtly than she had intended, since she was actually somewhat glad to see him, although she could not imagine what he was doing here. "I must say I was astonished to see you here, of all places!"

"Miss Verner," he said, inclining his head. "Yes, what a remarkable coincidence it is, that we should both be here at the same time. The ballet, by the way, was marvelous, and your dancing was superb!"

Michele nodded her head, accepting the compliment gracefully. "Thank you, sir."

"You have evidently established yourself well, here in France. Everyone speaks of you, of the lovely dancer from the English colonies. You have become well known in a surprisingly short time. That must be taken as a tribute to your talent, and your beauty as well, of course."

Michele was beginning to feel ill at ease under the barrage of his compliments. "I was fortunate to be accepted by an excellent teacher and ballet master, and I am fortunate to be a part of a fine ensemble. And you? May I ask how you . . . ?" Her voice died away; she could find no graceful way of asking how he came to be here without sounding insulting.

He started to laugh. "You are politely trying to think of a way to ask what I am doing here. How a young Scotsman of no particular renown happens to be at the court of the king of France. No, you needn't blush, it is a perfectly natural question."

Michele could feel her face growing hot, and as she looked away from Ian MacLeven, her gaze met that of the king; and he smiled at her, causing her to blush further. What was wrong with her tonight? She was usually facile with words. Why was she so awkward in the company of this young Scotsman?

She felt the touch of Ian's fingers warm upon her wrist, and she could not help but remember the feel and the taste of his mouth on hers that day on board the ship. The memory made her feel even more uncomfortable.

"I am afraid that I was not entirely honest with you, Miss Verner, on board the ship."

Surprise and curiosity drove away her feeling of self-consciousness. "What do you mean?"

"I mean," he said ruefully, "that I did not tell you the entire truth about myself."

Michele could not imagine what he meant. "I don't suppose any of us ever tells another person the whole truth."

Ian nodded. "That is no doubt true, but I carefully avoided telling you one fact about myself that is pertinent to who and what I am. However, there was a reason, the reason being that I was traveling incognito. Part of what I told you was true. It *is* customary in my family for the eldest son, the heir, to make a journey, a trip over the habitable world, before he takes his place as head of the family. The purpose, hopefully, is that such a trip will acquaint him with the world, and its affairs, so that he will have some knowledge of foreign places and will, presumably, gather some wisdom to bring home. What I did *not* tell you is that the trip is made incognito so that the young man in question may see the world as a common man and not as a nobleman."

Michele felt a little piqued at how she had been fooled, although the reason for the deception seemed logical enough as he explained it. So Ian MacLeven was a nobleman, a lord. She did not want to admit to herself that the feeling she was experiencing was disappointment; his background could create a gulf between them. Why this should occur to her, or even matter, was beyond her at the moment.

Her annoyance made her sharp of tongue, as it always did. "Well then, so you are a nobleman! It seems I was properly gulled. I don't believe I was entirely to blame for that, since your behavior aboard ship was scarcely that of a gentleman, was it?"

He winced, and a flush that had nothing to do with rouge stained his strong cheekbones. His gray eyes considered her gravely. "*Touché*, Miss Verner. I suppose I deserve that, but I should like to remind you that having a title is no proof against the lure of beauty, and I should also like to ask that we might now be friends. It seemed to me that, on shipboard, at least at one point, we were on the verge of becoming just that."

Michele felt a sudden shame at her petty behavior. He was a good man; she had felt it on board the ship, and she felt it now; and she had liked him then, and found herself liking him now. Also, she felt much older and wiser than she had the day she berated him for kissing her, recognizing that he had evidently felt for her something of what she had felt for Deampierre; and indeed, she had returned something of the sort toward him, although she had not wanted to admit it. Her anger had really been because she had not wished to become involved; and of course she still did not; but surely being friendly, enjoying Ian's company, did not, and would not, mean an involvement.

The voices at the king's end of the table had grown somewhat louder; and Michele glanced quickly in that direction, seeing that the king and those closest to him were laughing heartily.

She turned back to Ian. "I apologize for my sharp tongue, Lord MacLeven, and I should be pleased to call you my friend."

His smile almost overwhelmed her with its brilliance. "That is the best tidings I have heard since I arrived in this foul court," he whispered, leaning toward her, and raising his glass. "Let us drink a toast to the occasion!"

She lifted her own glass, staring at him curiously. "Why do you call this a 'foul' court?"

As they both sipped from their wine glasses, Ian grimaced. "I'm sorry. I am too frank spoken, perhaps, but I find the court here overripe, decadent. Look around you. Look at the gold, the jewels, the paintings, the china and plate. Look at the guests, tired of pleasure, constantly seeking something new, something to bring them for a moment out of their deadly boredom. And then go into the streets, carefully study the faces of the people there, and see the anger and despair. While the king and his court dine on roast pheasant and quail eggs served off gold plate, his people starve. And grow angrier, day by day. There will be a reckoning one day, I will wager."

Michele glanced around her, and was forced to agree with some of what he said. She too had felt antagonism toward the lush, overwhelming display of wealth, toward the vapidness of society life; but she had assumed that it was just because she came from a different place with different ways. She remembered that Arnaut Deampierre had seemed to feel something of what Ian was expressing. However, thinking about it made her uncomfortable, and she did not want to be uncomfortable on this night, not on the night of her greatest success.

She made a moue. "I know little of political things, Lord MacLeven, and tonight, I confess, I have little stomach for such matters. Could we speak of pleasanter things?"

His answering smile reassured her. "Of course, it was thoughtless of me. But I beg of you, please, no more of this Lord MacLeven! You knew me simply as Ian on board the ship, and called me that. Won't you please do so again?"

She nodded, grateful that he had suggested it, for using his title seemed awkward to her. "Now," she said, leaning toward him so that the person on her right could not hear her. "Tell me, which one is the king's mistress? I am dying to know."

He laughed richly, then put his hand upon her arm, bending his head down to place his mouth close to her ear. "It is the large woman on his immediate right. Look quickly now, for she is glancing the other way."

Michele turned her head toward the end of the table, and saw the woman under discussion. As she did so, her mouth fell open in shock, for the woman was not only very large, but of considerable ugliness, not much helped by the thick powder and rouge upon her face.

Michele turned back to Ian. "But she is ugly!" she said in astonishment. "*Quite* ugly!"

Ian muffled his laughter with his napkin. "I am forced to agree," he said when he was somewhat recovered. "I take it then that you have not seen her before?"

She made a face. "No, but my friends told me about her, although they managed to omit certain important facts." She shook her head in bafflement. "But why? I mean, why does the king choose such an unattractive woman for his . . . his mistress? I do not understand! They told me that the queen is plain, but she *cannot* be less attractive than this one!" Michele continued to shake her head. "I thought that mistresses were always beautiful, very desirable. A king can have, well, I suppose almost anyone he wants. But why does he want *her*?"

Ian shook his own head. "That, my dear young lady, is something no one has ever been able to reason out, for it *is* commonly said she is the ugliest woman at court, and her disposition, I am told, rivals her appearance for unpleasantness. Still, one can never tell where cupid's arrows will strike, and one does not question a king, particularly not this one."

Michele looked again at King Louis, who was laughing heartily at some sally of Madame de Mailly's. "He does not appear to be an unkind man," Michele said thoughtfully. "A bit willful, perhaps, and his mouth has a petulant cast."

"That is an apt description. You are most observing, but you must understand that a king's petulance is not like that of other men, since no one dares dispute him. I have heard stories of his behavior that are hard to credit. Incidents which he calls 'jokes,' but which are hardly humorous to those who suffer them."

"What kind of incidents?"

"Well, it is said that when he was twelve, for instance, he tortured three kittens to death. Of course, he was but a child then, if that is any excuse. Now that he is a man, King Louis amuses himself with such 'jokes' as inquiring kindly about the gout of one of his courtiers, then stamping upon the man's foot, asking, 'Is *this* where you have the gout?' Another time I saw him slap a courtier full in the face, simply to observe the man's reaction."

Michele grimaced. "He does sound unpleasant, and I must admit that I am somewhat disillusioned. I thought that a king would be better, nobler than ordinary men, exceptional somehow."

Ian said gravely, "Not so. A king is but a man who has had exceptional privileges all his life, and is usually the worse for it."

Michele's smile was mischievous. "And is the same true for the nobles?"

"Sometimes, milady, but at least most nobles have work of a sort to perform, at least in my country that is so. I have an estate to run, a castle to keep in repair, farmers and other estate workers to supervise. These matters keep me fully occupied. I have no time for intrigue, malicious gossip, and the pursuit of self-gratification." Ian sighed. "Truth to tell, I am quite ready to return to my own country. This was a 'visit of convenience,' as my father would have called it. He always felt it wise to stay on good terms with the powerful, even if one does not always agree with their politics."

"Will you be leaving soon?" Michele found that she was awaiting his answer with considerable trepidation.

He nodded. "Soon, very soon."

An ornately attired waiter was placing a new dish in front of Michele, some kind of fish; and she suddenly realized that she had been too busy talking to eat.

She dug into the white, flaky fish with a dainty gusto. Suddenly remembering the man on her right, she flashed him a beguiling smile, to which he raised his wine glass in a silent toast.

The fish was delicious; and as Michele ate, she gradually became aware of the conversation between the man and woman directly across the table from her. They were separated from her by at least six feet, yet the woman's voice had the carrying quality of a cawing crow, and Michele could hear her quite clearly.

"I cannot decide," she was saying earnestly to the man next to her, whose glazed eyes and empty wine glass intimated that he was hearing very little of what she said, "between the satin in Paris Mud, or the brocade in King's Eye. Of course, my dressmaker insists that the Goose Dung satin shows off my color to best advantage, but I do not agree. I think it is an ugly color."

The man, with the exaggerated care of the very intoxicated, signaled to the wine steward to pour him another glass of wine.

The fish eaten to the last bite, Michele turned again to Ian. "Perhaps you are right about the boredom here. If that one-sided conversation across the table is any indication of the witty conversation at the court."

"I'm afraid that it is," Ian said dryly, "although occasionally the wit expressed is a little more amusing. There is a tale current about the queen, for instance, that I find rather amusing, but a bit on the ribald side, I am afraid."

Michele, feeling contented and happy, and just a bit lightheaded from the wine, giggled behind her hand. "Well, tell it to me, nonetheless. The queen is supposed to be a lady, and if she was present during whatever happened, I should imagine that I can be present during the telling."

Ian hesitated momentarily, and then laughed outright. "All right! It *is* rather amusing. The tale concerns a member of the court who told the queen that the hussars were holding their annual war games. 'What if I run into a troop of hussars and am poorly defended by my guards?' asked the queen. 'Well, madame,' answered the courtier, 'they would "hussar" Your Majesty.'

" 'And what would you do, monsieur?' asked the queen.

"The courtier replied, 'Madame, I would imitate the dog in the fable, who after having defended his master's dinner, began to partake of it like the others.' "

Michele, a little shocked by the story, still found herself giggling. It *was* amusing.

She looked down the table to where Louis was seated next to a buxom and rather overripe woman wearing a bright blue satin gown, and an enormous, jeweled wig. Michele caught Louis looking at her and Ian, with a rather strange expression, a look far more serious than she could ever remember seeing upon his usually merry countenance.

When Louis caught her glance, he smiled, and gave a helpless shrug, for the woman had her plump, jeweled hand upon his arm, and her painted mouth was close to his ear. Michele felt her own flesh crawl with distaste. Poor Louis! How could he stand the woman, she looked more than old enough to be his mother.

The waiter set another dish in front of Michele, and still hungry, she partook of the fowl. It was a slice of roast swan, from one of several which had been brought in, seemingly with feathers intact. It was tasty, she thought, but not as good as turkey.

Dish followed dish, wine followed wine, until Michele could not remember how many courses had been served, and no longer much cared. She was very full, very sleepy, and now wished for nothing so much as a bed upon which she might retire.

Still, the courses came on—marzipan fruits, looking wonderfully lifelike; cakes; puddings; pastries; cheeses; and more and yet more wine.

Michele, unable to eat another bite, leaned back in her chair, gazing bemusedly around; slowly she became aware of the cacophony of false laughter and loud talk. She focused her rather bleary eyes on the raddled faces upon which rouge and powder had caked and run, showing patches of livid and blotched skin, so that the illustrious company looked very like a gaggle of clowns left in the rain to the detriment of their paint; and suddenly she knew that Ian was right, for the glimpses of the real people under the decorated and painted facades were not pleasant. The smeared mouths were cruel and weak, the blurred eyes sad and without sparkle.

She felt not only tired now, but depressed. She could not endure much more of this. When would it end?

She turned to Ian, and found him watching her. "I'm so tired," she said. "When will all this be over? Must we stay until the king leaves?"

He nodded. "I'm afraid we must, milady. No one must leave before His Majesty. But I think it will not be long now. Look at him, he is almost asleep in his chair."

Michele glanced at the end of the table, where King Louis, somewhat the worse for drink, sat with his head propped on his hands. He looked as if he was as near to sleep as Michele herself, and she sighed. What if he should go to sleep right here at the table? Would the rest of them have to remain in their places throughout the night? Certainly no one would dare wake him.

But then, to her great relief, the king rose from his chair, nodded to the table in general; and then, clutching the sturdy arm of Madame de Mailly, he made his way, somewhat unsteadily, from the room followed by his entourage, in various stages of drunkenness.

Michele sighed gustily. "Thank goodness! If it had gone on much longer, I should have disgraced myself by falling asleep in my chair!"

Ian stood, and offered his arm. "At this stage of the festivities, I doubt that anyone would have taken notice. May I see you to your quarters, Miss Verner?"

Michele, thinking only of the soft bed upstairs, nodded. "Thank you, sir, you may indeed."

Just as they were turning away from the table, Michele saw Andre coming toward them, his expression concerned. She was much too weary to feel curiosity at his expression, only annoyance that anything should keep her from her bed.

"Michele? *Chérie*, are you all right?"

She looked at him crossly. "Of course I'm all right! Why should I not be?"

Andre shrugged, his gaze first on her face, then on Ian's. "Well, it has been a long night, and there was a great deal of wine served . . ."

"Monsieur Leclaire," Ian said, "it is a pleasure to see you again."

Andre's expression changed from puzzlement to recognition. "Ian MacLeven, isn't it? From the ship. *Naturellement!* I didn't recognize you at first. But how is it you are here?"

Michele lifted her hand. "Please, Andre! It is a rather long story, and I would prefer that he tell it to you after I have gone to my bed. I am deadly tired."

Andre patted her cheek. "Of course, my pet. How very thoughtless of me. I shall see you to your room at once."

She shook her head. "Lord MacLeven has already requested that he might do so. I shall see you in the morning, Andre."

She was unable to control a yawn, and Andre nodded, although he looked dubiously at Ian. "I shall be interested in hearing your story. *Lord* MacLeven, is it? My curiosity is piqued. And I shall entrust you with her safekeeping, sir!"

Ian smiled. "I shall see Michele to her door, and no farther, monsieur, and you have my oath on that."

Andre flushed, but Michele was so drowsy that she scarcely noticed the byplay between the two men.

She leaned on Ian's arm as they went up the broad staircase; and when they reached the door of her room, she turned to bid him good night, hardly aware of what she was saying.

As she reached out to open the door, he touched her arm. "May I see you in the morning, Michele? I am quite familiar with the house and the grounds of Fontainebleau, and would enjoy showing them to you."

She nodded, smiling sleepily. "That will be fine. But not too early, if you please. I feel as if I could sleep for a week!"

"Of course. Till the morning then."

"Till the morning," she replied, and then slipped into her room, and made her way toward the bed, almost stumbling.

Slipping out of her costume, she debated making her toilette, but the lure of the bed and sleep was too strong. Pulling on her night rail, she crawled between the smooth linens and pulled the coverlet up to her chin, moving, she thought, quickly toward sleep.

Strangely, sleep did not come immediately. Her body, overtired, seemed to twitch and move without her willing it, and she was very aware of its separate parts. She grew aware that her nipples felt sensitive and that they were extended, and that her lower body felt warm and somehow expectant.

She tried to will herself to sleep, but disturbing thoughts kept intruding, thoughts of Ian MacLeven, and his hand upon her arm, his lips upon hers; and thoughts of Louis when he had playfully hugged her to him, the feel of his strong arms and hard body.

This, inevitably, led to thoughts of Arnaut Deampierre, and the day in the studio; and her wicked mind played back for her the scene as it had occurred, causing her body to tremble as it had when his hands had touched her here, and here, and when he had . . .

She groaned. What was the matter with her? Why was she thinking these thoughts, feeling these sensations? It was the body that was the traitor, she thought; the mind is clear on what it wants, but the body always betrays it. If only the body could be made to obey! If only these damnable urges could be overcome in some way. Life would be so much simpler.

Finally, after much tossing and turning, Michele fell into a deep sleep, troubled by erotic dreams which, upon waking, she tried so hard to deny to herself.

Chapter Fourteen

COURT was in a foul mood as his coach drove away from Malvern the next afternoon.

John had ridden into Williamsburg early that morning with word that Hannah wanted to see him, urgently. When he had arrived at Malvern, Court had found Hannah in a state of near hysteria. The moment she saw him she burst into tears, the first time he had ever seen her weep.

She flew into his arms, racked by sobs. "Oh, Court, I'm ruined!"

"Now calm down, my dear." He smoothed her hair against his shoulder. "I know you've lost your cotton. John told me something of what happened."

"It's gone, all gone! A whole year's work gone for naught!" She raised a tear-stained face. "What am I to do, Court? Without the proceeds from my crop, I can't pay Dade!"

"First, let's see if we can figure out what happened."

"Come, I'll show you." Taking his hand in a desperate grip, she led him toward the cotton shed. "All those buyers came out here this morning, prepared to bid on my cotton, and I had to send them away."

Inside the shed, she swept a hand around. "See? All the bins are empty. I know who's behind it. It was Nathaniel. Oh, why didn't I listen to you about him?"

"You are positive that Bealls was behind it?"

"He left in the night like a thief, and his clothes are

gone. He left without asking for his wages. Isn't that proof enough?"

He nodded grimly. "It would seem so . . ."

One of the field hands had wandered into the shed.

Hannah raised her voice. "Linus, would you come here, please?" To Court she said, "He is one of the three I left on guard here last night. All three were lying on the ground in here this morning. John thinks they were somehow given a sleeping potion."

The black man approached hesitantly, looking disconsolate. "Yes, mistress?"

"Tell Mr. Wayne here what you told me."

"We got sleepy around the midnight hour. Ben, he went up to the kitchen for a pot of tea, we thinking it would keep us awake. When he came back, we heard a terrible ruckus outside. Out there." He indicated the far end of the shed. "We hurried to see what 'twas. Ben had a torch, but we could see nothing. We came back inside and drank our mugs of tea. The next thing I know I got terrible sleepy. I tried to make it to the manor house to tell somebody, but I fell, halfway across the shed. Next thing I know, John, he's shaking me and it's daylight. The cotton was gone." He looked woebegone. "I'm sorry, mistress."

"It's all right. Linus, it wasn't your fault," she said gently. "You may go now." When Linus was out of hearing, she turned to Court. "You see? Nathaniel caused some kind of commotion. When they went to investigate, he dumped a sleeping draught into the tea. It had to be that way, Court!"

"It would appear so," he said with a nod. "But of course Jules Dade had to be behind the whole thing."

"Dade? I never thought . . . Oh!" Hannah clapped a hand to her mouth. "The last time Dade was out to Malvern, Nathaniel told me later that they had had a conversation. I never connected the two, but I'm sure you're right, Court. What can we do? Should we go to the constabulary in Williamsburg?"

"No, I don't think that is the best course of action to take."

"But they stole my cotton! That makes them thieves!"

"Not unless you can prove it. And can you? You can be sure that Dade has removed the cotton from this immediate vicinity, storing it someplace where it will be difficult to find."

"Then we just do nothing?" she said in despair.

"Oh, I am going to do something, of that you may be sure," he said grimly. "I am going to see to it that Dade returns your cotton to you."

"Can you do that?"

"I'm certainly going to try. I have some leverage to use against Master Dade."

She looked at him curiously. "What leverage is that, Court?"

"I'd rather not go into that at this time, Hannah. It is something that goes back a long way between us, and it's better you do not know."

Now, as his coach drew near Williamsburg, Court's thoughts traveled back to that long-ago time, when he not only met Jules Dade, but Michael Verner as well.

It had happened over twenty years ago, in the year 1718. Courtney Wayne, just past twenty, was serving under the king's command, on board a sloop, under Lieutenant Robert Maynard. They were under orders from the royal governor of Virginia, Colonel Alexander Spotswood, to find and put an end to the career of Edward Teach, the infamous Blackbeard.

The search had been long and arduous, Teach always managing to elude capture; in essence thumbing his nose contemptuously at his pursuers. Rumor on board the two sloops under Lieutenant Maynard's command was that the governor had a spy among Blackbeard's villainous crew. This rumor was confirmed when word reached Lieutenant Maynard as to where Blackbeard could be found. On the morning of November 19, the two sloops closed in on Blackbeard's pirate ship, the *Adventure*.

Court was on board the same sloop as Lieutenant Maynard. The battle began at nine in the morning. The two sloops sailed down on the *Adventure*, which fled toward the open sea. They had underestimated the firepower of the pirate ship, and the first sloop, desperately trying to halt the flight, maneuvered to within half a pistol shot of the fleeing vessel in an attempt to cut the ship off. Blackbeard swung his ship around and delivered a broadside. Half the sloop's crew was killed, including its commander, and the jib and foremast were shot away; out of the battle, the sloop began to drift helplessly.

The other sloop, under Maynard's direct command, had closed in on the *Adventure*, but not quite soon enough. Blackbeard's crew had time to reload and fire another broadside; twenty-one men were killed. Maynard, fearing a wholesale slaughter, ordered his men below.

Blackbeard, evidently thinking there were no longer enough of the king's men left alive to do battle, brought the *Adventure* alongside, and boarded the ship with his crew, leading the way himself, as was his habit.

Maynard immediately ordered his men back on deck, and the battle was joined. It was fierce and hot for a few minutes. Blackbeard, laughing, cutlass flashing, long black beard flying, looked like the devil out of hell to young Courtney Wayne.

Maynard and the pirate came face to face. Both fired pistols. Blackbeard's shot missed, but Maynard's pistol ball plowed into the giant figure of the pirate. The shot scarcely staggered him; he drove forward, and the lieutenant and the pirate had at it with clashing cutlasses. Then Blackbeard delivered a powerful blow, snapping the lieutenant's cutlass like a piece of wood. Laughing fiendishly, Blackbeard prepared to deliver the killing blow.

Court assessed the situation in an instant. His own pistol empty, he ran at Blackbeard with his dagger, slicing into the pirate's throat. By this time Maynard's men had surrounded the pirate. Pistol balls thudded into his body, and cutlass slashes opened great wounds in him. Still he fought on. Court watched in awe, sure that the man was invincible. Blackbeard jerked yet another pistol from his belt, started to cock it—and fell over dead.

It was later discovered that he had twenty-five separate wounds in his body, most of them severe enough to have killed an ordinary man.

The battle was done, having lasted approximately ten minutes. Most of Blackbeard's men were dead on the deck of the sloop, and others were jumping overboard; the remainder surrendered.

Busy reloading his pistol, Court saw Lieutenant Maynard standing over the body of the dead Blackbeard. He proclaimed, "Sever the villain's head, and swing it beneath the bowsprit of our ship. Let the world know that the prince of villains is no more!"

Court, faintly sickened by all the slaughter, turned away and worked his way to the stern of the vessel, where he stood leaning over the railing, wondering if he was going to vomit over the side.

There was no one in his immediate vicinity, but elsewhere on the ship he could hear pistols popping as the remaining pirates jumped into the water. He glanced to his right as another splash sounded, then heard a pistol shot, and saw the head of a man in the water explode in a burst of blood.

Court looked quickly away, toward the stern, just in time to see another pirate leap into the water. The man went under briefly, then surfaced just below where Court stood. Apparently no one else had seen him. Court stared down into the frightened face. Slowly, he took aim with his pistol. He could see the man's face clearly, and knew he would never forget a single feature—mouse-colored hair plastered close to his skull, a rather round face, and gray eyes wide with terror as he stared up at Court.

Court willed himself to fire, but he could not. He slowly lowered the pistol. A look of disbelief spread over the face of the man in the water; then he turned and began to swim vigorously for the distant shore.

Court watched until the swimming man was only a dot in the water. He was sure that someone would spot him any second, but no one did. Court felt no regret at not having killed the man—there had been enough death this day.

He turned away from the railing and returned midship just as Lieutenant Maynard came across from the *Adventure*, with a man in tow. The man had a full black beard and snapping black eyes; to Court he looked as piratical as any of Blackbeard's men.

Smiling broadly, Maynard motioned the man forward, raising his voice. "Here's the man to whom we owe our victory over Blackbeard, lads! This is Governor Spotswood's man in Blackbeard's crew, Michael Verner, known to the dead Blackbeard as Dancer. A cheer for Mr. Verner, lads!"

A rousing cheer went up from the king's men, and Michael Verner stepped forward, rubbing his wrists. "It is I who owe a debt to you fellows. Teach had gotten onto me. He knew me for a spy, and I would have been killed ere this day was over, if not for you lads coming to my rescue."

A few days later Lieutenant Maynard's sloop sailed into the bay at Bath, and the lieutenant allowed his victorious crew leave to go ashore. The news had spread, and the waterfront was crowded by townspeople come to look and marvel at the severed head of the pirate, Blackbeard, fastened to the bowsprit of the sloop.

A couple of hours after coming ashore Court was drinking ale in a waterfront tavern when Michael Verner came in. He got an ale from the innkeeper and looked around for a seat. The only one vacant was at the table where Court sat alone, and Verner came over.

"May I share your table, sir?"

"Gladly, Mr. Verner. Pray be seated."

Verner's black eyes showed surprise. "Do I know you, sir?"

"No, but I know you, Master Verner. I was on board the sloop when Lieutenant Maynard brought you up from the bowels of Blackbeard's ship. I am Courtney Wayne."

"Then a toast to you, Mr. Wayne. You, and your fellows,

have my everlasting gratitude." Michael Verner raised his glass.

Court looked away in some embarrassment. "I had very little hand in it, sir. I was just one of many."

"Not so, Mr. Wayne. I was told by your lieutenant that you saved his life when you attacked Blackbeard, else Teach would have run him through."

Court made a negligent gesture. "I only did what had to be done." He considered telling Verner about the pirate he had let escape with his life. Would he still think him a hero? He decided to keep quiet; for some reason he valued Michael Verner's good opinion of him, stranger though he might be.

Michael was speaking, ". . . making a career of the king's service?"

Court shook his head in horror. "Good God, no! At least I hope not. I joined up for a lark, a bit of adventure, and frankly, to put food in my belly. I do believe that the battle with Blackbeard's crew is quite enough adventure for me. Besides, the pay is terrible."

"I suppose that is the reason I became a spy for Governor Spotswood, a seeking after adventure. That and the fact that I was not getting along well with my father." His face darkened and became sad. "Perhaps matters are better now at Malvern. I will be happy to return, that I know. I can see now that a great deal of the trouble was of my own making." His laughter was rueful. "Almost two years with a bloody buccaneer like Edward Teach tend to turn a callow youth into a man very quickly."

"Malvern? What is that?"

"That's the family plantation, outside of Williamsburg." Michael took a sip of ale, his features taking on a melancholy look. "My father is running it alone now. I didn't take to running a plantation. I thought it tedious and boring. My father and I quarreled about that. Although it hasn't been all that long in time, I've grown up somewhat, and it doesn't seem all that boring to me now." He grinned sardonically. "I was pretty wild back then, occupied with wenching, horse racing, and gambling. We said some things

I'm sorry for now. I don't know about Father. But as soon as I'm able, I'm going back to Malvern and find out . . ."

Over several more glasses of ale, Michael reminisced about his youth and Malvern. Court felt envious of the man, and thought it very foolish of him to leave such a fine life. As for himself, Court had never known his father; he had died right after Court was born, leaving Court alone with his mother. Their life had been a struggle merely to survive, and in the end it had killed his mother, who died a few months before Court joined the king's service. That, in large part, was the reason he had joined. He had no calling, and he had to eat.

Michael asked no questions of Court's past, and Court volunteered nothing. When they parted, Court felt that he knew the other man well, and he had developed a liking for him. Evidently Michael shared his feelings, for his parting words were: "If ever you get to Williamsburg, Court, you would be more than welcome at Malvern."

Almost twenty years were to pass before Court got to Williamsburg, and he did not see Michael Verner in all that time. He did see Jules Dade, however, at least two times; he never learned whether or not Dade was the man's real name, or if he had taken a new one for himself after he left the life of piracy.

The first time was in Charleston, South Carolina, five years after the episode with Blackbeard. At that time Court was a mate on a sailing ship out of Boston; his ship was beating its way up the coast after a long and wearying journey to the Orient for spices and other trade goods, bound for Boston town. It was necessary to put into Charleston harbor for repairs and fresh water. Laying over for three days, Court found idle time on his hands; and he wandered the romantic, picturesque town of Charleston, a port city that he had come to love.

On the second day he found himself on the waterfront as a ship sailed into port. From a conversation between two portly, apparently affluent, planters standing nearby, smoking cheroots, he gathered that the ship was a slaver, returning from Africa with a load of slaves. The planters were there to buy several slaves for their plantations.

Although Court had never approved of slavery, he lingered on the docks, having nothing better to do, and watched as several longboats left the ship and rowed toward shore. The boats were heavily laden with blacks, men and women; and two white men rode in each longboat, armed to the teeth. As the boats neared the docks, Court could see that the slaves were chained together. He made a face of disgust and had started to turn away, when his attention was caught by one of the white men in the first longboat, the man facing toward the dock. He looked familiar; and when the boat bumped against the dock, and Court had walked closer, he realized that it was the pirate he had let live in the water that long-ago day.

Now the man in the boat clambered up onto the dock, and looked around before giving the order to unload the blacks. His gaze encountered Court's, and he froze, his face paling. There was no doubt that he recognized Court. If any further proof of that was needed, his hand strayed to the pistol in his belt. They stood thus for a long moment, gazes locked, before Court made a contemptuous, dismissing gesture, and turned on his heel.

It had been in his mind to reveal the man as a former pirate to the bystanders, but he decided against it. What good would it do? He might not even be believed, and even if he was, what could be gained? Clearly, the man was no longer a pirate; and while Court viewed slaving as little better than piracy, he well realized that this view was not shared by the people around him; least of all by the planters who were flocking around now to get a peek at the blacks before they were put on the auction block.

Five more years passed before he saw Dade again, once more in Charleston. Court had just arrived from Boston. He had been working on a whaling ship for three years, and was weary of the bloody slaughter, although it had made him a relatively wealthy man. He had decided to leave the sea for good, and was in Charleston in search of some endeavor in which to invest his money.

After three days of investigating various enterprises, he finally settled on one—a farm a few miles outside of Charleston. Court had never owned any land, and owning his own place appealed to him. It was certainly not a plantation, but only about thirty acres, and he had no intention of farming it; he was going to raise mules. It was a lucrative business; and although he knew absolutely nothing about raising mules, he figured he could learn—he had already learned a number of trades and had done well at all of them.

After the transaction was completed in a solicitor's office in Charleston, Court wandered down toward the waterfront. Before he reached the docks he came across a slave auction in progress. He had no intention of watching—it was always a revolting spectacle—but something caught his eye as he maneuvered around the edges of the large crowd in attendance. An open carriage was parked in the street, with a black, liveried driver in the front seat; and sitting in the back, dressed in finery and smoking a cigar, was the pirate he had let live.

Court paused, studying the man who had not noticed him. Court turned to a man nearby. "Pardon me, sir, but do you happen to be acquainted with the man in the carriage?"

The man glanced at the carriage. "I am indeed, stranger. That's Jules Dade. The slave ship in the harbor is his. He just unloaded this load of slaves last night."

Court nodded slowly, thanking his informant, and continued to stare at the man in the carriage. Finally, he made up his mind and walked over.

"Mr. Dade?"

At the sound of his name Dade's head snapped around. The cigar fell from his mouth into his lap, and he scrambled to retrieve it and throw it over the side of the carriage.

Court was smiling grimly. "I see that you recognize me, Mr. Dade."

Dade stared at him, tight-lipped, but remained mute.

"I must say that you have improved your situation in

the world since you swam for shore that day, like a water rat, after Blackbeard was killed."

Dade's glance darted about fearfully. His lips drew back in a snarl, and he whispered, "Watch your tongue, sir!"

Unheeding, Court went on, "Although you seem to be prospering, I cannot say that I think much of your new profession. Slaving, in my opinion, is on a par with piracy."

"What I am doing is legal!" Dade hissed.

Court nodded. "That is true, but I wonder what these good people would think should they learn that you were once Blackbeard's man?"

"You will not tell them!" All of a sudden Dade had a pistol in both hands, the barrel resting on the side of the carriage, pointed at Court's heart.

"You will kill me, your benefactor? The man who saved your worthless life?" Court said mockingly. "Such ingratitude!"

Dade had recovered some of his aplomb now. "It is only your word against mine," he said with a sneer. "And I am a respected member of the community."

"I wonder how long you can continue to fool them, Mr. Dade?" Court stared calmly at the pistol. "Once a blackguard, always a blackguard."

"I could kill you now, and none would fault me for it. I would tell the good people that you tried to rob me."

"I doubt that you have the courage, sir. Besides, methinks you are concerned more with profit than that. Think what it would do should you cause such a commotion. It would disrupt your precious auction. Besides, I have no intention of revealing your villainy. It is too late for that. I can only regret that I did not kill you that long-ago day. You have naught to fear from me today. But do not disillusion yourself, Mr. Dade. It is not from fear that you might do me bodily harm. You do not possess the courage. A man such as you needs darkness to perform his foul deeds."

Dade glared at him in frustration, literally gnashing his teeth. Court motioned contemptuously, and strode away.

Court did not see Jules Dade again until he settled in

Williamsburg. Many events had transpired in Court's life in the interim. He had sold his mule farm at a profit after two years. He had gone on to other, even more profitable things. He had met and married Katherine, and then lost her within a short time.

But oh, how sorely he regretted that he had not killed Dade that day of Blackbeard's death! Or even that he had not revealed Dade for the villain he was that first day in Charleston! If he had done so, Hannah would not be in such dire straits now.

Court was really not sure what had caused him to settle in Williamsburg. He had stayed a night there once in his many travels, and it struck him as a quiet, peaceful town. He desperately sought peace and quiet now. He had worked hard all his life, since his early teens, and he had accumulated a great deal of wealth. He no longer had the need to possess more worldly goods, and he realized all the drive had gone out of him with Katherine's death; he was perfectly content to spend the rest of his days in idleness, in a quiet town, among good neighbors. That, of course, was before he learned of Dade's presence. But by the time he learned that Dade also resided in Williamsburg, he was already well-settled in and content. The fact that Dade lived in the same town troubled him, yet he never really considered leaving. If Dade caused him any grief, he would reveal the man for what he was, although Court knew that would raise questions in many minds—why had he not told what he knew of Dade's past long ago?

Although he knew that Michael Verner still lived on Malvern, Court was reluctant to approach him. The invitation to visit Malvern was twenty years old, and Verner might wish to forget the days with Blackbeard. Also, Court learned in town that Michael was married, with a daughter nearly grown.

Then, one cold winter's day, while Court was enjoying an ale in a tavern, his head bent, a voice spoke above him, "Do I not know you, sir?"

Court looked up into the face of Michael Verner. "Mr. Verner!" He sprang to his feet. "You do, sir, and I you.

We last shared drink and good talk in a tavern much like this."

Michael nodded, beginning to smile. "Yes, in Bath, after the demise of Edward Teach. And you're Courtney Wayne, I believe?"

"That is right, sir. My friends call me Court." He reached out for Michael's hand.

"It would pleasure me to become your friend, Court."

Noticing that Michael carried a mug of ale, Court motioned. "Won't you share my table?"

"That will also be my pleasure." The two men sat down, and Michael stared across the table. "You have changed little, friend Court."

Court smiled. "I am twenty years older."

"Aren't we all? I had heard that a stranger had taken up residence in Williamsburg, I may even have heard the name, but I did not connect it up until just now, seeing your face. You have been here some months, I believe?"

"Yes, since shortly after Christmas."

"Why didn't you ride out to Malvern? I do recall inviting you."

Court drained his ale, vaguely embarrassed. "Well, that was long ago, spoken to a passing acquaintance in a tavern, and I did not wish to impose."

Michael nodded. "Well said, sir. But we shall have to rectify that. Tell me, what has happened to you in the meantime?"

Court gave him an abbreviated version of what had transpired in his life.

Learning of the death of Katherine, Michael said, "My condolences, Court. I am, of course, married now, and I know what sorrow I would suffer should I lose my precious Hannah." Once started, Michael launched into the story of what the intervening years had brought to him—the death of his father; his later marriage to Hannah, his father's young wife; and his life on Malvern.

"Well then, it seems that you have taken to life on a plantation very well, Michael."

"But perhaps not as successfully as I would like." Michael looked down into his ale, his face mirroring a melancholy close to despair.

"What is it, my friend? What troubles you?"

Michael looked up with a heavy sigh. "I am in dire financial straits, Court. My stubborn pride has prevented me from relating this to any close friends, not even dear Hannah. Last year I had a crop failure. It left me desperately short of funds. But even more, I did something much worse. I recall telling you in Bath that I was a wild young blood, wenching, dueling, and gambling. I put all that behind me when I married Hannah . . . until recently. Hoping to win enough to tide me over until this coming year's crop, I started gambling. The more I gambled, the more I lost. It was foolish of me, Court, but there it is." His face was gray, his eyes bleak. "I am destitute. I have not enough funds to see me through. I have been considering going to a moneylender here in town, one Jules Dade. It goes against my nature to go into debt, but I can see no alternative."

"Jules Dade?" Court said with a gasp. "No, do not go to him, I beg of you, my friend."

"Why not?" Michael shrugged. "One moneylender is as good, or bad, as another."

"Not in this instance. Let me tell you about Jules Dade . . ."

He told all he knew of Dade, beginning with the day of Blackbeard's defeat, and brought Michael up to date.

Michael hailed the innkeeper over and ordered another ale apiece. When it was served, he said thoughtfully, "This Dade is a proper blackguard, isn't he?"

"The blackest."

"I should think he could still be hauled before the authorities on the charge of piracy."

"Perhaps. But it would only cause an uproar and likely accomplish little. Just do not go to him for money, I beg of you."

"No, of course not," Michael said, staring off. "But I still face a dire shortage of funds for the coming year."

"Let me loan you the money, Michael."

Michael stared. "You, friend Court?"

"Yes. I have a sufficiency. You may borrow whatever you need, and repay me when your harvest is over."

Michael fell into a brown study for a little. Finally he sighed and nodded. "I will avail myself of your kind offer. It galls me, but I have little choice. But I must exact a promise from you."

"And what is that?"

"Hannah must never know of my foolishness, that I gambled and placed myself deeply in debt. If she ever learns of the loan, which I pray she won't, promise me you won't reveal my reason."

"You have my solemn promise."

"I realize that you are doing this as a favor to a friend, but I insist on a proper note being drawn up, for your protection, should something happen to me."

Well, I kept my word, Court thought, as his coach entered the outskirts of Williamsburg; I did not tell Hannah why her husband needed money so desperately.

And likely, if Michael had lived, Court thought, he would never have pressed for payment, giving Michael all the time he needed. Actually, the motive behind the loan was as much to thwart Dade, as it was to help Michael. He had waited a decent interval after Michael's untimely death, yet a business transaction was a business transaction. When he received no indication from Hannah Verner that the debt was even owed, he sent her the letter. After all, he did not know her at the time; and he thought it proper that she should at least acknowledge her husband's obligations.

He interrupted his thoughts to lean out the window and direct his driver to Dade's residence. It was just dusk when the coach clattered up before the moneylender's home, and there was a dim light showing in the front window.

Court rapped loudly on the door, then waited until he heard footsteps inside. The door opened a crack, and Dade peered out. His eyes widened. "You!"

He started to swing the door shut, but Court had been expecting just such a move. His booted foot was jammed in the door. The door slammed against it, and Court used his shoulder to push it open. Dade was backpedaling, his face showing fear.

Court stepped inside, and closed the door after him. "I want a few words with you, Dade . . ."

All the while Dade had been sidling toward the side table just beyond the entryway, where a pistol lay. Just as Dade reached for the weapon, Court took two quick steps and kicked the table hard. It skidded across the floor, overturned, and the pistol fell to the floor.

Court caught Dade's wrist in a firm grip. "No pistols this time, Mr. Dade."

"What do you want of me, sir?" Dade demanded in a quavering voice.

"Hannah Verner's cotton mysteriously disappeared last night."

"What has that to do with me?"

"You stole it, Dade, or had Nathaniel Bealls steal it for you."

"I know nothing of this Bealls fellow, whoever he is."

"Dade, I have no patience to listen to your lies."

"You can't prove a thing!" Dade said shrilly.

"I have no need to prove it. I *know* that you are behind this deed, that is sufficient. I also know that you haven't had time to sell it as yet. You have it secreted away somewhere."

"Lies, all lies!"

Court continued calmly, "You will see that Hannah's cotton is returned to her by the morrow."

Dade drew himself up. "You, sir, are mad. How dare you come into my house with such insane accusations!"

As if the man had not spoken, Court continued, "If her cotton is not returned to her by noon tomorrow, I will reveal to the good people of Williamsburg just how villainous you are. And you will probably hang for a pirate. The people of this community well remember Blackbeard's depredations in this area."

"You cannot prove that, either. It will be my word against yours!"

"Even if they don't wholly believe me, it will cast doubt on your character, and you will be finished in Williamsburg."

"I will tell everyone that *you* are the pirate, lying to protect yourself and to discredit me."

"Tell them what you please," Court said with a shrug. "I can always prove otherwise. But you, sir, if you try to flee . . ." He seized Dade by the shirt front and shook him. "I will track you down and kill you. I will devote my life to it, if necessary. I will do what I should have done over twenty years ago. I was young then and had not the belly for it."

He let the man go, and Dade shrank away from him in terror.

"So, consider carefully, Mr. Dade. You have a choice. Return Hannah's cotton, and that will be the end of it. As much as I despise you, I will do nothing more. I will even allow her to sell her cotton and repay her loan to you, although it galls me. On the other hand, if you do not do what I ask, you face disgrace, in the very least, or death, at the worst.

"Consider very carefully, Dade. You will lose nothing but the cotton, which was not yours anyway, and you will have your money returned to you, with interest. You should be content with that."

Court backed up toward the door. "Remember, Master Dade, you have until noon tomorrow to carry this out. If you do not, you will sorely regret it. You have my solemn promise on that."

Chapter Fifteen

AFTER Ian MacLeven had left Michele at her door, he headed toward his own room with a light step. The delight that he felt at seeing Michele Verner once more was overwhelming, and he could not help but be hopeful that something good might come of the renewal of their acquaintance.

Often, since that scene aboard the ship, he had thought of Michele—too often, in fact, for his peace of mind. In the short time that he had known her she had made a profound impression upon him; and it was not simply her beauty of face and figure, extraordinary though these were, that charmed him; but her beauty of spirit and nature as well. Even her strong will and arrogance intrigued him, for they spoke of the intensity of the flame that burned within her. She was not one of those insipid, curds-and-whey girls who flutter about a man, attempting to cling to him; nor was she one of the bitchy, self-centered creatures interested only in their gowns and toilettes, like those here at the court. Michele was a real woman, and Ian wanted her with a desire that was both frightening and thrilling.

He could not remember ever feeling quite this way about a woman before, and it worried him that she did not seem to feel the same way about him.

As a nobleman, with acres of land, a castle, and many people at his beck and call to serve his every whim, he was, of course, considered an excellent catch; and he was accustomed to having women seek him out, and pursue his favor. The fact that Michele did not intrigued him mightily, and yet puzzled him at the same time, for he considered himself a good judge of people, and on board the ship, he had been quite certain that the attraction that he felt toward her was returned; yet, when he had kissed her, she had suddenly flailed out against him in what had appeared to be real anger. Was she one of those women who abhorred a man's touch, who hated anything sexual? He could not believe that, for the flame of life burned too brightly in her. Was she fighting her feelings for other reasons? This seemed more likely. Well, he would just have to be very, very careful; for this, he was quite certain, was the woman he wanted to marry, and now that he had found her he did not want to lose her again.

His room, as he opened the door, smelled of scent, and the air was very close.

Impatiently, Ian went to the windows, and despite the evening chill, flung them open. Everything here, he thought disgustedly, is overperfumed, oversoft, and overripe. After a week here he already longed for the clean, spare elegance of MacLeven Castle, and the sweeping lines of the moors. Paris was a beautiful city, and he admired its grand buildings and spacious *places*, but he never felt quite at home there. Fontainebleau was a beautiful, grand chateau—*too* grand, for his liking. It was, he knew, because of the life style here at court that he always felt out of place. The king, and the members of his court, seemed to have no concept of what life was actually like for the common man. They did not seem to care that much of the populace was always hungry, ill-clothed, and ill-housed, that dreadful diseases prowled the streets and lanes unchecked. They seemed interested in only their own pleasure, interested in trying to amuse themselves with greater and greater excesses.

Well, that was not his problem, Ian thought. At home, in Scotland, his father, Laird MacLeven, had run his estate with a firm but fair hand. None of MacLeven's people went hungry, or were in want of a decent roof over their heads. The MacLevens looked after their own, and in return they received loyalty and hard work from their tenants and servitors; and Ian was determined to carry on the tradition set by his father, and other MacLevens before him.

He smiled as he thought of the old man, visualizing the stern, craggy face that could change in an instant when his father smiled, which he did often enough to keep him from seeming totally forbidding.

It was usually the custom for a lord to keep command of his holdings until death released his property to the eldest son, but it had long been the custom of the MacLeven clan that the patriarch should step down at a certain age, if he was still alive, and turn over the management of the estate to the next in line, so that a strong hand would always be in charge. And now it was Ian's turn to take on the responsibility of MacLeven Castle, its lands, and its people; a task he both looked forward to, and dreaded, for it meant the end of his youth, in a sense; and certainly it meant the end of his freedom to do what he pleased, where he pleased. Also, it saddened him to see his father growing old and feeble. Malcolm MacLeven had always been a giant of a man, heavy-shouldered, with a broad chest that looked capable of withstanding any blow; but old age and sorrow had shrunken him, and had taken the edge off his fine, sharp mind so that he now occasionally spoke of his son, Douglas, and his long dead wife, Jane, as if they were still alive.

Ian, himself, sometimes had difficulty in remembering his mother. She existed for him mainly as a faint picture in his mind; a beautiful woman—as her portrait in the great hall at MacLeven Castle attested—slender, with an intelligent, narrow face, fine, brown eyes, and a sweet smile. Certain fragrances, certain things, could bring her back to Ian in an instant, and he would remember his sorrow and despair at her death. He knew that his sisters missed her even more than he; for Elizabeth had been only a baby at the time, and girls stood more in need of mothering.

His father evidently had loved her very much, for he had never married again, although he had had his share of women. And now the old man was past even that. If only Douglas had lived, Ian thought. It was his death that had broken his father's health, and made him age.

For a poignant moment Ian visualized his dead brother's strong, handsome face, so like their father's. Despite a difference of ten years in their ages, the brothers had been very close, and Douglas' tragic and untimely death was an event that greatly affected Ian, as well as his sisters, Margaret and Elizabeth. They were a close family; and although it had been three years since his brother's death, he still lived strongly in their minds and hearts.

Often Ian would think of Douglas as if he were still alive; he would think of some occurrence or some story—"I must tell this to Douglas," and then experience again the shock of realizing that Douglas was gone. They had shared so many happy times—sailing and fishing at Loch Leven; riding across the moors, the smell of crushed heather and gorse powerful in their nostrils, the wind in their hair; the dances at the castle; the sound of the pipers; Douglas had been an excellent piper. So many memories—Douglas with his sisters, carrying little Elizabeth piggyback down the great staircase; dancing with Margaret, five years younger than he and the next eldest; and of course walking and dancing with Mary, his betrothed, a beautiful girl with great masses of copper-colored hair and serious gray eyes.

It was partly because of the memory of Douglas and Mary that Ian felt such a pressure to declare his intentions to Michele, and to hasten her into accepting him. Douglas, although quite foolishly in love with Mary, had delayed their wedding until he had returned from visiting his friend, young Robert Campbell. Of course, he had not returned; and the fact that he and Mary had never been able to consummate their love, seemed to Ian to be the greatest tragedy about his brother's death.

It was Douglas, as the eldest, who should have been taking over the care and control of the MacLeven clan.

Now that responsibility and honor fell to Ian, who had made a promise both to himself and the precious memory of Douglas that he would carry out his duties and responsibilities in a manner that would have made Douglas proud.

Ian sorely missed his home and his family, and he would return to them as soon as decently possible. He was weary of traveling, and would not have returned to France at all if it were not for King Louis' invitation, which his father had told him would be unwise to ignore. Louis was always hungry for new people at his court, particularly those who were attractive, intelligent, and of noble blood. The king had taken a liking to Ian upon first meeting him, several years ago, and had extended a number of invitations since.

This time, of course, Ian was pleased that he had come, for he had met Michele Verner once more. She was, he knew, only going to be at Fontainebleau for the weekend; but that, hopefully, would be enough time for him to convince her to see him again. And despite his desire to return home, he would stay in Paris at least a few days longer, or even a few weeks, if necessary, for as long as it took him to persuade Michele to come and visit him at MacLeven Castle; and once he had her there, all to himself, so to speak, he hoped to convince her to marry him.

Michele slept late the next morning, and breakfasted upon fresh hothouse strawberries with thick cream, warm bread and butter, and tea.

She had slept well and deeply, and now felt refreshed and expectant. She was looking forward to seeing Ian MacLeven more than she cared to admit to herself. Spotting his familiar face among the strange countenances of the king's court had been almost like seeing someone from home. She had almost forgotten how truly handsome he was, and how witty and entertaining; and it was good to be with someone with whom she could speak English. She had grown quite used to conversing in French, but often she yearned for the sound of her own mother tongue. Of course, she spoke to Andre in English sometimes, but more often than not they were in the company of others, and so spoke French.

After finishing breakfast, she called the maid in to help her dress and complete her toilette. She chose a soft green velvet gown and wide-brimmed hat, as suitable attire in which to stroll about the chateau grounds, and had the maid dress her hair in soft curls, pulled back from her face. Since the day was clear, but chilly, she chose a short, dark green velvet cape to top off the ensemble, but refused the maid's suggestion that she wear a mask to protect her complexion against the sun and the chill wind. It would be worth a freckle or two, she thought, just to feel the fresh air on her face; and besides, she found the masks uncomfortable and hot. The maid was just putting the last touches to her hair, when there was a knock upon the door. The maid went to answer the knock, and Michele, fighting back a mounting excitement, arose from her dressing table bench.

She could hear Ian's voice at the door. He had a good voice, she thought, deep and strong; and was rendered more attractive by the slight Scottish burr that made both his English and his French distinctive.

The maid turned away from the door and came over to Michele, wearing a sly smile. "It is Monsieur MacLeven, mademoiselle. He says you are expecting him?"

Michele nodded. "Yes, Nicole, thank you. We are going walking this morning."

Nicole's smile widened. "Have a nice walk, mademoiselle."

Michele found herself flushing under the other girl's knowing gaze. The French, Michele thought, always seem to see things in terms of love; I don't imagine that they can even *conceive* of a platonic relationship.

The look in Ian's eyes as she went to the open door, more than made up for all the effort she had taken to dress. He took her gloved hand in his, and made a leg. "The day is beautiful," he said, in French, "but you put it to shame, mademoiselle!"

Michele felt her cheeks grow warm, but managed to

nod, she hoped, regally. "Thank you, sir, but could we speak in English, please? I am afraid that I shall forget my own language otherwise."

His smile was understanding. "I know what you mean. When I am in France, I always grow hungry for the sound of my mother tongue."

As Ian escorted her down the long, ornate hallway, Michele glanced covertly at him. He was wearing a different tartan this morning, and a short, dark jacket instead of the ruffled linen shirt. She found the kilts unusual but attractive. He had strong, well-muscled legs, which were shown to good advantage; and the sturdy woolen and bold pattern of his clothing looked masculine and rugged; a nice change, she thought, from the velvets, silks, and satins of the French nobles.

"You will like the gardens," he was saying as they walked. "They are very beautiful, although you should really see them in the spring. Still, the day is clear and sunny." He smiled down at her. "You will also, I think, enjoy the clean country air. It should remind you of your own home."

She could not help but respond to his friendliness and warmth of manner. "Do you know Virginia?" she asked curiously.

He nodded. "Aye. I passed through there on my tour of the world, and I will have to admit that it is a fair land. I must also confess that I envied you your soil, so rich, so fertile. I saw acres and acres of tobacco and cotton, fields of vegetables. And your homes, so fragile and lovely, like great white swans sitting in green parks."

She laughed with delight at his description. "But why do you say fragile? Our homes aren't fragile. Malvern, my own home, has been standing for over fifty years, and, I hope, will be standing for many more."

He echoed her laugh. "Ah, lass, I did not mean to insult your homes. They are, as I said, beautiful, and well suited to your temperate climate, but in Scotland the great homes and castles are built of stone. We have no ample supply of wood for building, such as you have in the colonies, but we do have stone, and stone withstands the fierce winter winds and storms, the rain and snow. Too, we are an older land. MacLeven Castle was built over two hundred years ago, and God alone knows how much longer it will stand."

Michele sighed. "So old. And the colonies are so new, at least new in civilization. I imagine Scotland is very beautiful, at least I have heard so."

Ian nodded. "Aye, I think so, although it is different than your Virginia, harsher, bolder, but it has its own beauty, and a history that lives in all Scottish hearts." He gestured sharply. "But enough of your country and mine, for the moment. Now you must view the beauty here."

While they had been talking, Ian had led her out of the chateau and into the grounds.

"This," said Ian, waving his hand toward a lovely fountain capped with a bronze statue of a hunting Diana, surrounded by four stag's heads and four sitting dogs, spouting water, "is the Garden of Diana, or the Queen's Garden."

Michele, peering out from under the shade of her wide-brimmed hat, smiled with pleasure. The garden was indeed lovely, with banks of autumn flowers setting off the rich green of orange trees, and the gleaming marble of the statues which were artistically situated among the trees and flowers. Gratefully, she inhaled the sparkling air, which was redolent with the odor of newly cut grass.

"It does remind me of home," she said wistfully. "Except that it is more formal and grander."

She was feeling very relaxed and happy. It was nice, for a change, to be able to forget about everything except enjoying herself, enjoying the moment; and she realized how seldom she did that—forget about lessons, forget about dancing, and just enjoy doing nothing but being with pleasant company.

Of course, she enjoyed the company of the other dancers, and she considered Louis and Marie to be her best friends; but when they were together, they almost always talked exclusively of dancing. Michele had not realized just how narrow her life had become of late.

"Would you care to sit for a while? There is a nice bench near the fountain."

She nodded. "Yes, please. It is so peaceful here, you might think that we were the only two people on the grounds."

He took her hand in his, and even through the fabric of her glove, she was very aware of the heat of his strong, well-formed fingers upon hers.

"I wish we were," he said softly, his deep voice husky. "The only two here, I mean."

She glanced at him quickly, then away. She could feel her pulse begin to race, and a familiar warmth spread throughout her lower body.

Damn Arnaut Deampierre! she thought despairingly. He had awakened something in her that she would be far better off without. Before that afternoon with him, her body had expressed inconvenient urges, but she had been able to ignore them. Now, knowing what pleasure a man's body could bring, her own body suffered. Yes, suffered, for although the feelings she experienced were thrilling, she felt frustrated, for there was no relief for them.

Of course, she should not damn the ballet master. It was she, after all, who, afflicted by some kind of momentary madness, had pressured him, had tempted him beyond his control—in short, she had seduced him. And some part of her, she knew, wanted to do the same with this stalwart young Scotsman.

She could see the fine hairs on Ian's strong wrists, red-gold in the afternoon light, and she could sense the controlled passion in him, for his hand trembled slightly upon hers. She could feel her own body begin to tremble, and a kind of panic overwhelmed her. She must keep herself under control, she must!

Gently, she moved her hand out from under his, as if to arrange her skirts, pretending that she had not heard what he said. Her mind frantically searched for another subject, one less upsetting.

"I am curious about your Scotland," she said hurriedly, in a voice that sounded to her own ears false and too bright. "And I would find it interesting to hear how your family lives. Is it a large family? Do you have many brothers and sisters?"

Ian gave no sign that he understood what she was doing, and why, yet she felt that he understood very well. It was one of the disconcerting things about him—his ability to make her feel that he could always see and understand her reasons for what she did.

He did not attempt to take her hand again, but he was still sitting very close to her. "There are three of us now, besides my father; myself and my two sisters, Margaret and Elizabeth. Margaret is several years older than I, and Elizabeth is the youngest, about your age, Michele. We had an older brother, Douglas, but he was killed three years ago."

Michele, touched by the sorrow in his voice, forgot her own emotions for the moment, and put her hand upon his. "Ian, I am so sorry. I have never had a brother, or a sister either, but I can imagine how it would be to lose one. Were you very close?"

Ian nodded. "Very close. He was ten years older than I, but I worshipped him. He taught me so much. He was a fine man, aye. We all still bear the scars of his death. It was all the more tragic for being so unnecessary."

"How did he die?" Michele said in a soft voice.

"In a shameful way," said Ian, his voice burning with bitterness. "He had gone to visit a good friend, Robert Campbell of Glencoe. The MacLevens and the Campbells have been friends for over a hundred years, and have been enemies of the MacDonells for just as long, ever since the MacDonells massacred the Campbells at Glencoe Pass. Aye, it was a shameful thing, and it is a bitter thought for us to bear that it was the MacDonells who slew Douglas and Robert Campbell. They ambushed the two of them while they were out fishing. They bore no arms. They were just out for a pleasant afternoon, two young men cut down in their prime.

"It was my father who suffered the most. Douglas was his eldest, you see, the heir. Oh, he got revenge, did my father. He personally slew at least three of the MacDonells, but although their deaths may have upheld his honor, they did not bring Douglas back to us."

Michele shuddered to hear this man speak so coldly and casually of fighting and violent death. "Does this sort of thing happen often in your country? It seems so . . . so bloody!"

He looked at her with eyes from which all the warmth had fled. "I am afraid so, Michele. Although we generally get along together most of the time, there are always clans who are traditional enemies. Or it might come about from present hurts or insults inflicted. I see that this idea disturbs you, and I suppose it does seem strange to someone who is not familiar with our ways. I am so accustomed to it, that I do not think it unusual. It is just one of the facts of our lives in Scotland."

Michele shuddered again. Having changed the subject once, she now wished to do so again. "Come," she said finally. "You promised to show me the rest of the grounds."

Ian arose, and helped her to her feet. "Aye, Michele. It is too lovely a day to spend it speaking of war and death. If we go this way," he motioned, "we can see the Grand Parterre. King Louis' father, Louis the XIV, had it redone by LeNotre. There is a particularly fine fountain there with a bronze sculpture of the Tiber. You can also get an excellent view of the golden gate, and the outside of the grand ballroom."

The remainder of the afternoon went all too quickly, and by the time they had visited the Grand Parterre and the fine tree garden, where Michele saw the legendary Fontaine-Belle-Eau, from which the chateau drew its name, and a rustic grotto supported by colossal caryatids sculptured in stone; Michele, despite her excellent physical condition, felt as if her feet would fall off soon.

"We must have walked miles," she said, as they approached the chateau again.

Ian looked at her in chagrin. "I'm sorry, lass. I didn't think. I am so used to walking miles over the moors at home that I didn't notice how far we'd come. I didn't mean to overtire you."

Michele smiled. "It wasn't the distance, really, but my shoes. I'm afraid that I chose for fashion rather than comfort today, and I must confess that this attire is ill-suited for walking."

He looked down at the dainty slipper that she extended, and her hooped, panniered skirts. "It is very fetching," he said with a laugh, "but I can see that it is not very practical. I imagine that men would not be able to walk long distances, either, in such shoes. They look painful!"

Michele began to laugh, and could not stop, for she was envisioning Ian in a woman's dress, and the image was extremely comical. He stared at her quizzically, and she could only point at him, and continue laughing helplessly; and he, finally understanding, began to laugh as well.

As they stood there, helpless victims of their own mirth, Michele saw Louis and Cybella coming toward them down the path.

Cybella, in sympathy with their mood, began to laugh with them, but Louis' face remained deadly serious; and even in her undone state, Michele noticed this fact, for such seriousness was not at all like him.

"Well, there you are," Louis said somewhat crossly. "We've been looking everywhere for you."

Michele finally managed to control her laughter. "I'm sorry, Louis, but I have been walking with my old friend, Ian MacLeven. Ian, these are members of the dance troupe, Louis and Cybella." She looked at Louis. "Why were you looking for me?"

Louis' gaze went from Michele's face to Ian's. "Do friends need to have a reason to seek out one another? We wanted you to accompany us as we toured the chateau."

His glance, now settled on Ian, was somewhat accusing, and Michele felt some annoyance. Louis was her friend, true, but did he think that she must account to him for what she did, and where she went?

Still, in the face of his obvious disappointment, she found herself apologizing against her will. "I'm sorry, Louis, but I haven't seen Lord MacLeven in some time, and I wished to spend some time with him. I can always see the inside of the chateau tomorrow."

Louis bit his lip. "We also wished to tell you that the king has arranged a gala for this evening. There will be dancing, and wine, and a repast, and we are to be his guests of honor."

Michele, trying to improve Louis' mood, smiled sweetly at him. "That sounds very pleasant." She turned her glance to Ian. "If we are going to be entertained this evening, I had best get out of these shoes, and rest a bit before the festivities. I thank you for your company, Lord MacLeven. It was nice seeing you again."

Ian looked at her, than at Louis and Cybella. Michele could tell that he wished to say something more to her, but hesitated to do so in front of the other two.

Cybella, reading the situation, took Louis by the arm. "Come, Louis, you and I should take a bit of rest, also."

Louis looked again from Ian to Michele, and after a moment's hesitation, he allowed Cybella to lead him away.

Ian watched his retreating back with an odd look on his face, then slowly turned to Michele. "That is the young lad who danced the role of the Beast, is it not?"

Michele stared at him curiously. "Why, yes, he is. Why do you ask?"

Ian took her arm, and they began to walk slowly to the chateau. "He is in love with you, you know."

Michele stopped dead still, and stared into his face incredulously. "What are you saying, Ian? He is my friend, that is all."

Ian smiled tightly. "Perhaps that is all he is to you, a friend, aye, but I would be willing to wager that you mean a great deal more to him than that."

Michele felt her face flame, and her first inclination was to stoutly deny such an outrageous statement; but as she thought over Louis' reaction to Ian last night, coupled with his attitude just now, she was not so sure. Was Ian right? And how should she reply?

She finally decided that the light approach would be best. If she made too much of it, it would only add credence to Ian's theory; so she smiled slightly, and said, "I am sure you are mistaken, Ian, but at any rate we do not have time to discuss it now. I really need time to prepare for this evening, and I'm sure you do as well."

Ian put his fingers under her chin, and looked deep into her eyes. "Will I see you tomorrow? Will you permit me to show you the interior of the chateau? I warn you, I will be desolate if you do not!"

Michele hesitated for a moment, thinking of Louis. No doubt he would be upset if she did not spend some time with him and her other friends; but then, she thought, she saw them almost every day in Paris, where they were constantly together. Surely they could spare her for the short time they were at Fontainebleau.

"I will be most pleased to have your company," she said, and was surprised at the pleasure this decision brought to her.

Chapter Sixteen

THE grand ballroom was golden with light shed by the many gilt candelabra which hung from the arches of the consoles, lining both sides of the long, hall-like room. Each candelabrum held dozens of white candles.

Michele paused at the entrance to the great room, feeling a nervous flutter in her stomach; and Andre, who held her arm, looked down at her in concern.

"What is it, *chérie*? Are you nervous?"

She swallowed and nodded, all at once realizing that tonight she would really be mingling with the members of the royal court, and the thought was somewhat unnerving. "Very nervous, but I will be fine," she said, squeezing his arm. "Just let us stand here and watch for a few minutes."

Andre chuckled. "Before we plunge in? An excellent idea." He patted her hand.

Michele fixed her gaze on the elaborately dressed dancers, moving with studied grace in the pattern of a quadrille, which she recognized as "The Feast of Paphos." The light of the candles caught and glittered on the fine fabrics and jewels of the dancers. It was a sight that Michele knew she would never forget. Nowhere in the world, she thought in awe, could wealth be more lavishly displayed.

"Come," said Andre, as the dance finished, and another began. "It is time to join them, my pet. They are playing 'The All Too Brief,' and that is one of my favorites."

Michele, still bemused by the scene around her, allowed Andre to lead her out onto the floor; but as they danced, her eyes were busy. She saw the king, dancing with a woman who was not Madame de Mailly, but who resembled her a great deal, and was, if possible, even larger, and less attractive.

"Who is that woman dancing with the king?" she whispered in Andre's ear.

He followed the direction of her gaze. "That is Madame de Vintimille, Madame de Mailly's sister."

"At least he's keeping it in the family," she murmured wickedly.

Andre stared at her for a moment, then burst into laughter.

A few minutes later Michele saw Louis, dancing with an overpainted woman in a gold gown and wearing a heavy diamond necklace; and then Ian, dancing with an attractive young woman in bright pink.

And then the dance was ended, and there was a general milling about, as dancers either returned to the sidelines, or changed partners; and Michele suddenly found herself looking up into the smiling countenance of King Louis.

Michele's heart jumped in her chest like a frightened rabbit as a surge of panic struck her. She was face to face with the king of France, and by all indications, he was going to ask her to be his dancing partner!

She shot Andre a pleading look, and he gave her a faint smile and a shrug, as if to tell her that for the moment she was on her own—there was nothing he could do to help her.

Even though she was flustered, Michele still retained enough of her wits to make good use of this opportunity to observe His Majesty at close range. As she had noticed from a distance, his face tended to be pretty, rather than handsome, a fact that was only enhanced by the painter's art. His eyes, large and dark, were beautiful, and his features fine and even.

His dissipations were expressed by a slight plumpness of the face, a puffiness around the eyes, and the small, cupid's bow mouth, which showed signs of petulance and self-indulgence. He appeared to be in his late twenties, and Michele could not help but think of what she had been told about his siring ten children; but then she recalled that she had also been told that he had married at fifteen.

He was attired in a suit of gold cloth that outshone the suits of any of his guests. The skirts of the vest and coat were quite full, and his white silk hose showed off his legs to great advantage. His buckled shoes matched his suit, and the buckles were gold, encrusted with jewels, and the heels were quite high. His shirt was white, of the finest silk, and generously ruffled at throat and cuff. The whole ensemble was topped off by a magnificently curled wig, powdered to perfect whiteness.

The king smiled, obviously amused by the effect his immediate presence was having upon Michele.

"I should be delighted," he said in a soft voice, "if mademoiselle would consent to be my partner for the next quadrille."

Michele, feeling as if her tongue was glued to the floor of her mouth, and forgetting everything that Andre had ever told her about how to behave in the presence of the king, finally managed a deep curtsy, and got her voice working long enough to say, "I should be extremely honored, sire."

The king tendered Andre a slight, imperial nod, and presented his arm for Michele's hand.

As he did so, the orchestra, on its platform, struck up the music and the king moved, with Michele's hand upon his arm, into the patterns of the dance.

This time Michele's gaze was not on the other dancers, she was far too intimidated by the man at her side. She did notice that the king moved gracefully and well, and that he often glanced at her in appreciation. This, of course, only made her all the more nervous, for it brought to mind what she had been told about his behavior with women. What would she do if he approached her in the same fashion? It would not do to insult a king, yet she certainly would not submit to him, no matter that he was the king of France.

It seemed to Michele that the dance went on forever, and several times she wondered if she could manage to maintain her aplomb until it ended; but at last the music stopped, and the king escorted her toward the sidelines, where Andre was still standing, speaking as they went, "You dance most gracefully, Mademoiselle Verner, although that is to be expected by a professional of your caliber." As he talked, his dark eyes roamed appreciatively over her body and face, until her face grew hot.

"I should like to dance with you again, before the evening is over," he added, as they approached the spot where Andre was waiting. "But first I must pay my respects to the rest of my guests."

Michele, at a loss as to what to say, could only nod, and again made a deep curtsy, from which she would have had trouble rising if Andre had not taken her by the elbow.

When the king was out of hearing, she said vehemently, "Oh, my lord! Andre, I thought I would die! I have never been so distraught, not even at my first appearance on stage!"

Andre laughed softly. "I know, it is passing strange that a mere man, because he is the king, can have that effect on one. But you carried it off well, my dear, at least you did not faint, as some would have done."

Michele, fan unfurled, fanned her fevered face furiously. "Well, I was afraid that I might. It was a wonderful occasion, I am sure, and certainly later I will enjoy being able to say that I danced with the king of France, but while it was happening, it was pure torture!"

"I should certainly not like to see you tortured, lass."

The voice belonged to Ian, and Michele turned to see him smiling gently at her.

She shook her head ruefully. "Well, if you were watching as I danced with His Majesty, you certainly saw it happening, nonetheless."

Ian chuckled. "Why, I have always heard it said that

Louis is an excellent dancer, light upon his feet, and the feet of his partner."

Michele folded her fan and tapped his wrist with it. "You know that is not what I meant, Ian. I was simply undone at the thought that it was the king of France with whom I was dancing."

Ian made a low bow. "Well, milady, if you think that you could put up with the presence of a mere mortal after having danced with His Royal Highness, may I request the pleasure of the next dance?"

Michele lowered her head, then lifted it, elegantly. "I suppose that I might find it in me to make that adjustment," she said with mock hauteur.

"Very well then, milady. Shall we step onto the floor?"

Andre watched them go with mixed feelings. They made a handsome couple; there seemed a balance somehow between them.

And Ian MacLeven certainly came from a good background. He was a noble, heir to lands and a fortune, and, as far as Andre could ascertain, of good temperament and morals. In fact, he was perfect, if Michele was looking for a husband; and she was certainly of an age that she would normally be doing so. However, she was a dancer, very much in love with her profession, and right now she was on the threshold of real fame and fortune in her own right.

And yet, Andre wanted what was best for Michele, and who was to say that she might not be happier married to a good man, than pursuing a career on the stage? The ballet demanded much, and often offered little more than a life of loneliness in return.

He wondered if Michele's own feelings toward the handsome Scotsman were as ambivalent as his own. He only wanted her to be happy. It was natural to want love; and she was of an age where her body's physical urges must already have begun to plague her. It was true that some dancers managed to have both careers *and* a family; yet it did not often work out if the spouse was not also involved in the arts. Ian MacLeven was a nobleman, and must, of necessity, reside in Scotland most of the time to manage his estate. Would he want a wife who was away from him a good part of the year? Andre thought not. He sighed. In the final reckoning, the decision would be Michele's. He could do little more than wait and watch, and try to give her wise counsel if she came to him for it.

He laughed wryly at himself. He was a fine one to counsel anyone about love, considering his own many failures in that particular facet of life.

Michele enjoyed dancing with Ian far more than she had with King Louis. She was relaxed, at ease, and Ian was a marvelous dancer.

When it was over, she felt a touch upon her arm, and turned to see Louis, resplendent in a suit of blue brocade, and almost unrecognizable under a powdered wig. He bowed extravagantly, with a flourish, and Michele could not help but smile, for she had never seen him so attired.

"Mademoiselle, may I have the honor?" His voice mocked the formality, and Michele experienced a surge of happiness. At least, he seemed to be his old self once more.

"I would be delighted, sir," she said, taking his arm, and smiling over at Ian, "although I am not sure that I know you. There is some resemblance to . . . But no, you cannot be him, he is a raggle-taggle young fellow, a dancer, not an elegant gentleman such as yourself."

"I would never even associate with a fellow such as that," said Louis. "The music is beginning. Shall we?"

With a sidelong glance at Ian, Michele took Louis' arm, and they moved out onto the floor.

Michele, happy to see Louis apparently over his bad humor, or whatever it was that had made him act so out of character last evening and earlier today, began to chatter, "Oh, Louis, hasn't it all been grand? Our performances went very well, and the king and his court seemed to really enjoy it. And I've seen Madame de Mailly! Shame upon you and the others for leading me on the way you did. I would never have believed it, a king having such an ugly mistress!

"And today I saw the grounds. They are so beautiful! It has been such an experience, and we still have another day here."

Louis was smiling, but it seemed to Michele that his smile had a bitter twist to it. "Is it Fontainebleau, the king and his court that please you so, Michele, or is it seeing your old friend, Lord MacLeven?"

She stared at him, dismayed by the bitterness in his voice, and she began to feel the faint stirring of her temper. "Louis, why do you make such a nasty remark? You've not been like yourself since dinner last night. I thought you were over whatever was bothering you. What *is* wrong with you?"

His smile was suddenly gone. "I might ask, what is wrong with you, Michele, that you do not have time for your real friends?"

She gave him a sharp look, trying to keep a part of her mind upon the steps of the dance. "Are you implying that you, Marie, and the others are my only true friends? Am I not allowed to have others? The fact of the matter is that I was friends with Ian MacLeven before I even met you!"

She did not feel it necessary to tell Louis that her shipboard friendship with Ian had ended unpleasantly, for it was none of his concern. He had no right to be displeased or angry because she had friends other than himself.

Could Ian be right? Were Louis' feelings for her more than just friendly? *Was* he in love with her? His present manner had the appearance of jealousy.

Suddenly, her anger drained out of her. If this was true, then she should not quarrel with him. She well remembered her own jealous feelings concerning Arnaut, and recalled the pain she had experienced. She was very fond of Louis, and certainly had no wish to cause him pain.

"Louis," she said gently, "I am quite fond of you, and do not wish to hurt you, or make you unhappy. You are my friend, and you have been a true one, but I have other friends also, and will sometimes wish to spend time with them. You must not be jealous! It does not become you."

At that moment the dance ended, and Louis began to propel her toward one of the consoles. Michele wondered where he was taking her.

When they arrived at the alcove formed by the huge pillar and its curved arch, she realized that they were fairly secluded from the rest of the crowd; and it was as she noticed this that Louis took her into his arms, pulled her to him, and pressed his mouth against hers.

The suddenness of it took her quite by surprise. His kiss was hard and demanding, pressing her own lips painfully against her teeth so that she made a small sound of complaint, causing him to lessen the pressure a little, but he did not remove his mouth from hers. In fact, he held his mouth on hers so long that she began to feel the stirring of panic. While it was true that she was fond of him and found him attractive, now that he held her so intimately, she knew that her feeling for him was like that of a sister, rather than a lover; and a great sorrow washed over her, for the hurt she would have to inflict upon him.

Pushing hard against his chest, she managed to pull her face away. His eyes, so close to her own, held an expression that she could not interpret.

"Louis, Louis," she said in a soft voice, feeling that she might weep.

He was still looking deep into her eyes, and his mouth twisted. "It's no use, is it." It was not a question. "You don't care for me in that way, do you? To you, I am just someone who amuses you. You do not see me as a man at all!"

She looked back at him sadly. "You *are* a man, Louis, and a wonderful man. The very best, but I do not love you in the way you mean, no, although you are as dear to me as the brother I never had."

"A brother!" He almost spat the words. He released her, and turned away.

She could not bear to see him go like this. "Louis, do

not blame me, or hate me. We have no control over the dictates of our hearts, none of us. You know this as well as I."

"I watched you with Deampierre," he said, "and I could see your infatuation, but I waited patiently, and it ran its course. Now there is this Scotsman. I do not think I want to wait again!"

Michele gave a sigh that came from her heart. "Louis, it has nothing to do with Ian. What I feel for you has only to do with yourself, and what I feel for you *is* love, but it is not romantic love."

"You have made that very clear!"

Turning away, Louis quickly disappeared into the crowd, leaving Michele feeling dismayed and drained. Suddenly, all the joy had gone out of the evening, and she stood there with tears of anger and sorrow in her eyes, wondering why and how life and its relationships always seemed to become so complicated.

The following day, as Ian had promised, he took Michele on a tour of the interior of the chateau, showing her one magnificent room after another, until her mind was reeling; yet she could not enjoy it as much as she might have, for her thoughts kept straying to Louis and what had transpired last evening.

It was when they were in the Gallery of Francis I that Ian turned to her, tilted her chin up with his forefinger, and asked her quietly, "What is amiss today, Michele? Is it something that I have done, or not done?"

She lowered her gaze. "Whatever do you mean? Nothing is wrong, nothing at all."

"Michele," he said softly. "It is not difficult to read your moods, your face is like a mirror. You have been so quiet today, and when I catch you unawares, you look so sad. Can't you tell me what is the matter?"

Slowly, she raised her eyes. His kindness made her ache to tell him, but she could not speak of such a matter to a man; and even if she could, she felt that doing so would be a betrayal of Louis in some way.

So she smiled, and looked into Ian's eyes, telling him as much of the truth as she felt she could. "I am a little depressed today, Ian, that is true, but I cannot discuss the reason with you. I can only say that it has nothing to do with you. You have done nothing to hurt or displease me. To the contrary, you have been very kind, and I have enjoyed your company, more than I can ever say."

He gave vent to an exaggerated sigh of relief. "Well, at least that takes a worry from my mind, and also leads to something else that I have been wanting to discuss with you. This evening you will be returning to Paris. I should like to know if you will allow me to visit you there?"

She looked at him in some surprise. "But I thought you said you were leaving very soon for Scotland? You told me you were anxious to return home."

His expression turned rather sheepish. "That is true, aye, I did say that. But I find now that I have some unfinished business to conclude in Paris, and that I will be there for at least a week or two, perhaps even more. It would please me very much if you would let me see you."

Michele was quite unprepared for the surge of pleasure that she felt at his words. As much as possible, she had avoided thinking about the fact that he would be returning to Scotland right away, and that she would not be seeing him again. His words were like a welcome reprieve.

Still, she felt wary about letting him see her feelings, so she simply nodded coolly. "Why, yes, Ian. I would be pleased to see you in Paris. I will tell Madame Dubois, and I am certain that she will wish to have you at one of her salons."

"And perhaps you will let me take you to the theater, and to supper?"

"Perhaps, although you must know that I will often be performing myself, and that I practice and rehearse a great portion of each day."

"But you will try to make time for me?" he pressed.

"I think that I can safely promise that," she said, not able to contain the smile that lifted the corners of her mouth.

"That is all a man could ask," he said gallantly, bowing over her hand; and his face mirrored the happiness which she tried to control, but could not prevent from bubbling inside.

Despite the thrill of the performance and the visit to Fontainebleau, within days of returning to Paris things had settled back into the routine with which Michele had grown so familiar. However, there were two factors that made things different for her; one was Louis, the other Ian.

Louis, to her dismay and consternation, continued to avoid her, and treat her with coldness. He ceased joining her and the others during the noon break, and instead went off on his own—where, no one seemed to know.

The third time this happened, Marie, who was the first to notice his absence, asked Michele where he was, and did she know the reason Louis was absent.

Michele, embarrassed because she could not tell Marie the real reason, simply shrugged, and lowered her gaze. "I don't know," she said—at least that much was true. "He disappeared the moment Monsieur Deampierre announced the break."

Café au Lait, reaching into Michele's basket, which she always made free to her friends, took out a piece of roast chicken. "He's been acting awfully odd since we returned from Fontainebleau. Something is troubling Louis, but he won't talk about it." He glanced at Michele. "You sure you know of nothing that could have happened there which would affect him this way?"

Guiltily, Michele shook her head, not meeting his gaze. "Perhaps it's something personal, something that he cannot discuss with us."

Café au Lait snorted. "That strikes me as most unlikely. Usually Louis will talk about anything. The problem often is to get him to shut up. It is all very strange."

Marie nodded, her face shadowed. "Yes, it is. I wish I knew what was bothering him. Perhaps we could help him. I miss him."

Michele, looking into the face of her friend, was struck by Marie's expression. Good heavens, she thought; how blind I have been, thinking only of myself! Marie cared for Louis in a way that she could not.

The thought made her very unhappy. Why was it that fate had arranged things so cruelly? Marie wanted Louis, but Louis wanted her, Michele; and she wanted . . .

Time to change the subject, she thought firmly, and quickly spoke before Marie could say more. "Have either of you noticed that Denise has been awfully quiet lately? Do you suppose she has decided to mend her ways?"

Marie shook her head. "People like Denise never change, Michele, no more than a leopard changes its spots. If she is quiet, it is because she is planning something. You can depend on that, just you wait and see."

Café au Lait, finished with the chicken, took some cheese from his own basket. "She is right, Michele. When Denise is quiet like this, is when she bears watching the most. She is still furious about your getting the role of the sister in *Beauty and the Beast*. It is my opinion that she is trying to think of some way of getting back at you. You must be careful. Anyway, I don't care to talk about Denise. The thought of her always spoils my appetite. I would much rather talk about your handsome Scotsman. A lord, no less! He is really too, too gorgeous!"

Michele felt her face flame. "He is simply an old friend," she said defensively. "I met him on the ship when we were coming to Paris."

Café au Lait smiled archly. "You can keep saying that, if you wish, but Marie and I watched you together, and the look upon his face told us that he wants to be a great deal more than just an old friend. Your own expression, by the way, was not one of casual friendship. You appeared to be quite taken with him."

Michele, desperately seeking a change of subject, jerked away her basket. "If you keep talking like that, I shall share no more food with you. Besides, how can I trust the judgment of anyone who would tell me that the king's mistress was beautiful?"

"I never said that!" Café au Lait said in outrage. "The woman is a pig, a baptismal font in which every passerby has the right to clean the tips of his fingers."

Then he caught her sly expression, and laughed at himself. "Ah, our innocent Michele is learning to fool as well as to be fooled. I shall have to watch myself. Yes, it was a neat device to turn the conversation away from your handsome Scotsman. A neat device indeed!"

Michele smiled and turned her attention to her basket, wishing that it were as easy to turn her own thoughts away from Ian; since their return to Paris, he had been much on her mind. He had already called upon her at Madame Dubois', and had taken her once to supper and the theater. Each time she saw him, her feeling for him grew, and this fact was both a matter of concern and delight to her; for although she thoroughly enjoyed his company, and the time they shared together, his continued presence in Paris was distracting her from her work, and kept her off-balance just at a time when she needed to focus all of her faculties upon her dancing.

Deampierre was preparing another ballet in addition to *Beauty and the Beast*, for the winter season, and the rumor was that there were several very good principal roles, besides the leads. Everyone was naturally excited about this, and everyone was dancing their best, hoping that Arnaut Deampierre would choose them when the time came. Since dancing the role in *Beauty*, Michele dreaded going back to the corps de ballet; and she was hoping that she would again be picked for one of the featured parts; but she would have to work, and work hard. Deampierre would never choose her simply on her prior performance.

Also, every time they were together, Ian talked to her about Scotland and MacLeven Castle, telling her how handsome it was, and how beautiful the countryside was in the spring.

At first Michele thought that he was simply homesick for his own land, as she was sometimes for Virginia; but then he finally spoke of what was really on his mind. He asked her if she would come to visit him in the spring at MacLeven Castle.

Michele had to admit that the idea appealed to her. She was curious about Scotland; and she was drawn to Ian, but again, there was her dancing. Things were going so well for her now. If she continued to improve, she might soon be dancing leads. It was what she had trained for, longed for, and it was growing so near, so possible! How could she possibly leave at a time like this?

So she had tried to put him off, but he was very persistent about it. Thinking about it now, she sighed. At home, in Virginia, she was rarely ever required to make an important decision from one year to the next. Since she had arrived in France, her life had been nothing but one decision after another. She supposed that was what it meant being out in the real world. She could see now that Ian had been right when he had told her, on the ship, that she had been overprotected, and was inexperienced in the ways of the world. Well, she was certainly getting that experience now!

Marie broke into her thoughts. "Why the big sigh, Michele?"

Michele laughed wryly. "I was just thinking how complicated life can be at times. Ian keeps asking me to visit him in Scotland, in the spring, and I would love to go. Yet I don't see how I possibly can. It would mean leaving the company for at least a month or two, and I couldn't do that!"

Marie shrugged. "It would mean missing classes, yes, and some performances, but it wouldn't be all that impossible. Deampierre would probably let you go."

Michele shook her head dubiously. "I don't know if I could risk it. I might . . ."

"You might miss something, am I right?" Café au Lait's smile was white and wide. "You are frightened that a great role will come along, and it will go to someone else."

Michele flushed, and he laughed heartily. "Don't be so embarrassed, Michele. We all feel the same way, you can be sure. Dancing is a harsh mistress, or master, as the case may be. Sometimes I believe that we are all enchanted, under a magic spell that holds us in thrall. You remember the old fairy tale? The one about the girl and the enchanted slippers that made her dance without stopping until she died? Sometimes I think that story fits us very well. We all are given such slippers, invisible naturally, at birth, and we wear them all our lives."

Michele moved her shoulders in a nervous gesture. "You make it sound so . . . so grim!"

He shrugged. "I suppose any compulsion is grim, in a way. But enough of this philosophical chatter. Deampierre will be summoning us shortly, and before that happens, I must answer a call of nature."

Michele watched him leave, thinking of what he had said, finding his theory both fascinating and yet a little frightening.

Chapter Seventeen

HANNAH stood in the center of the cotton shed, turning all the way around. Her cotton was back! Her happiness was such that she was close to tears.

Wagons had begun pulling in shortly before the noon hour, and the drivers started to remove the cotton from their wagons, dumping it into the bins. The drivers were all black men, and they refused to answer her repeated questions: Who had employed them? Where had the cotton been? Who had stolen it? Who had told them to return it?

One man finally informed her: "We were told not to say a word, mistress. We were told we would be beaten sorely, that we would not be paid for our work, should we speak one word. Please do not ask us."

She softened at the look of fear he wore, and nodded slowly. After all, what did it matter? Her cotton was being returned to her, that was more important than anything else.

After the last wagon was unloaded, she watched them drive off. They were all in great haste to depart, even spurning her offer of food.

She had not heard a word from Court since he had left her yesterday, but she was confident that he was responsible for her cotton being returned. She was already very grateful that Court had come into her life, and now she was doubly grateful.

She decided to send John into Williamsburg this very

day with orders to contact all the cotton buyers, telling them that she had retrieved her cotton, and the auction would take place two days hence.

With this in mind she turned toward the house and froze dead still. Standing in the north entrance of the cotton shed was Nathaniel Bealls, his feet planted wide apart, the quirt swishing against his leg.

"What are you doing here, sir?"

He started toward her. "I have come for my pay." He stopped before her, his handsome face set in angry, sullen lines.

"Your pay?" Hannah laughed harshly. "You expect me to *pay* you after you stole my cotton?"

"You cannot prove that I stole anything of yours," he growled.

"Then why did you sneak away like a thief in the night?"

"None of that matters. You still owe me. You asked me to wait for my pay until after your crop was harvested. Well, it has been harvested. What happened after that is not my responsibility."

She stood firm. "Anything I may have owed you is canceled by what you did. Go to Jules Dade for your money."

"Dade refuses to pay me . . ." He broke off. "I have not worked all these months for naught, Mistress Verner. One way or another, you will pay me."

"If you don't leave at once, I shall call for someone to throw you off Malvern!"

"Who will you call, madam?" He sneered. "Your high and mighty niggers? They are all afraid of me. I saw to that. They dare not touch me."

"We shall see about that."

She started past him, and he seized her arm in a tight grip, pulling her against him. "Oh, yes, we shall indeed see," he said gloatingly. "If I cannot get my pay one way, I will get it another."

He had a sour smell about him, and his touch was

offensive to her. She tried to pull away, but could not. "What do you mean by that remark?"

"The day we were in your study . . ." He grinned lewdly. "It would be a most expensive tumble, in view of what you owe me, but I will settle for that if I must."

She gasped. "You wouldn't dare!" She motioned with her head. "There are people within hearing distance. I will scream." Belatedly, she remembered that John was not on Malvern at the moment; she had dispatched him on an errand to a neighboring plantation.

"Scream," Nathaniel said indifferently. Then he raised the quirt, his fingers still clamped around her wrist. "A touch of the quirt will bring you to heel. You'll be more than happy to cock your leg for me."

She began to struggle, and the quirt whistled down, across her shoulder just above the neckline of her dress. The pain was immediate and excruciating. She screamed shrilly, and then screamed again as the quirt struck another time.

The second blow drove her to her knees before him.

"Kneel, madam. I have always wanted to see you kneeling, proud bitch that you are."

This time the quirt lashed across her bowed back, cutting through the flimsy material of her dress, all the way to the flesh.

"Just tell me that you will submit, and I will cease. Then we may go inside, in the study where you have so often lain with your dandy man. You think I didn't know that he was tumbling you?"

Her anger blazed, and momentarily forgetting the pain, she glared up into his face. "You are a foul-tongued monster, sir! I will thank you not to . . ."

He broke in, "Still full of spirit, I see. Perhaps another few lashes will subdue you."

He raised the quirt, and a harsh voice lashed at him from behind. "You strike her again, Bealls, and you are a dead man."

Nathaniel froze, the quirt still raised over his head, and started to turn slowly. Hannah took advantage of his inattention to scramble back, and then to her feet. Court stood a few feet behind Nathaniel, a pistol aimed at the overseer.

A cry came from Hannah. "Court, darling!" She ran toward him.

Without taking his eyes from Nathaniel, Court motioned her to one side. "Stay out of the way, Hannah."

Hannah backed up against a nearby cotton bin, gaze darting from one man to the other.

Lowering the quirt, Nathaniel said sneeringly, "Well, Mistress Verner's dandy man."

"You are finished here, Bealls. I should shoot you like the cur you are for what you've done to Hannah."

Composed, Nathaniel flicked back the tails of his long coat. "I have no weapon on me, sir. You wouldn't shoot an unarmed man?"

"I should, for what you've done. But if you will turn around and take your leave this instant, I will let you live, perhaps to my everlasting regret."

Nathaniel did not move. "I demand the money due me."

"You will get nothing here, Bealls. Get your money from Jules Dade."

"He refuses to pay me."

"And so does Hannah, and I stand by her decision. Any debt owed to you is canceled by your behavior, not only for stealing her cotton, but for using your quirt on her. Now I'd advise you to go, sir, my patience is wearing thin." He brought the cocked pistol up to eye level. "While it is true that I would not shoot an unarmed man, were he a gentleman, you are far from a gentleman."

Finally, Nathaniel wavered before Court's unyielding stare. He flicked a glance of burning hatred at Hannah, then turned on his heel and strode out of the cotton shed. Now Hannah could see his big gray tethered at the end of the shed. She waited with bated breath until she saw him mount up and ride off at a gallop.

Court lowered the pistol, gently let the hammer down, and put it into his waistband. Hannah hurried to him, burying her face against his chest. Now that the tense scene was over, she began feeling the pain again, burning like fire across her shoulders and back. A sob shook her.

Court touched her back tenderly, exhaling a shocked breath at the sight of the ribboned dress on her back, and the seeping blood.

"That son of a bitch! I should have killed him! I didn't realize, I only saw him strike you once," he said in a voice taut with anger. Then he said gently, "Come, Hannah, let's go up to the house, and have those cuts tended to."

Leaning on his arm, Hannah let him help her into the house. Frightened faces peered out at them as the front door swung open, and Hannah knew that they had been aware of Nathaniel's presence. Apparently Nathaniel had been correct—they were terrified of him. She did not fault them for that; clearly she was about the only one on Malvern who did not know the overseer's true nature. Although John had watched Nathaniel closely and had not observed him abusing her people, he either must have abused them secretly, or there was something about him that hinted at how vile and vicious he was; and she had been too blind to see it.

Inside the house, Court handed her over to the house servants. "I'll wait in the parlor, my dear, and have a glass of sherry while they take care of you. Come to me when you are tended to."

Hannah's clothes were removed, her wounds washed tenderly, and she was eased into a hot bath. After she had soaked in hot water for awhile, which helped to ease the stinging of the cuts, she was helped out of the tub, her wounds treated with a cooling ointment; and a robe was wrapped around her.

Feeling considerably better, she went into the parlor to join Court.

He asked, "Feeling better?"

"Much." She smiled palely. "At least my wounds are better, but my injured pride still pains me."

He poured her a glass of sherry, and she sat down with a sigh. "I know I have you to thank, darling," she said, "for the return of my cotton. I assume that Dade was behind the theft?"

"He must have been. I told him to see that your cotton was returned by midday, or else. It was returned, was it not?"

She took a sip of the wine, her gaze on him. "Or else what, Court? It must have been pretty dire, whatever you threatened him with."

He looked at her, then away, and shifted uncomfortably on the divan. "I'd rather not say, Hannah. It's something you do not need to know, nor would you be better off for knowing. It's not a pretty tale."

Hannah was still curious, and would have pressed him on it; but in that moment he set his wine glass down, and turned to her, taking her into his arms. It crossed her mind that he was doing it purposely, to distract her thoughts from whatever was between him and Jules Dade.

Then his lips were on hers, as soft as a butterfly's wings, and she relaxed with a sigh. She would question him another time.

"I am sorry that Bealls hurt you, my dear. It's partly my fault, I sensed what he was. I should have chased him off long since."

"Hush, darling." She placed a finger across his lips. "It's my fault, you warned me, but I was too stubborn to listen. Now, let's talk of it no more."

She closed his mouth with hers, but there was nothing soft about her kiss—it was firm, demanding, afire with ardor.

After a moment he took his mouth away to say, "You know what this will lead to, Hannah. With those cuts on your back and shoulders, are you sure you want to . . ."

"I want to," she said fiercely. "I want to very much. But not here, not with the servants running all over the place."

She took him by the hand and led him out of the parlor. As he started on past the staircase, she tugged at his hand. "No, I want you to love me upstairs this time."

He cocked an eyebrow at her. "But you've always said you didn't want the household help to know."

"You think they don't already know? I was only fooling myself. Besides . . ." She feigned a pout. "I've been wounded, so I'm entitled to the comfort of my own bed."

In Court's arms, in her own bed, Hannah soon forgot the sting of the cuts, and lost herself in all-consuming passion.

Nathaniel Bealls rode the gray hard halfway to Williamsburg, until its hide was flecked with foam, and the animal's mighty chest labored like a bellows. His anger cooling a trifle, Nathaniel reined in by the side of the road. There was no need to kill the horse, the only thing of value he had left to him.

He had worked all summer for Hannah Verner, and he had nothing to show for it.

He had contrived to steal Hannah's cotton for Jules Dade, and just this morning, Dade had refused to pay him. Not meeting Nathaniel's gaze, Dade had said, "The cotton has to be returned, and therefore I cannot pay you a cent."

Nathaniel was incredulous. "It has to be returned! Are you daft, sir? After all the trouble I went to to steal it for you, now you're returning it, and I don't get paid for my services?"

"In having to return the cotton, I will receive no profit, so why should you? Our agreement was that we were to split the proceeds. Now there are no proceeds."

They were in the mean little room Dade used for an office, and as usual Nathaniel had to stand. Swollen with rage, nearly inarticulate from it, he strode back and forth, the few steps provided him, the quirt swishing against his leg.

"I left Malvern without even asking for my wages, knowing that would give me away. Now I will receive no money for nearly a year's labor!"

Leaning forward, hands under the desk, Dade smirked. "That, sir, is your problem. Mayhap the bitch of Malvern will pay you, being she is thought so honorable by all."

"She is more likely to have the constabulary on me,"

Nathaniel growled. He stopped before the desk. "You still have not told me why you had to send the cotton back. It was well hidden, no one could prove a thing."

"I had no choice in the matter." Dade's face wore a look of pain. "You think I wanted to?"

"But why?" Nathaniel pounded on the desk. "You owe me an explanation at least."

"I owe you nothing. It is a personal matter, and no affair of yours."

"I want my money, by God, and I intend to have it!" His fury overflowed, and he leaned toward Dade. Dropping the quirt onto the desk, he reached for the man's neck with both hands.

Dade pushed away from the desk, and his hands came up, holding a cocked pistol. "Back off, Bealls, or I'll blow a hole in you. I want you to turn and leave now, and don't come near me again. Do, and I'll kill you without compunction. Ah, yes!"

Nathaniel stood bent over, breathing heavily. After a moment he slowly straightened up, reached down for his quirt, and quickly left the room, and the house.

Now, astride his horse by the side of the road, he took a deep breath, trying to control his renewed rage. Dade had gulled him, but Nathaniel knew that he could do nothing about it. He had known that he would get no money from Hannah Verner, but he had thought he might get his pound of flesh from her; it would be little enough for all the time spent on Malvern. He would have had her, too, if not for Courtney Wayne!

The thought of Wayne caused him to straighten up in the saddle. He knew suddenly, as convinced as if Dade had told him in so many words, that Wayne was responsible for the cotton being returned. And Wayne would be coming along this very road soon; he never spent the night at Malvern.

For the first time Nathaniel looked about him. The road here dipped into a small glade. Trees and bushes grew thick and close on each side of the narrow coach road, some meeting overhead, forming a sort of tunnel.

He began to grin. Maybe he would not be able to recoup his money, but he could end Wayne's life. Nathaniel knew that he was finished in this area anyway. After killing Wayne, he would ride on, far away; even if he was suspected of killing the dandy, he would be long gone before any hue and cry was raised. Not only would killing Wayne be sweet revenge, it would be a blow struck at Hannah Verner! Nathaniel gloated to himself as he imagined Hannah prostrate with grief over the death of her dandy man.

He started the gray along the road toward the other side of the glade, where the road began to climb again. About halfway up the grade, he found a place where he could tuck the gray in out of sight from the road, between two beeches. The coach would have to slow along here, the horses laboring up the grade.

Dismounting, he got a short, cruel rein on the horse, and forced him back into the underbrush until the animal was not visible from the road. Then Nathaniel mounted again, taking his pistol from the saddlebags. If only he had thought to take it with him when he had approached Hannah, he could have shot Wayne then and there; but it had not once entered his mind that he would need the weapon. He primed it, loaded the pistol ball, and then settled down to wait, with the patience of a duck hunter in a blind.

He had a long wait, but his patience seemed endless, well worth it, in view of the revenge he would get before this day was over. The sun had set, and shadows were long on the road, before he heard the thunder of horses' hooves and the creaking of the coach coming from the direction of Malvern.

He pushed a branch aside to peer up the road, and saw that it was indeed the Wayne coach. As he had surmised, the coach began to slow as it hit the grade, in spite of the driver's shouts and the laying on of the whip.

Nathaniel waited until the coach horses were almost abreast of him before he sent the gray charging out of concealment. Pistol in his right hand, Nathaniel stood up in the stirrups, seized the driver by one arm, and yanked hard. The driver yelled and started to fall off the seat. Nathaniel struck him alongside the head with the pistol barrel, then let him fall to the ground. He had to let the gray run a few yards before he could rein him in enough to wheel the animal back toward the coach.

The coach had moved on, but the horses were slowing. Driverless, the coach labored to the top of the grade, and came to a full stop. Just as it stopped, Nathaniel reined in his horse on the left side of the coach, and slid to the ground. Crouching slightly, he grabbed the door handle and jerked the door open.

He shouted, "All right, Mr. Dandy Wayne, come out here! *I* have a pistol now!"

There was no sound from inside the coach. "Come out, I said! No need to cower inside like a frightened hare, I'm bound to kill you anyway. Face your fate like a man."

When there was still no answer, Nathaniel cautiously peered inside. His mouth fell open. The coach was empty!

Court had been dozing slightly when he heard a commotion outside the coach—first, a scuffling sound, and then a strangled yell from the driver.

Snapping fully awake, he drew the pistol from his belt. Through the lefthand window, he saw a big gray horse pounding past. He waited, poised with his hand on the latch of the righthand door. Then, just as the coach breasted the grade and came to a stop, he pressed down on the latch, and slipped quickly outside.

He hugged the side of the coach, waiting, as he heard the sound of the horse returning, and caught a second glimpse of a big gray—Nathaniel Bealls, of course. Silently, Court cursed himself for being stupid; he should have anticipated that Bealls might waylay him, and been prepared.

Then he heard Bealls shouting at him to come out of the coach. On tiptoe he moved around the back of the vehicle until he could see Bealls' back as he leaned into the coach. Court gripped the pistol in both hands and raised it to point at the other man's back. He was strongly tempted to shoot him down where he stood, but he could not bring himself to do it.

"Over here, Bealls," he said tersely, and cocked the pistol.

A startled grunt came from Bealls, and he whirled, bringing his own pistol around to bear. Just before he could properly aim, Court fired. The pistol ball sped true to its target, and Bealls went reeling back, his own pistol going off, the ball whistling harmlessly over Court's head.

The overseer's horse, startled by the pistol shots, bolted up the road. Court walked over to where Bealls lay. He was on his back, his eyes staring emptily; the pistol ball had found his heart.

Court turned to look back down the grade. His driver was trying to get to his feet. Ramming the pistol into his belt, Court hastened to help him. Blood was streaming down the side of his head.

Court asked, "Are you all right, Lucas?"

"I . . . I think so," Lucas said dazedly. He felt the side of his head, and stared with widening eyes at the blood on his fingers.

Court examined the wound, then gave a sigh of relief. "It's only a cut, Lucas. You'll have a nasty lump there for a few days, but you'll be fine." He clapped the black man on the shoulder.

Lucas was staring past him at the prone figure of Nathaniel Bealls. "What was he about, Master Wayne?"

"A highwayman, what else?" Court said brusquely. "At least that's what we will tell the constable in Williamsburg. Come along, you ride in the coach. I'll drive the rest of the way. Help me get the body into the coach. You'll have to ride in with him, Lucas. I'm sorry about that, but there's no help for it. We can't leave him out here, as much as I'd like to."

Hannah's cotton auction was highly successful. She received enough from the proceeds to pay her notes to Dade and to Court, and see her through until the next crop harvest in fine style. She debated with herself for a little, but finally decided to send John to Dade with the money to pay the moneylender. As much as she would have liked to see Dade's face when she paid him, she did not trust herself. She hated the man so much for his perfidy, that she felt nauseated just thinking about confronting him.

She was expecting Court on the day she sent John into town with the money for Dade. Shortly before Court was due to arrive, the post rider came by Malvern with an envelope for her.

The only address on the envelope was: Hannah Verner, Malvern, with no indication of the sender.

With some trepidation Hannah opened the envelope. Inside was a single sheet of paper, which she began to read:

"Mistress Verner: In the interest of your own future welfare, it behooves me to warn you about one of your acquaintances, one Courtney Wayne. Beware of this man, madam! He is not at all what he seems. He is a scoundrel and a blackguard of the vilest sort.

"Be it even so that he professes to be an upstanding citizen of the community, he was once one of Blackbeard's pirate crew, a minion of Edward Teach, the infamous pirate who ravaged and pillaged not only poor, hapless vessels at sea, but also the area along the York and the James Rivers, and the town of Williamsburg.

"Mistress Verner, be it also known that this man Wayne is a murderer. He killed your husband. With murder in his heart, he waylaid Michael Verner on the Williamsburg road and slew him.

"Yrs, in friendship, a concerned neighbor."

Hannah could only gape in disbelief at the import of the letter. She read it again to make sure she had read it aright. The same damning words were there.

Her first coherent thought was to burn the letter and not even mention it to Court. It had to be a calumny, a defamation of character most outrageous. Then caution stayed her hand, as she remembered bits of gossip heard here and there, about Court's past. No one seemed to know about his origins; the only thing known about him for sure was that he was wealthy, but none knew where the money came from. There had been rumors that he *had* once been a pirate, one of Blackbeard's men; another story she remembered was that his wealth came from loot garnered from pirate expeditions.

At the time she had heard these rumors she had paid them little heed, knowing Court only slightly. There had been a time—when he had written her the note demanding payment of Michael's loan—that she had been so incensed with him that she had been prepared to believe the stories.

Then, as she got to know and love him, she put the tales down to malicious gossip, nothing more. She had rarely ever questioned him; but she realized now that he had managed to evade even those few she had asked. And how had he managed to coerce Dade into returning her cotton? She was grateful, of course, yet it was an unexplained mystery.

She remembered what Michael had told her many years ago. While she, Hannah, had been living on Malvern as Malcolm Verner's young wife, Michael had been a spy in the camp of Edward Teach, and it had been with Michael's assistance that Blackbeard had been made to pay for his crimes. Many had been the horror tales Michael had told her about the terrible, almost unbelievable atrocities the pirate and his men had committed. She had grown to hate Blackbeard and all he stood for; so how could she love a man who had once been one of his perfidious crew?

She forced herself to read the last paragraph yet a third time. She had shied away from that, but there it was—the damning accusation. Court had killed Michael? She did not want to believe it; it was simply not possible!

Dazedly, she sank down into the wicker chair nearby.

She was still sitting in the chair, the letter dangling from her hand, as Court's coach drove up. She was a little surprised to see him driving the coach himself.

She got to her feet as he came up the steps. "Why are you driving, Court, instead of Lucas?"

"We had a . . . a little accident on the way home the other day."

"An accident?" she said sharply. "What kind of an accident?"

He hesitated briefly, then shrugged. "We encountered Nathaniel Bealls. He clubbed Lucas with his pistol. Lucas is all right, but I told him to take it easy for a few days. He got a nasty bump on his head."

"And Nathaniel?"

"Bealls is dead," he said flatly. "He waylaid me with the intent to kill me, but I got in the first shot. I told the constable in Williamsburg that he tried to rob us. Lucas backed me up, not really knowing otherwise, and I would appreciate it if you would not enlighten anyone, either. It's much simpler this way."

Before she could say anything else, he moved toward her, clearly with the intention of taking her into his arms. She forestalled him by holding the letter out. "This came by post today."

He looked at her keenly, then down at the letter. He took it, almost reluctantly, it seemed to Hannah. She watched his face as he read it, watched it turn hard and cold. When he finally glanced up at her, his eyes were like ice, and there seemed to be an air of violence about him. He motioned with the letter. "What am I to say to this?"

"Just tell me whether or not it's true."

He seemed remote, distant. "Do you need to ask?"

"Yes! I don't think it's too much to ask," she said a little wildly. "I think I'm entitled to an answer, Court."

"Considering what we have been to each other, it seems to me you should take me on faith."

"On faith? But why should you refuse to answer?"

"Because you have no right to ask it of me," he said tightly. He was angry now; Hannah knew the signs very well by this time.

"I have every right. I know nothing about your past. Every time I ask a question you usually evade it."

"My past has nothing to do with what we are to each other now. I've asked you nothing about yours."

"But I've told you everything, mostly everything. Anything else, all you have to do is ask."

"Hannah, I'd advise you not to push me."

"I want to know! Were you ever Blackbeard's man?" Her voice rose as her own temper blazed.

"And if I said yes?"

"Court . . ." She stared at him in shock. "Michael was once the governor's spy in Blackbeard's crew. He told me about all the atrocities that vicious pirate and his men committed. And Michael came within an inch of losing his own life." She drew a ragged breath, and confronted the unthinkable. "And the other thing the letter charges, about you having killed Michael . . ."

He stared at her with burning eyes. "You would believe that I am such a man?"

"I don't want to, but I don't know what to believe!" she cried. "But I could never love a man who was a pirate, who killed my husband!"

"Then there's nothing more to say, is there? Except that you disappoint me, Hannah."

Without another word he turned on his heel and strode down the steps and toward the coach.

She stood without moving. She could not believe that he was just walking away from her like this! As he reached the coach and started to climb up onto the driver's seat, all the while not looking back, she broke free of her inertia and started down the steps.

"Court, Court! Wait, you can't leave like this!"

He gave no sign that he heard her. Picking up the reins, he flicked them, calling out to the team in a snarling voice. The horses strained into the harness, and then the coach was moving.

Hannah ran a few steps after it, still calling. Finally her steps slowed, and she stopped.

"Damn, damn!" she said aloud, kicking the dirt furiously with her toe.

She had handled it all wrong, she realized that now. She should have remembered that scratchy pride of his; and she should have gone about it another way, or burned the letter without his ever knowing about it. Yet she had a right to know!

"Damn you, Courtney Wayne!"

It would be all right, she was confident; he would come back to her once his fury had subsided.

She waited impatiently for three days, but there was no word from Court. On the fourth day, she told John to hitch up the coach for the trip into Williamsburg.

The house where Court lived had a forlorn, almost deserted look, and Hannah's heart sank as she stared at it. Refusing to consider the unthinkable, she hurried up the steps and pounded on the door.

To her surprise the door was opened almost immediately, and her hopes soared.

A sour-faced, bony woman, wearing an apron and a dust scarf around her head, peered out at her. "Yes?"

"I'm here to see Courtney Wayne," Hannah said brightly.

"Well, he ain't here." The woman started to close the door.

"Wait!" Hannah caught the door just in time, and pushed it half open. "When will he be back? I can wait for him . . ." Her voice died as she looked past the woman, and saw objects piled haphazardly on the floor. What furniture she could see was shrouded with cloths.

"You wait, it'll be a long one, I'm thinking," the woman said with a harsh laugh. "Master Wayne is long gone. He left yesterday."

"Left? Left for where?"

"He didn't bother telling me. He just hired me, payment in advance, to pack up his things and store them, and put dust cloths on the furniture."

"But he must have told you where he was going!" Hannah said desperately.

"I asked, but he told me he didn't want a soul to know where he was going, and that he would be gone a long time."

"Oh," Hannah said faintly. Then she said hurriedly, "Maybe he left a message for me? I'm Hannah Verner."

The dour face brightened a trifle. "Yea, that he did, Mistress Verner. He said you'd likely come looking for him. A minute, and I'll fetch it."

She was gone for a few minutes before she came back with an envelope in her hand. She gave it to Hannah, and then closed the door firmly in her face.

Hands trembling so badly they would hardly function, Hannah tore open the envelope, praying that it would be a message from Court informing her as to where he had gone.

But inside was the note of indebtedness that Michael had given to Court in exchange for the loan, and written across it in Court's sprawling hand were the words: "Paid in full."

Hannah's hands sank down to her sides, and she stared straight ahead without seeing a thing. She had never felt so desolate in her life, not even after Michael's death. That, at least, had been none of her doing, but this time she had been instrumental in driving Court away.

She turned away from the house and walked toward the coach. As John held the door open for her, his expression was sympathetic.

"He's gone, John. Court is gone."

He nodded. "I am sorry, mistress."

Her gaze sharpened. "You knew?"

"Yes, I heard the rumor that Master Wayne had left Williamsburg for . . ." He broke off, then added quickly, "But I am certain that he will return."

Hannah knew better. Court was gone, gone for good. She rallied herself, and said determinedly, "Drive me to the house of Jules Dade."

John showed dismay. "Not to that house, mistress! He is one sorry white man, if you will excuse me. Your business with him is concluded."

"Not quite," she said. "Just drive me, John, and do not argue. I am not in the mood to brook dissent."

A short time later she was knocking on Dade's door. John stood by the open door of the coach, arms folded, scowling in disapproval. He had wanted to accompany her inside, but she would not allow it. As the door opened, Hannah braced herself to face the man she hated so much.

Dade frowned at her in astonishment, then began to smile. "Well, Mistress Verner! This is a pleasant surprise. I thought our business was concluded."

Hannah gave him the same answer she had given John. "Not quite, sir."

He made an awkward bow and opened the door. "Then please come into my humble abode."

Inside, he closed the door and turned to her, still smiling slyly. The brown man was clearly pleased about something, and Hannah knew it was not her presence. His eyes glinted with some secret knowledge, and all at once she knew, knew what she should have realized all along—Jules Dade had written the letter. Who else would be so vicious? But how could she prove it?

Dade was saying, "To what do I owe the pleasure, madam?"

She said steadily, "Could we go into your office?"

"Ah, yes. After you, Mistress Verner."

He made another mocking bow, and she started toward the room he used for an office. Hands hidden from him, Hannah reached into her reticule, her fingers closing around the anonymous letter. For some reason she could not fathom, she had not destroyed it; and now she was glad she had not.

In the office she headed directly for his desk. On the untidy desk were a number of papers. Her gaze quickly ran over them; seeing one covered with handwriting, she scooped it up, and had it hidden in the folds of her cape before he went around behind the desk.

Dade sat down and looked at her expectantly. "Now, what may I do for you, madam?"

Hannah handed him the anonymous letter. "Would you have any idea who penned this?"

Dade took it gingerly, glanced at it briefly, then looked up at her with a smirk. "So the truth is out at last about Master Courtney Wayne!"

"You didn't answer the question, sir. Did you write it?"

Dade assumed a look of outrage. "Most certainly not! Why should I do such a thing?"

He tossed the letter onto the desk, and Hannah snatched it up. With the letter in one hand, and the paper from Dade's desk in the other, she held them side by side. The one from the desk had Dade's signature on the bottom. She quickly compared the handwriting on both, and went weak with relief. Her surmise had been correct!

She stared down into his face. "Then perhaps you can explain why the handwriting on this," she waved the paper she had picked up from his desk, "is identical to that of the letter? This one was signed by you, sir. Evidently, you were too cowardly to attach your name to the letter defaming Court."

His face went mottled with rage, but after a moment he leaned back, and sneered at her. "Granted that I wrote the letter, madam, it is no crime to write a letter, especially when every word of it is the Lord's truth."

"How can you be so sure of that?"

That maddening sneer still lingered on his face. "I have my sources."

"The only way you could know that Court was one of Blackbeard's crew is that you were Blackbeard's man as well." A sense of elation filled her as she saw the blood drain from his face. She was right! "But Court never was. I know that now, even if I did not before. In that filthy letter you wrote, you just turned it around, accusing him of something you had done. And if that is true, it also follows that you killed Michael. You murdered my husband!"

Dade shot to his feet. He whispered, "You're mad, coming in here accusing me like this!"

"You killed him, I am convinced of it," she said

relentlessly. "I don't know the reason, but I know that you did."

He was silent, staring at her with murderous eyes.

Hannah turned quickly and started for the door. She heard his footsteps come around the desk, but she willed herself not to turn around. Suddenly, she was very frightened, realizing that John had been right—she should not have come in here alone.

"You have no proof," Dade said from behind her.

"I will find proof. If not, I'll shout your guilt from the housetops. You shall be forced to leave in disgrace." She was just two steps from the door.

She felt rather than heard him rush at her. Just as she reached for the door handle, Dade had her in his grasp. One arm went around her neck, the other around her waist. The arm around her neck forced her head back, shutting off her breathing. She was amazed at the strength he possessed.

As he increased the pressure on her throat, Dade said in her ear, "Yes, I killed your damned husband! He had talked to me of a loan, but before we could complete the transaction, Wayne talked against me, loaning him the money himself. Courtney Wayne!" His voice began to rise. "He has hounded me for years, thwarting me at every turn. I accosted your fine husband on the Williamsburg road, and demanded that he honor his commitment to me. He said he had made no such commitment, and threatened to tell one and all that I had been one of Teach's crew. So I killed him. It's people like your husband who have stood in my way for so long. All I wanted was respectability, and Malvern would have given me that."

His voice took on a self-pitying whine. "Is that too much to ask? Yes, people like you, Mistress Verner, people of the gentry have always balked me." His arms tightened even more, and he began to haul her back toward his desk. "But no more, no more. You do not leave this room alive. Perhaps I shall never have Malvern, but neither shall you!"

Spots danced before Hannah's eyes, and her lungs burned for lack of air. She knew that she would be unconscious in another few moments; but she refused to let this monster do her in. He had killed Michael, and had been the cause of Court leaving her.

She gathered her fading resources; and doubling up her one free arm, she drove her elbow into his stomach, just below the rib cage. It was a weak blow; yet it was enough to drive the breath from him, and caused him to loosen his grip slightly around her throat. Hannah drew in a breath of sweet air, and then screamed as loudly as she could.

Dade uttered a foul oath, and again tightened his grip upon her. This time he locked the fingers of the one hand around his other wrist, and applied brutal pressure, muttering curses all the while.

Hannah tried to struggle, but she was too weak to have any effect. She was about to lose consciousness, when there was a splintering crash; and the door burst inward. John stood there for a moment, taking it all in. Dade again involuntarily loosened his grip, and backed up a few steps. John began to advance toward them.

"Stay back, you black bastard!" Dade yelled. "Don't you dare lay a finger on me, or I'll horsewhip you!"

John had reached them now. He fastened his hands around Dade's arm, and broke the man's grip. Hannah swayed and would have fallen, but John took her gently by the arms and sat her on the desk, his gaze never leaving Dade, who suddenly broke for the door.

John caught him halfway there. From behind he wrapped both hands around Dade's neck, his powerful hands beginning to squeeze. A strangled shout came from Dade. Slowly, John raised him almost a foot off the floor, his hands tightening like a vise. Dade struggled desperately, arms flailing the air, heels drumming against John's legs. John ignored it all, and squeezed.

On the desk Hannah had been breathing in ragged, frantic gulps. Gradually, she began to realize what was happening. She gasped out, "No, John, no . . ."

The big man did not heed her. Dade's face was slowly turning purple, and Hannah knew that he would be dead in another minute or so. She pushed herself away from the desk, and stumbled to the interlocked pair. She clawed ineffectually at John's hands. "No, John, don't kill him."

Without loosening his grip, John turned a dazed stare on her. "He is an evil man, mistress, one of the devil's own. He sold my people into slavery. He should not live."

"That is true, he should die. But not at your hands, John." Her voice gathered strength. "This way you will be in trouble, John, a Negro killing a white man for whatever reason. Let him live for now. He has just confessed to me that he killed Michael. I shall see him hanged for that, if it is the last thing I ever do!"

Chapter Eighteen

WINTER arrived in Paris full of storm and bluster. The practice hall, despite the steady fire in the huge German stove, was drafty and chilly; and the dancers, muffled in woolens, looked, Michele thought, like dancing bears.

Deampierre had announced the name of the new ballet—*The Three Sisters*—this time from an idea of his own conceiving. The music was being composed by a young composer Deampierre had discovered the previous year, an Italian named Giovanni Bartolo.

The story line centered on the three sisters of the title, who lived in an isolated cottage in a magic wood with their brother. The only other person on the property was a hunchbacked gardener, who kept the grounds in order.

Michele read the script with great interest.

In the story the elder two sisters, Lily and Rose, were vain, lazy, and selfish; and made the youngest sister, Violet, do all of the housework and cooking, at the same time managing to convince their brother that it was they who did all the work. They also told the brother lies about Violet; that she was lazy and insolent; and that she said disrespectful things about them, so that he was always angry with the youngest girl, which she could never understand, for she worked very hard indeed.

Her brother's attitude toward her, and her sisters' cruelty, made life very hard for Violet; but because she was a good girl, and sweet-natured, she tried always to see the best side of things, and would go singing about her work, looking for the beauty and good in life. She was kind to the hunchback, whom her sisters mistreated as badly as they did her; and he was the only person who was kind to her in return.

Her sisters, angry because whatever they did to her Violet always remained cheerful, hated her more and more, for her goodness seemed a reproach to them, and together they plotted constantly for ways to make life more miserable for their sister.

One day when the two sisters were absent, shopping in the village, Violet sat under her favorite tree, a slender willow, and a small redbird appeared on the branch overhead, and fixed its small, bright eyes upon her. Violet gazed up at the bird, waiting for it to sing; but instead, the bird spoke to her in a human voice, saying, "Violet, I have come to bring you a gift from the prince of the wood."

Violet cried out in astonishment. "But how is it you speak, little bird? And how is it you know my name?"

"That is not important," said the bird. "What is important is that I come from the prince of the wood, and that I bring you a gift. He has taken note of you, and has seen that you are as good and pure as you are beautiful."

Violet smiled, for these were the first kind words she had heard in a long while. "That is very kind of the prince," she said politely. "No one has given me a gift since my mother died."

"Now listen carefully," said the bird, "for your sisters are even now returning. Your gift is in this tree, for it is magic, and can give you whatever you wish. You must stand under the tree, facing the trunk, and place your hand upon the bark, and then you must say, 'Willow tree, what I desire, bring to me.' As you speak these words, you must picture in your mind whatever it is that you desire, and whatever it is, gold, or jewels, or rare fabrics, fine foods or wine, it shall appear on the other side of the tree. Can you remember the verse?"

Violet repeated the verse in her mind. "Yes, little bird, I can remember."

"Good!" the redbird said. "You must remember that you are to tell no one of the source of your gift, for it is for you alone. Now, I can hear your sisters approaching, so I will take my leave."

As he flew away, a spot of bright color against the trees, Violet called out, "Give my thanks to the prince of the wood, for I appreciate his gift most kindly."

That evening, quite late, when all but herself were abed, Violet, anxious to try out her magic gift, stole from the house, and approached the willow tree which stood bathed in the light of the full moon.

She placed her hand upon the trunk, as she had been told to do, and then wondered what she should ask for. The first thing that came to her mind was food, for her sisters always managed to eat so much that there was little left for Violet.

She thought of a chicken, plump and savory, with crackling skin and a chestnut stuffing; and of hot bread, crusty and smelling of yeast, dripping with good yellow butter; and then strawberries with thick, white cream.

As hunger squeezed her stomach with a hard hand, she repeated the words: "Willow tree, what I desire, bring to me!"

There was a soft, popping sound, and then her nostrils became aware of the odor of roast chicken and hot bread. She hurried around the trunk of the tree, and there, just as the redbird had promised, was what she had wished for.

Hungrily, she fell upon the food, and feasted until she was satisfied. The redbird had spoken the truth—the tree would give her whatever she wished for.

Wiping her hands upon her much-mended apron, Violet went back to the other side of the tree, and placed her hands once more upon the trunk. This time she wished for decent clothes—a dress, shoes, apron, and undergarments.

Again she heard the soft, popping sound, and again, behind the trunk she found the items she had requested.

After that she wished for a nightgown—so that she should not have to sleep in her ragged shift—an ivory comb for her long, golden hair; and then, because she was a good and kind girl, who bore her sisters no animosity despite their treatment of her, some trinkets and baubles for them, as well as a new pipe and aromatic tobacco for her brother.

Happy and replete, Violet then crept back into her bed, and for the first time in a long while, slept well fed and content.

In the morning Violet, who was in the habit of rising earlier than the rest of the family so that she could prepare their morning meal, placed the gifts by the table settings of her brother and sisters, and innocently awaited what she was certain would be their pleased surprise.

When the meal was ready, and the family came to the table, their initial reaction was all that she could have hoped for. Her brother picked up the handsomely carved pipe, and looked at it in wonder. "Where did this come from?" he asked Violet.

Delighted by his surprise and pleasure, Violet told him that it was a gift from her. Her brother was very pleased; he thanked her warmly, and kissed her cheek.

Her sisters, although busy looking at their own gifts, still noticed this, and were displeased.

After examining their presents closely, they studied Violet with deep suspicion. They had never let her have any money of her own, and so there would have been no means for her to buy such lovely things. They also noticed her new dress, shoes, and apron, and her neatly combed hair.

Not wanting to say anything in front of their brother, and desiring to keep up the pretense that they were kind to their younger sister, they waited until the meal was finished and the brother had gone outside; and then they turned on Violet with greed in their eyes and on their lips.

"Where did you get all these things?" Rose asked in a cold voice.

"You have no money," said Lily. "How could you come by such fine things?"

Violet, who had thought they would be pleased, could not understand their apparent displeasure. "Don't you like the gifts? I thought they would please you."

Lily and Rose exchanged meaningful glances. "Oh, we are pleased enough with them, mean as they are, but we are curious as to how you obtained them."

Violet hung her head, remembering the redbird's warning that the secret of the willow tree was hers alone. "I cannot tell you," she said miserably, "for it is a secret."

Lily and Rose exchanged looks again. "You had better tell us," Rose snapped angrily, "or it will go hard for you. You know how difficult we can make matters for you."

Violet only shook her head stubbornly, and would not tell them; so the sisters, in anger, scattered the ashes from the hearth all over the floor and threw the dishes about, telling Violet that she was a dreadful housekeeper, and that she had better have the room clean by the time they returned from their morning walk.

As they went out the door, they brushed past the crippled gardener coming in to bring some cut flowers to the table; and they roughly pushed him aside, so hard that he stumbled, and then laughed cruelly at his lameness.

When the gardener entered the kitchen, he found Violet crying, for even her pleasant disposition was saddened by this new cruelty from her sisters.

"Why do you cry, little one?" he asked in a soft voice.

"I cry because I thought to please my sisters, and instead I have made them angry," Violet said, wiping the tears from her eyes. "And because I have a secret they wish to know, but which I cannot tell them."

"Do not cry, my child," the gardener said, handing Violet the flowers. "I have the gift of second sight, and my sight tells me that all will come out well for you in the end."

The gardener's words cheered Violet, and she finished cleaning the house before her sisters returned, hoping that the walk would ease their temper.

And when they returned, they did seem to be in a better mood. They even thanked her nicely for the gifts, and Violet was very happy, for she sought only to please them. She did not notice the sly look in their eyes, or see that the smiles upon their faces were false.

"Do you suppose," Rose said offhandedly, "that you could get me something else, sister dear? There is something that I have longed for for some time."

Thrilled by their apparent change toward her, Violet nodded eagerly. "Yes, of course. Anything you wish. You, too, Lily."

"Well," said Rose, "I really need a new silk bonnet, in blue, lined with white."

Lily said, "And I would like a silver-handled brush and silver-backed mirror. Can you get these things for us?"

"Oh, yes!" Violet said happily. "I will have them for you tomorrow morning. Oh, I am so glad that you are no longer angry with me!"

The sisters smiled and smirked at one another, but Violet was so pleased with the turn of events that she did not notice. Free of guile herself, she did not suspect it in others.

That night, after the rest of the family were supposedly asleep, Violet again crept from her bed and went to the willow tree, unaware that her two sisters had followed her, and were watching her from the cover of the wood.

Smiling happily, Violet placed her hand upon the tree, and spoke the verse twice, once for the bonnet, and once for the silver-backed brush and mirror.

No sooner had she retrieved the items from behind the tree, than her sisters rushed out from hiding and pounced on her.

"Ha! So that is how you do it!" Lily exclaimed, pushing her aside and facing the tree. "Well, your secret is out now, dear sister, and from now on you will stay away from this tree. Only Rose and I will be allowed near it. Now, I am going to wish for silver candlesticks for my room!"

Knowing that she had been tricked, Violet sank down upon the earth in dismay, all her happiness gone. So they had not changed, after all; they still did not love her!

She watched sorrowfully as Lily placed her hand upon the tree and confidently began to recite the verse. As she spoke the last word, Violet could hear the now familiar popping sound, and Rose shrieked loudly, "It's here!"

Quickly, both sisters rushed around to the other side of the tree, and then their voices cried out in unison, a cry of surprise and shock, for behind the tree they found no silver candlesticks, but only the hunchbacked gardener, looking at them out of angry eyes.

"What are *you* doing here?" Rose demanded.

"What have you done with my candlesticks?" Lily cried.

"There will be no candlesticks for you, and nothing else, either," said the gardener in a strange and unfamiliar voice.

The sisters fell back in astonishment, for his voice was now that of a young man. Rose said angrily, "How dare you speak to us this way?"

"You will be disciplined, you can be sure," Lily exclaimed.

The gardener merely laughed, and walked around the tree to where Violet sat upon the ground.

"I dare speak thus to you because I am the prince of the wood," he said loudly enough for the sisters to hear. And with a flash of light and a puff of smoke, he disappeared, to be replaced by a handsome young man in elegant clothing, with a golden crown in the shape of twining branches upon his head.

Lily and Rose cowered back in fear and trembling, as he lifted Violet to her feet, and kissed her cheek. "I am the prince of the wood," he said again, "and your sister will be my princess."

Violet gazed up at him in awe and wonder, as her sisters looked on in dismay.

"You do not deserve her," the prince said. "I am taking Violet with me to my castle in the wood, where she shall have the finest of everything, and be waited on hand and foot, forever and always. As for you two, I have a parting gift for you!"

He waved his hand, and the two sisters began to shrink and change, until there stood in their place, illuminated by the moon, two large crows, both cawing angrily.

The prince smiled tenderly at Violet. "I have put them under a spell that befits their nature. They will still complain, and they will still steal, but their activities of whatever nature shall henceforth be on a much smaller scale."

And with that, the prince and Violet vanished from the sight of men, although it is said that they have occasionally been seen, by those clear of eye and pure of heart, living in a wonderful castle deep in the wood, where trouble never visits and happiness is everlasting.

Michele found the story enchanting, and desperately wanted to dance the role of Violet. The difficulty was that *everyone*—all of the female dancers at any rate—wanted to dance the role also. So far Deampierre had not announced his selections for the cast, and tension was running high.

Denise was working furiously, and, Michele was forced to admit, dancing very well. Also, Denise was due for a featured or even a starring role. Cybella, of course, wanted the role, and had the edge because of her experience; and she was, after all, the *première danseuse* of the troupe.

Michele realized that it was unlikely that she would get the role, but, like many of the other young women in the troupe, she could not help hoping for a miracle. If she could not have it, she hoped that Cybella would get it, for besides the fact that Denise was such an awful person, Michele really believed that she was all wrong for the part. As Marie put it: "Can you imagine Denise portraying goodness and purity, much less humility?"

Michele was able to focus all of her attention upon her dancing now, for Ian had left for Scotland, after eliciting from her a promise that she would at least *consider* visiting him in the spring. Of course, with the new ballet coming up, there was little chance she would be able to go.

Now that Ian was gone, Michele found that she missed him desperately; she missed his good company, his touch, and the expression in his eyes when he looked at her.

At night she dreamed of him, and would awaken in the dark with her body throbbing. Although they had never been intimate, she could imagine how it might be with him; and she finally had to admit to herself that even as she denied it in her mind, she had wanted him to make love to her. Damn Arnaut Deampierre, and herself, for what had happened that afternoon! If it were not for that, her body might not have been awakened, and she would not now feel this yearning for intimacy with a man.

It was strange, she thought, that she no longer felt the overwhelming attraction she had once felt for Deampierre. She still admired him, of course, and thought him attractive; but the infatuation for him seemed to have passed, and their relationship was in fact far more comfortable than it had been before.

One morning in the practice hall, as she bent and stretched at the barre, muffled in thick stockings, and a heavy woolen skirt and jacket, she reviled the cold. The heavy clothing made moving awkward, and would make learning the new ballet all the more difficult.

It was almost time for class; and when the door opened, admitting Deampierre, he had Giovanni Bartolo with him. Both men were talking animatedly, their faces intent on each other, and both were smiling.

Michele felt her breath catch, for she had a sudden premonition that Deampierre had finally made his selection for the lead dancers. When he called them to attention, she learned that her feeling had been true.

"Ladies and gentlemen," he said sardonically, "I have

good tidings for you. The selection of the dancers to play the lead roles in *The Three Sisters* has been completed.

"Now, before I announce the names, I wish to speak to those of you who are *not* chosen. I realize that you will be sorely disappointed, and perhaps angry with me. Many of you will feel that my choices are unfair, that you are better suited to dance the role than the one chosen. This is understandable, for we all have a strong belief in our own abilities. I would have it no other way. If you are not confident of yourself and your talent, how can you ever handle an important role? But you must remember that since this is my company I must use my own best judgment, relying upon my experience and wisdom to make the choices. I will confess that I also listened in this instance to the suggestions of the composer, since Giovanni is also involved in this, our joint effort. Remember that there will be other ballets and other chances for featured roles.

"And now, the names. Cybella, you will dance Violet. Michele and Denise, you will dance the roles of the other two sisters. Roland will dance the prince of the wood, Louis will dance the brother, and Café au Lait, I am going to give you the role of the gardener. Do you think you can dance a hunchback?"

Café au Lait grimaced and then grinned widely. "It will certainly be different from my own dashing image, but to dance a featured role, I will play *anyone*!" All of a sudden, he slumped into a hunched, grotesque stance, and he *was* a hunchback.

The rest of the group laughed, although Michele could see a long face here and there, and she knew that many of them were hiding their disappointment.

As for herself, Michele felt excited and elated. True, she had really wanted to dance Violet; yet she had known there was little chance of that as long as Cybella was available.

She shot a covert glance at Denise, to see how the other girl was taking it, and Denise's expression told her that the young dancer was not taking Deampierre's choice with good grace. Her face was set and cold, and she was talking heatedly with Roland, whose eyes were narrowed in thoughtful concentration.

Michele experienced a shiver of apprehension. Would Denise take up her old habits again? There had been no "accidents" since Michele's warning to her; surely now that the other girl knew that the others were all aware of her actions, she would not dare try anything. Would she?

"Michele! Pay attention! Your mind is not on what you are doing!"

Deampierre's crisp voice summoned Michele back to the present, and she focused her mind upon her movements, letting the knowledge that she was to dance another solo part wash over her, making her feel warm and happy. She was a fortunate girl, she knew, very fortunate indeed!

The weeks of winter went by more quickly than Michele could have imagined. Despite the damp cold, despite the rain and the snow, and despite rooms that were never quite warm enough, she managed to get to class and practice every day; as did most of the others. There were, of course, some who were out with illnesses, but this was common during the cold months in Paris.

It was the new ballet that kept them all going to the point of exhaustion; almost all the dancers were in love with it. Deampierre had created some very innovative choreography; and the solo dancers were masterpieces of the dancer's art, the steps and movements delineating so well the personalities of the characters that they seemed to really come alive.

There was only one dark blot on the white landscape of the winter, and that was the death of Minette, one of the young dancers of the corps de ballet, who had died of a chest ailment early in December.

It was not until late December, when Christmas was drawing near, that Michele had another wave of homesickness. It was the advent of the holiday season, naturally, that brought it on, for Christmas at Malvern had always been a jolly time, with parties and sleigh rides, culminating with a Christmas Eve gathering. At least it had been so while her father was alive.

What would it be like at Malvern this year? Would her mother, now that she was alone, observe Christmas at all? Michele had not heard from Hannah recently, for mail was even slower during the winter months; and suddenly she longed for her mother, and for Malvern, with an almost physical ache. Almost, at that moment, she would have given up everything just to be home again; almost, but not quite.

Then the Christmas preparations began at Madame Dubois' home, and the round of holiday parties started; the ache of homesickness lessened, although it did not disappear entirely.

Michele, much in demand since her new celebrity status, was invited, it seemed, to all the parties. It was all very gay, and she enjoyed herself in a way, yet she found herself wishing that Ian was there to act as her escort. Of course, she had no lack of admirers, or dancing partners, but she found herself comparing each of them to Ian; and when she did, she found them wanting.

She would have been pleased if Louis would have escorted her, for she missed his merry company; but he was still treating her with reserve, and avoiding her as much as possible, a fact which somewhat dampened her holiday spirits. He even refused to come to the party which Madame Dubois gave for the ballet company—a lovely party which they all very much enjoyed. However, the others were all there, even Roland and Denise, who, however much they might disdain Michele, attended every function they were invited to, as if they were, as Café au Lait jokingly put it, "afraid they might miss something."

And so the cold months passed. The winter season went well for the company, for they performed always to packed houses. Michele was particularly pleased, for she was given a featured role in one of the repertory ballets; and she felt that she was making progress, that it was not too ambitious to dream that someday she might have a chance at a leading role.

As they worked on the new ballet, Michele became more and more enamored of the role of Violet; and if she could possibly be present when Cybella was practicing the role, she would carefully observe the other girl, memorizing the steps, which she would later practice alone.

Deampierre, who believed that everyone should learn all the roles in the new ballet, approved of this. He appointed official understudies, of course, but he encouraged the dancers to learn all the roles if possible. He had chosen Denise to understudy Cybella, and Marie and Celeste to understudy Michele and Denise. Louis was understudying both Roland and Café au Lait, and also had an understudy himself.

Michele had been severely disappointed when Deampierre had chosen Denise to understudy Cybella, for she had hoped she would get that opportunity, at least; and she still thought Denise wrong for the role. Yet, she thought she understood why Deampierre had done it. Denise *was* a fine dancer, and she had been very unhappy when she had not been chosen for *Beauty and the Beast*. Deampierre had to keep peace within the company as much as possible, and it was, so to speak, Denise's turn.

It was the middle of April before the weather began to really ease, and hints of the arrival of spring began to appear.

The Three Sisters was nearly ready for performance. The sets had been constructed, the music scored, the dances polished and repolished. All had been going very smoothly—too smoothly, Michele was to think afterward.

It was on the first fairly nice day that tragedy struck. Cybella and Roland were practicing the closing *pas de deux* in front of the assembled company, who were watching enthralled.

It was a beautifully constructed dance, graceful and innovative; and watching it, Michele felt her heart ache, for it seemed to represent all that was good and noble of love between a man and a woman. If love could truly be like that, she thought; then it might be worth giving up everything else for.

Cybella, her wandlike arms graceful as reeds, seemed to be the epitome of femininity, and even Roland's essential coldness seemed changed by the configurations of the movements designed for him. It was a beautiful moment that touched them all, and then it happened.

Roland, raising Cybella in the majestic lift that crowned the dance, suddenly appeared to lose his balance. Those watching let out a collective gasp as Cybella hit the floor with a jarring thump, her right leg twisted grotesquely under her.

Deampierre, his face ashen, rushed to her side, kneeling beside her, angrily motioning the others back.

Michele, numb with shock, had an urge to look at the faces around her, and saw her own feelings mirrored there; and then she spotted Denise, and drew in her breath with a hiss—Denise's face bore no signs of shock or horror. Her eyes were bright, and upon her thin lips was a smile, faint but unmistakably a smile!

Later, after Cybella had been taken away, her leg broken, Michele, Marie, and Café au Lait had brief talk.

Michele said angrily, "I know that Roland dropped her purposely! He and Denise planned it today, I am sure of it. If you two had seen her face . . ."

Marie sighed, and put her hand on Michele's shoulder. "I am reasonably certain that you are right, Michele. But how could we prove it?"

Café au Lait's voice was sad. "Marie is right, Michele. We all know what Denise is like, and she and Roland may very well have planned this, as you say, but we have no proof, and we must not disrupt the new ballet just because of a *feeling* we have. We could destroy it, and it would never be produced. Denise is the understudy, and she knows the role. Granted that she will not bring the sympathy to the part that Cybella would, she is an excellent dancer, and will carry it off well enough. Now you must admit that."

Michele wanted desperately to cry out that *she* could do the role better, but she kept silent. If she said anything of that nature, it would only sound as if she were jealous because she had not gotten the part herself. That was not entirely the truth, but it would sound that way to others. In her heart, she was convinced that Denise had been responsible for the "accident," and it sickened her that the other girl should profit from such perfidy.

She went on with the rehearsals, dancing her role as well as she could, but her heart was no longer in it; she was sorely disillusioned. She also felt unhappy at Deampierre for not realizing what had happened, and angry with Marie and Café au Lait for counseling caution. Was this really what the professional world was like? Did you always have to be on guard against your fellow performers? Did you always have to view the people with whom you worked with suspicion and distrust? Did you have to bite and claw and cheat on your way to a successful career? If that was the way of it, perhaps success was not worth the price.

As the days grew warmer, and the trees and flowers began to bud and then to bloom, the spirits of the company did likewise. They all felt sympathy for Cybella, who was immobilized with a broken leg; but they knew that the rest of them must go on, for that was the nature of the ballet.

As the time drew near for the first public performance of *The Three Sisters*, the excitement mounted, as it always did when a new ballet was about to have its premiere. Everyone shared in the breathless anticipation, except Michele; her disillusionment still plagued her; and she could not keep her thoughts from Cybella, forced to spend the days in her room, with her leg splinted and still, wondering if it would heal straight and true, wondering if she would ever be able to dance again. It could happen to anyone, Michele reasoned; and the one who was the cause of it was going unpunished. It was simply not fair!

She watched Denise closely, keeping an eye on her at rehearsals and at practice. The girl looked smugly happy and pleased with herself. She easily slipped into the role of Violet, and she had all the dances mastered, for she was undeniably an excellent technician. The only thing she did not bring to the role was soul. Although she was small and delicate enough to make Violet physically believable, Denise could not project the vulnerability or sweetness that the character should project, abilities that Cybella had possessed in abundance.

And so that was how matters stood when the letter arrived from Ian MacLeven, reminding Michele of her promise to consider his invitation. Michele did not this time dismiss the idea out of hand.

As she sat in her room, pondering the letter and looking out at the awakening garden below, which was bathed in pale, early morning sunlight, she suddenly longed to see him. Ian had described his highlands to her as having a wild and clean beauty—a beauty that she needed just now to wash away the taste of what had happened to Cybella, and the feeling that had been subsequently aroused in her. She felt weary and discouraged, and sick of the rich, lavish life she had been living. It would be good to be somewhere less effete, some place more real, if only for a little while. Excitement began to build in her. She would go! Marie could take her place in the new ballet.

If Deampierre was upset, then so be it! She would tell him a small lie—that she was not feeling well, that she needed the fresh air of the country for awhile.

For a moment she hesitated. What would Andre say? He would not be particularly pleased, she well realized. Still, it was *her* decision to make. It was her life, not his. She would go. She would send word to Ian right away to expect her.

* * *

It had been a dreary winter for Hannah, seemingly endless. The weather had been terrible, cold and wet, keeping her indoors much of the time. Even the Christmas season had given her no joy this year. Court had not returned, nor had there been any word from him; what faint hope she had had that he would relent and come back had long since evaporated.

The one bright spot in the winter was the fate of Jules Dade. He had been turned over to the authorities, given a speedy trial, convicted of the murder of Michael Verner, and had been hanged for his crime.

Hannah did not know when the idea of going to Paris germinated in her; probably some time after Dade's execution, which took place in late January. She had received three glowing letters from Michele, and a couple from Andre. Both had written that Michele was in good health, and faring well in her career as a dancer. One of the letters from Michele, telling of her triumph in Paris and the command performance at Fontainebleau for the king of France, was especially cherished by Hannah. At least her daughter's life was going well!

Evidently, the idea had been brewing in her mind for some time, for she suddenly awoke on a dreary March morning with it full-blown in her thoughts. Why not go to Paris to visit Michele and Andre? If nothing else, it would be a nice visit between mother and daughter; Hannah had the feeling that Michele would never return to Malvern, except for visits, and such a trip should go far toward lightening her mood of melancholy, which seemed to grow bleaker as the days passed. She could afford the trip now, she had never been out of the country, and she was not needed on Malvern at the present time. It would soon be time for spring planting, but John could oversee that well enough.

She discussed it with him. "I know that I mentioned it to you once, John, running the plantation for me, and you said you didn't want the responsibility, and my neighbors would not look favorably upon a black overseer on Malvern. But I won't be gone too long, perhaps four months all told. I will be back in plenty of time for the harvest." She leaned toward him with a look of pleading. "John, after all that has happened this past autumn and winter, I need to get away." She laughed ruefully. "I never thought the day would come when I would say that I needed to get away from Malvern, but I *do* need just that. And I want to see Michele."

John nodded judiciously. "I agree, mistress. I have watched you this past winter. You have been restless and unhappy."

"It showed, did it?"

He nodded again. "Yes, mistress." He smiled slowly. "You take your journey, and I shall see to Malvern the best that I am capable."

She touched his hand. "You will do fine, John. I would trust you with my life. In fact," she remembered Dade's hands on her throat, "I do owe you my life, and I shall never forget that."

And so it was arranged—Hannah was to journey to France, and John was to run the plantation in her absence.

Now that the decision was made, Hannah fretted, impatient to sail for Europe; but crossing the Atlantic in winter was not advisable. Great storms raged across the ocean, and the weather was not suitable for such a voyage until late spring. So she was forced to wait until early May before sailing. She did not write to Michele of her coming, wishing to surprise her.

Hannah had never been on a ship crossing the ocean, and she was miserable much of the way. The weather was still not too good, and the ship was buffeted by two fierce storms. Hannah was sick often, she could not keep food down, and she spent a great deal of time in her tiny cabin, until she was driven on deck by a feeling that she would die without a breath of fresh air.

She, fortunately, became acclimated to the sea just a few days short of landing on French soil; but at least she was feeling well again, and looking forward with great anticipation to seeing her daughter and Andre as she rode the coach into Paris. When she had left Virginia, the countryside had still been drab, with only a few signs of spring; but here in France, everything was green and lush, the countryside a riot of spring flowers.

Entering the outskirts of Paris, Hannah gawked in breathless awe at the things she saw on every side—much as her daughter had done a year earlier. Paris, she realized, was like no other city she had ever seen, and she was already glad she had come, even before seeing Michele.

Once in Paris, she hired a carriage, and in her limited French, asked the driver to take her to Madame Dubois' address. Eventually, Hannah found herself at the door of what she hoped was the proper residence. A maid answered her knock.

"I am Hannah Verner. Is either Madame Dubois or Michele Verner in?"

The maid curtsied, led Hannah to a sitting room down the hall, curtsied again, said something in French, and left. Hannah, knowing little French, assumed that she had been told to wait, which she proceeded to do, composing herself on the divan.

Michele had written her that Madame Dubois had a splendid home, but Hannah was not quite prepared for such grandeur. The furnishings, the draperies, the fine carpets on the floor—all spoke of wealth and social position.

She came out of her musings with a start as a rather spectacularly attired woman swept into the room. Hannah got to her feet.

The woman said something in French. Hannah shook her head. "I'm sorry, I don't speak your language. I am Hannah Verner."

"Ah!" the woman said in English, her face broadening into a smile. "You are dear Michele's mother, from the English colonies, of course. I am Madame Dubois. How do you do, Mrs. Verner? But I am afraid that your daughter is not here."

The woman's words came out in such a rush that Hannah had to smile. "You mean Michele is rehearsing?"

Madame Dubois shook her head. "No, Mrs. Verner. Your daughter is presently in Scotland."

"In Scotland?" Hannah said in dismay.

"That is correct." Madame's smile turned roguish. "There is a romance in bloom, with a Scottish lord, and Michele is visiting him in his castle. She departed less than a week ago. With dear Andre chaperoning, *naturellement*."

Chapter Nineteen

WHEN Michele and Andre arrived at Inverness, they found a coach awaiting them.

As the driver stepped down from his seat, Michele recognized him immediately; it was Angus Lowrie, the man who had been Ian's traveling companion on the ship from the colonies.

"Why, Mr. Lowrie!" she exclaimed. "How nice to see you again. We met on the ship coming over from Virginia last year."

Lowrie nodded, his face a study in reserve. "Just Angus, if you please, Miss Verner." His voice had more of a burr than did Ian's. "You see, I am Laird MacLeven's man."

Andre glanced at Michele with a smile. "So Lord MacLeven was not the only one traveling incognito."

Angus permitted a slight smile to soften his craggy features. "That is correct, sir. The Laird came down a step, and I came up a step, so that we might travel as equals. If I may say so, it is a pleasure to see both of you again. The master has been fair atingle with anticipation, waiting for you to arrive. He would have come himself, but there was some urgent business he had to attend to, but he'll be waiting for you at MacLeven Castle. He has obtained rooms for you at the best inn in town for tonight, so that you may rest from your journey, and then, if it meets with your approval, we will set out for MacLeven Castle in the morning."

"That sounds fine to me," said Michele. "I could do with a good night's sleep after that boat trip."

Andre laughed. "The sea was quite rough," he explained, "and the ship ill-constructed and appointed. We will be happy to avail ourselves of your inn. Thank you, Angus."

Within a few minutes, Angus had their baggage loaded atop the coach, and they were settled within. It was a fine coach, Michele noted, large and comfortable; and she leaned back against the well-padded seat with pleasant anticipation.

After the coach got under way, Michele let her thoughts wing back to Paris. She had been afraid that Deampierre would be angry when she told him that she wished to leave the troupe temporarily, and that she would not be dancing in *The Three Sisters*, but to her surprise, he had taken it very well. In fact, he seemed to understand.

"I believe that I know how you feel, Michele," he had told her as they shared a cup of tea following an afternoon class. "I know that you feel that Denise influenced Roland, so that he would purposely drop Cybella. Perhaps you are right in thinking so, but I have no proof of this, and perforce must act as if it is not true.

"I also know that you feel you would make a much better Violet than Denise, and again you are probably correct. However, Denise *is* a good dancer, and she is the understudy to the role. If I ever find out that Roland did drop Cybella intentionally, then he and Denise will pay for their deed, but until then I must proceed as if it was a regrettable accident. Do you understand?"

Michele nodded. "And I am grateful that you understand the way I feel, and that you are not upset at my leaving."

Deampierre smiled. "But you will be back, will you not?"

Michele nodded again. "Oh, yes. It is just that I need a rest. I need to get away for awhile."

"I understand and agree wholeheartedly," he said. "You have been working hard. I cannot recall having a student with more dedication. I only ask that you continue your exercises while you are away, so that it doesn't take you too long to get back into condition when you return. I will tell you something in confidence, Michele. Truthfully, since Cybella had her mishap, I have lost some of my enthusiasm for *The Three Sisters*. Oh, we will perform it, as planned, but my heart will not be in it, not to the extent that it was in the beginning. When Cybella is well, we will perform it again, later in the year, when you have rejoined the company, and then we shall see it done as I conceived it."

"But what if Cybella never dances again?"

Deampierre shuddered. "Please! I refuse to harbor such thoughts!"

Michele, touched by this out-of-character confidence, noticed for the first time that the ballet master's eyes looked tired, and that his face showed lines of tension and worry. It must not be easy, she concluded, managing a company such as his, making all of the decisions, taking care of everyone, trying to keep peace between fiercely competitive dancers.

Leaning forward, she touched the back of his hand. "Take care of yourself, Arnaut. You look tired. Perhaps you need a holiday, also?"

"There are no holidays for me, my dear Michele. I told you once that I consider the dance a demanding mistress. She will not let me go."

Michele felt a surge of affection. He gave so much to them all! It was no wonder that he sometimes lost patience, that he was often tired. "Well, if she will not let you go, at least petition her to be a little easy on you." She smiled fondly. "We all depend on you, you know. And we all love and care about you, even though we may not always appear so."

He patted her hand. "I know, but it is nice to hear it said. Go with my blessing, Michele, and do not worry. I promise that your place will be waiting when you return. And give my regards to Lord MacLeven. He is a fine young man."

Telling Andre proved to be more difficult, for as Michele had supposed, he was upset by the idea.

"*Mon Dieu!* We came all this way, Michele, so that you might make a career of your dancing. You have worked very hard, and you have achieved some success. I am proud of you, but why, now when things are going so well, do you want to run away?"

"I am not running away, Andre," Michele said in exasperation. "I am only taking a holiday. Arnaut understands, so why can't you?"

Andre looked at her thoughtfully. "If Cybella had not been hurt, if things had gone as planned, would you still be going?"

She shrugged. "I don't know, Andre. Truthfully, I do not. Perhaps not."

"Is it because Denise got the role of Violet?"

"No!" she said hotly. "It's because I know that Denise and Roland *planned* to hurt Cybella so that Denise would get the role. It's so . . . cruel, and heartless. It's entirely possible that Cybella may never dance again. If it is going to be like that always, I am not sure that I want to be a part of it!"

Andre took her hands in his, his eyes showing compassion. "Oh, my dear Michele, I had no idea that this matter had affected you so, touched you so deeply. Just because there are selfish and evil people in the world does not mean that *all* people are like that. Think of your good friends in the company. They have been supportive, have they not?"

Michele nodded quickly. "Yes, in the main. But now Louis is not speaking to me, and the others are more interested in getting on with the ballet than in what happened to Cybella. Oh, I will not give up dancing, Andre, but I do need to get away. I really do!"

Andre's look was probing. "And I suppose that you really have no interest in seeing young MacLeven?"

Michele felt herself flushing. "As a matter of fact, I have," she answered sharply, annoyed by Andre's acumen.

"I find him very entertaining, and quite good company, and I see no reason why I should not visit him."

Andre held up his hands. "All right, *chérie*. It is only that I want you to have what you have worked so hard for. If you were to become emotionally involved with a man such as Ian MacLeven, if you were to marry him, certainly it would mean the end of your career."

"I know that! I have no intention of becoming involved with Ian in that way. I only want to get away, and to see a part of the world that I have not seen before. Is that too much to ask?"

Andre finally admitted reluctantly that it was not; and since Michele wanted him to accompany her, he was somewhat mollified, and had made the arrangements for the trip in good enough grace.

And now here they were, in Scotland, and Michele felt as if a great weight had been lifted from her shoulders. As much as she loved the ballet, the thought of not being held to a rigid schedule of practice and performance for a time appealed to her, as she realized for the first time just how insular her life in Paris had been. Dancing, as Deampierre had said, was indeed a jealous mistress; and it was pleasant to escape from her rule for a time. The freedom Michele experienced was exhilarating.

"The best inn in town" proved to be homey and comfortable—a large, half-timbered building, with a thick, well-trimmed, thatched roof that crowned it like a farmer's hat.

Inverness seemed a pleasant little village, full of simple but attractive cottages, quite different from those Michele was used to at home, and those she had seen in France.

Her room at the inn was not large, but it was clean and comfortable; and marvelous odors of food came up from the common room below, reminding Michele that she was very hungry. The food on the ship from France had not been of the best.

As soon as she had refreshed herself, she and Andre went downstairs to a simple but hearty meal before the warmth of the fireplace; the warmth was welcome for the afternoon had grown a bit chill, with the lowering of the sun.

That night Michele slept so well that in the morning she did not remember her dreams; and after breaking fast with a large bowl of oaten meal, topped with sugar and thick cream, she felt ready to face any sort of adventure. Angus had already loaded the coach with their baggage, and was ready to go as soon as Michele and Andre had eaten.

The morning had dawned clear and sunny, but a bit cool; and Angus settled Michele into the coach with a pile of cushions, and a fur laprobe that made her feel warm and cozy.

Andre, seated across from her, stared at her sleepily. "Well, *chérie,* you seem chipper enough this morning, although how anyone can be cheerful at this unholy hour is beyond my understanding. We could have slept in and started out a bit later. Only peasants arise at such an hour!"

Michele laughed. "Andre, you are a shameless sybarite! No wonder you didn't want to leave Paris. It is a glorious morning, and being in another country which is new to me is very exciting. Wake up and look at the scenery. It is very beautiful."

Andre yawned. "I have seen it before, love, and to my notion it is somewhat rough and intimidating, particularly after Paris."

Michele snorted in an unladylike manner. "Any place would seem rough after Paris. Everything is too artificial there. I'll admit that the land here looks untamed, but it has its own beauty. I think it looks clean and bold, and in *my* opinion, a fine change from the hothouse atmosphere that we have been living in."

Andre smiled lazily. "Do I detect the words of Ian MacLeven coming our of your pretty mouth, my pet?"

"He may have said something of the sort, but I happen to agree with him," she said hotly.

Andre shrugged. "There is, I suppose, something to be

said for both kinds of life. The English kings, I am told, come to Scotland for the hunting, and for a touch of the rough life. As for myself, I do not hesitate to admit to a preference for the sophistication of Paris. This is no country for a civilized man!"

Michele looked at him sharply, and then noticed his self-satisfied smile. "You're teasing me, aren't you? Andre, you can be a brute!"

He raised an eyebrow in mock surprise. "But I thought that was what you liked. A rugged, rough-talking man?"

She made a face at him, pulling up the laprobe. "I think even you will have to admit that Ian MacLeven is a perfect gentleman, at the same time being far more manly that those courtiers of King Louis!"

"He is indeed a proper gentleman, and certainly manly, if mere observation can be a proper judge. I just hope that you will be careful not to find out just *how manly!*"

Michele's face flamed. "Andre, if you do not shut your wicked mouth, I shall stuff this robe into it. Now look out the window and admit that the view is very fine."

"It is very fine," he said dryly. Then he laughed, and she could not help but join him; her spirits were, she had to admit, very high.

As the coach jolted over the narrow dirt road, swaying and rattling as the wheels ran over ruts and potholes, Michele hung on to the side strap, and studied the countryside. It was, as Ian had told her, far bolder than that of Virginia; but she found it wild and beautiful. The hills were well greened, and covered with a purplish, low-growing vegetation that she assumed must be heather. The air was thin and crisp, and very invigorating, full of the fresh smells of growing things.

As the day wore on, the chill left the air, and Michele was able to throw aside the laprobe.

They stopped at midday atop a small rise, to eat and allow the coach horses to rest, and to take care of the necessities of nature. All of them were glad of the stop, since they were all feeling jolted and bruised from the coach ride. They made a very pleasant meal from a large hamper packed for them by the innkeeper, and washed it down with two bottles of very good wine.

After the meal, Michele, despite the rough movement of the coach, fell asleep, and did not awaken until Andre shook her by the shoulder, saying, "Wake up, *chérie*. We are approaching MacLeven Castle. You had better make yourself presentable for your young lord."

Michele, knuckling sleep from her eyes, looked out the coach window. The vehicle was climbing a long, gradual incline, atop which stood a building the like of which she had never seen. Built entirely of stone, its size was such that it made Malvern look like a cottage in comparison.

With awe, she studied the turrets and towers that reared up starkly against the blue of the darkening sky. The great building looked grand, but somehow formidable; and she tried to imagine how a family, how *people*, could live in such a home.

She realized that her heart had started to beat very fast, and that she felt a bit faint. Hurriedly, she smoothed back her hair, and searched in her reticule for the small mirror she always carried. Peering into the glass, she tried to see if her face was smudged, or her eyes red. She looked, she thought, a bit tired, but presentable enough.

"You look fine, my pet, just smooth back that strand of hair near your right temple."

Michele looked into the glass again, rearranged the offending strand, then put the mirror away. In a few moments they would be there, at MacLeven Castle, and she would be seeing Ian again!

As the coach clattered to a stop before the wide entrance of the castle, the wooden doors swung open, and a manservant appeared, followed at once by Ian MacLeven and two young women; Michele took them to be the sisters he had mentioned.

Ian looked handsome and dashing in his kilt, and he wore a broad smile; Michele, her face craned out the window, waved and gave him an answering smile. He was obviously glad to see her, and her heart set up such a hammering that she was certain everyone within earshot could hear it.

He beat the manservant to the coach door, and opened it wide, holding up his arms to help her down. "Michele! Lass, I am so glad you are here at last!"

She moved to the door, and let him lift her to the ground. She felt a touch giddy from the long, uncomfortable coach ride, and, she had to admit, Ian's presence.

"You, too, Andre," Ian added. "I didn't mean to exclude you from my greeting. Welcome to MacLeven Castle."

Andre stepped down onto the stool the manservant had now placed by the coach step. "That is quite all right," he said dryly. "I should not expect to be greeted as eagerly as a pretty young lady."

Ian laughed with his head thrown back; and Michele flushed, realizing that she had been standing with Ian's arm around her much longer than the situation called for.

Turning toward the two young women, disengaging herself from Ian's arm, she smiled. "And are these your sisters, Ian?"

"Aye." He reluctantly switched his gaze from Michele to the young women. He took the hand of the taller girl, whose hair was as light as his own, and who bore a remarkable resemblance to him. "This is Margaret. And," he took the hand of the small, dark-haired girl, "this is Elizabeth."

Michele smiled again at both young women, and they returned the smile, their faces reflecting polite interest, and, Michele fervently hoped, approval of her appearance. Both women were very attractive, in different ways—Margaret so tall and fair; and Elizabeth so small and delicate, with fair skin, but dark hair and eyes.

"I am delighted to meet you both," Michele said.

"And we you," Margaret said, laughing winsomely. "We have heard little else this past winter, and you must forgive us if we act overly familiar, for in our minds we already know you quite well."

Elizabeth took Michele's arm as she might that of a

sister. "Of course, it is difficult to believe that *anyone* can be as perfect as Ian claims you are, but we are willing to be convinced." She tilted her head to one side. "Certainly you are as beautiful as he swore you were. He tends to exaggerate, great hulk of a man that he is, but not this time. Welcome to MacLeven Castle, Michele!"

Michele, her cheeks flushed, let Elizabeth lead her through the castle portals and into the entryway. Feeling both embarrassed and pleased, she did not know quite what to say in answer to Elizabeth's remarks. Shooting a sidelong glance at Ian, she saw that his cheeks were fiery as well.

The interior of MacLeven Castle was as impressive as the outside. The entryway was large, the stone walls adorned with family portraits, and various arms.

"We will show you to your room first, for I know how tiring that coach ride can be," Margaret said. "You will have time to freshen yourself and rest a bit before dinner."

"Thank you, Margaret," Michele said with sincerity, for every bone in her body seemed to ache, and she longed to stretch out upon a bed.

Her room was very large, and very different from the highly decorated lushness of her room at Madame Dubois' in Paris.

There was a beautiful, wooden four-poster bed, with a velvet canopy, coverlet, and bed curtains in a rich burgundy, trimmed in gold braid; a carved wooden chest at the foot of the bed; and a heavy, carved clothes cupboard against one wall.

Near the narrow window, there was a small, well-crafted writing desk, with a simple wooden chair; and by the fireplace was a settee, padded and covered in the same rich burgundy of the bed fittings. A low, padded slipper chair, covered with deep blue velvet, completed the seating arrangements.

A lowboy, against one wall, held a magnificent china pitcher and wash basin, next to which was a clean white towel and face cloth.

The cold stone of the walls was softened by heavy wall

hangings, mostly tapestries, and the whole effect, while rather somber, to Michele's mind, was of a richness of taste and restraint. A solid room, where a person could feel safe. Not as pretty, certainly, as her room in Paris, but attractive enough in another fashion.

A small, red-haired young woman came bustling in the moment Margaret and Elizabeth had showed Michele into the room.

"I'm Annie, Miss. And I'll be looking after you while you are at MacLeven Castle. If there is anything you need, anything at all, you let me know. Annie will take care of it." The girl's burr was so thick that it took Michele a few moments to decipher what she had said.

She gazed down into the freckled, wide-eyed face, and was immediately captivated. The girl was so small and slender that she looked little more than a child, and her bright-eyed enthusiasm was contagious.

"Thank you, Annie," Michele said, laughing slightly, "but right now, all I want to do is get out of these clothes and stretch out for a little to take the ache from my bones."

Annie's small face immediately assumed an expression of deep concern. "I know how it is, miss. A long coach ride can shake a body up something fierce. Let's get you out of those clothes and into your dressing gown, and then you can rest while I unpack your things. You'll feel a lot better after a good wash and a lie down. Mark my words."

Michele laughed again. The idea of being mothered by this elf child was amusing; and yet she had the definite feeling that Annie knew whereof she spoke, and what she was doing. She let the girl help her out of her traveling clothes and into her wrapper, and watched as Annie poured water from the pitcher into the basin, and laid out the soap and another wash cloth.

"Now while you have a nice wash, I'll put your things away, miss, and then I will brush your traveling dress and dust off your shoes. If you will tell me which dress you wish to wear this evening, I'll lay it out for you."

Michele thought for a moment. She wanted to make a

good impression upon Ian's family, particularly his father whom she had not yet met. She had the feeling that the elder MacLeven might not care for the daring Paris styles, and was glad that she had heeded Andre's warning that she should pack her plainer, more sensible dresses. She had realized that Andre was right when she first caught sight of Ian's sisters, who were soberly dressed, certainly by Paris standards.

"I shall wear the blue," she finally said. It was elegant enough, but simply made, and it flattered her.

"If I may be so bold, miss, I recommend that you also take along a shawl, for the nights are still a bit chilly, and the castle halls are often drafty."

Michele nodded, thanked Annie for her advice, and then literally fell onto the high bed, which, although it was a bit harder than she was accustomed to, felt like heaven after having been sitting for so long.

She did not see how carefully Annie put her things away, for she was asleep at once.

The evening meal was served in a huge, high-ceilinged room, at a table that looked large enough to accommodate a small army. Here again, the cold stone walls were hung with heavy tapestries, shields, battle axes, swords, and various military implements, as well as family portraits. Suits of armor stood in the corners, causing Michele to think of posted sentries. With all the visible armament, Michele could not help but be reminded of what Ian had told her about the warlike proclivities of the clans. She shivered, and pulled the heavy shawl more closely around her shoulders. Annie had been right; it was chilly in the huge dining hall, despite the blazing fire in a fireplace so large that it easily could have accommodated an ox.

Ian had been waiting for her, to escort her to the table; and as she took his arm, the temperature was forgotten, for she felt warmed by his nearness. His gaze held hers for a long moment, his eyes telling her just how glad he was that she was here at last.

And then they were entering the hall, where Ian's

father was already seated at the head of the table. Later Michele was to learn that the elder MacLeven experienced great difficulty in walking, which he could only manage by supporting himself with two heavy canes; and preferring that no one see him in his awkwardness, he always came to the dinner table alone, before the others.

Margaret and Elizabeth, escorted by Andre, had preceded Ian and Michele into the room, and the girls went first to kiss their father's cheek before taking their places. Michele and Ian were seated to Lord MacLeven's right and left, and Michele looked into the old man's craggy face with some unease, for he looked very fierce; and she hoped that his expression did not reflect his opinion of her.

Ian said, "Father, this is Michele Verner, the girl I have been telling you about. Michele, this is my father, Laird Malcolm MacLeven."

"How do you do, sir?' Michele said, trying to keep her voice steady. And then she blurted, "What an odd coincidence! My grandfather, on my father's side, was named Malcolm!"

Lord MacLeven said nothing, just looked at her out of faded blue eyes that still had the look of an eagle about them, shrouded as they were by heavy lids, and separated by a nose that could easily be mistaken for the fierce beak of an eagle.

He stared at her for so long without speaking that she was almost ready to run from the room; and then, like a spring sun, he smiled, and the fierce eyes brightened.

"You spoke true, my son. She is a winsome lass, and a feisty one, too, if I'm not mistaken. Tell me, lass, is your family a healthy one? This grandfather you speak of, was he a healthy man, of good, sound stock? Are *you* strong? You look to be a little bit of a thing, but you seem wiry."

"Father!" Ian said in a shocked voice.

The old man merely laughed, a booming sound that struck echoes in the huge room. He twinkled at Michele. "There's one great advantage to growing old, lass. You may say whatever you damned well please, and if it sounds outrageous, you can always blame it on your dotage. But it is a reasonable question, I think. A woman must be strong if she is to bear a man many sons. I say again, are you strong?"

Michele felt a wave of embarrassment roll over her, and then a prick of annoyance. How dare he ask such a personal question in front of them all like this? He *was* outrageous! And he seemed to be enjoying her discomfiture. She strongly suspected that despite his physical enfeeblement, this man's mind was as sharp as a needle. Well, she would not let him see that he had upset her.

"My family is very healthy, sir," she said spiritedly, "and I am quite strong. What of your family, sir? Are they strong as well?"

The old man fixed her with a stern eye, but both Margaret and Elizabeth burst into laughter.

"Ah, you might as well stop it, Papa. Michele is on to you," Margaret said, giving Michele an approving glance.

"Yes, Papa," Elizabeth said. "She won't allow you to tease and harass her like you do us."

"Tease and harass, is it? I tease and harass you two? Is a man to have no respect and honor in his own household? Aye, 'tis an awful thing to grow old, and to be abused and rebuked by thankless children."

His face was serious as he looked at Michele, yet there was a twinkle in his hooded eyes; and Michele understood that this was a game of sorts, one of the few amusements left to an aging man. As his face lightened again with his craggy smile, she realized that she had passed some kind of a test, and she began to relax.

The dinner, served on snowy linen, with fine plate and crystal, was hearty, and for the most part delicious, except for an odd-looking pudding that she did not care for at all. She managed to swallow the bite she had put into her mouth, but she pushed the rest of her portion to the side of her plate.

The old man saw her do it, and laughed heartily. "So, you do not care for the haggis? I thought you said you were strong?"

Margaret waggled her forefinger at him. "Papa, shame on you, for talking so to a guest!" She looked over at Michele. "Take no notice of him, Michele. Haggis is not to everyone's liking, particularly when they are unaccustomed to it."

Michele looked down at her plate doubtfully, and then up at Margaret. "What is it? I mean, how do you make haggis?"

Lord MacLeven said, "It's made of sheep's innards, lass. That's what's in it."

Michele attempted to keep her dismay from showing. Was the old man teasing her again?

"Oh, Papa!" Elizabeth said in exasperation. "You make it sound so dreadful. It's made of sheep or calves heart, liver, and lungs, Michele, mixed with suet, onions, oatmeal, and seasonings, and boiled in the animal's stomach."

Michele swallowed, and said stoutly, "I'm sure that it is very tasty, when you become accustomed to it."

"Aye, that it is," said the old man, taking a large bite and masticating with gusto. "That it is!"

"Well, I have never cared for it much, as you very well know, Papa," Elizabeth said.

"Sure, and you're the runt of the litter, aren't you, lassie? More haggis, that is what I should have done, made you eat more haggis!"

Elizabeth shook her head. "Papa is impossible sometimes, Michele, and he is a great tease, but not nearly so fierce as he would have you believe."

The old man lowered his heavy, white eyebrows and glowered at his youngest. "That is calumny, Elizabeth, calumny! What are you trying to do, damage my reputation?"

This time Michele laughed, too, and the dinner progressed famously after that, with no more unpleasant surprises.

During the rest of the meal, the girls plied Michele and Andre with so many questions that they had difficulty in finding time to eat. Both young women were very curious about Paris and the king's court, and about the colonies;

and their questions came so thick and fast that Ian, finally, called a halt.

"Allow our guests to eat!" he thundered. "The poor things will begin to think that this is the inquisition. And why so many questions about the court? I have been there, and although I will admit you questioned me, it was nothing like this!"

Margaret laughed. "Oh, pooh! It was no use asking all those questions of *you*, brother!"

Ian glared. "And what does that mean, sister dear?"

Elizabeth said, "She means that it never does any good to ask you questions about what the ladies wore, or about how the rooms are decorated. You never notice such things. This is the first chance we have had to talk to someone who can really tell us what we want to know."

Ian scowled in mock anger. "Well, that is the last time I shall bring news home to *you*."

But he was smiling when he said it, and Michele could see that he harbored a real fondness for his sisters, and for his father, also. They were a fine family; and thinking this Michele was reminded of her own family, consisting only of her mother now, and for just a moment her pleasure in the evening was dampened.

When dinner was over, Michele all at once was conscious of how weary she was. It had been a long day; and despite her restless nap in the rocking coach, she was very tired.

She realized that with all the questions from the sisters, she had not had much of a chance to speak with Ian; but she would be here for a time. There would be many days, and many other chances.

As she looked over at him, she sensed that he also felt frustrated by the presence of the family; and her thoughts jumped, despite her efforts to curb them, to the memory of his lips on hers, and she shivered slightly. That, too, would have to wait until another time.

Michele had almost forgotten how nice simple pleasures could be. The days at MacLeven sped by, filled with such pleasant pastimes as horseback riding, fishing, walking upon the newly greened moors, picnicking, and rowing on the loch.

She, who had never had any sisters, now felt as if she had two, for both Margaret and Elizabeth treated her as such, and they often accompanied her and Ian on their rambles.

But at other times, they remained behind in the castle, as it was Margaret's place as the elder daughter to manage the household, and Elizabeth was her helper in this chore.

Michele enjoyed the times they shared with the girls, but she also looked forward to the instances when she was alone with Ian. Seeing him here, in his own homeland, she realized that he was, indeed, ill-suited to be a royal sycophant. During their outdoor activities, the sun had burned his face a golden tan, and her own face, without her mask, was growing darker, and freckles were sprouting across her cheeks and the bridge of her nose. Andre scolded her severely for this; but she did not care, and even thought it attractive.

Andre ventured outdoors as little as possible, spending a great deal of time in Lord MacLeven's great library. He had also made several acquaintances in the neighborhood, during a gathering that Lord MacLeven had held in their honor; and he seemed content enough at the moment.

He did make Michele practice for at least two hours a day, grumbling that it was not nearly enough; and she dutifully went through her exercises and routines, knowing that she must keep her body in good condition; but strangely enough she did not really miss the ballet, or the company; she was too occupied enjoying the luxury of getting out of bed whenever she pleased, and of having the freedom to do just what she wished.

The thing uppermost in her mind, of course, was Ian. When they were alone she could feel the strength that held him back from taking her into his arms, and she did not know whether this pleased her or angered her, for her body ached for him; and she lived for the casual, accidental touch that would often set them both to trembling. She sensed that the situation rested in her hands, for she had rebuffed him once. She knew that he was at least as proud as she, and that he would not touch her again until she made it clear that she wished it. And oh, did she wish it! But somehow she could not make up her mind to show it.

She had been at MacLeven Castle a little over a week when the decision was taken out of her hands. They had just dined in the great hall, and a thunderstorm moved in as they ate. By the time the meal was over, the rain was drumming steadily on the windows, and lightning was splitting the sky like a fiery sword. It was a fierce storm, fiercer than any that Michele had ever seen, back in Virginia or in Paris; and she was more than a bit nervous, since she had always been somewhat afraid of thunderstorms; they always seemed so angry and violent.

After dinner, they all sat for a while in the small side room where it was warmer, and where Margaret and Elizabeth often entertained them with musical selections, for both girls played the harpsichord and the harp, and both had sweet voices; but tonight the sound of the storm precluded that; and so after a bit both girls and Laird MacLeven excused themselves, leaving Ian, Michele, and Andre alone in the room.

Andre read for a time, while Michele and Ian talked together in low voices. Once Ian glanced over at Andre and then looked at Michele with a frown. Michele nodded; she was growing angry with Andre, sure that he was playing the part of chaperone deliberately; and she was about to remonstrate with him, when he suddenly put down his book. He sighed in an exaggerated fashion, stretched, and glanced over at them with a slight smile. "All of a sudden I find myself fatigued. I hope that you young people will pardon me if I leave you all alone. And *do* refrain from leaping up and down and shouting at my exit, if you please."

Michele made a moue and blew him a kiss, and Ian arose as Andre did, and bowed slightly.

Laughing softly, Andre took his leave, and now there

were just the two of them in front of the crackling fire. The sound of the drumming rain seemed to shut out the rest of the world as their glances locked; and Michele felt her heart begin to beat as fast as the rain, as loud as the thunder, as a quick fire ran through her veins. Just at that instant, a gigantic roll of thunder rattled the windows, and the fire flared high as the wind gusted down the chimney. Before she could even think, Michele cried out, and coming to her feet, she found herself in Ian's arms.

He drew her against him, close and hard, and his kiss was fierce and gentle at the same time. His lips seemed warmer than the glow from the fire, and Michele felt her own body flame. She felt herself go limp with desire, and knew that this night she would not deny Ian MacLeven, for she no longer had the will to resist him or her own passions.

"Michele, Michele!" he whispered when at last he took his mouth from hers for a moment. "How I have longed to do that, lass, to hold you so. You cannot know!"

I do know, she thought, but did not speak the words, only fitted her lips again to his, as they kissed. No words were necessary; she let her mouth and body speak for her. His right hand moved up her back and around to the swell of her breast, and she felt the nipple rise to his touch. A tingle sped along her nerve-ends, until it reached the innermost core of her, and she could not help but moan aloud with her need.

In response he held her even closer, until it appeared to her that they were one body; and as the thunder crashed outside again, it seemed like the sound of their bodies meeting.

Later, she did not fully remember going up the stairs. All at once, they were there, in her bedroom, the only illumination coming from the fireplace and from the lightning that flickered and flashed over their naked, straining bodies.

And then they were on the bed, beneath the thick mound of covers, and it was like being in a small, dark cave, alone together and unobserved. In his arms she felt safe. Only the storm created by her own raging senses was a threat, but if such it was, it was most welcome.

Michele cried out as Ian lowered his head and touched her sensitive nipples with his tongue, and then his lips. His hands urgently caressed her body, making her acutely aware of its lineaments, making her aware of her own urgency.

She answered by touching his body, feeling the smooth curve of muscle, the soft brush of hair upon his chest, the moving tendons of his back.

And then his hands moved down to her hips and buttocks, and sought out the juncture of her thighs; and forgetting everything, she joyously and wantonly opened herself to give him easy access to the center of her desire; and as he touched her there, she gasped and opened her mouth against his, feeling his tongue softly probing, knowing the intense pleasure of it, and experiencing the answering response and need in the place he was touching.

Ian's breath was coming as fast as a running man's, and she could feel his heart thrumming wildly against her breast.

Gently, he spread her thighs farther, and inserted himself in one smooth thrust. Without conscious thought she raised her hips to meet him, and sighed in ecstasy as he entered and filled her. And then, as he began to move more and more rapidly, she was wholly lost except for the sensations of her body, the delight and need and hunger and pleasure that his movements brought her.

Soon, her own body was moving as rapidly as his as she rose again and again to meet him, twisting herself under him to increase the delicious pressure which mounted until, with a shuddering climax, she clung to him as he gasped out his own passion; and they collapsed in one another's arms, their breaths and their sighs coming as one.

Chapter Twenty

THE night of the storm was the beginning of many nights that Ian spent in Michele's bed. Once Ian had made love to her, she found that love was all she thought of. It was as if a dam had burst somewhere inside her; and now that the water was pouring forth, there seemed to be no way to stop it. She did not *want* to stop it. They made love almost every night, and often, when they were alone during the day, upon the moors, in secluded ruins, any place where they had enough privacy; it was as if they could never get enough of one another.

Ian, on the average of at least once a day, asked Michele to marry him; and although she had not said yes, she was sorely tempted. She loved her dancing, yes; but she also now knew that she loved this man as well. The delight of being in his arms, of having him take her, exceeded even the pleasure she felt upon the stage. But would this pleasure last? When they were married, when there were children to care for, and a home to run, would the passion fade, as she had seen it do so often in so many others?

Also, there was the life she would lead as Ian's wife—wealth and social status; the lady of the castle; and a life of luxury that the ballet would never offer her.

Of course, she realized that she was in grave risk of having the matter taken out of her hands, for she knew very well that there was an ever-present possibility of

Ian's getting her with child. If this happened, she would *have* to marry him.

Truthfully, sometimes, she almost wished it would happen, for then the decision would be made for her; she would have no other choice open to her. But perversely, it did not happen. Her menses came on schedule; and she found that she almost resented it, particularly as during this time she was unable to make love to Ian.

These weeks at MacLeven Castle, she decided, were both the happiest and most confusing of her life. She felt much as she had during the long coach ride—thrown first to one side, and then the other. One day she was sure she loved Ian and wished to stay with him forever; the next she felt that she could not possibly give up her dancing.

She finally discussed it with Ian. They were alone, taking a stroll through the castle grounds, and had stopped to rest upon a stone bench surrounded by blooming azalea bushes.

"Ian, may I speak to you seriously?"

He smiled down at her, squeezing her hand gently. "Of course, my darling."

She hesitated, trying to get her thoughts in order, before she said slowly, "Ian, if I were to marry you . . ."

His face lit up with a brilliant smile.

She said hastily, "I didn't say I would, Ian, I only said if. If I were to marry you, would you allow me to continue with my dancing? I know it would mean that I would be away at least a part of every year, but . . ."

She watched with dismay as his smile faded, and his expression became grim. "Michele, I know how you love the ballet, but it would not be possible. I would need you here. Your place would be here, with me, by my side."

She sighed. "I was afraid that you might say that. Couldn't you come with me to Paris, for at least part of the year?"

His mouth was set; and she recognized his stubborn look, and her hopes plummeted.

"You know what I think of Paris, Michele, and besides, it is not a man's place to follow his woman. It is her place to remain with him." His face softened, and he took both her hands into his. "Lass, I would make you happy, you must know that. You are happy with me now, I can tell. What more can you seek?"

Michele felt the sting of tears, but blinked them away. "I have been happy here with you, Ian, that is true. In fact, these weeks have been the most wonderful of my life, but I don't know if I can give up dancing. It means too much to me. It would be like cutting a part of me away."

"You could dance for me, and for our children, right here at MacLeven."

Michele began to laugh, envisioning herself, pregnant and with stomach extended, trying to execute ballet steps, but the laughter was from pain, not pleasure.

"Please stay, Michele," Ian urged. "Stay and become my wife, and I promise you that I will never make you unhappy. I will make you so happy that you will forget about your dancing!"

It was that very afternoon, when they had returned to the castle, that Michele's mind was made up.

They were barely inside the door when Elizabeth came running up to them, bursting with excitement. "Michele, there is a messenger here, from Paris! He has a letter for you that requires an immediate answer. He was instructed not to return without one. I do hope that nothing is wrong!"

Startled, Michele stared at her. Had something happened to Madame Dubois, or Deampierre? An even more terrifying thought came to her—her mother! Had something dire happened to Hannah?

"The letter is waiting in the library," Elizabeth said. "The courier is resting, and having a repast in the kitchen."

Quickly, Michele and Ian followed Elizabeth into the library, and Michele's gaze went immediately to the large, white fold of paper upon the library table, and then to Andre, who was seated in one of the large chairs before the fireplace.

He rose at once and came to her, taking her hands.

"Michele, *chérie*, do not fret until you know that it is necessary. It may not be bad tidings at all."

He handed the letter to her, and she took it hesitantly, knowing intuitively that it contained something that was going to change her life forever.

Her fingers trembled as she broke the seal, and read:

"Dear Michele: Please forgive the haste, but I must have an answer from you concerning this matter as soon as possible.

"*The Three Sisters* has not yet been performed. I will explain in detail when I see you. Sufficient for now is the fact that I now wish to schedule the ballet, and I wish you to dance the role of Violet. If you accept, it will be necessary for you to return to Paris posthaste. Please let me know by return courier, and please give your consent. I beg of you to accept. I think you know what this role could mean to you, and to me as well. Yrs. affectionately, Arnaut Deampierre."

Michele gasped in surprise and delight. She could scarcely believe the contents of the letter. Deampierre wanted her to dance Violet! At long last, a starring role!

She whirled on Andre, her face alight. "Oh, Andre, look! Read it! It is from Deampierre."

Andre took the letter and scanned it quickly, and his face broke wide with a glowing smile. "*Chérie*, this is absolutely divine! *Mon Dieu*, we must pack at once, but first your answer. Quickly, quill and ink."

Ian stepped to Michele's side and touched her shoulder. "What is it, Michele? *Why* do you have to leave so soon?"

Michele turned to him, clapping her hands together. "Oh, Ian, I have been offered the leading role in Arnaut Deampierre's new ballet, but I must return to Paris at once. Isn't it marvelous?"

His face turned dark and forbidding. "Do you mean that you're really going? Is that your answer to me, Michele?"

Andre, seeing that Ian and Michele desired to be left alone, gestured to Elizabeth, and they slipped out of the library.

"Will you really leave me, spurn my offer of marriage just to dance another role on the stage?" Ian demanded.

Michele stared at him helplessly. "Ian, you must understand. It is not just another role, it is *the* role, the chance of a lifetime!"

"No, I do not understand. You said you loved me. If you do, how can you leave me now?"

"You would deny me the chance that I have been dreaming of, the chance that all dancers hope for all their lives and almost never get?"

"Would you deny our love? That is what you are doing, if you go back to Paris."

"I am not denying our love, darling! Of course I love you, and I always will. But if I denied myself this opportunity, I would be miserable, never knowing if I was good enough. Can't you realize that?"

"I realize only one thing," he said stolidly. "If you love me, you will stay here and become my bride."

She cried, "Darling, if you would only agree to let me dance and still be your wife. I would say that it comes down to whether or not you love me enough."

Ian, his features set, began to turn away. "No, Michele. You have made your choice, do not put the onus on me. So be it!"

The rest of it—the writing of the reply to Deampierre, the packing, the farewells to Margaret, Elizabeth, and Malcolm MacLeven—was all a jumble that Michele could barely remember later.

Ian did not see her off; he had not spoken to her since the scene in the library. At the very last moment Michele wavered, feeling that she could not go away and leave matters between them like this; but somehow she did. She rode away in the MacLeven carriage looking back, hoping for a last glimpse of his face, but she did not see him.

The trip to Paris seemed to take an eternity, made worse by the fact that she thought her heart would surely break, yet she finally decided that hearts were much stouter than tney would seem. Andre, sensitive to what she was going through, was very gentle with her, and said not one word about Ian. He always steered the conversation around to the new ballet and her role in it. Consequently, she arrived in Paris tired, but filled with excitement engendered by the thought of dancing Violet; and she found that another, entirely different surprise awaited her.

As Michele and Andre, weary and travel-stained, entered Madame Dubois' house, Madame herself came trotting to meet them, her face ablaze with excitement. She cried, "Oh, my dears! You will not believe the surprise I have for you!"

Michele experienced a strong sense of *dêjà vu*. Had she not been through this same scene in Scotland, or one much like it?

She glanced quickly at Andre, who shrugged and rolled his eyes. "It appears that this is our season for surprises, *chérie*." He turned to Madame. "Just what is this wonderful surprise? We are very tired. Could it not wait until tomorrow?"

Madame Dubois, fairly bouncing with suppressed excitement, shook her head so violently that powder flew from her wig. "No, no, NO! Not possibly! For once you know what it is, you would not want to wait, believe me. Here, my pets, see for yourselves!"

With these words she flung open the door to the small salon, and Michele gave a cry of delight, for standing in the center of the room was a figure she had been longing to see—her mother.

In the next instant she was in Hannah's arms, and Andre was holding them both, as they alternately wept and attempted to speak.

Finally, Hannah held Michele away from her, and looked at her long and hard. "You look wonderful, I must say," she said with an approving nod. "I was afraid that you would be pale and thin from all that practicing indoors, but you are blooming!" She glanced at Andre. "Old friend, you have looked after her well." She laughed exuberantly.

"Oh, how I have missed you both! I have so much to tell you, but it should wait until after you have rested. I know you must be very tired."

Michele shook her head, smiling fondly. "Truthfully, when I came into the house, I wanted nothing in the world more than to go to bed, but now I feel as if I had slept for a week. Oh, Mother, I am so glad you're here!"

It took quite awhile before they all calmed down enough to talk sensibly. Madame Dubois had a cold supper brought in, and as they ate and drank, they brought each other up to date. Hannah told Michele of the success of their cotton crop, omitting most of her troubles of this past year. She did not tell Michele of the lien against Malvern; to do so, would reveal that her father had borrowed money, which would only distress the girl. Neither did she mention Courtney Wayne; since that was over and done with.

In her story of the past year, Michele did not mention Ian MacLeven. She talked instead of the new ballet and her role in it, which pleased Hannah immensely. Michele finally ran out of words. She spread her hands. "That brings you up to date, Mother."

Hannah looked at her shrewdly. "Not quite, my dear daughter. According to Madame Dubois, you have been visiting a young man in Scotland. She hinted at a budding romance."

Michele stiffened. "Madame Dubois is a fine woman, but she is a bit of a gossip." She got to her feet. "I find that I am tired after all, Mother. If you will excuse me, I'm going to my room now. Oh, Mother!" She leaned down to embrace Hannah. "I *am* glad you came."

As Michele went out of the room, Andre started to follow her.

Hannah said sharply, "Andre, come back here!"

"Dear Hannah, I am weary as well," He gave an exaggerated yawn. "I am also ready for the arms of Morpheus."

"I have never known a time when weariness stopped you from talking. Now, you come back here and tell me about this young Scotsman and my daughter."

* * *

They all slept late the next day, and spent the afternoon and evening talking; so it was not until the morning of the second day that Michele went to see Arnaut Deampierre.

Andre and Hannah accompanied her, for Hannah wished to meet Deampierre, and to see where her daughter spent so much of her time.

Deampierre greeted them with delight. Michele could see that he was obviously impressed with Hannah, with her beauty and youthful appearance.

"One can see where Michele gets her beauty of face and figure," he said gallantly, speaking English for Hannah's benefit. "And you, Michele. You look in good health. Have you been practicing, as I asked?"

Michele laughed. "Oh, yes. Andre saw to that."

"Good! I wish to do *The Three Sisters* as soon as possible, and it would take that much longer if you were out of condition. Are you ready to begin work this afternoon?"

Michele nodded. "But I must know what happened. I'm dying of curiosity. Your letter said you would explain. Why did you postpone the performance, and how is it that you want me to play Violet?"

Deampierre sighed. "Much has happened during the weeks you have been gone, Michele. The doctors who had been treating Cybella say that it is doubtful that she will ever be able to dance again. Her leg has mended, but it mended somewhat crooked, and it is far from strong. She is exercising it, and strong woman that she is, Cybella has not given up hope. But if she does ever dance again, it will not be for some time."

"And Denise?"

Deampierre shrugged ruefully. "I finally had to decide that she was not suitable for the part. Physically, yes. As you know, she is a good technician, but after rehearsing her in the role, it became apparent to me that I had made an error in judgment. She is simply not right for the part. I could not bring myself to give our first performance with Denise dancing Violet."

Michele experienced a surge of guilty pleasure. So, if Denise had plotted Cybella's accident, it had done her no good. There was some justice in life after all!

Deampierre was going on, "I have also changed some of the male roles around as well. Roland will now dance the brother, and Louis will dance the prince of the wood. I thought you would not wish to be partnered by Roland."

"That makes me happy. I was wary about dancing with Roland. I wouldn't care to end up like Cybella!"

Deampierre nodded gravely. "Yes, I was sure you would feel that way, thus the change."

"And how are all the others? Have they missed me at all?"

Deampierre grinned teasingly. "You shall see for yourself. But I can tell you this . . . I practically had to threaten them to let me talk to you first alone. Shall I let them in?"

Michele said eagerly, "Of course. I want them to meet my mother."

Deampierre went to the door of the main studio, and opened it, beckoning. The entire company poured in with cries of greeting. Past them Michele saw Denise standing in the doorway, her face set in a spiteful grimace, her eyes burning with hate.

Then Michele found herself being hugged, lifted, and kissed by her friends. How could she have ever thought that they did not care about her?

"Oh, Michele!" Marie said, embracing her. "I am so glad you are back. I have missed you so. We all have."

Behind Marie stood Louis, smiling at Michele in the old way. He said, "Yes, Michele, we are all glad to see you back."

Michele gazed into his eyes, and saw that he spoke the truth. "You have forgiven me then?" she asked, in a soft voice, just loud enough to be heard over the other chattering voices.

His smile was warm. "It is I who should beg forgiveness. I was an unreasonable beast!"

"And now you feel differently? We are friends again?"

He stepped forward, pushing Café au Lait aside to do

so, and kissed her cheek. "Friends now and forever. For I now know what you meant when you said that we have no choice over whom we love."

Michele caught her breath. "You mean . . . ?"

"Yes." He reached out an arm and pulled Marie to him. "Marie and I. It was not until you went away that I began to realize how much I cared for her."

Michele had only to look at Marie's face to know how happy she was. She said softly, "I am so happy for both of you." She felt the sting of tears. Her heart was so full that she feared she might make a spectacle of herself. Louis was her friend again, and he and Marie had found happiness together.

For just a moment she thought of Ian, and tears again threatened; but she resolutely turned her thoughts away from him. She had made her choice, right or wrong, and she was happy. Her mother was with her, her friends were around her, and she was about to dance the role she had longed for. What more could she possibly want?

As soon as rehearsal was over the following day, Michele went to visit Cybella. She had expected to find the dancer bitter and depressed; but to her surprise, she found Cybella in good enough spirits, and looking in good health.

There was a practice barre in her room, and a large mirror; and when Michele arrived, it was apparent that Cybella had been doing exercises at the barre.

Cybella limped toward Michele, greeting her with an embrace and a kiss. "I am glad to see you," she said, showing Michele to a comfortable chair. "Arnaut had told me that he had asked you to return."

Michele looked at Cybella closely. "How are you, Cybella? You look quite well, I must say. I had been expecting to find you thin and pale."

Cybella laughed. "Oh, I was, for awhile. But the leg is pretty much healed now, and I am able to get about, if still limping a little, and that has much improved my spirits. I am able to practice now, and each day I get a little stronger."

Michele, thinking of what Deampierre had told her, frowned slightly. "Arnaut told me that . . . that it would be some time before you can dance again."

Cybella smiled wanly. "You don't have to spare my feelings, Michele. The doctors did say I would probably never dance again, but they are wrong. I shall prove them wrong. It may take some time, I know that, but eventually I will dance again. I am determined of that. As I told you, each day I grow a little stronger. I will keep practicing, exercising my leg, and in time it will be as strong as ever."

Michele smiled, heartened by Cybella's positive attitude and determination. "I believe you. It will happen just as you say."

Cybella held out a box of fancy chocolates. "Have one of these, Michele. They are quite good. By the way, I am so pleased that you will be dancing Violet. Denise was not at all right for the role."

Michele took a nibble of the sweet chocolate. "Speaking of Denise, and of Roland, do you believe that Roland's dropping you was inadvertent?"

Cybella shrugged. "I have no way of knowing. I spent much time thinking about it, after the accident, but I finally decided that it did not matter that much."

"Did not matter! How can you say that, Cybella?"

"Because whether or not it was an accident does not change what happened. However it came about, I was crippled, at least temporarily, and since there is no way to prove what happened, I decided that I would not brood about it, but spend my energies upon getting well and dancing again."

Michele shook her head. "That is a commendable attitude, Cybella, and admirable, I'm sure, but I am not as generous as you. I believe that Roland dropped you deliberately, and that it was at Denise's suggestion, and for that I think they should both be punished!"

Cybella said, "But there is no way to prove it, Michele, no way at all."

"Well, I am going to keep a close watch on both of them, and I am going to ask the others to do the same. I don't want the same thing to happen to me. Thank heaven, Arnaut has changed the male dancers around, and I will not have to do the *pas de deux* with Roland. I would almost rather turn down the role than be partnered with him."

"I think it is wise to watch them," Cybella said, "but I don't think you are in any real danger now. Denise is not stupid, she must know that everyone is suspicious."

"She was warned once before, but that didn't stop her. Denise does not take easily to being replaced. She is the kind of person that cannot stand to see someone have something that she wants, and I believe she is capable of going to any lengths to get revenge, in the hope that Arnaut will be forced to use her as Violet."

"Perhaps you are right." Cybella looked unhappy. "I often wonder why we go through what we do."

"I think you know why, Cybella," Michele said softly. "There is nothing else like it. I have never experienced it fully, as you have. But I got a taste of it in *Beauty and the Beast*. The applause, knowing that you have danced well, knowing that the people in the audience love you. It's worth any sacrifice, isn't it, Cybella?" Michele was distressed by the sudden note of urgency in her voice.

Cybella stared at her searchingly before saying, "Yes, I suppose it is. It must be worth all the sacrifices we make, or we wouldn't keep making them, would we?"

Chapter Twenty-One

ON the day of the premiere of *The Three Sisters*, Michele was sure that she would never be able to go on. She had slept very little the night before, could scarcely keep food in her stomach, and had vomited more than once.

Her mother, Andre, and Madame Dubois all tried to comfort her, with reassurances and extravagant predictions of what a splendid performance she would give, but this did not help. She finally locked herself into her bedroom until it was time to leave for the theater. Strangely enough, she wished that Ian was here. With his steadying presence and strong love, he might have been able to calm her irrational fears.

Madame Dubois had proposed that they all go to the theater in her coach, but Michele had refused. "I must be there at least two hours before the overture, and I wish to go alone."

Andre took her side. "It is better, madam, that Michele go alone. She must have no distractions until she is on the stage, she must concentrate all thought, all energy, on the coming performance. I have been in her position, waiting to dance the most important role of my life, and I can appreciate what she is suffering. Not even her mother, dear Hannah, can offer her any solace now. After it is over and Michele has taken her rightful place in the world of ballet, she will want all of us there, to share in her triumph. Until then, we must be only a part of the audience. Do not fret, *chérie*, I shall have a hired carriage and driver waiting to take you to the theater."

Michele did not know why she should be so nervous, why this time should be any worse than her first appearance in a role other than the corps de ballet, or the command performance at Fontainebleau. There was not all that much difference; and yet she knew this was not wholly true. This time the success of a ballet rested on her performance. If she did not dance well, better than she ever had before, *The Three Sisters* would be a failure; and the fault would be largely hers.

In a sense, everything depended on her. If she failed, she knew that she would be crushed, that she would never dance again. She recalled what Deampierre had told them when he announced his selections in the beginning: "If you are not confident of yourself and your talent, how can you ever handle an important role?"

Thinking back to that day, Michele laughed without humor. If Deampierre had any suspicion of the state she was in, he likely would dismiss her out of hand, and turn the role over to Denise, in spite of his opinion that she was not fully capable of the part.

Then Andre knocked on her door. "The carriage is here and waiting, *chérie*. It is time."

Michele was already dressed—she had been for over an hour. Still, she dallied for a moment, calling out, "In a moment, Andre. I'm not quite ready."

She took several deep breaths, composing herself as best she could, before she picked up her reticule and opened the door for Andre. The knowing look in his eyes told her that she had not fooled him for a moment; he had known that she was ready and waiting.

"Michele, do not fret so," he said softly. "You will dance tonight as you never danced before, or may never again. This is *your* moment, now make the best of it." He framed her face with his hands, and kissed her on both cheeks. "Would you like me to accompany you to the theater?"

For a moment she was strongly tempted, but again she

decided she wished no company. Besides, she knew Andre well enough to realize that he would be a poor companion. At this moment he was calm, reassuring; but if he was with her, he would become more and more distraught as the time drew near.

She shook her head. "No, dear Andre. Thank you, but I think I will fare better alone."

He gave her his arm and accompanied her to the carriage waiting just outside the door. Michele saw no one on their way out—apparently everyone was keeping out of her sight.

"We will be in the audience, Madame Dubois, your dear mother, and I, all cheering for you. Now, go dance your heart out, *chérie*."

"Thank you, Andre, for everything." Impulsively, she threw her arms around him, and embraced him fiercely. "I don't know how I'll ever repay you for all you've done."

As he stood back, tears were in his eyes. "Dance well, that is all the repayment I ask."

He handed her into the carriage, stood back, spoke to the driver, and the carriage was in motion. It was not too far to the theater, less than a half-hour's drive, and Michele rode all the way with her eyes closed, wishing nothing to distract her, trying to free her mind of everything but the ballet. She thought only of Violet—she *was* Violet.

To her own surprise, as she thought of the character of Violet, much of the tension flowed out of her; and she fell into a light doze, despite the rocking of the carriage and the street noises. She did not even awaken when the carriage came to a stop. The first thing she knew the driver was shaking her shoulder gently. "Mademoiselle Verner, we have arrived."

She awoke with a start. Opening her reticule, she fumbled for coins to pay him. Something pricked her finger, causing her to cry out. She jerked her hand out and stared at the drops of blood oozing from her finger. Lying on top of the jumble of items in her reticule was a long hatpin, and she had jabbed herself with it. She pushed aside the hatpin, found the coins, paid the driver, and he helped her out.

The carriage was stopped in front of the theater. Michele knew that the main doors were locked at this hour. She could probably attract enough attention to gain admittance, but she decided to go down the side of the building to the performers' entrance, which was not used too often. A narrow alley ran down between the theater and the building next door. It was a dark, smelly corridor, and she always viewed it with misgivings, but it was the quickest way to the dressing rooms.

She started down the alley, hurrying as fast as she could. It was about sixty yards to the rear door, and halfway back was a recessed doorway to the building next door. As she hurried past the doorway, she felt rather than saw someone in the recess—it was often a refuge for human debris from the streets, hiding there to drink away the day. Many times when she came along this way, she saw both men and women sleeping, a huddle of rags.

Then, to her horror, she heard footsteps behind her. Taking a deep breath, she started to run. She could hear the pound of footsteps behind her; and far short of the stage door, she was caught from behind, two powerful hands clamping down on her shoulder and the upper arm on her left side.

She was hauled around and slammed hard up against the wall on her left. As she spun around, she glimpsed a brutal, scarred face leering at her. Pain shot down her left arm, and she felt her dress tear, and her bare skin scraped against the rough stone wall.

Eyes glared at her, and liquored breath brushed her face as her assailant opened his mouth, exposing missing teeth. "Well now, missie," he said in English, "you're that fancy dancing girl, ain't you? Michele Verner by name?"

Involuntarily, she nodded before she could catch herself. Her heart was pounding madly, and her glance darted both ways along the noisome alley, seeking help. There was not another soul in sight.

The man laughed gratingly. "I'm going to fix you good,

missie. When I'm done with you, you ain't going to be dancing for a bit!"

She opened her mouth and screamed piercingly. He loosened his grip long enough to cuff her alongside the head. Head ringing from the blow, Michele had presence of mind enough to try to scramble away while he did not have her in his grip. He caught her again before she had taken two steps. This time, when he pushed her against the wall, he placed both hands flat on the wall on both sides of her, his body pressed hard against hers, effectively holding her penned in.

He smiled unpleasantly. "Now let me think . . . What would be the best thing to break to keep you from dancing this night?"

"Who's paying you to do this?" she said quickly.

"Now why would you think that?" But his look of surprise, quickly hidden, gave him away. "Nobody's paying me. I just don't like to see swells like you making all that money for doing nothing, whilst somebody like me starves." His eyes suddenly blazed with hatred. "Break your leg mayhap? Naw, an arm would be easier, and that should do it. I seen one of you fancy dancers once, tripping around up there, waving your arms about."

He clamped his fingers around her left wrist, and stared at it appraisingly. Michele's thoughts raced desperately, trying to calculate a way out of this without being maimed. She could scream again—he could not very well hold a hand over her mouth and break her arm at the same time. But the likelihood of being heard here in this alley was small; better to conserve her energies for something else.

Abruptly, he slammed her hand and arm against the stone wall. Despite herself she did scream; the pain was excruciating. He laughed cruelly. "Hurt, did it, dancing lady? A couple more times like that, missie, and it'll snap like a dry stick."

Then Michele remembered something. She still had her reticule clutched in her right hand. Holding it awkwardly against the jut of her hip, she managed to fumble it open. She groped blindly inside, her fingers finally closing around the hatpin. Again, he smashed her left arm against the wall. She gasped from the pain; and her reticule fell to the ground, but she managed to hold on to the hatpin. Bracing herself, she brought the hatpin straight up, aiming for his face.

Her outrage was such that she aimed for his eye. She was never to know whether or not she might have changed her aim at the last instant, for her assailant chose that moment to turn his head aside to expectorate; and the sharp end of the hatpin plowed into his cheek. Michele felt it penetrate the flesh, going in an inch or so.

The man yowled in agony and lurched back a few steps, his eyes wide and staring at her in disbelief. His hand went to his cheek and touched the protruding hatpin in wonder.

Michele broke away then. Leaving her reticule where it had fallen onto the ground, she ran as fast as she could for the doorway to the theater. She prayed that it was not locked, and it was not. She threw it open, and paused for just a moment, risking a glance back down the alley. Her assailant had not moved, but was trying gingerly to remove the offending hatpin.

Michele did not wait to find out if he succeeded. She went inside, closed and bolted the door behind her, and leaned against it, gasping for breath. Her heart still pounded from fear; but at least she was safe now. If any of the other dancers wished to use this door, they would just have to pound on it to attract someone's attention; she was not about to leave it unbolted, in the event the man dared to come inside after her.

Still leaning against the door, she turned her thoughts to what had just happened, trying to make sense out of it. From what her assailant had let slip, there was no doubt in her mind but that she had not been a random selection; someone had given him her name and description, and that could only mean that that same someone had hired him to cripple her so that she could not dance tonight.

Well, at least that intent had not succeeded. She flexed her left arm carefully. Pain shot up her shoulder, and she noted there was a slight swelling of the wrist; but nothing seemed to be broken. Stepping away from the door, she stood up on her toes, waving her arm above her head. There was some pain, yet she could move it well enough. She would just have to ignore the pain; it could have been much worse.

As she turned about, she saw Denise standing a few feet away, pale as a ghost, and staring at her as if she *were* a ghost.

Michele knew then, as she should have known when her assailant gave away the fact that he was paid to harm her. Fury raged in her, and she advanced on Denise threateningly.

The other girl turned to flee, and Michele snapped, "Don't bother to run, Denise! There's no place to run, and anyway it's too late for that."

Denise stopped, and drawing herself up haughtily, she said, "I don't know what you mean."

"Oh, I think you do. I think you know very well. I was just assaulted in the alley outside, and was fortunate to escape without being seriously harmed."

"Well, I'm sorry about that, of course, but I fail to see what that has to do with me."

Michele was face to face with her now, prepared to grab her if she tried to escape. "It has this to do with you . . . You employed that thug to do me bodily harm, so that I could not dance tonight, hoping that Arnaut would let you dance in my place."

Denise's cat face showed fear for the first time. "You must be mad, accusing me of something like that!"

"Not mad at all. I know what you've been up to all along, you and Roland," Michele said relentlessly. "I warned you once before. This time you're not going to get away with it. If I let this go unchallenged, the next time your hired thug might succeed, and I would be in Cybella's position, likely never again able to dance."

"You have no proof of any of this," Denise said with a toss of her head. "And there is nothing you can do about it, anyway!"

"We shall see about that," Michele said grimly, and marched on past Denise toward her dressing room.

Just before she reached it, Deampierre hurried along the passageway toward her. "Michele, just a moment! I want to discuss . . ." He broke off, staring at her in horror. "What on earth happened to you, you look ghastly!"

"I was assaulted in the alley just outside the building," she said shakily. "Someone did not want me to dance tonight."

"Are you all right?" he asked anxiously.

"I'd like to see someone else try to stop me."

His gaze sharpened. "What do you mean, someone did not want you to dance tonight?"

"Just what I said. Right this moment I am supposed to be lying out there with a broken arm or leg."

"Who would . . ." He broke off, then said thoughtfully, "Denise?"

"Of course." She gestured. "And don't ask me if I have proof. I don't need any. One look at her face when she saw me a bit ago, relatively unharmed, told me all that I needed to know."

He nodded slowly. "All right, Michele, I will dismiss her from the company. You'll not need to worry about her again."

"Now? Today?" she said insistently.

He hesitated. "Well, if you wish. Denise's understudy can dance the other sister, but that will mean that you will have no understudy until I can work another dancer into the role, and that will take a few days."

"We won't need one," she said strongly. "I will dance Violet, no matter what. I do not intend to let anything stop me now, not after what I've given up . . ." She broke off, her glance skipping away.

"Given up?" He took her chin in his hand, turning her face to his. "You mean you had a choice, either give up your young man, or give up dancing?"

Her head went back. "If you must know, yes. But I have made my choice."

"I told you how demanding a mistress is the ballet," he said gently.

"I realize that now, but I will survive."

"I'm sure you will, Michele. You're a strong woman, and I admire you for it."

"How about Roland? I'm reasonably certain he had nothing to do with this today, and with Denise gone, he'll no longer be under her influence. We need Roland, Arnaut."

"I agree, we do," he said soberly. "But I will give him a word of warning. If he is the cause of any more mishaps, he is finished." He stood back, smiling gently. "I wish you well tonight, my dear, although I know you will dance brilliantly. Now go and prepare yourself for your starring debut."

As Michele entered her dressing room and began to get ready to go on stage, she realized something that both surprised and pleased her. The nervousness that had plagued her last night and today was completely gone. The encounter in the alley and the outrage it had produced in her had dissolved her fears. She was as confident as she had ever been. She was going to do well tonight; she was convinced of it.

As a patroness of the ballet, Madame Dubois had a private box, which she naturally shared tonight with Hannah and Andre. They arrived a good half-hour before the overture, and settled into the box. Madame was dressed in the height of fashion; in Hannah's opinion she was overdressed, but Andre had assured her with a sardonic smile that it was customary with Madame Dubois. Madame sat crowded against the railing of the box, waving her fan at acquaintances in the audience, and calling out to them. She seemed to know everyone present, including a large number of men, with whom she flirted outrageously.

"Madame really comes to the ballet to be seen," Andre said behind his hand to Hannah, "and not so much to see the ballet."

"I heard that, Andre," Madame said. "And it is a canard. I enjoy the ballet immensely. But I do come early so I can see and speak to my friends. Once the performance begins, I will be as attentive as anyone in the theater."

Hannah felt somewhat overdressed herself. When Madame had seen the skimpy wardrobe Hannah had brought from Virginia, she had been horrified. She simply would not *allow* Hannah to attend Michele's debut as a star wearing such out-of-fashion garments! She bullied Hannah into going to her own dressmaker to have a new dress made, and then took her on an exhausting round of the shops for the other accessories necessary. Hannah was alternately proud of her new wardrobe, and embarrassed . . .

Her thoughts were interrupted by Andre, who was staring past her with a frown. "Sir, this is a private box. Evidently you have made some error . . ."

A voice behind her said softly, "Hannah?"

Hannah's head snapped around, and for a long moment she was positive that she was imagining the tall, splendidly-attired figure standing with the box curtains parted, staring at her.

"Court?" She managed to get to her feet. "Oh, dear God, it *is* you!" She took two steps forward, and stopped, swaying dizzily. Court moved quickly to her, taking her by the shoulders in support.

Her gaze was on his face, hungrily searching out each beloved feature. She groped for his hand. "How did you . . . ?"

Andre ranged alongside her. "Hannah, do you know this fellow?"

"Yes, yes." Dazedly, she turned and somehow managed to make the introductions. She could only take her gaze away from Court for a second or two before she had to look back, as if to reassure her senses that it was really he, that he was really here; and she never once let go of his hand.

Andre was studying her quizzically, and she saw realization dawn in his eyes. He drawled, "This is quite a surprise, my dear. You have been keeping something from us. For shame!"

She felt color sweep her face. In confusion she turned to Court. "How did you find me?"

"It wasn't easy," he said gravely. "Could we talk in private?" She could only nod. "If we may be excused, sir? And madam? I shall bring her back shortly."

"Of course, Mr. Wayne," Madame said regally. "And you are most welcome to share my box to watch dear Michele's performance."

"Thank you." Court's gaze was on Hannah's face. "But that will be Hannah's decision to make."

He led her out into the passageway, letting the curtains fall back into place. The passageway was crowded by latecomers hurrying to their boxes. Court led her down the way to a relatively quiet nook.

"Court, how did you learn where I was?" Her gaze clung to his face. "Did you return to Williamsburg?"

"Yes. When I left I thought I would never return, but I found that I had to. I returned some time after you left. John told me where you had gone and where to find you. I arrived in Paris this very day, and went to Madame Dubois' in search of you, and was told that you were here. But first, before we say more . . ." He cleared his throat. "Can you ever forgive me?"

"Must you ask?" she said simply. "It is I who should beg forgiveness, for not taking you on faith, as you asked of me."

He was shaking his head. "No, you had every right to question me. That damnable pride of mine! I humbly beg your forgiveness, Hannah."

She brushed the plea aside with a wave of her hand. "You learned about Jules Dade?"

"Yes, John told me everything. That was a courageous thing you did, Hannah. It should have been me handling Dade, had I not been such a fool. And if I had had any sense, I would have realized that Dade killed your husband. Michael was too good a horseman to be thrown by accident. Dade wrote that letter to you, didn't he?"

"Yes, Court. He hated you and wanted to discredit you. There is still one thing I do not know . . . Why did Michael need to borrow money? Do you know?"

He was silent for a moment. "Yes, Michael told me his reasons, but he also made me promise never to tell you. I must keep that promise, Hannah."

"Yes, of course you must. But can you tell me this much . . . He must have been ashamed of his reasons. Was it all that terrible?"

This time he answered without hesitation. "No, it was not so terrible, that I can promise you, although he evidently thought it was. He was a proud man, also, your husband. It is a flaw in the male of the species, I do believe." He raised her hand to his lips. "These past months have been pure hell, Hannah. I finally realized that I had to see you again, to at least try to make amends for any hurt my foolish pride did to you."

"You did hurt me terribly, Court. And these past months have been agony for me as well. That is why I came to Paris, hoping to forget."

"And have you?"

"If you mean have I forgotten you, no. The pain I still remember, but that will go away now that you're here with me. Unless . . ." She looked at him questioningly. "Unless you intend to go away again?"

"Not without you, dear Hannah. If I have my way, I'll never be separated from you again."

"Oh, Court! Darling!" Her eyes swam with tears.

One step, and he had her in a crushing embrace, his mouth on hers. Sweet fire coursed through her, and she clung to him with all the love she possessed.

She heard low laughter from people passing by. They both ignored the passersby, holding the kiss until Hannah began to feel faint from lack of breath.

Finally, Court took his lips away, holding her slightly away from him. He gazed deep into her eyes. "Hannah, will you be my wife?"

"Yes, oh, yes!"

"Will you marry me here, in Paris? So that we can sail back to Virginia, when it's time, as man and wife?"

"I will marry you in Paris. I will marry you anywhere on earth." She gazed at him with moist, shining eyes. "It *would* be nice, if we were wed here, so Michele could be in attendance."

"Paris it is then."

She gave a start as the sounds of music came to her. "The overture, Court." She tugged at his hand. "The ballet is about to begin. Come on, I don't want to miss any of it!"

The applause broke over Michele like continuous thunder. She bowed again and again—they would not let her go. She was weary to the bone, so weary she could scarcely stand on trembling legs; and she was drenched with perspiration, but she was deliriously happy.

She had danced beautifully; she knew it, and the audience knew it.

"Bravo! Bravo! Bravo!"

Flowers rained onto the stage around her feet. She bowed again, almost touching the stage floor with her forehead.

As the applause lessened perceptibly, she started to run off-stage, toward Deampierre, standing in the wings, holding out his arms, a happy smile upon his face.

Voices rose from the audience, "No, no!" And the applause thundered again.

She bowed again, twice more. She picked up a rose at her feet, kissed it, and tossed it out into the audience. She glanced at Deampierre, and saw him motioning her off. She turned back to the audience briefly, throwing kisses. Then she ran into the wings, running right into Deampierre's arms. He hoisted her high, swinging her all the way around.

"You did it, Michele!" he shouted exuberantly. "My God, I have never seen a better performance! I have never been so proud of one of my students. You will be the toast of Paris tomorrow, mark my words!"

He set her on her feet, and kissed her on the lips. Then the others were swarming around, Louis and Marie in the forefront, everyone kissing and hugging her, yelling congratulations.

Even Roland took her hand and bowed over it. "You were magnificent, Michele, truly magnificent," he shouted in her ear.

Now Deampierre waved his arms for attention, and shouted, "All right, all right! Michele must get to her dressing room and change! All of you must change. We shall have a celebration of our successful performance in my studio later. The preparations are underway now. I anticipated our success." He laughed aloud. "Which is not entirely the truth, unless hoping made it come true."

With a wave Michele hurried to her dressing room, where she found her mother, Andre, Madame Dubois, and a strange man, waiting outside.

With moist eyes Hannah said, "Michele, I am so proud of you!"

They embraced fervently, and then Andre was tugging at Michele's elbow, almost dancing up and down. "Did I not tell you, *chérie*?" he crowed. "I knew that you would enchant the audience tonight!"

Madame Dubois said, "Congratulations, my dear. You did indeed dance superbly tonight."

"I thank you all." Her curious gaze rested on the stranger. "But let's go into my dressing room. Arnaut Deampierre is giving a celebration in his studio, and you are all invited, of course. I must change out of my costume."

Inside the dressing room, her mother said nervously, "Michele, I wish you to meet a friend of mine, from Virginia, Courtney Wayne. Court, this is my daughter, Michele."

Court bowed over her hand. "May I also add my congratulations to the others, Michele? I have never seen a ballet danced more beautifully."

Flustered, Michele glanced at her mother.

"Michele," Hannah said shyly, "I am going to be wed to Court before we leave Paris. He proposed to me before the ballet began." Color stained her cheeks. "I wanted to be married here, so you can attend."

Michele swallowed her astonishment, and threw her arms around her mother. She thought, Oh, Ian, Ian, why couldn't you have been here tonight? That would have made it the most perfect evening of my life!

In a choked voice she said, "I'm very happy for you, Mother."

A knock sounded on the door. Michele made a face, and turned toward her dressing table. "Answer that, Andre. And whoever it is, send them away. I shall never get changed."

At her dressing table, back to the room, she began cleansing her face. She heard the murmur of voices behind her, then the sound of the door closing.

Andre said in a strange voice, "*Chérie*?"

She faced about, and he held out a bouquet of red roses. "These are for you."

Madame Dubois said archly, "Unless I am mistaken, this room will be filled with flowers from gentlemen admirers before this night is over."

Michele gestured impatiently. "I can't be bothered now, Andre. Put them down somewhere."

Still in that strange voice, he said, "I believe you will wish to see these. They are not just from any admirer, and there is a letter attached. The delivery fellow said they received the order a week ago, along with the letter, and instructions not to make delivery until *after* the first performance of *The Three Sisters*."

A premonition set Michele to trembling inside. She took the flowers, inhaled their sweet fragrance, then placed them on her dressing table, and unfolded the letter that Andre held out to her.

"My dearest Michele: My most sincere congratulations, lass. I do not need to see the ballet to know that you will be a great success.

"I have much agonized over my decision, but I know now, without any lingering doubt, that I would rather have you to myself for only a part of a year, than to never have you at all.

"My darling, if it is not too late, will you be my wife? If you say yes, I will agree to your being away from me when your career requires it. My heart will ache for you in your absences, I know, but I shall be grateful for the time you can spend with me.

"Please reply as quickly as possible. If your answer is yes, as I pray it will be, I will hasten to Paris on receipt of your answer, and we shall be married at your convenience. With love and a full heart, Yrs. Ian."

Michele blinked back the sting of tears, but it was a moment before she was able to control her emotions. From Andre's knowing, almost mournful smile, she realized that he sensed what was in the letter.

Her glance went from Andre to Hannah. "Mother, what would you think of a double wedding?"

Hannah's expression showed first surprise and then delight. "So I am not the only one who has been keeping secrets. Is it the young Scotsman you were visiting?"

Michele nodded. "Oh, Mother, this is the happiest day of my life!"

Hannah raised her arms and Michele moved into them. As mother and daughter embraced, Hannah smiled at Andre over Michele's shoulder. "Well, old friend," she said, "do you think you are up to raising another generation of Verner women?"

FLAMES OF GLORY
by PATRICIA MATTHEWS

Sultry Tampa, crossroads for gallant soldiers of the Spanish-American War, was the beloved home of young Jessica Manning. Her elegance and beauty fascinated not only Lieutenant Neil Dancer, one of Teddy Roosevelt's Rough Riders, but also the ruthless and hot-blooded Bill Kroger. Unable to resist the emotions that she had aroused in him, Kroger abducted Jessica, and swept his anguished prize on a blazing seaward quest for Aztec gold. Through it all, Jessica clung to her one aching wish – that she could return to the glorious moments spent in the arms of Neil Dancer.

0 552 12309 9 £1.95

EMBERS OF DAWN
by PATRICIA MATTHEWS

In a violent age of war and turmoil, she rose from the ashes of battle to seize a wild and passionate dream.

In the fiery aftermath of Civil War, Charlotte King was penniless, possessing only a ravaged farm and a cache of prized tobacco. Everything was gone but the determined spirit that drove her on. Two men would kindle her dreams, ignite her ambitions, set her aflame. Ben Asher gave her wisdom and tender love. Clint Devlin introduced her to passion and swept her into a stormy romance.

Torn between two men, pitted against sworn enemies, she battled to find rapture and wealth beyond compare, to see her beloved South reborn.

0 552 12080 4 – £1.95